CUNARD

Thank you for using the Cunard Library and we hope you enjoy this book as much as your holiday.

This book is for enjoyment during your voyage, please return it to the Library the day before disembarking.

Replacement and damage fees apply for books not returned or significantly damaged. The fee will be charged to your on board account.

For assistance please contact the Library Team.

D1514714

00002001077

THE
FALL

THE
FALL

Gilly Macmillan

CENTURY

1 3 5 7 9 10 8 6 4 2

Century
20 Vauxhall Bridge Road
London SW1V 2SA

Century is part of the Penguin Random House group of companies
whose addresses can be found at global.penguinrandomhouse.com.

Penguin
Random House
UK

First published by Century in 2023

www.penguin.co.uk

A CIP catalogue record for this book is available from the British Library.

ISBN 9781529135381 (hardback)
ISBN 9781529135398 (trade paperback)

Typeset in 11/17.6 pt Palatino LT Std
by Integra Software Services Pvt. Ltd, Pondicherry.

Printed and bound in Great Britain by Clays Ltd, Elcograf S.p.A.

The authorised representative in the EEA is Penguin Random House
Ireland, Morrison Chambers, 32 Nassau Street, Dublin D02 YH68.

MIX
Paper | Supporting
responsible forestry
FSC
www.fsc.org   FSC® C018179

Penguin Random House is committed to a
sustainable future for our business, our readers
and our planet. This book is made from Forest
Stewardship Council® certified paper.

In memory of Milo Macmillan
Also a very good dog

LANCAUT

N

RIVER WYE

RIVER BANK

GLASS BARN

COACH HOUSE

MANOR HOUSE

RUINED CHAPEL

ABANDONED VILLAGE

NATURE RESERVE

CLIFFS

RIVER WYE

TO LANCAUT VILLAGE (1 MILE)

TO CHEPSTOW (3 MILES)

KEY
ROAD
TRACK
PUBLIC FOOTPATH

AUTHOR'S NOTE

Lancaut is a real place but the houses and characters in this novel, as well as some of the locations, are fictionalised. The fictional locations, names, characters, businesses, events and incidents are the products of the author's imagination. Any resemblance to actual persons, living or dead, or to actual places is purely coincidental.

1

SATURDAY

Nicole

I'm so lucky, Nicole tells herself. If the first thirty-two years of her life were exceptionally ordinary, the last two have been anything but. It's almost impossible to believe. There are so many younger versions of herself she'd like to travel back in time and describe this new life to and not one of them would believe her.

The car's soft top is down and sun glints off the bonnet. Nicole's new Chanel sunglasses filter everything the prettiest blush pink, even the lovely sheep grazing in the fields. She doesn't think she's ever felt so hopeful or so happy before, not even on her wedding day or the day it was confirmed that she and Tom were lottery winners and were about to become filthy rich.

Even so, she drives carefully, hands at ten and two on the wheel. Maybe she's gripping it a little tighter than usual as her endorphins surge, but she doesn't consider putting her foot down. Nicole is risk averse; never in her life has she craved an adrenalin rush. Before they were rich, there was nothing impulsive about the tenacious way she sought promotion to the position of Administrative Manager at Carter, Carter & Dun, solicitors specialising in conveyancing, and persuaded Tom they should put aside every spare penny to save up for a deposit to buy their first home, a tiny house in Swindon's dormitory suburbs. She put in long hours, turned herself out well on a tight budget, and everything she did was for her and Tom, her childhood sweetheart, the love of her life.

Even now that their life has become a fairy tale, she's proud of what she achieved then and she's proud of how she's handled things since they won the money. When the people from the National Lottery arrived at their home to confirm the win and Tom was acting, well, as shocked and stupefied as someone who had won the lottery, she listened attentively to their advice, took notes on everything they told her, twice underlining the advisers' suggestion to think carefully and take their time before making any radical decisions. The only decision Nicole made swiftly was not to go public with the win. The thought of people knowing appalled her. She's instinctually private and Tom is incredibly laid-back, so he didn't welcome the idea of the fuss it would bring, either.

She also paid special attention to the financial adviser who opened new accounts for them to take receipt of the money and she took heed of the cautionary tales he told, about previous winners who behaved rashly and lost it all, and decided that would not, ever, be her and Tom. Over her dead body. Tom

2

might have been happy working as a mechanic and going to the pub with his mates on Friday, but she always dreamed of having a bigger, better life and this was their chance.

She slows the car as she approaches a neglected wooden sign that points left, towards Lancaut Nature Reserve, and makes the turn onto the lane that leads to their home, which is also their biggest investment to date. She and Tom built the Glass Barn on the Lancaut Peninsula, an outcrop of land formed by a dramatic bend in the River Wye, on the border between England and Wales. Her father, a keen birder, brought her there as a child. He called it a lost, special place, and it hasn't changed.

Woodland envelops the car, throwing dappled shade across the lane. Trees cover the peninsula like lichen. She drives past the small lay-by where her dad used to park, from where they would walk along the lane and down the steep track to the nature reserve, binoculars swinging from their necks. The walk took them past the Manor House gates, which were, and still are, tall and imposing and offer a tantalising glimpse of the house behind them. As a girl, she marvelled at the place and wondered who lived there. She never dreamed that she might be a neighbour one day in the future.

She doesn't drive as far as the Manor House today. Within minutes, the view opens out to her right and the woodland shrinks back, forming the only large clearing on the peninsula. A patchwork of fields and meadows slopes down towards the river. Nicole's heart rate quickens. It's some months since they moved in but still, every time she arrives home, she feels as if she's reached the end of the rainbow and found a pot of gold.

On a level piece of land in the middle of the area, the Glass Barn rises stark and proud from the remains of a cluster of eighteenth-century farm buildings. In Nicole's eyes, the contrast between the strong angles and uncompromising materials of the new building and the mellow stone ruins at its base is stunning. The sun's reflection flares hotly in the swathes of plate glass. The house is the dominant feature in the landscape, appearing to own not just its site, but the views around it and even the sky above it. Nicole loves it with her whole heart.

They've lived here for six months. She wants to raise a family – they've started trying for their first baby – and grow old here. She told Tom she won't leave until they carry her out in a coffin.

She makes a right turn onto her long, straight driveway. She has so much to tell Tom about the County Show. She saw the cutest farm animals. They need to talk again about getting some sheep, just a small ornamental flock, to graze the fields beside the Barn. Tom's not keen, but she hopes he's persuadable. She parks beside his Maserati in their capacious driveway and grabs her bag from the passenger seat. As she approaches the Barn's front door, she hears music playing from inside. Opera. She smiles. Tom must be in the living area, right behind the door. The Barn has smart systems installed. They track individuals through the house and are programmed so that if you play music, it follows you when you move from one room to another, coming from speakers hidden in the walls.

She looks directly into the camera that will scan her face and let her in. Usually, this is a smooth process and the door clicks open, but it doesn't always work first time. She gets closer to it, stretches her eyelids wider, stares into the lens intently and, after a pause when she thinks the system might have gone wrong, it opens.

The system glitches, sometimes. There are days when it acts like a cranky relative who needs pacifying before they'll do anything nice for you. If it had been up to Nicole, they'd have had a security system installed but none of the other features. She prefers things old school, but Tom got carried away with the tech. He wanted the Barn to be a state-of-the-art smart home.

'Thank you,' she says to the door and shuts it behind her. She's happy to escape the heat. The Barn is climate controlled, each room kept at an ideal temperature. She drops her sunglasses and keys on the console table in the atrium and walks into the living area. The music is playing at top volume but Tom's not there. 'Hello!' she shouts. 'I'm home!'

There's no answer. She sighs. She doesn't know how to turn the music down manually. 'Tom!' she yells. *'Nessun Dorma'* drowns out her voice. Tom recently decided to try to get into opera, one of a series of self-improvements he's embarked on since they won the money. He's had the Three Tenors playing on a loop for weeks.

'Music down!' she shouts. The volume is way too high. But the system still doesn't respond. Perhaps it needs her to do something on her phone, or Tom's. She's still foggy on the details where the music system is concerned. That's Tom's department. 'Tom!' she yells again. 'Turn the music down!'

The tenors answer her yell with a soaring crescendo, and she covers her ears with her hands. Tom could be anywhere in the house, or he could be outside on one of the decks. Ironically, the house probably knows where he is, but that doesn't help Nicole.

The Glass Barn is enormous, a series of buildings linked via a quirky floor plan based on the original structures that were here. She messages him, I'm home where r u? and waits for a reply but the message remains undelivered. That's odd. She proceeds through the kitchen, pausing to wipe the frother on the coffee machine which is scaly with dried milk and to pick up a used cereal bowl from the central island and put it in the dishwasher.

When the architect told them that their starkly minimalist interiors had to be kept immaculate to look good, she listened to him, too. And she's determined not to hire a cleaner. Her mum worked two jobs and kept a tidy home and Nicole doesn't want anyone to think she's got above her station since winning the money.

She makes her way deeper into their home. The music is playing at full blast in every room, which it's not supposed to do, and it's giving her a tension headache. She checks their gym where the lights are all blazing, but there's no sign of Tom. 'Where is he?' she asks the house. He's not in the steam room, the sauna, or the shower.

Upstairs, she finds their bed unmade, and she sighs once more. Tom knows she likes it to look tidy once they're both up. He should have made it. She straightens it out with a few deft movements and notices that one of the doors to their balcony is ajar. She steps out, expecting to find Tom dozing on one of the recliners, iPad on his chest, but he's not there.

She shades her eyes and looks out over their grounds, down the meadow, through the fringe of woodland at its base, and towards the glinting river which shapes and encloses the peninsula. Tall limestone cliffs rear up steeply from its far bank and follow the river's curve.

Wow, you've got your own private natural amphitheatre, the architect said when he first saw it. *We need to make the most of that view.* And he did. They can see a version of it from many of the rooms in the Barn. It's spectacular. Nicole smiles as her eyes drink it in. She never tires of it; it reminds her of her childhood trips here with her dad and makes her heart feel full. I'm so lucky, she thinks to herself for the second time that day. But she doesn't want to linger outside. The heat is intense, there's no shade out here at this time of day, and the tenors are still singing at top volume.

She's about to step inside and resume her search for Tom when she sees him.

He's directly below her, in the swimming pool, floating, face down and motionless.

She screams and after a beat, in which all the light seems to be sucked out of her world, the cliffs echo the sound faintly back at her.

2

SATURDAY

Sasha

Sasha strides out of the Manor House and lays her yoga mat in a patch of shade beneath the oak tree on the front lawn. It's the middle of the day and it's hot, but the tree casts a deep shade, and the lawn is encircled with woodland. The greenery always makes her feel good, no matter how warm it is, maybe because the towering trees give the place a sort of spiritual feel, as if an ancient ritual might have taken place here.

The Manor House overlooks the lawn. Built from stone, the roof tiled in old Welsh slate, its façade is a mix of styles. The oldest, medieval part of the building is sandwiched between later additions, built over a period of five centuries. Some of the windows are gracious, generously sized; others are smaller, set deep into the stone and leaded. One part of the building retains its original arrow slits. Out here, you could easily feel like you were being watched from inside, but Sasha knows she's not.

Olly is in his study, at the back of the house and Kitty, their housekeeper, is ironing in the laundry room that overlooks the walled vegetable garden to the side. Sasha can enjoy a rare moment of privacy and peace.

She moves into her first pose and holds it, focusing on taking and releasing measured inhalations and exhalations, which help her to let go of some of the tension she's been feeling. She wants to get out of her head and back in touch with her body.

It's been a long morning, a long night, and a long few weeks. She taught a private yoga class this morning and that's on top of running a full programme of classes lately, and two weekend retreats. It's taken a toll on her. She continues her practice, focusing hard as she transitions from pose to pose and imagining that she's inhaling the essence of the woodland surrounding her, its goodness and life force, and that it's feeding into her, strengthening her mind and the bones and tissues in her body, until she feels a part of the ecosystem, and at one with the natural world. It's a blissful feeling, delicious, bigger than her, and when she finishes, she feels sated and calm, almost post-coital. She doesn't get up but lies in Shavasana and opens her pellucid green eyes to gaze up at the oak tree's canopy, taking in with wonderment the spread of the branches, the glimpses of cobalt sky through the green.

She senses Olly before she sees him, his wound-tight creative energy, the gangly height of him, the short shadow that follows him across the parched lawn, and she smiles as he lies down beside her.

'Hey,' she says.

'Hey.'

'Paradise, isn't it?' she says, stretching an arm up, as if it was possible to grab a piece of the beauty above.

'I know.' He reaches for her arm and pulls it towards him, taking her hand in his and laying it palm down on his chest. She feels the steady beat of his heart.

If she could, Sasha would lie here forever, leaving the rest of the world shut out, sensing the heat of their envy of her and Olly's connection. It terrifies her sometimes, how strongly she feels about him.

But their moment of tranquillity can't last; it never does. They raise their heads at the sound of footsteps, pounding the gravel drive. Olly looks up. 'It's Nicole,' he says, and Sasha hears possibility in his voice. She props herself up on her elbows.

Nicole is coming, but she doesn't look right. She's running, her large frame moving awkwardly, her head tilted back. She looks as if she might stumble. Sasha gets up to meet her and Nicole hits her like a freight train, collapsing into her arms with such momentum that Sasha's knees buckle.

'It's Tom,' Nicole sobs. 'Tom's dead.'

Sasha feels the words travel through her like an electric shock. 'What?' she says. Nicole's clothes are soaking wet and dripping.

'I found him in the pool. Dead!' Nicole shakes as she says the word. 'I couldn't drag him out. He's too h—' she stutters. The 'h' won't make itself into a word.

'Heavy,' Sasha says and Nicole stares at her and nods before her face crumples and collapses.

'I tried to take his pulse,' Nicole says. 'I couldn't feel anything. He's floating in the pool. Help me.' Her eyes are glassy with disbelief and horror. Sasha supports her as she sinks to the grass.

'Oh my God,' Sasha says. She looks at Olly. He's staring at Nicole. She knows how he feels. Sasha feels strangely detached from the situation, as if it's happening to someone else. She tries to think what she *should* do. 'Did you call an ambulance?' she asks.

'They're coming,' Nicole says.

She wails, almost more beast than woman, and it occurs to Sasha that there's a chance that Tom might still be alive, that Nicole didn't check his pulse properly. It might be an infinitesimal chance, but they need to check. 'Go,' she tells Olly. 'Quick!'

He looks confused. 'To the pool!' she yells, and he jerks into action, sprinting off across the lawn and up the driveway. It should only take Olly a few minutes to run to the Glass Barn, but if Tom's floating in the water and has been since Nicole found him, there's surely no chance he's alive. That's got to be at least ten or fifteen minutes ago by now. She wants to ask if Tom was face up or face down, but it feels like a cruel question, the last thing Nicole needs. They'll know soon enough.

She crouches beside Nicole, puts her arms around her and thinks about how Tom is a big lug of a man, and while Olly might be six foot tall, he's slender and not very muscular. It could be a struggle for him to pull Tom out of the pool on his own.

'We need to help Olly,' she says. Nicole looks at her, but there's nothing behind her eyes. She's still lost in the horror of finding Tom. 'It's okay, I'll go,' Sasha says, standing up, but Nicole claws at her clothing and grabs her arm. 'Don't leave me,' she says. Her grip is painfully tight, and Sasha wrenches her arm away. She suppresses an urge to slap Nicole in return for the pain she's inflicted. This is so raw it's overwhelming, she thinks. It's animal.

'I need to go with Olly to see if we can help Tom, but I'll fetch Kitty to sit with you. Okay? Do you remember Kitty? Our housekeeper?' She doesn't wait for an answer but turns her back on Nicole and races to the house.

She bursts through the Manor's heavy front door. Shards of coloured light pattern the wooden staircase and the floor, where sunlight filters through a stained-glass window. Her bare feet slap the flagstones as she runs down the long corridor that leads past the Yellow Room, the Music Room, Olly's study, the kitchen and into a warren of small utility rooms behind it.

'Kitty!' she shouts. 'I need you!'

She bursts in on Kitty who's in the laundry room, ironing, Radio 4 on low in the background competing with the hiss of steam. Kitty wears cropped cotton trousers and a vest top; a scarf ties her greying hair back from her face. The scene is a picture of domestic serenity and Sasha is conscious that she's about to shatter it. Kitty looks up as she comes in. 'What is it?' she asks before Sasha has said a word, and Sasha explains what just happened, and how distraught Nicole is. 'She needs some dry clothes. Can you bring her in and look after her while I go to the Barn?'

Kitty doesn't hesitate. She turns off the iron and rushes outside. Sasha knew she could rely on her. As Sasha hurriedly slips on some shoes in the front porch, she watches Kitty kneel beside Nicole and put an arm around her. Sasha runs right past them as Kitty is helping Nicole to her feet. She needs to get to the Barn as quickly as possible in case there's any possibility of Tom being alive.

3

SATURDAY

Olly

Olly wades into the pool and swims towards the body, which is bobbing in the deep end, face down. The water drags at Olly's clothes. He's a poor swimmer.

It's a natural pool, beautifully landscaped, the edges planted with iris and reeds alive with iridescent dragonflies. If circumstances were different, it would be like wading into paradise, which is how Olly felt last week when he and Tom sat on the deck out here drinking beers and taking a dip whenever they got too hot, or just for the hell of it. They didn't have much in common, it turned out, but who needs to when a pink sunset and alcohol soften the edges of an evening? You just put your head back, close your eyes and life feels good, even if your companion is talking about the smart features of his swimming pool lighting and how the engine of his car was tuned based on data from motorsport races and all you want to discuss is Hemingway's prose.

Olly reaches Tom and tries to flip him onto his back, but it's too difficult while he's out of his depth, so he takes the sleeve of Tom's polo shirt and swims then walks, pulling the body towards the steps, where he drags Tom partially out of the water, twisting him so that he's face up, before collapsing exhausted. He reaches to feel for a pulse in Tom's neck, noticing how mushy and white Tom's skin looks, like toes that have been in bathwater too long; he looks closely at a wound on Tom's hairline, a small bump, the skin damaged but not broken enough to bleed. He isn't surprised to feel nothing. Tom has well and truly gone. There's no trace of the man left in this soggy lump of flesh and clothing.

Olly sits on the steps beside the body, feeling the sun beating down onto his head and warming his wet clothes. He pushes his dripping hair back off his face and thinks of Sartre's words about the death of Camus, the 'unbearable absurdity' of it. This feels like a perfect illustration of that. The luxury of this place, the beauty of the setting, and at the centre of it all, a pudgy corpse in overpriced, ugly designer clothing. It makes Olly feel strangely powerful to witness this and to think these thoughts. It's profound, he thinks. He wasn't expecting that.

Sasha arrives, panting. Standing at the edge of the pool she casts a shadow over him. 'He's dead,' he says, and notices Tom's body looks like it might drift back into the pool. 'Help me.'

They take a side each, put their hands under Tom's armpits and drag him to a more secure position. His head lolls and Sasha straightens it. As if he's a doll, Olly thinks.

'How did you find him?' she asks.

'Over there.' He points to the deep end of the pool.

'What do we do?' Sasha is very solution focused, sometimes to a tiring extent. Olly prefers to have time to consider things, to muse.

'We wait,' he says. 'As if for Godot.'

'What?' she asks, and he says, 'We wait for the ambulance.'

She sits on the side of the pool, hugging her knees. Olly notices Tom's shoes lying beside the pool. He gets out and his clothes drip, forming a puddle around his feet. He wants to take his T-shirt off, but he's embarrassed by his scrawny figure and doesn't want to be judged by the paramedics when they arrive. He considers borrowing something of Tom's before realising that it's not a good idea to be wearing the dead man's clothes.

The sound of an approaching vehicle cuts through the bird-song and the drone of insects. Olly nods at Sasha and walks around the side of the house. A police car pulls in as he gets there, which surprises him. He understood that Nicole had called for an ambulance, but perhaps the emergency services operator sent both. He wonders what Nicole said, to trigger that. Perhaps it's just protocol.

The driver cuts the ignition, and Olly takes a breath. He's surprised to find he's a little nervous about answering their questions correctly. I guess, he thinks, this is where I find out if I'm a good witness, or not. A writer should be, he believes, because a writer observes.

A female and a male officer get out of the car. Both put on hats. They look as if they're going to overheat quickly in their uniforms.

'I'm the neighbour,' Olly says before they've even spoken. 'Olly Palmer. I live in Lancaut Manor, the house just up the lane. This is Sasha, my partner. Nicole, who called you, she's the wife of Tom, the guy in the pool, Tom Booth. She ran to our house when she discovered him, and we came here to see if we could help but he was already dead.'

They look at his wet trousers and T-shirt, which are clinging to his body. He might as well be naked. He feels acutely self-conscious and plucks his T-shirt away from his skin. 'I tried to pull him out of the pool,' he says. 'In case, you know, he wasn't dead. But he was.' Neither of them replies; they look up at the house. 'Yeah,' he says. 'It's amazing.' He laughs. They don't. Shut up, Olly tells himself. You sound like a jerk.

The female officer is about his own age, Olly reckons, average height, slim as a whippet, much like himself, and too young for her blonde hair to be thinning as much as it is. Her partner is a big lad, older, way older. Olly feels intimidated by male authority figures and this guy is no exception. 'Lead the way?' the man asks, nicely enough but his eyes look dead, and instead of feeling important, as he was beginning to, Olly feels small and put in his place.

He shows them around the side of the house. Sasha has moved away from the pool and is standing by a pot blooming with fuchsia, popping the flowers between finger and thumb. She looks stressed as she introduces herself and Olly feels for her. He thinks that he needs to remind himself sometimes that she's not as well read or educated as him, not as accustomed to considering the darker, more complex things in life like he is when he's writing. He should have sent her home and dealt with this alone.

The police look at the body. The female officer pulls on a plastic glove and checks Tom's pulse. She shakes her head.

'The ambulance is coming,' Sasha says.

'Too late for that,' the male officer says. 'Did you find him like this?'

Olly explains what happened, how he pulled the body from the deep end to the steps. 'I wanted to get his head out of the water,' he adds because he'd like them to know he didn't move Tom thoughtlessly.

'Did you see any signs of life?'

'Zilch.' Zip, nada, niente, the words run on in his head. A quote from a film. What was it now? No, don't try to think of it. Focus.

The female officer strips off her glove with a snap. The male officer stares at the body dispassionately. Olly wonders how many corpses the officers have seen. The male officer steps away and mutters into his radio. Olly feels empowered to talk to the female. He approaches her beside the pool. She's staring intently at it. 'What happens now?' he asks.

'Step away, sir, please,' she says, pointing to a spot beside Sasha where she wants him to stand.

Olly resents being spoken to as if he's a child; he's trying to help, after all. The female police officer scrunches up her eyes and squints at him as if sensing his resistance. He nods and moves towards Sasha, but he's had enough of being patronised.

'Can we go home?'

'Home is next door?' the officer asks.

'Yes. The Manor House. It's just a bit further up the lane from here.'

'And that's where the wife of the deceased is currently?'

'Yes. She came to us for help when she found the body. As I said. She's a wreck so we left her there in the care of our housekeeper.' He feels it necessary to reiterate this, to show the officers that he and Sasha are good, helpful neighbours.

She consults with her colleague, and they agree that it's fine for Olly and Sasha to go home. They will follow shortly, they say, to take statements and to interview the widow. CID will need to be called. Detectives, she adds, as if Olly didn't know that already. We have to treat this as a crime scene now, her colleague says. In case it wasn't an accident.

Olly and Sasha walk slowly until they're out of sight of the Glass Barn. He stops beside a five-bar gate that's almost swallowed by overgrowth, pulls her towards him and hugs her.

'Stop,' she says. 'What are you doing? Someone might see us.'

The adrenalin has lifted him high as a kite. Every nerve in his body feels as if it's jangling. But she's right. It's not the time or the place.

They walk on. Olly glances at her. He has so much admiration for Sasha. She is without a doubt the best liar he has ever known.

4

FIVE YEARS EARLIER

Anna's Journal

'It's time you moved on,' Kitty said. I was reading my book in Nick's study, minding my own business, when she just walked in and blurted it out as if she'd been thinking about it for ages.

I didn't know how to reply. 'That's none of your business,' is what I wanted to say but I don't like confrontation. Instead, I felt ashamed, as if I'd failed at being a widow.

'You've shut yourself up in this house for too long, Mrs Creed,' she said. 'It's not healthy. Mr Creed died six months ago.'

As if I didn't know that.

Kitty has worked for Nick and me as a housekeeper since we moved into the Manor House ten years ago, but she and I have never become close. Over the years, I've concluded that I'm not the kind of person that other people naturally like. There's something off-putting about me, though I'm not sure what. So far as I can tell I look like your average fifty-two-year-old woman, I keep myself to myself and I don't do or say anything to upset or offend, so I don't know what the problem is. Nick said it's just because I'm shy, which means I can sometimes come over as stand-offish, but that can't be helped. We have each other, he said, and a few friends. If you want to meet more people we can try, but I'm happy as we are, if you are. Why would we need more people?

I should have said, 'In case one of us dies.' Those friends dropped me like a hot potato after the funeral.

'Thank you, Kitty,' I said, hoping she'd go away, but she stood there for so long that I was forced to put my book down and talk to her.

'I'm grieving,' I said.

'And you should be. Mr Creed was a wonderful man, but there are other good men out there. You can't shut yourself away.'

'I don't want another man.'

'You need a friend, or a hobby.'

'There's a lot to do here.' The Manor House is one of those buildings that becomes your life. In the ten years since Nick and I moved in, I've dedicated myself to looking after it. We weren't able to start a family of our own and this place has become my passion, instead.

'Can I speak plainly?'

'I thought you were.'

'You need to change into some better clothes and go to town for a haircut and get your nails done. It'll make you feel better. Wouldn't you like that?'

'I feel fine as I am, thank you,' I said, though I was a little bit insulted and thought that she'd crossed a line.

'I'm not saying this to make you feel bad. Mr Creed would hate to see you this unhappy and he'd hate to see the Manor House become your prison. Before he died, he asked me to look out for you.'

'He did?'

She nods. 'And if I don't say anything I won't be doing what I promised him. He said you might do this.'

I was shocked. I'd been keeping my memories of Nick to myself. The pain his death caused me felt intensely private, something I instinctively wanted to deal with alone. It hadn't occurred to me that he and Kitty might have talked about how his death could affect me. When he tried to talk to me about what I would do after he was gone, I would always tell him I'd be fine and change the subject because it was too painful. It was touching that he'd predicted my behaviour so accurately and taken steps to try to help me. But he was my soulmate, so it also made perfect sense.

She held out a note and I took it. It was one of those slivers of paper that you tear off an advertisement that's been pinned up. It said, 'Sasha. Yoga.' There was a phone number.

'What's this?' I asked.

'Yoga classes. Sasha's a good teacher, brilliant with beginners. Will you try it?'

I felt sceptical and tired by the thought of it. 'I've never done anything like this before.'

'It's only an hour a week and Sasha is very welcoming.'

'Do you go?'

'I go to one of her evening classes, but you could go during the day. It would give you some structure and you might meet some people.'

I looked at the piece of paper, and back at Kitty. She seemed so solid standing there, and it can't have been easy for her to tell me these things, even if Nick made her promise to. It felt hard to say no.

'I'll try it,' I said.

'You won't regret it,' she said, 'I promise.'

I wasn't sure why she seemed so excited that I'd agreed to try yoga, but I supposed it must have been hard for her watching me withdraw into myself. I guess sometimes you don't realise how much you're affecting others.

'Thank you,' I said. 'It's very good of you to look out for me.'

She smiled awkwardly and, though I still felt surprised, I thought, if something good can come out of Nick's death, if Kitty and I can get closer, then it's something to be grateful for.

5

SATURDAY

Hal

'Steen,' the detective says. He answers his phone on the move, on his way to an interview room, walking fast, shouldering through doors, questions he wants to ask a suspect running around his head. The response he expects to get is 'No comment', but it hasn't stopped him preparing thoroughly and tenaciously.

If you look like Hal Steen, tenacity is a useful quality. He isn't blessed with smooth skin or even features. Nobody ever admired him for his looks.

'Hal,' his boss says. 'A body has been found in a swimming pool out at Lancaut, on the Wye.'

Hal stops and wedges himself against the side of the corridor as colleagues pass. He knows the Lancaut Peninsula a little. He's hiked a winding trail near there, high above the River Wye, and remembers its beauty, how peaceful and detached from its surroundings its geography made it feel and the sense he had of time ticking backwards, of his brain slowing down and repairing when it sorely needed to.

'I want you to lead this,' his boss says. 'Okay?'

'Yes. Absolutely.' He speaks calmly, but he doesn't feel it. Best to keep a lid on his excitement so he doesn't say anything to make the boss change his mind. Hal's been waiting a long time for an opportunity to investigate something that could be meaty. He's watched colleagues who are slicker and more skilful office politicians, get opportunities that he hasn't, though he's as good as any of them. Better, often. 'I'm interviewing now, but I can head out to Lancaut as soon as I'm finished.'

Hal sees his partner, Jen, walking down the corridor towards him. She's three things he would like to be: tall, good-looking and tolerant of bucket-loads of caffeine. He holds up a finger to halt her.

'Can someone else interview for you?' the boss asks down the line. 'You're going to want Jen on this, yes?'

Hal pauses before answering, thinking about all the prep he's put in, his doubts over who else could run the interview the way he wants. It's hard to let go, but the suspect is a minor drug dealer who they've seen before and they'll see again. He needs to let go if he wants this case. 'Yes,' he says. 'On both.'

He ends the call and turns to Jen. He can feel that his face is flushed. 'There's a body in a swimming pool out at Lancaut. Boss wants me to lead. I want you on it with me.'

Her eyebrows rise. She's as surprised as him. 'Thank you. So, are we still interviewing?'

'No.'

'You agreed to let that go?' She knows him better than he thought.

'I'm going to have to.'

Jen waits by the office door, while he over-explains his interview notes to their colleague. 'Hal!' she says after a while. 'Let's go.'

They pick up a pool car and Jen drives, taking them through Chepstow, its town centre dominated by the ancient castle. It towers over the River Wye which snakes along one side of the town, forming a natural boundary. There are plans to close the Criminal Investigations Department here and move their team to a featureless office block beside the motorway. Hal will miss it if they do. He likes the history, and the border-town mentality. Chepstow is in England, but Wales is on the opposite bank of the River Wye.

A few minutes and a few sets of lights and they're free of the outskirts of town and heading into the countryside. Hal feels his allergies come to life. He blows his nose and gazes out of the window. Poppies flare red at the base of the hedgerows. They drive past stubbled, golden fields then scruffier, grassy meadows occupied by Holstein-Friesian cattle, standing in the shade of oak trees, dirt dried on their flanks, their ears and tails twitching in the heat. Soon they reach a village, houses and bungalows scattered alongside the road, a post office and small convenience store amongst them. They see a church set back behind its graveyard, where a mass of stones tilt and list, undermined by centuries of gentle subsidence.

Jen takes a sharp left turn at a sign indicating Lancaut Nature Reserve and she slows the car, avoiding potholes. Within seconds they're enclosed by dense native forest. The tyres spit up small stones. Just as suddenly the landscape opens up to the right of the lane.

'We're here,' Jen says. She pulls into the gated entrance to a driveway, where a brand-new sign saying 'The Glass Barn' is mounted prominently. The gates stand open, and the driveway stretches out ahead of them, long, perfectly straight and newly made, its surface a fresh, tarry black. There's no planting to soften it. It seems to cleave the undulating landscape rather than sit within it.

'Wow,' Hal says. The Glass Barn is visible at the end of the drive, dominant and uncompromising. His first impression is that it's an uneasy mix of ultra-modern architecture and over-restored ruins. The glass structure grows out of what he assumes are the remains of old agricultural barns, but the juxtaposition makes them look as if they've been built in a Disney park. They've lost any charm they might have once had.

'That's a house,' Jen says.

'You like it?'

'Hell, yes.'

He shakes his head, says, 'No taste,' and she laughs, but reapplies her poker face before they get out of the car. A uniformed officer is standing in the shade at the front of the house. His shirt is damp under the armpits. He shows them around the side of the Barn to the pool.

The body is lying by the pool, the face covered with a blanket that the paramedics must have put there. The deck is damp beneath it, soaked by the wet clothing, though everything is drying out fast in the sun. He puts on a glove, squats beside the body and gently lifts the towel. The victim's eyes are shut. Hal notes a small bump on his hairline. It seems to be a recent injury. The expression on his still face is benign. He looks relaxed, like a nice guy.

'Poor man,' Jen says, and he knows she's thinking the same as him, even though experience has told them that a lot of people aren't nice, even when they look it.

'His wife spotted him face down in the pool from up there,' the uniformed officer says. He points to a balcony on the first floor of the house. 'It's the master bedroom.' Hal notes that the balcony is too far from the pool for the victim to have fallen directly from there into the water. He scans the rest of the scene. The poolside area is decked and the planting is lush. The pool has been made to look as if it's a natural feature. Beyond it, on one side there are tall grasses. On the other, the land slopes steeply down towards the river. Hal can't see it from here but he knows it's there, and he can see the far bank, where limestone cliffs overhang the water, rising tall and straight, pockmarked with birds' nests and clutches of foliage.

It's a beautiful spot to die in, he thinks, but he doesn't say it out loud.

The pool area is tidy. Six sunbeds are arranged in a neat row beside a couple of parasols, which haven't been opened. There's no sign of a towel or any other personal effects. It doesn't look as if the victim was intending to swim. But it's too early to say anything for sure. There's no obvious indicator as to whether this was an accident or the result of foul play. But he wasn't really expecting anything. That would be too easy.

'Where's his wife?' he asks. He's not looking forward to meeting her. Other people's sorrow weighs heavily on him. It creeps beneath his skin and burrows deep. He feels like he can never get rid of it. But it's why he does his job. It's the reason he's tenacious.

'She's still at the neighbours' house,' the uniformed officer says.

Hal stands up. The heat is intense, beating down. That body needs to be moved. Jen has stepped into the shade. She's looking at the scene, absorbing the detail. She'll take care of the widow, he thinks. She'll make an excellent Family Liaison Officer. He intends to ask her to assume that role.

They walk back to the car. Hal gets a text from the forensics lead. She's young, but meticulous. He respects her. Almost there, the text says. I need to speak to the wife now, he replies. She's with neighbours. Let's talk at the scene afterwards.

He looks around. There's no other property in sight. The sky is almost white, the sun burning a hole in it. He squints at Jen. 'Shall we drive next door?' She nods. They get into the car.

'Right.' Hal settles back in his seat. The heat in here is worse than outside. 'Let's see what the wife has to say.'

'The widow,' Jen corrects him as she turns on the ignition.

He consults his notes to remind himself of her name. 'Nicole Booth,' he says.

Of course, the widow might not need looking after. She might be delighted her husband is dead. At this stage she's undoubtedly their prime suspect. Jen isn't just the right person to comfort her, but also to observe Nicole Booth closely, to see whether there are any fractures in her widow's mask.

Jen rolls down the window. 'Where's the neighbours' house?' she asks the uniformed officer.

'Turn right out of the driveway and it's almost immediately on your left. You can't miss it. The Manor House.'

6

SATURDAY

Kitty

Deftly and unobtrusively, she clears up the used tissues from around Nicole Booth and puts a fresh box in front of her. They're waiting for the detectives. Everyone is sweltering. In spite of its thick walls, which usually keep the place cool in summer, heat has crept into the Manor House. The almost constant low-level smell of damp has disappeared, and the air has become stuffy with new smells of old materials gradually, reluctantly warming and shifting.

It feels like change. Everything in her life does, right now.

Last week, she saw something that turned her world upside down and she can't tell anyone about it. She wants to see it again, to be sure she believes it, but she hasn't had a chance yet. She needs Olly and Sasha to leave the Manor at the same time, which they hardly ever do.

The windows in the Yellow Room are wide open, trying to catch a breeze, but nothing in the room stirs. She feels enveloped by the muggy warmth, by Nicole's grief, by the emotional whiplash of her discovery and of what they're all going through right now. What's happening has the potential to shatter the status quo and to affect her home, her identity, her memories, her future.

When Sasha burst into the laundry room so violently this morning, disturbing her ironing, for one terrible moment she thought that Sasha somehow knew what she'd discovered, that there was going to be a confrontation. But no. Horrifyingly, it was the news of Tom's death that Sasha brought, spreading even more seismic tremors through their little world.

She says, 'Would anyone like anything else? More water? A cup of tea?'

She looks at Nicole, who shakes her head. Since she arrived here a couple of hours ago, Nicole's either been crying or staring into space. Clearly, she's in shock. Earlier, she was shaking so much that it was hard to help her out of her wet clothes and into dry ones. Her eyes are red, swollen and glassy, her cheeks wet with tears, her expression pallid from horror and desolation.

She feels strongly drawn to Nicole, desperate to offer her whatever solace is possible at a time like this. She liked what she saw of Tom. She's never chatted to him in any meaningful way, but he was friendly and polite to her when he and Nicole came for drinks here after they moved in or when they saw each other on the lane. She liked that neither Tom nor Nicole had any airs or graces in spite of their obvious wealth. She's enjoyed watching them build their new life. Seeing the Glass Barn rise out of those old ruins has been amazing. Olly and Sasha complained bitterly about the noise and disruption, even though a good deal of money was made from the sale of the land to Tom and Nicole, but she enjoyed watching the progress of the build.

She sits down beside Nicole and takes one of her hands in her own. Sasha, on the sofa opposite, watches, and nods. Olly sits in the wingback chair beside a window. He stares down the drive-way, his profile still and serious. She wonders about the detail of what Olly and Sasha saw at the Glass Barn this morning and tries not to imagine what the body must have looked like. They haven't said much about it. She hears a car engine. 'The police are here,' Olly says.

'I'll let them in.' She stands and smooths down her house-coat.

At the door, the detectives introduce themselves to her. They make an odd couple. The woman, Jen, has pretty, curly hair, the physique of an athlete and a courteous smile. The man, Hal, has the face of a criminal. She supposes that might work in his favour professionally, but it's a little intimidating. She hopes he'll be gentle with poor Nicole.

'Who are you?' he asks.

She hesitates, nervous. 'I'm Kitty. I take care of things around here.'

There is something about seeing them here, law enforcement in the Manor House, that reminds her that a wider world exists out there, and that she might have some agency, if she can find the courage.

'Is Mrs Booth here?'

'She's in the Yellow Room. She's very upset. It's this way.' She indicates that they should walk ahead of her, but he pauses. He has small eyes. It's difficult to read anything into them in the gloom of the hallway. The heavy staircase, dark wooden panelling and densely patterned wallpaper suck light from the space, and the stained glass in the window on the half landing steals brightness from any daylight that gets through it. The chandelier is lit, but its ornate design – all brass and antlers – directs light upwards and casts shadow beneath.

'We'd like to talk to you after we've spoken to Mrs Booth.'

'Yes,' she says. She feels excited and scared. Words start to run from her mouth. She spends so much time being silent or subservient around others that this happens sometimes. She feels a need to tell. 'It was such a shock. We were just having a normal morning. Sasha gave a yoga lesson and Olly was working on his novel. I was doing the ironing. It was a regular Saturday until Nicole appeared. She ran here after she discovered her husband's body in the pool at her house. She was soaking wet. I stayed with her while Olly and Sasha went to the Barn to see if they could save him. But—' She chokes up a little thinking about the awfulness of the moment when Olly and Sasha returned to the Manor and quietly confirmed that Tom was dead. *I knew he was,* Nicole responded. *I wouldn't have stayed here if I thought there was any hope.* 'But—' she repeats and finds she can't finish her sentence.

'Have you already given a statement?' the detective asks.

She nods. 'To one of your officers.'

'We'd still like to talk to you again later if that's okay. Can you take me to see Mrs Booth now?'

She indicates that they should walk down the hallway ahead of her. They look around as they go, taking in the dark oak staircase and the oil paintings that line the hall, layers of them, almost reaching the tall ceilings; some are large portraits, others are landscapes and hunting scenes. Usually, she tells first-time visitors all about the house if they look interested, pointing out its most significant features and informing them about the centuries of history. Everyone likes to see the ornate Tudor fireplace in the Great Hall and the medieval graffiti carved into the stonework, especially the witches' marks.

She's the perfect guide because she's made it her business to know everything about this place, every quirk and snippet of history. Whenever she moves through its corridors, she's aware of all the people who have trodden here before her and who will come after her. She's always felt privileged to be a custodian of the Manor.

But today is not the time. She only says, 'It's the second door on the right.'

She lingers in the doorway as the detectives enter the room. Olly and Sasha are sitting where she left them.

'We'd like to speak to Mrs Booth alone, if you don't mind,' the detective says. 'Is there somewhere you can wait?'

She steps aside as Olly and Sasha leave the room. The female detective closes the door, and they're shut out. She faces Olly and Sasha in the gloom. 'We're going to wait in Olly's study,' Sasha says.

'I should clear up the kitchen,' she says, though she knows it's immaculate.

34

Olly and Sasha disappear into his study and shut the door behind them.

Voices are audible from behind the Yellow Room door, but not what's being said. But there's something she can do about that. There are secret spaces in this house that only she knows about.

She walks down the hall and into the Music Room, which shares a wall with the Yellow Room. A grand piano fills most of the space. She walks around it to the corner of the room and releases a mechanism hidden in the panelled wall. Two of the panels move and she slips behind them, into a narrow space between the walls, closing, but not locking, the panels softly behind her. She can hear the detectives and Nicole perfectly from there.

She knows she shouldn't be snooping, and it's not that she wants to learn Nicole's secrets; she just wants to make sure that the police treat her right, and it's extremely hard to resist because there are places in the Manor House that were built for hiding in and for spying from. There's a priest hole here, and other hidden passages like this one, dating from the sixteenth century. She can only imagine how terrifying it must have been to hide in these walls while you were being hunted, back then.

But she also knows how it's possible to use these secret places to your advantage, and it's time she stopped being passive.

She kneels, her ear to the back of the panelling that lines the Yellow Room. The female detective gently asks question after question, but Nicole's so distraught that she can barely answer. She manages to give them permission to review the Barn's security cameras and to search the Barn and take any of Tom's devices they can find. She writes down passwords for them, but she never stops crying. It feels like a mercy when they stop the interview after a short while.

As she climbs out of the wall and secures the panel back in place, she finds herself wiping tears from her face.

Poor, poor Nicole, she thinks. She didn't deserve any of this, and nor did I.

7

SUNDAY

Nicole

Nicole feels cold to her bones in spite of the early-morning warmth and the shaft of sunlight penetrating the leaded windows in the Manor House kitchen. She spent last night here. The police asked her to keep away from the Barn while they investigate. Olly and Sasha have been incredibly generous letting her stay, and it's just as well, because she had nowhere else to go.

'The detectives are back,' Sasha says. Nicole nods. She heard them arrive. Yesterday's interview was hopeless because she couldn't stop crying. Today she wants to get through it as quickly as possible, to get it over and done with so they leave her to grieve. Tom's death was surely an accident. It's impossible to think of it being anything else.

She stands as Sasha ushers them into the room because she's not sure what else to do. 'I'm sorry about yesterday,' she says.

'It's not a problem at all,' the female detective says. Nicole remembers her name: Jen Walsh. The man is Hal Steen. Jen looks to be in her mid-thirties – about the same age as Nicole – and Nicole feels an affinity with her. Jen presents as straight-talking but not aggressive. Nicole's unsure what to make of the male detective. He's quieter but his stare is unnerving, and he has a pent-up quality about him, a restless energy.

They sit around the kitchen table. It feels more relaxing than the formal room they were in yesterday. Nicole finds the Manor House daunting. It's so old, and grand. Kitty keeps it immaculately clean, but still the air smells musty and there's this sense that you could never scrub the history out of it.

'Did Tom have any accidents before he died, that you're aware of?'

'What kind of accident?'

'A fall, maybe. Or something like that.' He's looking at her intensely.

'No. Not that I know of. Why?'

'We observed an injury on his head.' He touches his forehead, at the hairline.

'What kind of injury?' She didn't notice it when she was trying to save him, but those were frantic, awful minutes.

'A bump,' he says.

She stares at them. 'He must have tripped by the pool and hit his head, on the edge maybe. He could have knocked himself unconscious and fallen in. Don't you think?'

'It's a possibility,' Detective Walsh says.

'I should have persuaded him to come out with me,' she says. This possibility has been tormenting her. If she'd convinced

Tom to come to the County Show he'd still be alive, but he doesn't share her love of farm animals; he wasn't interested in seeing the livestock shows or the horse jumping.

'Our technical team tried to access your security system on your husband's laptop,' Detective Steen says. 'But unfortunately, it seems it wasn't working either the night before or the morning of your husband's death.'

'What? Are you sure?' she says. This seems unbelievable, but also very believable. Another system that's malfunctioned. They have cameras all around the perimeter of the property. If they'd been working, they would surely have picked up what happened to Tom.

'We're sure. Nothing was recorded.'

'I don't know what to say. We sometimes have problems with the house systems.' She feels disloyal to tell him why, but it might help. 'When the house was designed our architect warned us not to instal too many different systems because they can interfere with one another, but Tom wanted everything he could get. He stuffed this place full of tech.'

'You didn't disable the security system for any reason?'

'I wouldn't know how to even if I wanted to.'

'Might your husband have disabled it?'

'I don't know why he would have. It probably glitched out. But look, he could have. That was his area. He liked to play with it all.'

She works hard to hold back tears. This grief feels violent in its intensity, the way it did for her when she lost her parents and for Tom when his granny died. Granny raised Tom, who was made an orphan at a young age, and protected him with the ferocity of a mother bear. Though, secretly, Nicole found it hard to be as sympathetic as she should have been to Tom when Granny died because Granny never accepted her, and this brings her a sharp pang of guilt retrospectively. The shock and irreversibility of bereavement, the stolen future, the intense longing to be able to see and talk to a loved one just one more time. It tears strips off you. She should have supported him more.

'Did Tom have any enemies?' Steen asks.

She shakes her head. 'No. Everybody likes Tom.'

'And how about your relationship. Was it good? Any problems?'

'I loved my husband, and he loved me.' If she sounds defensive, she doesn't care. It's a horrible thing to ask.

Jen intervenes. 'We're sorry we have to ask such personal questions but it's important we build up a picture of Tom's life.'

'His death was an accident,' Nicole says. She shakes her head firmly. She doesn't want to hear anything else.

Hal Steen leans forward. 'It might well have been an accident. That's what we're here to find out. I don't know if you remember me telling you yesterday that Jen here has been appointed to liaise between you and our department. She'll be your Family Liaison Officer. It's her job to look after you and make sure we're updating you on everything, and that you have someone you can call when you need to.'

Nicole looks at Jen, who smiles. 'We're on your side, I promise,' Jen says.

'This is all so awful.'

'I know. And I promise we'll get through it as quickly as possible.'

'When can I bury him?'

'That will be up to the coroner. I'll keep you posted.'

'Are they doing a post-mortem?'

'It is the protocol in cases such as this, yes.'

Nicole tries to keep her chin up and her eyes free of tears. She can't stand the idea of Tom being cut open. It makes her feel sick to her stomach, even if it is necessary.

'It's hard being brave,' Nicole says. 'I don't know if I can.'

'You can,' Jen says.

Steen waits a moment before asking, 'How much did Tom drink?'

'He liked a drink in the evening, we both do, but not in the day unless the rugby was on. Then he'd have a couple of beers.'

'Did he take any medication?'

She shakes her head.

'Recreational drugs?'

'He hated drugs. Never even tried them.'

Steen looks at his notes. 'You told us that the last time you saw Tom was early yesterday morning. Can you talk us through that again?'

Nicole can't remember what she said last time. She can barely remember anything that happened after she found Tom in the pool. She knows she will never, ever listen to opera again. Steen smiles but it doesn't reach his eyes. The room feels doused in silence, only interrupted by a grandfather clock chiming somewhere in the Manor. Nicole hates the sound of it.

'As much detail as possible,' Jen says, her voice smooth as honey.

Nicole nods. 'I got up at eight because I wanted to go to the County Show.'

'The County Show?'

'Up near Monmouth. They have all the farm animals, the cows, and sheep. Beautiful shire horses and ponies, too. They show them and give out rosettes and prizes. And they have food stalls. It's a fun day out. I love animals. I really love sheep – I know that sounds funny, but I do. I'm even thinking of having a little smallholding here. Tom doesn't feel the same, he can take it or leave it, he's a city boy, so he didn't want to come.' She swallows. 'He was still asleep when I got up, so I left him in bed while I got ready, and I snuck out. It's a bit of a drive and I wanted to be there early. I left him a note on the kitchen counter to remind him where I was going.'

'What time did you leave?'

'Around nine. The show opened at nine-thirty.'

'Was it normal for Tom to sleep late?'

She feels embarrassed by the question, not wanting them to judge Tom. Nicole is instinctively private about how she lives. When they bought their little house in Swindon, before they won the money, they didn't socialise much with the neighbours, but kept themselves to themselves. They worked hard. All she wanted to do when she got home from her office job was kick off her work shoes, take off her bra, eat and sleep. It was a quiet, ordinary life. And while she's been keen to make friends with the new neighbours here, that feels different. It's about making something of their new life.

The truth is that Tom was a bit lazy before they won the money and he got lazier afterwards, but she's not going to speak ill of him.

42

'He didn't sleep in every day,' she says. 'Only sometimes.'

Steen writes something down.

'What kind of tea did you make?'

The question surprises her. 'Mint tea. Why?'

'We found two unfinished cups of coffee in the house, but no tea.'

'I put my cup in the dishwasher. Tom isn't, wasn't, as tidy as me.'

She thinks back to her walk through the house yesterday morning, when she got home and was looking for Tom, when the opera was blaring so loud, she couldn't hear herself think. She didn't see any coffee cups and it's the kind of thing she notices, especially since moving into the Glass Barn. She remembers cleaning the milk frother on the coffee machine, so he did use it. 'Where were the cups?' she asks.

'In a room we assume is Tom's den.'

'With the Maserati prints on the wall?'

Steen nods. 'That is his den,' she says. She finds this strange. She didn't look there when she was searching for him because he doesn't spend much time in there. He prefers to be wherever she is. It makes her feel a little funny to think of him in his den that morning. Why would he break his usual routine of having coffee at the kitchen island?

'We were wondering whether Tom might have had coffee with someone else yesterday morning,' Jen says.

'Who?' she asks. 'He probably had two cups of coffee. He drinks a lot of it.'

'You're not aware of any guests Tom might have been expecting?'

'No. Nobody was coming. Tom didn't really invite people around without me. I'm the one who organises all our social stuff. I mean, he has his old friends, but they're mostly in Swindon. We don't know people here yet, apart from the neighbours.'

'What time did you arrive at the County Show?'

'Sometime between nine-thirty and ten.'

'Did you meet anyone there?'

'No. I walked around, looked at the animals and the stalls. I watched a couple of the competitions. Time just disappeared.'

'Did you buy anything at the show? Chat with any of the stallholders?'

For the first time she feels a sense of trepidation. She's done nothing wrong so why does she feel as if they think she has? For a hot moment she thinks she might be sick, or faint, but it passes. She hugs her midriff. 'I bought some fudge. And just for the record, I didn't kill my husband.'

'Like I said,' Jen interjects. 'These are things we have to ask.'

Steen nods slightly but he doesn't look sorry. 'Do you have a receipt for the fudge?'

'I paid cash.'

'Do you have the fudge?'

'I ate it, and I threw the packaging away at the show.' She'd got rid of the evidence of her purchase because she felt guilty at allowing herself a sweet treat when she'd recently cleared the cupboards and fridge at home of anything fattening and insisted that she and Tom go on diets.

'Did you buy anything else?'

'I didn't. Don't you think it's premature to treat me like this when it's obvious that Tom died of an accident? You said he had

44

a bump on his head. He must have tripped and fallen into the pool. It must have knocked him out.'

Steen acts as if she hasn't spoken. 'We found Tom's phone in his pocket. It was cracked and waterlogged. Effectively dead.'

'Oh,' she says. She's not sure if he's implying something.

'Was it cracked when you last saw it?'

'No,' she says. 'We charge our phones in the kitchen overnight because I don't like them in the bedroom. His phone was fine yesterday morning. But Tom's clumsy. Maybe he dropped it.'

'Maybe,' Steen says. 'We found something else in his pocket, too.' He passes her a photograph. 'Do you recognise it?'

He hands her an evidence bag with a business card inside it. The card is matte and cream coloured, quite firm in spite of the water damage; it feels like quality, the kind of card that people have been eager to press into Tom and Nicole's palms since they won the money. There's text in the middle of the card: SADIE'S MASSAGES. A phone number beneath it.

'What's this?' Nicole asks. 'Who's Sadie?' She's never heard of this person. Tom didn't get massages.

'We were hoping you could tell us.'

'I can't.'

'We tried calling the number and didn't get an answer, but we've left a message asking for a call back and we'll keep trying. We're working on tracing the owner of the phone.'

Nicole turns the evidence bag over. The card is blank on the other side. She flips it back and stares at the text.

'Is this a sexual massage?' she asks.

'I don't think you need to jump to conclusions.'

Nicole can't understand it. Tom had no secrets from her. He was an open book, *her* open book. She knew the passcode for his phone and his computer because he was unimaginative enough to use the same one as she did. She knows what websites he looks at and what he searches for online, who he talks to and the very few people he messages.

She peers at the card again, hoping it might spark some recognition or memory, but nothing comes to her. It's frustrating. 'Can you find this person?' she asks.

'We'll do our best,' Jen says.

'Tom doesn't collect business cards.'

'Did he meet anyone new lately that you know of?'

She tries to think and shakes her head. 'No one. I mean, there have been people coming to the house to do things for us who we've met together. I'll give you details. But otherwise, he hardly leaves the Barn. He loves it here.'

'Does he have hobbies?'

'Not really. Not yet. We're getting used to living here. Like I said, he spends a lot of time at home. We both do.'

'Can I ask why you moved here, to Lancaut?'

'My mum and dad used to bring me walking here when I was a kid. My dad said it was the most beautiful place in the world. He was from Chepstow originally, but I grew up in Cardiff.'

'Do you have any family here now?'

'No, my parents died.'

'Where were you living before?'

'In Swindon. We had a little house. We'd still be there if we hadn't won the lottery.'

'You won the lottery?'

'That's how we got all this. We're just getting used to it all, really.'

'How much did you win if you don't mind me asking?'

'Ten million pounds.'

She watches that sink in. Usually, she keeps the win to herself, but they'll find out anyway. If they're going to treat her as a suspect, they're bound to factor money into their thinking.

'But we didn't go public, and I don't want people knowing now,' she says.

She pushes the card back towards Detective Steen. She hates it. It was in Tom's pocket when he died, an intimate place, and yet it seems like a suspicious, alien object, both to her life and to his.

He puts the card away and says, 'If you want to, you're free to move back home now. We've finished our work there.'

She nods. 'Thank you,' she says. Her mind is racing. Was there something I didn't know about Tom? she asks herself. It doesn't feel possible, because they've been together since childhood, and they are, were, each other's best friend, but then none of this felt possible twenty-four hours ago.

8

FIVE YEARS EARLIER

Anna's Journal

Yoga was fantastic! I was so nervous about going but I didn't need to be. Sasha was as welcoming as Kitty said she would be, and I wasn't the worst in the group! I'm stiff as a board today but I'm going to go back again. Sasha said I'd get the most benefit out of going more than once a week, so I've decided to attend class on Tuesdays and Thursdays. I bought Kitty a bottle of wine as a thank you for suggesting it and she said she was pleased for me and that she knew Sasha would look after me.

I had a haircut, too, though I drew the line at getting my nails done because it felt extravagant, and I also bought myself some new leggings and a T-shirt for yoga.

When I got home, I showed Kitty my new things and she said the haircut was lovely and made me look much better. I was pleased to hear it because Sasha has invited me for a coffee after class on Thursday. She likes to go for a hot drink with all new pupils, she says, and get to know them. Her approach is that she wants to treat the whole person, not just the body.

Even that one session of yoga has made me face up to the ways in which I've been declining. I'm stiff when I wake up. My muscles are getting weaker and complaining more. It's the ageing process, I know, but I feel as if it accelerated while Nick was ill and in the aftermath. And it's not just that. I've been mislaying things, too. This morning I put down my reading glasses in the kitchen and, when I went back to get them, they weren't there. Eventually I found them in the bedroom. I told Kitty and she said it happens to her a lot. Apparently, she searched for her glasses everywhere the other day and they were on her head all along. I took some comfort from that, but it was confusing. I was certain I left my glasses on the kitchen table. I remember wearing them downstairs.

My memory isn't what it used to be.

9

SUNDAY

Sasha

'What are you doing?' Kitty asks and Sasha jumps away from the kitchen door.

'Don't creep up on me like that!' she hisses, cross with herself for having been busted. But who could resist listening to Nicole's interview with the detectives? She was intrigued to learn about the business card the police found in Tom's pocket and the coffee cups. What did he get up to the morning he died? Her brain is popping with possibilities.

'Are you eavesdropping?' Kitty asks.

Sasha steps out of the hallway and into the Yellow Room, gesturing to Kitty to follow her. She pulls the door to behind them. Even though she asked it lightly, it's a surprisingly bold question from Kitty and Sasha's not going to admit she was listening. 'I thought I heard them finishing up the interview and I wanted to see if Nicole is okay. But I think they're still talking.'

Kitty sighs. 'It's terrible. How long do you think Nicole is going to stay here? Should I get some more groceries in?'

'I don't know. For as long as she needs to, I suppose.'

'Doesn't she have family she can go to?'

'Nope. She and Tom are both orphaned. He was raised by his granny who's also dead, apparently.'

Kitty raises her eyebrows. 'What about friends, or siblings?'

'She's an only. I asked about friends, but she said they either had babies and she couldn't impose, or she wasn't close enough to them. I didn't want to pry. I felt sorry for her.'

Kitty makes a 'that's awkward' face.

'I know,' Sasha says. 'She doesn't seem to have a support network at all.'

'I hope the detectives are treating her kindly.'

'If they think it's murder, she'll be a suspect.' And from what Sasha has heard, Nicole already is. She watches Kitty's reaction to her words. Sometimes she wants to shock Kitty, because Kitty always seems so comfortable, so lacking in ambition and imagination and so accepting of her role, and occasionally Sasha would like to see her display some reaction to the fact that she spends most of her days cooking and cleaning for other people. How can she possibly be happy like this? Sasha would never settle for it. Though, obviously, she doesn't want a full-on revolt from Kitty. What a nightmare it would be to roll back the years to the time when Kitty had the upper hand over Sasha and Olly, when they've worked so hard to be where they are now.

But Kitty doesn't seem shocked. 'It's usually someone you know,' she says. 'The police always look at partners first. I learned that off the TV. You know I like my crime programmes.' Sasha pictures her sitting alone in the Coach House, her face bathed in the light of the television screen.

So far as Sasha can tell, Kitty never has visitors there. She lives an extremely modest life within the Manor's grounds. Sasha knows she should be grateful for that because she's no idea what she and Olly would do without Kitty, but still, she can't help feeling contemptuous of the smallness of Kitty's life, too, though she would never dream of letting it show. She's not stupid.

Kitty runs a finger across the top of an old chest of drawers. It's hundreds of years old, Sasha learned when she first moved in here, the top of it warped with age. She finds it ugly.

'Needs a wipe,' Kitty says, though Sasha can't see any trace of dust and sometimes suspects that Kitty creates tasks, to keep herself feeling useful. 'I might add this room to today's list.'

'Can you help me prep the Great Hall first?' Sasha asks. 'For my class at eleven.' She wants Kitty out of the way. What she overheard needs consideration, and she needs to tell Olly about it. She thinks he'll be pleased.

'I dusted in there first thing this morning, and tidied the kit, but I think the flowers could do with refreshing,' Kitty says.

'Thank you.' Sasha manages a smile. Kitty responds well to gratitude and to praise. She likes to be liked.

'You're welcome.'

Sasha feels momentarily unsettled by Kitty's tone. Was it sarcastic? No, she thinks, I'm being paranoid, that's all. Kitty's fine, she's always fine. Though Sasha can't deny that occasionally she's afraid that Kitty hates her, and this is one of those moments, but it passes as they go their separate ways and Sasha's mind returns to processing what she overheard.

As she steps into the hall, the detectives emerge from the kitchen and Nicole follows, looking worn out as she shows them to the front door.

Sasha watches from the shadows as they say their goodbyes, then steps out into the light once the detectives have gone. 'Are you okay?' she asks.

Nicole's face collapses. 'They treated me as a suspect,' she says.

'Oh, God no,' Sasha says. 'Why? Come here.'

She puts her arm around Nicole, takes her back into the kitchen and sits her down. Nicole stares out of the open window. Sasha gives her a few moments. Fronds of wisteria creep through the window and onto the sill, tendrils reaching for something to grip. I need to ask Kitty to prune that, Sasha thinks.

'I didn't do it,' Nicole says. 'I told them I was at the County Show, but they acted like they need proof I was there, and I don't know if I can get it.'

Sasha listens with interest. Is Nicole really so naïve as to think the police will just take her at her word? How useful.

'It's stupid to act as if I did something to Tom. Why would I? Why are they wasting their time? He fell. He tripped and fell. *It was an accident*. What other explanation is there?'

Well, Sasha thinks, *there's the money*. If you wanted it all for yourself that would be a hell of a motive. Or it could have been a burglary gone wrong. Or, based on what Sasha just overheard, there could be suspicion that Tom was buying sexual services, which could have really upset Nicole if she found out. Enough to kill? The police will wonder.

She says, 'Of course you didn't hurt him. You loved Tom. It was plain to see.'

'Was it?'

'Oh, sweetie, yes. You had a fantastic connection, so special. You were soulmates. Even though we haven't known you for long, I could see it. Olly said so, too.' She's lying; all she saw was a pair of unremarkable people sharing a dull life together. The only interesting thing about them was their lottery win.

Nicole looks at Sasha gratefully. 'Thank you. We did. We really did. We were childhood sweethearts.'

Sasha smiles. 'That's so lovely,' she says.

This time, she thinks, might even be easier than the first. Nicole is as dumb and innocent as a lamb being led to the slaughter.

10

SUNDAY

Nicole

Sasha leaves to greet her yoga students and Nicole is relieved to be alone. She feels uncertain about what she just shared with Sasha and regrets being so open because Sasha's smooth reaction was unsettling. It's like everything Nicole told her just rolled off her. Nicole isn't used to people like that. Her parents – God rest their souls – and Tom wore all their emotions on their sleeves. Sasha says all the right things, but Nicole's not sure what's going on behind the eyes.

Were Tom and I too co-dependent? she wonders. She should have worked harder to keep her friends close, especially after her parents died, and then again when they won the money and everything changed, but she didn't, because Tom was all she needed. It never occurred to her that she would lose him young.

She watches through the window as a few cars pull in and disgorge Sasha's yoga pupils, all women. Sasha greets them from the porch with a 'Namaste' and a serene smile. Nicole feels jealous of them. Their lives haven't been blown up. It's almost insulting that they get to have a normal day.

Once they've gone inside, Nicole is left gazing at the empty front lawn. I must get out of here, she thinks, I want to go home now that I can; but she doesn't move and can't find the energy or the courage to get up and walk back to where she and Tom lived because it's where he died, too.

At first, she doesn't react when she sees a man walk through the gate. He's probably come for yoga. Even from this distance he looks outdoorsy and fit. He wears shorts and a T-shirt and is carrying a small pack. But unexpectedly he swerves to the right and disappears behind some tall hedging. She waits for him to reappear, but he doesn't. It makes her feel nervous.

It's probably nothing to worry about, she tells herself. He must have a good reason to be here. Maybe he's a gardener or a friend of Olly or Sasha. But there's something about the furtive quality of his movement, the way he slipped so quickly out of sight, and glanced over his shoulder as he did, that makes her feel something wasn't quite right about him. Could he have had something to do with Tom's death?

She stands up abruptly, the chair legs scraping the flagstone floor. Her heart thumps. She's about to run to get Olly, but then she sees the man again, emerging from the hedge and slipping back out of the gate and onto the lane. He turns left, in the direction of the path that leads to the nature reserve. He's probably a hiker who wanted a private spot to take a pee. She mustn't overreact. Her adrenalin ebbs and she sits back down. All of this feels so surreal.

She thinks about the detectives and what they said. The card they found in Tom's pocket preys on her mind the most. She didn't tell Sasha about it because she felt ashamed of it, of the fact that, no matter how much she doesn't want to believe it, it opens the door to the possibility that Tom might have been paying for sex and she can't bear the thought of anyone else suspecting that he was unfaithful.

His death must have been an accident. Nothing else is plausible in her mind. Nicole could tell Sasha thought she was dumb when she insisted on this, but she's certain of it. Surely the police will come to the same conclusion soon enough.

She turns away from the window and surveys the large kitchen. Banks of painted wooden units line two walls. There's a pine table scrubbed pale, shelves of cookbooks, a Welsh dresser stacked with china and a rocking chair in one corner, a cushion sagging on its seat. Fresh flowers from the garden sit pretty in a vase. She watched Kitty arrange them yesterday. The place feels homely, Nicole supposes, though it's too shabby for her taste. Even the grander rooms and areas in the Manor feel a bit unkempt to her. You can see and sense the wear and tear of centuries of history everywhere, even in here, one of the more modernised rooms. She misses her own kitchen, the coolness of its immaculate hard surfaces, the gleam she can achieve with a bit of elbow grease.

The old-fashioned and somewhat creepy vibe of the Manor House also seems strangely out of sync with what she's observed of Sasha. It fits Olly better, with his corduroy trousers and baggy knitted sweaters, the slight stoop to his narrow shoulders. She's never asked them how they came to live here, but she'd put money on Olly having inherited the place. Nicole wouldn't want it. She doesn't feel at home in the Manor and is certain she never would, not unless she renovated it from top to bottom.

But no matter how little she knows her neighbours, or what she thinks of them and does or doesn't understand about them, or how mortified she feels about having to endure the worst hours of her life in front of them, she's grateful to them for having her to stay. They've been so kind.

Her phone buzzes. Word of Tom's death is spreading amongst her friends and former acquaintances. Nicole knew it wouldn't take long once she posted it. She has almost no followers but Kath, her friend from school, can be relied on to amplify anything. Not that she considers Kath to be much of a friend any longer. Since she found out about the lottery win (Nicole told her but quickly wished she hadn't), Kath's been funny with Nicole, as if the money puts distance between them. I'm still me, Nicole said to her, but it didn't seem to make a difference. I know you are, Kath said, but you're different, too. It's like you're not one of us any more. Other so-called friends had similar, hurtful reactions.

The memory makes Nicole feel bitter. Will I be considered one of you again now that Tom's dead? she wants to ask. Have I been knocked down enough pegs for you?

She scrolls through her messages, barely bothering to read what people have said, because it's too painful to see the bland condolences, to sense the *schadenfreude* from those who she knows don't like her and are just jumping on the sympathy bandwagon. The police have warned her that the press will get hold of this story soon and a press conference will have to be held. They've said they'll try to keep a lid on the story, to protect the investigation, but there's only so much they can do. Once it's out, it's out. This will undoubtedly get worse when strangers are able to pile in, too. Nicole knows it'll be a juicy story, because of the money, and their rags-to-riches trajectory. A resourceful journalist will doubtless dig up the fact that they're lottery winners, if one of her 'friends' doesn't tip them off first.

She resolves that she's going to stay off social media from now on and decides to delete the few lines she posted letting people know Tom died unexpectedly. One name in the comments gives her pause: Patrick Young. Tom's best friend from their school days. It feels weird to hear from him. It's been a while – at least six months – and angry words were exchanged. After the win they gave him a sum of money which she felt was generous, and Tom did, too, but Patrick came back begging for more just a few weeks later. They refused and Patrick said some terrible things, accusing them of being greedy and selfish. It hurt Tom terribly. Nicole had felt extremely angry. Patrick always pushed her to the end of her tether. She insisted that they break contact with him temporarily and if Tom hadn't been so loyal to him Nicole might have been tempted to ease Patrick out of their lives completely.

She reads his message. He's distraught, he's very sorry for what he put them through, and he wants to come and see her. He's different now, he says.

She weighs this up. She's heard it before. Patrick had some bad years after school. While Tom and Nicole were at university, Patrick stayed in Swindon and did an apprenticeship. It didn't last. He dropped out and was evasive about why. When they went back home for the Christmas holidays, Patrick nearly killed a man in a brawl outside a nightclub. There were Santa hats, and there was blood. Nicole will never forget it.

Tom, always loyal, stood by his friend. Patrick was provoked, he said, which was true. Patrick was remorseful, he said, and this was also obvious. Patrick became a shell of himself afterward, for a while. He promised that it would never happen again. Patrick didn't mean to inflict so much damage on the guy, Tom said. Nicole wasn't so sure about that. She remembers the look in Patrick's eye as he lunged towards the man. It was chilling.

But, she tells herself, the incident and the money were only two bad times in almost three decades of friendship and, as Tom always said, Patrick never had the chances they did. His home life was fractured at best, abusive at worst. And then there's the fact that, his concerning behaviour notwithstanding, Nicole does have a grudging affection for him. He's a part of her past. The three of them were close at school. And there's also the compelling argument that if Patrick came to stay at the Glass Barn, she would feel safer. He could protect her from journalists if they come calling, or from people wandering in, because Patrick's a big guy, an ex-rugby player, like Tom was. Her only other option would be to stay in a hotel, and she doesn't want to do that. Hotels always seem to her to be the loneliest places in the world to be alone. This is better.

If he pesters me for money, she thinks, I'm going to kick him out immediately. No ifs or buts. She hopes it won't be like that. She's longing to share her memories of Tom with someone who really knew him. Her heart aches, and she knows that Patrick will be feeling the same way.

She messages him.

I'd love you to come.

He replies instantly:

Today?

The quick reply takes her aback, but she thinks, why not? These aren't normal times. She replies, telling him to come.

'How are you this morning, my love?' Kitty asks. She bustles into the kitchen, replacing the tea towels hanging on the range handle with fresh ones. Nicole likes her efficiency, the way she's always busy. She reminds Nicole of the women she grew up around, who weren't afraid to roll up their sleeves and get their hands dirty, and who took pride in their modest homes and lives.

'I'm going home today,' she says.

'On your own?'

'I've got a friend coming to stay. An old friend of Tom's. And mine, too.' It feels nice to be able to say this. Nicole has felt everyone's pity for what happened to Tom but also for the fact that she doesn't have a support network.

'That's a relief. I'd hate to think of you in that place alone.'

'I have to get used to it sometime.'

'I suppose you do. You wouldn't want to sell, would you, even after what's happened, because it's somewhere that the two of you built together.'

'Exactly that,' Nicole says. She's touched that Kitty would recognise this. Their housekeeper has more emotional acuity than Olly and Sasha put together. It makes Nicole curious.

'What about you?' she asks. 'Do you have family?'

'Oh no, dear. I enjoy living on my own. I do it by choice. Have you seen my little cottage? It's over on the other side of the old stable yard. It was originally the coach house.'

'I haven't noticed it,' Nicole says, trying to think if she even knows where the stable yard is. The Manor is a disorientating collection of very old buildings. It's easy to get lost within its walls and its grounds. 'How long have you been there?'

'Goodness,' Kitty says. 'I suppose it's a while, now. Let's see—'

She's interrupted by Olly calling her.

'Yes!' she replies and mouths, 'Sorry.'

'Can I have that coffee?' There's a note of impatience in Olly's voice that makes Nicole feel embarrassed for Kitty.

'Of course!' Kitty calls. If Olly's tone bothers her, she doesn't show irritation or embarrassment, but winks at Nicole. 'Master's calling!'

The wink interests Nicole. It's the only little sign of insurrection she's seen in Kitty.

Kitty hits a button on the coffee machine and waits as it busies itself preparing Olly's drink.

'I know you'll have a friend staying,' she says, 'but if you ever need company, you're welcome to come for a cuppa at the Coach House, or here. Any time.'

'Thanks,' Nicole says. She means it. There's something soft and welcoming about Kitty, something safe and familiar. She could possibly be a friend. Nicole feels more comfortable with her than she does with either Sasha or Olly.

She lets her mind wander a little further. I'd feel different about having someone work for me in the Glass Barn if it were a person like Kitty, she thinks. Or if it were Kitty.

There's a thought.

She remembers something else. 'I saw a man at the end of the drive earlier,' she says. 'He came in and disappeared behind the hedges then he left again. It made me a little nervous.'

'Was he a walker? They wander in sometimes, being nosy. Once we had an archaeologist asking if they could dig here.'

'I don't really know. I think he might have been. He went down the lane in the direction of the nature reserve.'

'You should report it to the police if you're worried.'

'Perhaps I will,' she says. 'But I'm sure it's nothing.'

Her phone buzzes with a notification. Patrick is on his way already. He'll be with her in three hours. That's very quick, she thinks. It's as if he has nothing else on. Because of their falling out she realises she has no idea what Patrick is up to these days. She doesn't know what his relationship status is, or if or where he's working. But no matter. She'll be able to ask him herself very soon.

Great, she messages back and hopes it will be.

11

FIVE YEARS EARLIER

Anna's Journal

Coffee with Sasha was amazing. We talked for so long that I thought we might get kicked out of the café, so I bought us some lunch. Sasha is lovely. I've never met another woman who I got along with so well so quickly. She's only in her thirties, which makes it more surprising, but the more we talked, the more she reminded me of how I was at that age. She spoke about how it took her a long time to know what she wanted to do in life. I told her that I'm still not sure!

She said she did a few things before she found yoga but, once she had, it was a love affair for her. I told her my passion was my home. We talked about how it feels to have found your soulmate. Her boyfriend is called Olly. He's a writer and he sounds fantastic. 'I can't imagine being with anyone else,' she said. I told her that I feel the same about Nick.

'Feel? Or felt?' she asks.

'Feel,' I told her. 'I still feel it, even though he's not here any more. I'll never look for another man.' She said she understood completely. She would never be able to move on if she lost Olly. I feel intrigued by that. She's a very beautiful young woman so he must be something special. She told me that they're about to move in together and it cheered me up to hear about their plans. I felt nostalgic for the days when Nick and I had everything ahead of us.

As we were leaving, she said it was obvious that Nick had left a huge hole in my life and that she understood I didn't want another relationship, but I should consider how to fill that hole.

'Honestly,' I told her. 'Apart from keeping the house going, I have no idea.'

I got tearful and she apologised for upsetting me. 'You need time, a little structure and some self-care,' she said. 'That's all. Keep coming to class and I can help with the structure and the self-care and time will take care of itself.'

I felt strange after we'd parted, as if something big had happened or some shift had occurred inside me. It made me think about the so-called 'friends' I had previously, the women who haven't stuck around to support me since Nick died. I think they only wanted to be friends when we were a couple who could fill two places at their dinner tables. Nick was so charming; he was an asset at a social gathering. I suppose I was the dull wife, not worth inviting on her own. Perhaps as a widow I'm a reminder that bubbles can burst, that the worst can happen, and who needs that when you think you're living a charmed life? Better to let me rot in the Manor.

But I mustn't dwell or be bitter. Sasha says she senses a lot of sadness in me, but she insists she can tell I'm a good person and that she's dying to get to know me better because I have a special quality about me. I'm not quite sure what she means by that, but it's made me feel worthwhile for the first time in ages.

It must have showed. When I got home Kitty said it was lovely to see me looking happier. I told her about Sasha and thanked her again for encouraging me to go to yoga.

I must admit, Kitty's an unlikely saviour, because in all the years she's been working for us and living in the Coach House on the estate, we've never bonded. Our relationship was quite formal, I suppose, and sometimes I even wondered if she resented me, but now I must give her credit for getting me out of a deep funk. Life surprises you sometimes, Nick said, when he got diagnosed with cancer. That was a bad surprise. This feels like a good one.

12

SUNDAY

Nicole

The Barn's door buzzer wakes Nicole up from a deep doze. Her cheek is sealed against the sofa's leather seat in the living area, which is awash with a glowing late-afternoon light. She's been dreaming of Tom. He feels present, as if he's here with her. The buzzer sounds again. Someone is pushing it hard, holding it for a long time. They're persistent.

She gets up too quickly and sees stars as she walks to the front door. Her hair must be a mess. She smooths it down as she walks and straightens her clothing. She glances at the clock and sees that it's only an hour and a half since she got home from the Manor House. She didn't mean to sleep, but she sat down on the sofa and must have been out in seconds.

'Who is it?' she calls through the door. She should have checked the video entry system, she realises, but who knows if it's working, and she's here now.

'It's me, Patrick.'

She opens the door, and he opens both arms. The hug lasts longer than she would like. He holds her tightly and for long enough that the scent of his aftershave becomes overpowering. She wonders when he started wearing aftershave. He says, 'I can't believe it.'

She pulls out of the embrace and studies him. He's dressed very well, in expensive jeans and a nice shirt, sleeves rolled up, a good watch on his wrist. 'You look great,' she says, trying to keep the surprise out of her voice. She's never seen him like this before. Behind him, she notices a smart car parked in the drive, a sporty dark green Jaguar. He sees her looking.

'I know,' he says. 'Isn't it beautiful? Things have changed for me. I'll tell you about it. But are you okay? Of course you're not. I'm so, so sorry. What are we going to do without him?'

She can't hold back tears and he hugs her again and this time she gives in to his tight embrace, and she feels a kind of lightness and realises how much she was dreading him turning up looking like he needed mothering, or funding. But he's done well for himself, somehow. It's such a relief. She can't wait to hear about it. Tom would have been delighted.

'Come in,' she says.

'Wow.' He stands in the open-plan living area, hands on hips, taking in the building and the view. He's been here once before when the Barn was almost finished. 'Just, wow. I mean, he was so proud of this place. I forgot how amazing it is. You've done a fantastic job with the furnishings.' He sounds as if he might tear up, and she looks away. Patrick never liked anyone to witness his vulnerability. He's a proud man.

She takes him to the panel that is the hub for all their smart home systems. In the drawer below it she finds a small, lozenge-shaped metal pin. 'This is for you,' she tells Patrick. 'It'll allow you to get in and out of the house and access all its systems as a guest.' She stares into the screen, and it recognises her. 'Good,' she says. 'It doesn't always work.' She tries to navigate the menus but finds it confusing.

'Can I help?' Patrick asks.

'I need to enable this, I think,' she says. Tom always did this stuff. She has no idea.

He takes over, clicking through menus until the screen offers an 'Enable Pin' option. Nicole holds the pin up to the screen and it beeps. 'Enabled,' it says. She hands the pin to Patrick. 'Attach it to your clothes somewhere and you're good to go.'

She makes him tea the way she knows he likes it, and they sit beside the windows. The house feels a little warm and she wonders if the climate control is working or if it's another glitch. 'So, he died here,' Patrick says. Even his hair looks good, and he's clean-shaven.

'He drowned in the pool. I found him.'

'God, Nic. I'm so sorry.' Patrick is the only other person apart from Tom who calls her 'Nic'. It jolts her to hear it.

'I can't face going out there yet.'

'The police came?'

'They searched everything. Took Tom's laptop. His phone was dead. It was in his pocket.' She debates with herself over whether to mention the mysterious card, decides not to. Patrick was competitive with her about having Tom's time and attention. She's long trained herself not to tell him anything that could make him feel as if he has an advantage over her. Any suggestion that Tom might have been paying for sex gives Patrick a win, in the old currency of their friendship, and that still counts while she's not sure what their future relationship looks like.

'They treat you right?'

'Yes. I mean, they act like I might have done it.'

'It takes him a moment to reply. They don't think it was an accident?'

'I don't know. They say they need to ask me things that make me sound like a suspect and I understand, but it was horrible. It *has* to be an accident. Who would hurt Tom?'

Patrick shakes his head. 'Nobody would.'

'They found something in his pocket.' She blurts it out. Her protective instincts have deserted her. She wants to know what Patrick thinks.

'What?'

'A business card from somewhere called "Sadie's Massages".' She feels dirty just saying the words, as if she's betraying their marriage.

He frowns. 'That doesn't sound like Tom.'

She feels grateful to him for that reaction. 'I know,' she says.

They fall into a silence which she finds awkward. Patrick stares out of the window, frowning. She sips her tea and glances at him nervously, half looking for more reassurance, half fearing that she's going to see something in his face she doesn't want to. For all the years she's known him and observed his friendship with Tom, she's been a little afraid that Patrick knows more about Tom than she does, and that if Tom were to have a secret and were to confide in anyone other than her, it would be Patrick.

Does he know something she doesn't?

He turns to her after a while, and those familiar dark eyes latch onto hers intensely, but to her relief she reads nothing in them apart from concern. He shakes his head. 'Whatever that card is, it's nothing,' he says. 'Tom would never do anything behind your back. This was an accident, Nicole, no doubt about it.'

'Thank you,' she says. Patrick moves to sit beside her, and she leans into him as he puts his arms around her. It's a weird feeling, being comforted by him. But it's not unpleasant. Any port in a storm, she thinks. He's not Tom, he'll never be anywhere near as good or as loyal a man as Tom, but he's the next best thing because he knows – or knew – Tom so well.

'I wish I hadn't been a dick about the money,' he says. 'I'm so sorry. It was stupid. I feel like I missed out on Tom. I was planning to get in touch with him, soon. I wanted to invite you both for an amazing night out, on me, to thank you for what you gave me and to apologise for my behaviour and to show you what I've made of myself, so you'd never worry about me doing it again.'

'He'd have been so thrilled to hear it.'

'I regret treating you both like that.'

It's a lot to hear. She wishes Tom could share this moment. After she'd decided they should cut off contact with Patrick for a while after the row over money, Tom hardly mentioned him, but Nicole knows the whole incident wounded him. Tom would have been hoping for a reconciliation like this, and now he'll never get it. She starts to cry.

'Hey,' Patrick whispers, pulling her in tight again. 'I'm here now. I'll look after you.'

13

TUESDAY

Sasha

Olly and Sasha walk hand in hand down the Manor House drive. They pass the entrance to the stable yard where Kitty is pegging sheets on the line. She waves and they wave back. The sheet she's holding billows in a rare breath of wind and Olly sniggers as Kitty fights to secure it.

Nicole returned home two days ago and they're going to call on her, but Sasha feels anxious about dropping in on spec. 'I should message her.'

'It'll be fine. Neighbours visit each other unannounced all the time.'

'They don't. They message first. It's polite. You wouldn't like it if she turned up and interrupted your writing.'

'That's why I have a Kitty to answer the door.'

Or a Sasha, she thinks, but says, 'But if you didn't.'

'But I do.'

Olly can be infuriating sometimes. She squeezes his hand hard enough to hurt. He stops and looks at her, surprised.

'What?'

'You know I'm only saying this because we want her to like us, yes? Not because I give a flying fuck about manners?'

'You think it'll upset her if we call in?'

'She might be sick of the sight of us.'

'It's been two days. And we have cake. Her favourite.' Over his shoulder, in a tote bag, Olly is carrying a tin containing a coffee sponge cake that Kitty made for Nicole. He mimes Nicole eating it, puffing his cheeks out like a guinea pig.

Sasha feels her anger rise at his flippancy. 'Is this a game to you?'

The smile drops from Olly's face, replaced by an ugly scowl, but she's not intimidated. He blows hot and cold constantly and at least she has his attention now.

'You know it isn't,' he says. 'I think it's more natural if we call round without warning her. It sets a nice precedent.' His tone softens. 'Casual neighbours, dropping in on one another. We don't have to go inside. We can hand the cake over at the doorstep. If her friend isn't there, we'll see him another time. We're going to ease in carefully, slowly. You remember how it works.'

She does. She often felt impatient in the early days when they were getting their foot in the door at the Manor, but the softly, softly approach worked in the end. In spite of his volatility Olly is more patient than her and always more confident that things will work out for them. 'You're right,' she says, though she still doubts it, but she needs to pick her battles.

They walk on towards the Glass Barn. It glints in the near distance. All that glass. She doesn't love how much attention the building attracts. When she first saw the plans, she'd thought that all the glass would reflect the landscape and help the building settle into it, but it's had the opposite effect. The Glass Barn advertises itself all the time, sticking out like a sore thumb, glinting in the sun. Anyone would think Nicole and Tom own the peninsula. Or just Nicole, now. That's money, Sasha supposes. It gets you property, and a big enough, fine enough property gets you a feeling of power. She and Olly know it first-hand. The Manor has transformed life for them both.

She had some respect for Tom and Nicole's wealth before Tom let slip to Olly that they won it all in the lottery, that they hadn't earned a single penny of it, and used to live in a tiny house in a dormitory suburb in Swindon before moving here. It was hard not to feel some contempt for them after that. Lottery winners haven't had to acquire the smarts to earn and retain money. That's the hard bit.

Olly whistles something complicated and irritating. Sasha bats away clouds of midges. The air is rich with loamy late-summer smells and the mud on the surface of the lane has dried to a crust.

They hear the vehicle a moment before they see it, barrelling along the Barn's driveway towards them, braking abruptly when it hits the lane and the driver sees them, stopping uncomfortably close.

'That's a very nice Jaguar,' Olly says. He walks to the driver's side and the window opens smoothly as he leans down. Music pumps, the bass offensively loud. The driver kills the volume and says, 'Hi. Can I help you?'

The lenses of his Ray-Bans reflect and distort Olly's face. The man has designer stubble and a wide smile. He's chewing gum.

He's attractive, Sasha thinks, and sort of smooth. She wasn't expecting this. She'd assumed that Nicole's old friend Patrick wouldn't have money, or any kind of class. If this is Patrick.

'You were going at quite a speed there,' Olly says and laughs, as if it's nothing to him, though Sasha knows it isn't. When Tom first got his Maserati, Olly took to dragging dead branches across the lane to discourage him from speeding. He said he found the cliché of a young man in a fast car cheap.

'Yeah, sorry,' the driver says. 'Hard not to in this beast.' His grin looks a little wild and Sasha feels disconcerted, because it's not the expression of a grieving man. Nicole told her that Patrick was Tom's best friend. Perhaps this isn't Patrick.

'Are you visiting?' Olly asks.

'I'm a friend of Tom's. I've come to help Nicole out. You know them?' He takes off his sunglasses and his expression seems softer; it loses its manic edge. Sasha sees exhaustion and vulnerability in the dark circles beneath his eyes. Maybe she'd misjudged him.

'We're the neighbours from the Manor House, just up the lane. I'm Olly and this is my partner, Sasha. We're so sorry about Tom.'

'It's unbelievable.' He shakes his head, pinches the bridge of his nose. 'I'm Patrick.' So, it is him. He sticks a hand through the window and Olly shakes it. Sasha reaches forward and shakes, too. Patrick's grip is a little too firm.

'I'm sorry for your loss,' she says. 'Nicole told us you were old friends.'

He nods in response. She thinks it seems self-conscious, as if he's faking it, and wonders if maybe he's high or just a little strange. Perhaps Tom's death has made him a bit crazy. Or he's

75

just socially awkward. Whatever it is, it's hard to get a read on him and she's not used to that.

'We were glad to hear that you were coming to stay with Nicole,' Olly says. 'It's not nice thinking of her being home all alone. Is she in? We have something for her.' He pats the tote bag.

'I can take it.'

'No. That's okay,' Sasha says. 'You're on your way out. It's cake. It might spoil in the car in this heat.' She fans her face with her hand and smiles at him, forcing herself to hold the expression in place as he looks her up and down. It's subtle, but unmistakable. Sleaze, she thinks. She feels a little tremor in the muscles holding up her smile.

'Sure, whatever you like,' Patrick says. 'See you again maybe. Good to meet you.'

Sasha and Olly step past the car onto the Barn's driveway and they watch it leave. Patrick puts his foot down hard and drives off too fast. A dust cloud envelops them.

'He's not what I was expecting,' she says. The car disappears around a bend and the sound of birdsong reclaims the landscape. She tries to remember what Nicole said about Patrick before she went home. It wasn't much, but enough to give Sasha the impression that he wasn't a larger-than-life character like this.

'His Rolex is fake,' Olly says. 'Did you see it? When he shook hands? Also, he didn't look too cut up about Tom.' He coughs drily, tetchily as the dust settles. 'We might be able to use it to our advantage.'

14

TUESDAY

Kitty

She drops the sheet she was pegging up, puts her hands on her hips and watches Olly and Sasha walk away down the drive, hand in hand. They waved at her nicely enough, and a week ago she would have taken that at face value, but now she wonders if they're going to mock her as soon as they're out of sight.

Before last week, it would never have occurred to her that they'd turn their venom on her, not even when they criticised other people, like Tom and Nicole. She thought of it as harmless, exaggerated talk. After all, they were good neighbours on the surface and isn't everyone a little two-faced?

She hurriedly pegs up a pair of pillowcases and then the final item, a matching sheet. Leaving the empty laundry basket beneath the line, she hurries towards the Manor. They might not be gone for long.

The building looms over her as she approaches, as familiar to her as the back of her own hand. It's a complex place. She always feels in awe of it. Sometimes it makes her shudder. There are pockets of cold air inside that don't feel natural and every space is layered with history, with all the things that must have happened over the years, good and bad, bleeding into the present.

This could be the start of another chapter, she thinks. A murder on the peninsula and the arrival of the police is a sign that things can change, and that she has an opportunity to act before things go back to normal and she reverts to feeling vulnerable.

She never thought it would be this way, that she would feel exploited, and of course it wasn't always. There were some happy years with Olly and Sasha at the beginning. They treated her well then. They *saw* her. Or at least she thought they did.

She realises now that she made some mistaken assumptions and some terrible choices and gradually, as a result, she's become invisible, unimportant, part of the furniture, a backdrop to their lives, an extra on the Olly and Sasha show, no more worthy of their attention than a fraying tapestry or a chair tucked into a forgotten corner. The grandfather clock in the hall makes more noise than her.

She's been used.

They don't even love the Manor House the way they should, she thinks, as she steps into the shade cast by the house. Sasha is most concerned about how it looks on her Instagram feed where she promotes the yoga business. Olly buries himself in the study every day, so obsessed with his novel that he hardly notices anything or anyone else. She's come to realise, far too late, that Olly and Sasha are not at all who she'd thought they were.

All of these revelations were triggered by her discovery, a week ago, of something that rocked her world and forced her to face some hard truths. But before she can find the courage to act, she needs to see it one more time, to be sure that she didn't imagine or exaggerate it.

Inside, she hurries to Olly's study.

She sits at the desk and opens his laptop. She knows his password because she's seen him type it in. That's one of the few advantages of being invisible: if people don't see you, they don't imagine that you might be watching them.

The document she wants is up on Olly's screen. It's his novel, the work in progress that he's been slowly writing for the past five years. He's nearly finished it. Unable to resist temptation, bit by bit, in snatched moments like this one, she has secretly devoured every page as he's written it. Olly is a good writer – superb, in fact. The book is gripping; it reads like a classic. She can see how Olly has carefully considered every sentence, every plot point, every beautifully drawn character. The story jumps off the page so vividly that she can imagine it as a film. Some passages made her heart race. She's read sad chapters which have brought her to tears and felt herself blush as she hasn't been able to tear her eyes away from the sexier scenes. They gave her feelings about him. Or, rather, they intensified feelings she already had, feelings she bitterly regrets now.

Reading the book became an addiction. She couldn't get enough of it. She craved the rare moments when Olly and Sasha both left the house, and she could sneak into the study and consume the next instalment. Until last week. Everything soured when she reached Chapter 28. She was reading eagerly, as usual, greedily, even, when she saw something that made her feel as if she'd been punched in the gut.

She reread the page once, then again and she was certain: she was seeing herself in the book; Chapter 28 contained her. A sense of dread unfurled inside her and bloomed into ripe shame. The picture of her that Olly painted wasn't flattering. Not at all. It was coruscating. She read it again. Nausea crept up her throat and had to be swallowed back down, bitter and hot.

The housekeeper was a dull woman, whose only role was to serve others, a woman without purpose of her own, servile, her mind more impoverished every time she rejected the inclination to seize life for herself, preferring instead to acquiesce to an existence devoid of meaning, mapped out for her by the actions of others. She had robbed herself of agency and might as well have never been born.

This paragraph caused her to feel uneasy, but mostly sympathetic towards this poor woman. She didn't see herself in the description until she read on.

Her outfits outwardly advertised her choice: she wore dowdy, mumsy, shapeless clothes, housecoats and flat shoes that rendered her soundless when she slunk through the domestic spaces that formed her cage. Her body took on the contours of servitude, her muscles moulded by the quotidian Sisyphean labour. Her hands were ruined. But her worst sin was the headscarf, a peach and aquamarine abomination. Stylish, she must have once thought it when she put it on; she probably entertained visions of soft-top cars on the Italian Riviera, of red lipstick, big sunglasses, silken strands of hair escaping the scarf. Dull minds can be prone to the most unrealistic of fantasies. The scarf in reality? A fishwife's rag. The meaning of the housekeeper's existence? An illusion. Subservient to the lives of others, she had probably even forgotten her own name.

She'd reached up to touch the scarf she was wearing over her hair. It was striped peach and aquamarine. She'd thought it pretty this morning but now it felt as if it was burning her scalp. She'd ripped it from her head and picked up a pair of scissors from his desktop and was about to cut it into pieces when something stopped her. This paragraph was one of the most recent he'd written. If she stopped wearing the scarf, would he suspect that she'd read his work? Would he notice the coincidence? Slowly, trying not to cry, she'd put the scarf back on, feeling as if her insides had turned to black tar, as if there was something fundamentally rotten and unlovable about her and she was as useless and virtually non-existent as he accused her of being. A shadow of a person.

But as she tied it, a thought rose from inside her, a stubborn, unexpected thought: I'll show him. She reknotted the scarf tightly and began to get used to a brand new feeling of rebellion that was unfurling inside her.

Now, she inhales deeply, steeling herself to reread that passage and to look at whatever Olly might have added to the book since last week. She scrolls through and reads with gritted teeth. The character based on her hasn't improved at all; in fact, he's portrayed her as an increasingly pathetic presence in the book and it hurts even more than it did the first time she read it.

Hold your nerve, she tells herself. She's been planning this. It will be her first act of revenge.

She scrolls back through Olly's document to an early chapter, a beautiful piece of writing that, when she read it at the time, moved her immensely.

She selects a paragraph which she cuts, then she scrolls randomly through the book and pastes the cut section somewhere that it doesn't belong. She repeats the action again and again, moving more paragraphs and sentences in the same way, jumbling everything up until almost no page is untouched.

Then she returns to the page that was on the screen when she accessed the document. She leaves that and the few before it untouched. Olly's word count hasn't altered so he shouldn't notice what she's done until he reads the book in its entirety again. Which he's often said he won't do until he's finished it. He'll never be able to unpick the damage.

She sits back, satisfied.

What's the expression? 'Hell hath no fury like a woman scorned.' She thinks it might be true. If Olly and Sasha are going to get what's coming to them, then this is a start, but there's more to do. Now that the police are here, she feels bolder. She won't do anything rash, though. Her situation, and what she knows, is complicated. The best revenge is planned slowly and lands all at once.

If she gets it right, they won't see her coming.

15

TUESDAY

Nicole

Nicole hears the buzzer and this time she remembers to look at the video entry system before answering, but the screen is blank. She taps it, even though she knows that won't help, and nothing changes. She needs to call the company to come out here and fix it. She feels angry with Tom for not getting on top of this. The Barn worked beautifully for the first few months, but these problems have been occurring more often lately. If he had sorted it out, the police might have had some taped evidence of what happened to him, this nightmare might be over, and she would be able to mourn him in private.

Immediately, she feels bad about feeling cross. It's so hard, this fresh grief. She knows Tom's gone, but part of her brain still hasn't accepted it and wants to feel all the normal emotions towards him, the day-to-day petty irritations, the urge to tell him about silly things that have happened. She wishes she could ask him about the card in his pocket. Doubtless he'd have an innocent explanation. He didn't have a bad bone in his body. It's what she's pinned her love on for all these years. Maybe I'll talk to Patrick about the systems, she thinks, ask him to sort it all out for me.

Patrick has been here for about forty-eight hours. Yesterday was strange. It should have been an ordinary, humdrum Monday but instead it felt like the longest, loneliest day of her life, just the two of them in the Barn, trying to be kind to one another, and supportive, but not quite connecting.

The female police officer called to check in but didn't have any developments to report. She asked how Nicole was doing and told her that they were pursuing enquiries. When she hung up, Nicole felt as if all of this should be happening to someone else.

She thought a lot about Tom's funeral, and it gave her some comfort. They can't hold one until the coroner releases his body, of course, but she wants to make sure he has the best of everything, a grand goodbye. She mentioned it to Patrick and that was the easiest part of their day, when they talked about Tom's favourite things, and how to incorporate some of them into the service and the wake. When she's up to it, she'll make lists and some calls. She wants it to be perfect.

She appreciates the effort Patrick's making, even if things have been awkward. He's very much the best version of himself. She's loved hearing about how he's found his feet working in recruitment. 'I've got a talent for it,' he said, and she heard pride in his voice. 'I'm actually making something of myself.'

'Can you spare time from work to be here?' she asked.

'Absolutely. They know the situation. I can do a bit of work from here if necessary.'

'How did you get the job?' she wanted to know.

'A friend of a friend offered to give me a shot. I was so lucky. And I'm a natural at it. I've never had a talent for anything in my life before.'

She knows that's true. Patrick survived rather than thrived academically at school. It was the same in sport and other extra-curricular activities. If he had a talent then, it was for getting Tom into trouble.

'I'm so pleased for you,' she told him, and meant it.

They've been reminiscing a lot. He's reminded her of stuff she's forgotten, told her things she didn't even know. It's been better than she could have expected.

The buzzer goes again. Oh yes, she thinks. There's someone here. She'd got quite lost in her thoughts. It's unlike her. She gives up on the video entry system and hurries to the atrium. Through the spy hole she sees Sasha and Olly. Her heart sinks a little, but she feels she owes them, so she puts a smile on and opens the door.

They're wreathed in sympathy-drenched smiles and hand her a cake. 'Come in and have a slice?' she asks. She doesn't want them to – it's been a relief to be out of their orbit and beyond their judgement – but politeness kicks in because they're her neighbours, they helped her, they brought cake and that's how she was raised.

Sasha looks as if she wouldn't dream of it. 'Oh, goodness, no, we don't want to intrude, and I hope we're not interrupting. We just wanted to give you the cake and check that you're managing okay. And to see if there's anything we can do?' Olly stands a pace or two behind her, hands behind his back, his head slightly inclined in a way that reminds Nicole, disconcertingly, of her sanctimonious childhood priest.

'Thank you.' She opens the tin and peeks in. The smell is instantly comforting. 'Coffee cake?'

'Kitty made it. We know it's your favourite.'

'Please thank her for me and thank you for bringing it.'

The silence is awkward; it lasts a little too long. Nicole tries to keep the smile on her face. Why won't they go away, now?

'We met Patrick,' Olly says.

She's interrupted by her phone ringing. 'I should probably check—' she says and pulls it from her back pocket. It's the police. Her heart skips a beat. 'I'm sorry. I need to get this.'

She steps into the house, pulling at the door, but it doesn't close completely behind her. Never mind, she thinks, they'll get the hint and leave anyway.

'Hello,' she says. Instinctively, she takes a seat on one of the chairs by the fireplace in the atrium, preparing herself for the emotional blow of whatever they might tell her. She puts the call on speaker.

'Hi Nicole, it's Hal Steen. Just a quick call to ask you a question, if you don't mind?'

'Go ahead.'

'We have a report back on possible causes for the injury to Tom's head.'

'Oh, yes,' she says.

'Our pathologist thinks it was the result of an impact from something made of metal, with a sharpish edge. Usually, the

86

pathologist will suggest a possible weapon. Often, the details visible in injuries correlate with specific weapons, like, for example, a baseball bat, and in this case, she has a few ideas, but none of them fit the injury perfectly. We wondered if you could think of anything in your household that might match the description.'

'A weapon?' she asks. 'But he must have tripped and fallen. Perhaps it was a rock. Or the tiles on the side of the pool.'

'The science is suggesting that it's not that. Can you think of anything?'

'Describe it again.' She shuts her eyes and breathes in and out deeply. This is horrible news. He repeats himself and she tries to focus but she can't think of anything.

'I have no idea,' she says. 'How can they be sure it wasn't something around the pool?'

'It's believed to be metal. They're firm about that.'

'I don't know,' she whispers. 'I'm sorry.'

Steen pauses, before saying, 'If you think of anything, will you let us know?'

'Of course.' She stands, the phone in her hand, and walks into the living area. She touches the little row of ornaments displayed on a shelf: sheep. Her favourite animal. In pride of place. They were the sweetest gift from Tom.

She tries to imagine what he might have been doing the morning he died, to visualise him moving through this space. He usually spent his Saturday mornings lounging in his sweats, maybe taking a slow walk around the house or grounds, a cup of coffee in hand. He would have lined up his sports viewing for the weekend, skimmed the news. Since the win, that's how he spent most mornings if they weren't expecting anyone at the house. She goes to the windows, where he loved to stand, and looks out. The sun is a white shimmer high above the cliffs, its harshness subduing the woodland greens, but scattering glinting shards across the surface of the river where it's visible through the trees.

'Thank you,' Detective Steen says. 'We didn't locate anything at the house which could have delivered his injury, which suggests that whatever hurt Tom might have been brought to your home and taken away afterwards.'

'You mean by a person?' she asks. 'Someone hit him?'

'Possibly,' he says. 'But the injury is likely not the cause of his death. Water was found in Tom's lungs, suggesting that he was alive when he entered the pool.'

'He drowned?'

'That's the official cause of death. But the injury is significant. It caused a small area of bruising to his brain. *If* it can be proved that he fell and drowned as a result of that injury and *if* the injury was inflicted on him by someone else, that could result in a charge of manslaughter, possibly murder.'

It's a lot for Nicole to take in. 'Significant' would seem to her to be an understatement when Tom's dead, lying in a morgue somewhere. She hopes they sewed him up neatly and with care. She would love to see him, to tend his body herself, however damaged it is. She might ask if that's possible.

Since she was a child, Nicole has wanted to nurture. There was only one person who didn't fall into that category, she thinks, and that was Tom's granny. Nicole tried to like her and in Granny's later years to look after her, but Granny made it clear from the start that she thought Nicole was competition and she had an acid tongue. Nicole never let on to Tom, but Granny's death, when it came, had been a relief. She felt too guilty to say it and couldn't even bring herself to point out that Granny was getting on and her demise was undoubtedly a respite from burgeoning medical needs that would have caused her suffering and burdened them. Tom wouldn't have wanted to hear it.

'Have you found out anything about the card you showed me?' she asks. 'Sadie's Massages.'

'Not yet. We're still looking into it. There are a lot of Sadies who offer massages. We're sifting through them.'

Steen reminds her that she can phone his colleague Jen if she needs anything or has questions.

'There is something,' she says. 'I saw a man on Sunday morning when I was staying at the Manor. He was sneaking around the entrance.'

'What was he doing?'

'He came in and disappeared behind one of the big hedges at the top of the driveway. At first, I thought he was one of Sasha's yoga students, but then he snuck back out after a few minutes. He looked furtive.'

'Can you describe him?'

'He was scruffy, wearing a T-shirt and cargo shorts and young, maybe in his twenties. He looked a bit like a vagrant. Or a hiker, maybe. I think he was carrying a small pack, but he was quite a distance away, so it was hard to tell.'

'Have you ever seen him before?'

'No.'

'Did anyone else see him?'

'Kitty didn't. I forgot to ask Olly or Sasha.'

'Do you feel unsafe?'

'I'm okay. I've got someone staying. Tom's best friend.'

'Well, that's good. Let us know if you see the man again, or anyone else behaving suspiciously.'

'I will.'

The Barn feels very silent in the aftermath of the call. She checks outside the front. Olly and Sasha have gone. She comes back inside and closes the door, realising as she does that someone could have crept in while she was on the phone. How long was the door unattended? A few minutes, at least. Olly and Sasha should have shut the door, but perhaps they didn't notice she'd left it open.

She thinks of the man she saw creeping through the Manor House gates and stands stock-still, listening, in case someone did creep in, in case he did, but she hears nothing unusual. Though it would be easy to hide in this house if you wanted to. It's so big. Her heart rate ticks up and she puts her hand on her chest to calm herself down. Patrick should be back soon. She could wait for him outside, but that's where Tom died. On the whole, she thinks she feels safer in here.

16

FIVE YEARS EARLIER

Anna's Journal

After a few weeks of yoga and a growing and wonderful friendship with Sasha my black mood caught up with me again. I knew it was too good to last.

I've been mislaying things more often over the past few weeks and it has sapped my confidence. I lost my purse and a necklace that Nick gave me. They both turned up, but I feel as if my brain just gets foggier by the day and I'm second-guessing myself all the time.

I made a mistake, socially. I tried to rekindle a friendship with one of the women I had felt closest to before Nick died: Lucy Samson. I woke up one day feeling confident and sent her a message asking if she wanted to have coffee. Stupidly, I built her response up in my mind. She would be pleased to hear from me, I thought; we would have coffee and then see each other regularly, just like I do with Sasha. It would be my introduction back into the lives of these women who always seemed so busy and purposeful.

But she didn't reply, even though I could see that she read my message, and it hit me hard.

I reverted to not being able to leave the house, even to go to yoga. My mind persuaded me that even friendship with Sasha was an illusion and I felt too bleak to do anything, even to write in here. All I could think about was the future that Nick and I had lost. For the first time since we bought it, the Manor House seemed more like a drag than a joy. It felt overwhelming and I blamed it for bringing me here ten years ago and ripping me away from my old friendship circles into those new ones which turned out never to mean anything. The feelings were hard to cope with because I've always loved this place, and Nick did, too. We were so aware of all its history and all the people who lived here before us. We bought it because we loved every part of it, every material that went into building it, every nook and cranny inside and outside. It's a precious piece of the past. But that didn't stop me wondering whether it was time to sell up and let someone else take it over.

Sasha called me right after the class I missed, and she's been calling me every day since, cajoling me into returning. 'I can't let you slip back into depression,' she said. 'What happened? You've been doing so well. Come to class again. All you need to do is to show up and I'll support you through the rest. I know you can do it.' I felt the tug of her words. It was nice to be wanted. 'I miss you,' she said. 'And I wouldn't say that to just anyone.'

Kitty encouraged me, too. 'This is just a dip you're having,' she said. 'Get back out there. You were doing so well. Nick would have been proud of you.'

I went back. It felt like the hardest thing in the world, but it was good to do it. Sasha was very attentive. Afterwards, over coffee, I told her how I'd been feeling. 'I wouldn't normally be as forward as this,' she said, 'but I care about you so I'm going to suggest something.'

'What?' I asked. I was feeling better in the glow of her attention. It was as if I'd stepped out of the cold, and she was warming me up. Being with her made me feel different, lighter, more hopeful. The attention she gave me was so intense and personal.

'I'd like to come to your house, to look at it. I want you to see it through my eyes, because I think your depression has, understandably, made you blind to what you have and to the possibility that you can be happy again.'

'Would you really do that?' I asked. I couldn't believe she wanted to visit me in person. Her classes were crowded, and she was charismatic. I'd seen plenty of other women trying to befriend her only to be gently, courteously rebuffed, and yet she wanted to come to my home.

'Yes,' she said.

I invited her to come for tea the next day. I said that she was welcome to bring her boyfriend, too, if he was free. She said they would both be honoured, and I felt thrilled as I walked back to the car. For a few minutes the darkness was pushed completely away. Of course, by the time I got home I was full of doubt. I hadn't entertained people at the Manor since Nick's funeral. It felt like a bad idea; I was convinced I wasn't up to it. They would be sure to see me as a dull old woman. I told Kitty I'd made a mistake. 'Nonsense,' she said. 'Let people help you.

I'll make a cake and tidy the Orangery. You can have tea in there and it'll be very nice.'

She was right. I picked them up because they don't have a car and drove them here. They were gracious and lovely. Olly was as charming as Sasha had described him. Both were polite to Kitty when I introduced them. I showed them around the Manor, and they loved it, especially the medieval parts. I told them stories about the house and Olly said that I was a born storyteller. It felt like a compliment coming from a writer like him. I started to wonder why I'd been so anxious. I felt as if I'd been silly.

'You can't give this up,' Sasha said, when we were about to say our goodbyes. 'Nobody will take care of this place the way you do. Nobody can love it as much as you.'

'It's too big for me on my own,' I said. 'Kitty and I barely keep on top of everything.'

'You're braver and more resourceful than you think,' Sasha said. 'Look, in the long term it might not be right for you to stay here but promise me you won't do anything hasty. It's not a good idea to make big decisions when we're in the grip of any sort of anxiety.'

She messaged me later that night:

Olly and I can't thank you enough for such a lovely afternoon tea and tour of the Manor. Olly said he could see why I thought you had a special quality. He said it's rare to meet someone so open-hearted and intelligent. See you at class tomorrow. Coffee after as usual? xxx

17

TUESDAY

Jen

Jen presses the doorbell of a terraced Georgian house in Chepstow. It's on a street she's long admired. The door is painted a pretty pale blue, with red geraniums blooming in pots on either side of it. She's here to interview the woman who'd had a private yoga lesson with Sasha on the morning of Tom Booth's death.

She introduces herself when the door opens. The owner is a middle-aged woman. A small dog yaps at her feet.

'Yes, yes. Come on in,' the owner says. 'Glad you called ahead because I'm going to visit my mother soon. She won't care if I'm late, she's got dementia, but I like to stick to my routine.'

'This won't take long,' Jen tells her.

They sit around a kitchen table overlooking a narrow back garden, beautifully planted and with a view of the castle.

'You had a private yoga lesson with Sasha Dempsey last Saturday at the Manor House at Lancaut?'

'I did.'

'What time was your lesson?'

'From ten to eleven.'

'Did you leave immediately afterward?'

'I did.'

'Did you see anybody else at the Manor?'

'No. Occasionally I see her partner, and I think there's a housekeeper because I've spotted her from a distance, but she isn't particularly friendly. I didn't see either of them this week. Can you tell me more about what you're investigating? I might be able to help you better.'

And gossip more, Jen thinks. 'I'm sorry but I can't at this stage,' she says. 'But it was a serious incident and we're grateful for your time. Did you see anything unusual on your arrival or departure?'

'I saw a young man on the lane, dressed like a tramp. There's a lay-by, before you reach that monstrous new glass building, and he was standing in it.'

'Alone?'

'Yes. And he stood right at the back of the lay-by, so he just caught the corner of my eye as I drove past. It gave me quite a fright because he looked creepy. But he wasn't there after my lesson.'

'Did you see a vehicle?'

'No.'

'Anything else you can remember about him?'

'Not really. Just that he had longish hair and possibly a scrappy little beard like all the young men seem to these days.'

'How old do you think he was?'

'He could have been anything between twenty and thirty. I honestly can't say more accurately than that. I only glimpsed him. I assumed he was on his way to the reserve. He had the look of a twitcher.'

'Was he carrying anything that made you think that? Binoculars?'

'Not that I can remember. Sorry.'

'You've been very helpful,' Jen says. 'Thank you.'

As she walks back to the station she thinks about this man. He might have been a walker, but there have also been one or two reports recently of young men sleeping rough in rural areas around Chepstow. She'll ask Hal if they can organise a search of all the woodland on the peninsula. The original search just took in the Glass Barn's grounds and the accessible areas close by. If this man did harm Tom Booth, he's probably long gone by now, but there might be traces of him.

At the station, she goes direct to Hal's office. His door is open and he beckons her in.

'I spoke to Nicole Booth,' he says. 'She can't think of anything that might have caused her husband's head injury.'

'Okay,' Jen says. This is fast becoming a strange, complicated case, where evidence is either lacking, like the failure of the security cameras, or hard to explain, like the business card found in Tom's pocket. Enquiries to masseuses called Sadie haven't thrown up any reasonable suspects. Most of them live nowhere near here. Locally, there are none who advertise publicly. They traced the number on the card and discovered that it's attached to a burner phone.

Jen shows Hal a message she's received from a local journalist, Dave Gittins, who has got wind of Tom's death.

'Ask him to put a lid on it,' Hal says. 'Do you want me to call him?'

'No, no,' she says. 'I'll handle it. I don't think I can put him off long, though.' The Glass Barn, the lottery win, the unexplained death in the swimming pool: the headlines will write themselves. She thinks Dave might respond better to a soft approach from her than to Hal laying down the law.

'How's Nicole doing today?' she asks. She hasn't made her daily call to Nicole, yet.

'She was upset that I asked about what might have caused the injury. She's still insistent it was an accident. She's presenting like a textbook grieving widow, but I feel uneasy about her.' He stands up. His energy is taut. Jen loves the intensity with which he approaches his cases. 'I mean, you can miss someone even if you murdered them. You can still feel grief for them. And she has no confirmed alibi yet. I don't love that the video cameras at the Barn were down. It's a heck of a coincidence.'

'Did anyone locate the fudge vendor from the show?' Jen asks.

'Not yet. There were over fifty food stalls. A lot of them sold fudge. Joe's still checking. We confirmed there was no CCTV anywhere on site, either.'

'Any road cameras between here and there?' Jen asks.

'Not one. The route's too rural.'

'I've been wondering if it's possible to see what actions were taken on the security system,' she says. 'Like, is there a log of what Tom or Nicole did to it? Is it possible to see whether the systems were disabled on purpose or if they malfunctioned?'

'That's a good idea,' he says. 'Make a note to get that followed up. Forensics have Tom Booth's laptop. What do you make of Nicole and Tom's relationship? Do you think they were happily married?'

Jen reflects for a moment. 'It's impossible to tell. I mean, she paints it as a happy marriage, and so do the neighbours. But you can be happily married until suddenly you're not. That's not the feeling I'm getting from her, though. I believe she truly loved him. But, like you say, you can murder someone you love. Maybe she knew all about the Sadie on the business card and couldn't forgive him for being unfaithful. If she did it, I can't believe money was a motive. They have so much they could divorce, and both walk away with millions.'

'It depends on whose ticket it was,' Hal says. 'In terms of who's entitled to the cash.'

'Would it, though? At this point? They claimed the win together and spent large sums of money together.'

He shrugs. 'I suppose that would be for lawyers to sort out if they split. But if she's greedy, she might want it all.'

Jen thinks about it. Did Nicole strike her as greedy? Impossible to tell from the little she's seen of her. 'We know they had a combined annual income in the region of 46K before they won the lottery, right?'

'Yes.'

'And now their combined wealth stands at ten million quid, which they won just over two years ago. So how do you get that greedy, that quickly, to go from living apparently happily on 46K to wanting all of the ten mill for yourself? I mean, wouldn't you still be getting used to having that much money? How do you even handle it?'

'It's enough to steal your daydreams if you have it all,' Hal says. 'But perhaps not if you have half.'

'What do you mean?'

'Ten million quid is enough to buy any ordinary mortal almost anything they want. Any house, car, bike, clothes, or whatever. And if you can buy anything you want without even thinking about it, what happens to your daydreams? What do you wish for?'

'I don't know,' she says. 'World peace? A superyacht? More houses. Bigger ones.'

'Exactly,' Hal says. 'You're in the realms of the silly. Your everyday dreams disappear, the dreams that give you something in common with the people you used to know, or to be. That's got to distort you somehow.'

'It'll alienate you.'

'Yes.'

She gets his point. 'I wonder if they adjusted well,' she says. 'Or agreed on how to spend it.'

'It might be a case of be careful what you wish for. But my point is that in Nicole's eyes half of ten million might not be enough to get everything she wants.'

'We should talk to her again.'

'We will. After we've spoken to the neighbours again, which I want to do today so we're crystal clear on the morning's timeline. Nicole also said she has a friend staying with her. A man she describes as "Tom's best friend".'

'Not *her* best friend?'

Hal shakes his head.

She frowns. 'She didn't mention him to me. He's on the scene very quickly.' She doesn't love that Nicole withheld this from her during their calls. Jen's the FLO. She should be telling Hal this, not vice versa. She feels guilty. She needs to do better.

'He is.'

'And he's just a friend?'

He shrugs. 'We'll speak to him, too, because it hasn't taken him long to get his foot in the door.'

She nods. This investigation is getting more complex by the minute. She's glad to be working on it with Hal. There are other detectives who wouldn't explore the possibilities the way he will. The downside is that he's not a good political player, and while she might not respect him as much if he was as smarmy and out for himself as some of their colleagues, they might be better at getting resources than Hal, and it's looking as if this enquiry is going to need all the money and manpower that it can get.

'I think we need to do a wider search of the peninsula,' she says. She tells him about the interview she just had, with Sasha's yoga student, and the man who frightened her on the lane leading to the Manor and the Glass Barn.

Hal says, 'Nicole Booth also told me she saw someone lurking around the Manor gates the day after Tom died.'

They compare notes. 'It could be the same person,' Jen says.

'I've already organised a more thorough search of the area for this afternoon. I'm not sure we went far enough the first time around.' Of course. He's on it.

Jen's phone pings, and she checks her messages. 'Here's one more thing. Forensics are saying that there are traces of lipstick on one of the coffee cups found in Tom Booth's den.'

18

FIVE YEARS EARLIER

Anna's Journal

Sasha offered to take me shopping because I told her that I was feeling dowdy. It was fun. She picked out some new outfits for me and was very patient while I tried things on. The sales assistant mistook us for mother and daughter, and we didn't tell her that we weren't! We giggled about it and Sasha got serious and said that she honestly felt that I was like a mother figure to her, which was a big deal because her own mother hadn't been present for her. I cried a little and she did, too. I told her that Nick and I tried for a family for a long time, but it wasn't meant to be for us.

We got me some basics then took a break and I treated Sasha to lunch. I wore the new clothes out of the shop because Sasha told me I should, and the waitress complimented me on my new blouse, which was lovely. It's been a long time since I felt that I looked nice. Sasha said I should try a soy latte because nobody has dairy these days. Nick would have scoffed at that, calling it a fad, but I thought, why not? It wasn't too bad. I wanted to buy us both a slice of cake, but she said she didn't think we really needed it.

I showed Sasha an invitation that I had from one of my old so-called friends. Not the person I invited to coffee who never replied, but another woman I used to know. The invitation was to a charity event. It came out of the blue and I was surprised and excited to have it. It had given me a real lift. I asked her if she could help me find an outfit for the event after coffee. I had a boutique in mind that I wanted to go to. But she was outraged. 'You shouldn't go to that,' she said. 'They just want money out of you. Have they invited you to anything else since Nick died? Didn't you say that your old friends have deserted you?'

'Oh,' I said. 'But I thought this was them trying to make things up to me.' I'd assumed she would be pleased.

Sasha said that she'd give the invitation a lot of careful thought if she were in my shoes. 'You have to make sure that people aren't using you, Anna,' she said. 'You know this woman, it's up to you, but ask yourself whether she's supported you at all since Nick died? Have you sat with her like you sit with me, and shared your thoughts, or does she just want bums on seats and money for her charity?'

'I hadn't thought of it that way,' I said. It put a bit of a damper on things. I felt my excitement dribble away.

'I'm sorry if that sounds harsh,' she said. 'But I worry people will take advantage of you. And look, the party is next week. Surely, her A list got invitations months ago.'

'It's a good charity,' I said. I resented her bursting my bubble. The evening looked fun. I didn't love parties, but a sit-down dinner and an auction would give the event structure and something to talk about if conversation flagged.

'Then donate to it, but don't mistake this for a heartfelt invitation. I mean, it *might* be, only you can be the judge of that, but it might not. Before you say yes, you need to have a good think about who your real friends are.'

When I got home, I asked Kitty what she thought, and she said that Sasha had a point. I dithered for twenty-four hours but decided to go to the event anyway and RSVP'd via email and sent the money for my seat at the banquet. For the first time since Nick died, I was feeling better about myself, mentally and physically. If I could get close to Sasha, I thought, I might be able to rekindle other friendships and make something of them. Sasha would get over it when she saw that these women cared about me genuinely.

When I told her I was going, she didn't see it that way. 'You're drawn to those women like a moth to a flame,' she said. She seemed sad. 'Don't blame me if they damage you again,' she warned. 'But if they do, know it'll be hard for me to witness.'

She didn't call the next day and cancelled our yoga class via a group message. When I contacted her directly to ask if she was alright, I heard nothing.

Kitty said that perhaps I'd upset Sasha. 'I expect she doesn't want to see you get hurt,' she said.

'She told me to be brave,' I said. 'And you did, too.'

'Brave,' Kitty said. 'Not foolhardy. Remember how upset those women made you feel. They were like rubberneckers at

Mr Creed's wake, nosing around the place, complaining about the canapés.'

'They complained about the food at Nick's wake?'

'And the service. I didn't want to tell you. It wasn't the time or place.'

That hurt. I started to second-guess my decision to go. I felt guilty that I'd given Sasha the impression that I didn't value her advice. Not seeing her for a few days was a jolt, too. Without her daily call and messages, I quickly began to feel unmoored again, the way I'd done right after Nick's death. I drove to the yoga centre, even though class was cancelled, and asked them to give a handwritten card of apology to Sasha if she came in, because she still wasn't replying to my messages.

The night of the party came around quickly. I decided to go because I didn't want to pull out at the last minute and give anyone a reason to be upset with me. As I arrived at the venue, I still had some hopes that it might be a nice evening, but as soon as I stepped through the door to the ballroom, I found myself crippled with social anxiety. My dress looked old and frumpy compared to the other women. I'd done my hair myself but nobody else had. The hairdressers in Chepstow must have been busy that afternoon.

I pushed through the crowd to find the hostess, but she barely acknowledged me after an initial air kiss. I expected her to introduce me to the people she was with, but she moved on and so did they. I went to look at the table where the auction prizes were and ran into another woman I knew. 'Oh! You're still in the area!' she said. 'Where have you been hiding?' It felt like implied criticism and my anxiety began to escalate. Everything felt too loud and too busy after the quiet and isolation of the Manor. I felt like putting my hands over my ears. I hovered at the edge of the party, lacking the courage to break into any groups. I had hopes that things would improve at the banquet, but I was seated at the worst table and was totally ignored by the strangers sitting on either side of me. I felt invisible.

I ate my dinner slowly, the food like ashes in my mouth, and realised that I'd made a terrible mistake. Sasha was right. This scene wasn't me and these people weren't true friends. I fled before dessert and the auction, telling the man beside me that I felt sick, but he barely seemed to listen, let alone care. I had a full-blown panic attack when I got into my car.

Back at home, I found that Kitty had already gone to the Coach House. I went to bed but couldn't sleep. For hours I could hear brushing sounds behind the panelling. It didn't make sense. There are openings behind the panelling downstairs that a person can hide in, but not upstairs. Unless it had been accessed by a rodent. When the noises stopped, finally, I plucked up courage to run down the landing to the spare room at the far end and tried to sleep there, but the wind whistles around that side of the Manor and a branch kept striking the window, the sound like nails dragging on the glass.

I woke late the next day, feeling horrible. It was Kitty's day off. I didn't bother to get up, only dragging myself to the toilet. I didn't shower, I didn't brush my teeth, I didn't eat. I felt ashamed of myself for ignoring Sasha – the one person who meant something to me in this post-Nick existence – and letting myself get snubbed and overwhelmed. Moth to a flame was right.

Kitty found me in bed when she arrived the next day. I told her what had happened. 'You've got yourself in a state,' she said, shaking her head, as if she'd known I would. 'Leave it to me.'

A few hours later the door to my bedroom opened softly. 'Anna,' Kitty said. 'There's someone here to see you.'

Sasha sat on the edge of my bed. 'Hey,' she said. 'I heard you were struggling.'

'I'm so sorry,' I told her. 'I should have listened to you.'

'You need to trust me.'

'I know. I will. I do.'

'Promise?' she said. 'Because it's hard to be friends, otherwise. I have to look after myself, too, and if you don't trust me it's damaging to me. It means we're not connecting properly.'

'I promise,' I said. 'I absolutely swear it.'

'I missed you,' she said, and my heart felt full.

19

TUESDAY

Hal

Hal makes his way down the path leading towards the nature reserve at Lancaut and Jen follows. They pass some of the search team, heading up in the opposite direction, looking hot and tired. The path is steep and strewn with loose stones. Occasionally, his foot slips. He's grateful for the shade cast by the trees. On a different day, if he was making the trip for a different reason, he would stop and admire the beauty, but not today.

The wider search of the peninsula is a long shot and an expensive one. There's too much terrain here, too densely covered with vegetation for him to be very hopeful of finding anything. Any stranger who might have harmed Tom has had plenty of time to remove traces of him or herself and to get far away. But he doesn't like to leave any stones unturned.

At the bottom of the path, they reach flatter ground. The river is just yards away, but silty banks discourage him from getting close to it. A half-rotted wooden pier overhangs the water. A new path stretches out to their left and right.

A uniformed officer is posted there. He indicates which way they should go: 'Past the ruined chapel, and on a bit. It's in the woods. Someone will show you.'

Hal turns to look at Jen. He won't ask her how she's doing because she's clearly fitter than he is and he doesn't want to insult her, but he would like to check on her.

'Isn't it stunning here,' she says. 'Feels like you're cut off from the world. You could easily camp out here without anyone noticing you.'

The path runs along the edge of the riverbank. The intensity of the day's heat is dissipating, which feels like a release, and the evening light is golden. One of the search team is waiting for them. He shows them the recently abandoned campsite, which is in a pretty glade just far enough from the public footpath to be out of sight, and on the other side of a wooden fence.

Hal tries to orient himself. He has a terrible sense of direction.

'So, the Glass Barn is up on the hill above us?' he asks.

'Yes,' Jen says. 'If you looked out of the living-area windows at the Barn, you'd be looking in this direction. This is the woodland that you see from there.'

'This fence is the boundary of the land belonging to the Barn,' the search team member confirms. 'I'm not one hundred percent sure it was worth your time coming here.'

Hal says nothing. He likes to see things for himself; it's that simple.

'How do we know it's recent?' he asks.

'They've cleared some nettles to make space for a small tent, you can see them there, beside the indentation where the tent was. The nettle roots look as if they haven't been up long, and there's a trace of a fire.' He points to a small, darkened area of earth. Hal sees some ash around it.

'In this heat?'

'I know. Stupid behaviour.'

'Anything else?'

'We haven't found anything, but I would say that it's been very well cleared up. We nearly missed it. Whoever left it, pulled some of the undergrowth back across the site, which might suggest an attempt to hide the fact that they'd been here.'

Hal nods. 'Thank you,' he says.

He's disappointed that there's not more. It was too much to hope that they might find something that would allow them to trace an individual, but he had hoped, anyway.

But there was someone here. And recently. It potentially throws the number of suspects wide open. Unless someone Tom knew camped out here and waited and watched.

20

TUESDAY

Nicole

'The detective phoned,' Nicole says to the empty room. Patrick's gone to bed, but she doesn't want to go to her room and lie there, staring at the ceiling. Sleep has been patchy. Her dreams have become nightmares. She imagines Tom standing behind the kitchen island, fiddling with his coffee machine, debating whether it was too late to have an espresso, and imagines him replying, 'Oh, really? What did they want?' She misses the sound of his voice.

If Tom was murdered, she thinks, did I set it in motion somehow? Is it my fault? Would it have happened if we hadn't cashed that lottery ticket or built this place? Patrick has told her not to let herself go down the rabbit hole of 'What Ifs'.

'Nothing was stolen,' he said. 'That's a big thing that points to this being an accident. Hang in there. The police will confirm it soon, I'm sure.'

It's dark outside and she can see her reflection in the glass. She imagines someone out there, looking in at her. 'Blinds down,' she tells the house, and she holds her breath, wondering if the house will obey or if she'll have to try to get them down manually somehow, but the system works. She watches with relief as the blinds descend the way they should, rolling smoothly and in synchrony from hidden recesses in the ceiling until they touch the floor.

She sits on the couch and tries to distract herself from thinking about Tom and the police by scrolling through Pinterest, where she collects interiors images, but she can't focus. It all seems pointless now. Her mind turns to Patrick and how amazing it is that he's turned his life around. But she can't stay focused on anything.

At first, she thinks she's imagining the music. She hears opera playing, quietly, from somewhere else in the house. She assumes it's coming from Patrick's room, although if it is, he's playing it loudly, because the room he's staying in is in another wing. She'll ask him to turn it off. It's too painful to hear it. She walks out of the living area, through one of the glass corridors. Floor lights come on as she enters the corridor and illuminate the way dimly. The night sky is a dark, velvety blue, the stars pinpricks of light. She hurries, conscious once more of being visible to anyone outside – there are no blinds in the corridors – only realising when she reaches the bottom of the stairs that the music is quieter, not louder.

The back of her neck prickles, as if someone is standing behind her. She turns around. Now, the music sounds as if it's coming from their cinema room, which she just walked past.

She backtracks down the corridor and opens the door to the room. Wall and ceiling lights come on, and floor lighting shows her the way down a short, carpeted aisle between sets of velvet-covered reclining chairs. A curtained screen dominates the wall ahead. Picture lights illuminate posters of Tom's favourite movies. There's no music on. No sound in here at all.

She hears it again, coming from behind her, and it's louder than before. Her anxiety level increases. 'Patrick?' she calls. Perhaps it's him, moving through the house, the music following him. Though wouldn't she have seen him pass her? He doesn't answer. Cautiously, she walks back into the main living area. Now, the music seems to be coming from the fitness wing. She passes through the second glass corridor, her head down this time, afraid to glance up and see her reflection in the glass, looking haunted, or to see someone outside. The volume increases as she walks down the corridor, passing the sauna and the steam room.

At the doorway to the gym, she pauses before entering. The lights remain off. She can see through the room, past the silhouettes of the exercise machines, to double doors on the opposite wall. They lead out to the swimming pool. Above it, coloured light is dancing, changing shade every few seconds, from red, to blue, to green, to pink then a soft white. The pool lights. Tom set them to come on in different configurations. This is one he called 'disco'. It's crazy. And why is it on now? She inhales sharply. Her heart thumps hard against her chest.

She lets herself outside. The night air is warm and close and the music is booming. Was it always coming from here? Did the sound just bounce around the building in unpredictable ways, or did it move around the house from room to room the way she thought it did, earlier? As if Tom was walking through the place. She doesn't know.

She stands by the edge of the pool. It's the first time she's been out here since he died. She's been avoiding it, hadn't even wanted to look at it, but now she feels drawn to it, afraid, yes, but compelled to walk into the lights, to let the music envelop her. It's the soundtrack to the end of Tom's life. The coloured light dances across the front of her T-shirt. It feels as if Tom is trying to communicate with her. Or maybe someone is trying to mess with her. Patrick? Someone else? Or is it just the house malfunctioning again? She begins to cry. All she wants is to have Tom back.

The breeze is warm. It lifts strands of her hair and drapes them over her face where they stick to her damp cheeks. She pushes them back. Beyond the lights, the night is very dark, the stars so high and so far. A sliver of moon is mostly obscured by a torn rag of cloud. Nicole kicks her shoes off, pulls her T-shirt over her head, takes off her skirt and walks down the pool steps until she's knee deep in the water. The music surrounds her – Tom had speakers installed all around the pool, even underwater – and the lighting does too, so brightly that the rest of the world disappears as if she'd walked into the Northern Lights.

She feels so detached from reality it's as if she has a fever or is dreaming. Her sense of danger is strong, but so is a sense that she doesn't care, right now, in this moment. She doesn't understand why she's doing this, even as she feels the bite of the waterline rising up her torso. Usually, she would flinch and complain, shriek and stall, and Tom would laugh, but she ploughs on steadily as if drawn to dive beneath the water.

And there it is. The music. She can hear it even though she's submerged; the sound of the opera reaches her. It feels as if she's crying but she's not sure if you can cry when you're underwater. She stays under for as long as she can and when she resurfaces she gasps for breath, and even though it's warm, she begins to shiver violently as she climbs out, her wet underwear clinging to her. Beyond the lights, the night seems darker than ever, and she feels very sad and very afraid.

'Nicole!' Patrick is standing by the side of the pool. When did he get here? 'What are you doing?' The opera is still so loud he has to raise his voice.

She has no words for him. Her teeth start to chatter.

'I'll get you a towel,' he says. He grabs one from the gym and is back in a moment. He hands it to her, and she wraps herself in it.

'Why are you out here?' he asks. He's wearing Tom's robe, she notices.

'I heard the music,' she says.

'Since when did you listen to opera?'

'I don't. It was just on. Tom has been listening to it. It was playing when I found him.' She can't remember if she told him that, already. She's not sure she's making any sense.

'You didn't put the music on?'

She shakes her head. 'I thought you did.'

'No.'

'It's the house,' she says. 'The systems are broken.'

'Come inside. Get dry.' He picks up her clothes and shoes.

115

She looks up at the Barn. It seems so inviting, all lit up, floodlights illuminating the old ruins, light emanating from the windows, but she feels intimidated by it, too. She knows it's ridiculous, but she feels as if her home has got a mind of its own.

Patrick is obviously thinking the same thing. 'We'll get everything fixed,' he says. 'I'll sort it out. We can't have this happening.' She feels the pressure of his hand, lightly pushing her upper arm, guiding her in, and she lets him steer her.

'He died out here,' she says. The paving around the pool feels warm beneath the soles of her feet. It's hung on to the heat of the day. 'I thought I'd never want to be out here again, but I felt close to him, under the water. Is that crazy?' Patrick doesn't reply. She thinks maybe she does sound mad. She walks obediently in front of him, back into the house. As they step inside, the outside lights and music go off, all at once, and Nicole clutches his arm. The silence seems almost more threatening than the noise.

'It's okay,' he says. 'The house was having a funny turn. We'll get it sorted.'

Thank God he's here, she thinks. I don't think I could cope on my own.

21

WEDNESDAY

Olly

Olly flexes his fingers. His manuscript is open on the screen in front of him, calling him to start on the next chapter of his novel. He's full of coffee and nervous energy, but he isn't quite primed to start writing yet. He needs that energy to build just a little more.

He stands abruptly and paces the room, pausing in front of the window, taking in the view of the orchard where the boughs of gnarled apple and pear trees droop under their loads of ripe fruit. It's another lovely morning and he wants to find the view bucolic and inspiring, but too much fruit has already fallen and is spoiling on the ground, making him think of maggots, worms and other creatures that get under the skins of things.

He looks at the few objects he's arranged on the mantel shelf, things he's found in the Manor House or in its grounds: a piece of stone carving that looks like a fragment of a Celtic cross, an old metal key, heavy to hold, and an ancient flint arrowhead that he found near the riverbank. All mementoes of the time he's spent here so far. They give him succour. He's ready to write. He takes his seat and shuts his eyes briefly before starting – it's his ritual – but there's a knock on the door, shattering the moment.

'Go away!' he shouts.

'The police are here.' Kitty's voice.

'Tell them to leave. I'm working.'

'They're here, with me, outside the door. Can we come in? They'd like to speak with you.' She sounds anxious, her voice wavering.

Olly's jaw clenches. Not now, he wants to scream, you stupid woman, but he knows better. He opens the door. Two detectives stand behind Kitty, the same pair who came here on the day Tom's body was found.

'Good morning. Do you mind if we talk elsewhere?' he says. He can't bear the idea of them in his study, his sanctum. Their presence will pollute it. He finds it impossible to write unless he can keep the outside world out.

'This will do fine,' Detective Steen says. He pushes the door open, and Olly is forced to step out of the way as Steen walks into the room and sits down on Olly's couch. 'I hope you don't mind us dropping in,' he says. 'We won't keep you long.'

Olly hesitates. He wants to tell the man to get out of his study and to get lost altogether, but it's important he doesn't rile him. Olly's a little rusty at being polite and acquiescing, though. It's a long time since he had to kowtow to anyone, not since he moved into the Manor, and he's got used to it.

118

He settles on the couch opposite the detectives, straightens some research papers that are on the low table between them and tries to adopt a relaxed posture, though a little twitch in his eye develops. 'How can I help you, detectives?' he asks and smiles at the female, who presents as plain but could be very much more attractive if she made more effort. Her figure isn't bad. She looks at Steen, who starts the questioning.

'Firstly, we'd like to confirm what you were doing on the morning of Tom Booth's death.'

'As I told you before, I was here, in this room, writing my novel. My partner, Sasha, can confirm it.'

'Didn't she teach a class that morning between ten and eleven?'

'She did.'

'Where did she teach?'

'In the Great Hall.'

'Where does it overlook?'

'Nowhere. The windows are set too high in the walls.'

'That's what I thought,' Steen says. 'So, she didn't see you for that hour? And she couldn't have seen if you or your house-keeper left the house?'

He feels irritated. 'I didn't leave the house. Novels don't write themselves. I can't speak for Kitty.'

Steen nods and makes a note.

'When we spoke to you before, you said you first met Tom and Nicole Booth approximately six months ago,' he says.

'Correct.'

'But you weren't neighbours in the ordinary sense, were you? The Booths bought the land they developed from you, is that right?'

'That's correct, yes, but how is this relevant to Tom's death?'

Olly's being disingenuous. He knows the detectives will be looking at this case from every angle, especially now they consider it a likely murder. He and Sasha paid attention when Nicole took the call from the police while they were delivering the cake. They loitered and overheard every word of that conversation until Nicole moved out of earshot, so they know the police think it likely that Tom's head injury was inflicted on purpose.

'We believe that Tom's death might not have been an accident,' Steen says.

Olly is careful to feign surprise. 'You mean murder?'

'It's one of a number of enquiries.'

'That's horrific. Well, obviously, I'm at your service if there's anything I can do to help.'

'That's why we're here, Mr Palmer.'

Olly resents it when people state the obvious. It implies he's a stupid man, when he's anything but, and nothing makes him madder than people insinuating that he's an idiot. His molars grate against one another before he says, 'Well, fire away then!' He adjusts his position, throwing an arm across the back of the sofa he's sitting on, balancing an ankle on his knee so that he looks more open and helpful. The twitch in his eye is still there. He hopes they can't see it.

'Where were you the night before Tom died and the morning of his death?'

The answer trips off Olly's tongue. 'Sasha and I spent the evening together here. She was watching TV and working on her website, I believe, and I was working on my novel.'

120

'Was your housekeeper with you?'

'Kitty lives in the Coach House, which is on the estate. She usually leaves us after clearing up supper, so I'd say she was probably back there by eight-thirtyish.'

'Do you know for certain she went back to the Coach House?'

'No. I suppose I don't. I only know that she left here in the evening and turned up again the next morning. Will this take long, detective? I have work to do.'

'You're a writer?' Steen asks.

'I am.'

'Are you published? Would I know your work?'

'This will be my debut novel,' Olly says. 'But I hope you'll be hearing a lot about me as soon as it's published.'

He smiles, anticipating the usual reaction he gets, some sign that he's impressed his listener, perhaps some interested questions, but Steen doesn't smile back, only clears his throat. The sound is ugly to Olly, unpleasantly guttural, and the lack of any curiosity or respect from Steen irks him.

'Were you and Sasha together all evening?' Steen asks.

Olly laughs. 'No! We were in separate rooms for a few hours. I can't work with the television blaring. I need silence to work. Absolute silence.'

He pauses to let this sink in, the importance of what he does, the conditions required to excel, a hint of what their intrusion means to him, the sacrifice it entails.

'I expect you get the silence you need here, don't you?' Steen asks, glancing through the window towards the orchard.

'Oh, yes.'

'You're not disturbed by your wife's yoga classes?'

'No. And she's my partner, not my wife. Thankfully the Manor is big enough to accommodate us both,' Olly says.

'When did you move in?'

'Five years ago.'

'You and your partner bought this place?'

'To cut a long and rather lovely story short, we were invited to live here, by the owner.'

'Really? Is the owner a relation?'

'A good friend.'

'Name?'

'Anna Creed.'

'Does she live here still?'

Olly works hard to keep himself relaxed.

'No. Not in the Manor. It's complicated. She lives elsewhere.'

'So, to be clear, she lets you and your partner reside here while she's away?'

'That's correct.'

'So, when I asked if the Booths bought the land from you, it was actually' – he consults his notes – 'Anna Creed, the owner, they bought it from.'

'Yes,' Olly says.

'Do you pay rent?'

'We maintain the property. As custodians.'

'But no rent?'

'No.'

'She's a very generous friend, then.'

'Indeed, she is. How is this relevant, detective?'

Steen emits a small sigh, through his nostrils. 'I'm just wondering how I can get myself a friend like that, because this place, it's something else. Not many people get to live like this.'

Olly laughs, though he's immediately afraid it sounds a little too wild. Steen unnerves him.

'Can you run me *precisely* through what happened here on the morning of Tom Booth's death?'

'So far as I can remember, Sasha and I woke up at around seven. We had breakfast together an hour or so later. Kitty always gets up to make it for us, so she was probably in the Manor by seven-thirty. That would be typical. It was a beautiful morning. As I've said, I was in here working. Sasha gave a private yoga lesson and when that was over, she went outside. She likes to work on her practice under the oak tree out the front. I took a break for lunch and went outside to join her and that's when Nicole Booth ran up the driveway shouting that her husband was dead in their pool. Sasha took care of Nicole while I ran to the Barn to see if there was anything I could do, but it was too late. Tom was dead when I got there. Sasha left Nicole Booth in the care of our housekeeper, Kitty, and came to join me. Your colleagues arrived while we were still there, and we showed them the body.'

Steen makes copious notes even though Olly has told him all this, in his first interview, the day Tom died. Olly starts to wonder if he's soft in the head. When he finally stops writing he seems pleased with himself, and Olly sees a sharp flash of intelligence in his eyes. He frowns. He can't get the measure of this man. His uneasiness ramps up a notch.

'One last thing,' Steen says. 'Circling back. What's the situation with your housekeeper?' He flicks a page in his book. 'Kitty Ellis,' he says.

'As I said, she lives here, on site, in a little grace and favour cottage, which was originally the Coach House. She takes care of all the domestic tasks. Sasha and I both work very hard.'

Steen nods. 'I'm sure you do. Has Kitty had much contact with Tom or Nicole Booth that you know of?'

Olly shrugs. 'I doubt it. She kind of does her thing here and goes home. Though I suppose I don't know what she does with her evenings.' He leans forward. 'Between you and me, she's a creature of simple habits. Not to mention a bit of a fantasist.'

Steen raises an eyebrow and Olly feels encouraged. 'She doesn't always tell the truth,' he adds and enjoys the effect of his words when Steen and Jen exchange a look.

'Can you give us an example?' Jen asks.

'Ah! She speaks!' Olly says. Jen's face remains impassive. He notes the snub and continues. 'Kitty. Yes. She lies about things. We've noticed that she sometimes takes things from the fridge and the pantry, but she'll never admit to it. And once she broke a vase and denied it. Little things.'

Steen doesn't write this down, which is disappointing, but looks at Olly as if assessing him and asks, 'Why do you employ her if she's dishonest?'

Olly clears his throat. He must be careful what he says. 'Every one of us is flawed, wouldn't you agree, Detective?'

He smiles at Steen, hoping agreement on this will connect them, but Steen, like his partner, keeps his poker face on. Olly feels irritated. He's used to being able to charm people.

'One more thing,' Steen says. 'Have you seen any strangers in the area lately? Especially around the time of Tom's death.'

Olly considers this. 'A few weeks ago, I noticed someone was camping in the nature reserve. Gosh! Do you think they could have had something to do with this? I'm so sorry I forgot to mention it earlier. It totally slipped my mind.'

He's lying. This didn't happen a few weeks ago, but a few months ago. It won't harm to throw some uncertainty into the mix, to keep the detectives busy. He likes the thought of messing with them.

'Not to worry. It's useful to know now. Did you see the camper or campers?'

'No. I saw a tent set back from the footpath, hidden in the trees. The reserve is public land and people usually move on quickly, so I didn't think much of it. It never occurred to me that it could be something to do with Tom. I'm so sorry. Is that bad?'

'It's a line of enquiry. Would we be able to have a word with Sasha, now?' Steen asks.

'Absolutely.' Olly can't help feeling relieved this is over. 'We're done, then,' he says, getting up. Jen half rises from her seat but sits back down when Steen doesn't move. 'Oh, you mean in here?' he says.

'If you don't mind.'

Olly does mind, he minds a lot, but he says, 'Of course.'

He finds Sasha in the kitchen, her laptop open in front of her. Kitty is at the range.

'Could we have a moment, please,' he asks.

'I'm so sorry I let them in,' she says. 'They were insistent.'

Olly holds up a palm. 'Not now. Thank you.'

Kitty's head is bowed as she goes. Olly shuts the door behind her.

'Was it bad?' Sasha asks him.

'No. Maybe. They want to talk to you.'

'Maybe? What do you mean?'

'I mean I think it was fine.'

'You "think"?' she hisses. 'That's not good enough. You didn't fuck it up, did you?'

'No, I didn't, and make sure you don't either.'

He grabs her wrist, not wanting to hurt her, but to convince her that they're together in this. She pulls her arm out of his grip and he moves to the door and watches her walk all the way down the corridor towards his study. She stops before she enters, facing the closed door, as if gathering herself. She looks back at Olly briefly, takes a deep breath and her body language transforms from tense to relaxed as she turns the handle.

Attagirl, he thinks, and he exhales. He hadn't even realised he was holding his breath. She'll be fine, he thinks. He can rely on her completely. They'll pull this off.

22

FIVE YEARS EARLIER

Anna's Journal

I feel as if my feet have hardly touched the ground since I last wrote in here! It's been a whirlwind.

Everything went more or less back to normal with me and Sasha and I've never been so relieved. Even so, I've been trying to think of ways I can make it up to her because she's had a few wobbles and questioned me about how much I trust her and whether she can trust me in return. Once trust is gone it's almost impossible to rebuild it, she told me. I wish I'd never let her down by going to the party.

At first, I wasn't sure what I could do, apart from keep turning up at class. I bought her a generous gift, but she said that was unnecessary and she couldn't be bought. It was hard not to feel despairing that I'd ruined things. Not completely, but enough that it didn't feel quite the same. I feel as if I owe her, after everything she's done for me.

But an opportunity to prove myself has come up! Sasha told me that she and Olly have accommodation problems. The landlord is putting up the rent in their flat and they can't afford it, so they gave notice, but now they're finding it impossible to rent another place. They're afraid they'll have to move out of the area, to somewhere cheaper, but it would mean she'd have to start yoga classes somewhere else as they don't have a car. I almost felt ill when she told me. The thought that they could disappear from my life is awful. 'Come and stay with me while you look for somewhere new,' I told her. 'For goodness' sake! Kitty and I rattle around the Manor on our own. I've got plenty of room for you. And you can borrow a car to get to class.'

She refused outright at first, saying that it would be too intrusive, that it was too generous of me. 'Sasha,' I said. 'After everything you've done for me, it's the *least* I can do.'

'It'll be strictly temporary,' she said. 'You have to concentrate on rebuilding your life, not on propping up mine.'

'Helping you will help me,' I said. 'You can trust me on that.'

I felt as excited as a little kid the day they arrived. I gave them the guest room at the other end of the Manor from my bedroom, to allow them some privacy. I was honest about the noises I've been hearing at night and Olly said he'd listen out for them and help me investigate. Kitty made a lovely dinner for the three of us the first night they arrived, and we ate together in the kitchen. I lit candles and got out the good china and we had a jolly time. Olly is a hoot! He's got so many good stories and I haven't laughed that much in ages.

It all went brilliantly for a short while. The Manor House hasn't felt this full of life for a long time. I don't think Nick and

I ever brought it alive this much; we were too old when we moved in. It is such a joy to see a gorgeous young couple here. But Sasha came to speak to me in private after they'd been with me for about a week. It wasn't going to work out for them, she said, because I was making such a fuss of them all the time. They found it uncomfortable. All they wanted was somewhere to live that would allow them to work and save. They didn't need mothering. I was being a bit suffocating. It was too intense. They didn't want all this special treatment.

I was mortified. 'I'm so sorry. The last thing I want to do is suffocate you. Please, stay. What will make it easier for you?'

'Olly's very grateful for the dinners and the wine and the use of the car, but what he really needs is a better working environment. He's been writing at the vanity table in the bedroom and the chair is terribly uncomfortable for him.'

I had a solution. 'Why doesn't Olly use Nick's study? It would be the perfect space. There's a fireplace, the desk is large, and Nick bought himself one of those ergonomic chairs.'

'We can't impose that much,' Sasha said. 'Nick's space must be sacrosanct to you.'

She was right; she knew me well. But this was my choice.

'Please. Let me decide that. It's my absolute pleasure to be in a position to be able to help you both. I promise I'll stop fussing over you and start making sure you have what you need.'

Sasha helped Kitty and me get the study ready for Olly. I packed some of Nick's bits and pieces away so that Olly could make the space his own. We were chatting about writing, and I'd admitted to them that I wrote a journal, but I said it was just my silly thoughts jotted down rather badly and it was exciting to think that a novel would be written in Nick's study. Kitty didn't seem surprised and for a hot moment I wondered if she'd ever found it and read it.

Sasha told us that Olly is exceptionally talented. She said she has feelings about things, and she has a feeling about this and she's always right. I asked her if she'd read anything he'd written and she said no, but she knew he'd wowed everyone in a creative writing class that he did. He was so good that people had been very jealous of him. But, she said, writing a journal is very valuable, too. You should keep that up.

Olly was delighted with the study. 'I'm going to be so productive in here,' he said. 'Thank you very much.'

'We'll have to get you teaching in the Great Hall, next,' I said to Sasha. It was a joke, and they laughed, but it gave me an idea. What if they lived here semi-permanently? I was already dreading them moving out. They were going to a lot of property viewings and every time they came back from one, I watched from the kitchen window to see their faces when they got out of the car, afraid that they'd look as if they'd just found the place of their dreams.

When they came back yesterday Sasha said that they'd seen one they loved but got outbid. She caught my expression; it must have shown fear and relief.

'What's wrong?' she asked.

'Nothing. I'm just going to miss you both when you go, that's all.'

I worried as soon as I'd said it that it might make her feel stifled again, but she hugged me. 'You are so lovely,' she told me.

I've made myself a lot more low-key when I'm around them in the Manor. I can see that I've been a bit present when they need space to be themselves. As Sasha says, 'We all need to grow.' This is going to work well if I keep it up. The last thing I want to do is to drive them out.

23

WEDNESDAY

Nicole

Patrick pours himself another glass of wine. He's necked half a bottle already, one of Tom's expensive ones. Nicole is drinking too, but more slowly. She shakes her head when he offers her a top-up. She's slightly tipsy already, and it's not a nice feeling. Her grief makes life feel hallucinatory enough.

It's been a bad day. She's processing a call she had from Jen this morning, telling her that the police found traces of lipstick on one of the coffee cups in Tom's den, asking again if she knew who it might be. She didn't know, she told them. How long will DNA testing take? About a week, Jen said, but we'll try to expedite it.

Nicole hasn't told Patrick about the cups yet. She's desperate to work out who it could have been. She has no idea, but she can't bear to speculate on it with Patrick.

Again, she remembers their old rivalry, born when they both vied for Tom's attention as children. Patrick would gloat if he discovered that he knew something about Tom that she didn't, or if he discovered that Tom had hidden anything from her, and Tom did do that now and then if he thought something would upset her. Sometimes he did it to protect Patrick, because he was protective of his friend. He would neglect to tell her of the latest trouble that Patrick had got into, wanting to avoid her cross or frustrated reaction. He wanted Nicole and Patrick to co-exist so that he could keep them both in his life, even when Patrick crossed lines. The memory of that old rivalry with Patrick is souring things for her a little this evening.

'Tom was clumsy,' Patrick says. 'It makes sense that this was an accident.' Their conversation has been circling on this, again. The wine is making them both repetitive.

'He could trip over his own feet,' she says. 'Once, in Swindon, he took an old radiator to the tip and when he tried to throw it into the skip it caught on his shirt, and he went over the rail and fell in with it. The men had to pull him out.'

Patrick snorts. 'That's so Tom.'

They sit in silence for a while.

'You hungry?' he asks. 'Do you want me to cook?'

She nods. He's been doing all the meals since he got here and the quality of what he's prepared has surprised her.

'When did you learn to cook, then?' she asks.

'Recently. I can't do my job unless I look after myself.'

'Who taught you?' She's fishing for information on potential girlfriends because he's been coy on the subject since arriving. She's heard all about his new job and new flat, but not about his love life, and she can't help thinking that the kind of radical change that he's gone through must involve a woman somewhere along the line.

'YouTube,' he says.

She decides to ask him outright. 'Any romance on the horizon for you?'

He blushes the way he used to if he thought a girl liked him, and it endears him to her. 'No. Nothing beyond the odd fling. I keep hoping.'

'It'll happen,' she says. 'Especially now you've discovered yourself a bit.'

'I wasn't a very attractive proposition before, was I?'

She considers how to reply because he can be touchy, but she doesn't want to lie.

'You were perhaps a bit lost,' she says. 'But they'll be falling over themselves now.'

He smiles. 'You think so?'

'I know so.'

'I hold up you and Tom as my ideal romance. I was jealous of you for a long time.'

I know you were, she thinks. 'Your time will come,' she says softly.

'I thought we could have tacos tonight,' Patrick says. 'Does that suit you?'

'Anything,' she says. 'Thank you.'

She stays on the sofa and watches him prepare their food. He puts on the lights in the kitchen. Everything glints: the knife, the surfaces. Deftly, he slices a pile of red peppers. It's mesmerising but strange because he's the wrong man in her kitchen. The sight of him there is jarring. Life seems to have slid sideways into an alternative reality.

She finds she has a familiar, bitter taste in her mouth. It comes with unwelcome feelings. Like guilt. Or too much hope. But now it's more or less permanent. She thinks of it as the taste of grief and she knows that Patrick's food, however beautifully prepared and cooked, will taste like ashes to her.

He pours oil into a pan and when it's heated he adds the vegetables he's been prepping. She watches him stir with care. The smells are good, and she appreciates him doing this for her. Her guard drops.

'Patrick,' she says.

'Yes?'

'They found lipstick on one of the coffee cups in Tom's den. They're testing it for DNA.'

'What?' He looks disbelieving and she nods. 'They did.' Painful though it is, she lays out the evidence that Tom might have been cheating: 'A card for a masseuse – Sadie – in his pocket, lipstick on a coffee cup in his den.'

'He wasn't unfaithful. He loved you from the moment he met you,' Patrick says. 'I knew I lost a bit of him the day you turned up in our class.'

'We were only nine.'

Patrick shrugs. 'I still knew.'

His answer emboldens her enough to ask him outright the question that feels as if it's burning a hole in her: 'Do you know if he's ever been unfaithful to me?'

'He never has. Not to my knowledge, and I can't imagine it, quite honestly.'

135

'Do you promise?'

'I promise, Nicole. You were everything to him.'

'He was everything to me,' she says. She turns away, not wanting him to see the tears that she can feel sliding down her cheeks. Outside, the evening has clouded over, and the cliffs seem to be dissolving into the flat, grey light. Seabirds shriek and wheel as if defending something.

'Evening lights on,' she tells the house. Nothing happens. She sighs.

'We will get a handle on those systems,' Patrick says. 'I don't want what happened yesterday to happen again. The lights and the music coming out of the pool was freaky.'

She has no idea how she's going to do that. She can't think about it yet. Hopefully, Patrick will keep his word and sort it out for her.

She turns back to the windows. The dusky light and fast-moving clouds are creating a patchwork of shadows that are constantly transforming in shape and scale. She thinks how easy it would be to lurk outside, unnoticed, on a night like this. They built this place to give them exceptional views but never really considered how easy it would make it for them to be observed, too. Why not? It's not as if nothing bad had ever happened to either of them.

'Blinds down,' she says, and they obey. The evening lights come on in the living area.

'Don't you want to enjoy the last of the daylight?' Patrick asks. He's chopping again. Yellow peppers. The knife is moving so fast she worries he might cut himself.

'I don't want anyone looking in. If it wasn't an accident, it must have been a robbery gone wrong, don't you think?' she asks. She wants reassurance. Again. She's asked him this countless times already.

'In my mind, knowing Tom and you, it's one of the most likely explanations. Even considering the coffee cups.'

'But who drank coffee with him?'

'I don't know. A neighbour?'

She frowns. Could it have been? She thinks it unlikely. 'I guess the police will look at that.'

'How long will the DNA results take to come back?'

'Jen said up to a week. They'll only get a match if the person is already in the system.'

'Then we have to be patient,' he says. He adds the yellow peppers to the pan. Steam rises as he stirs them in and the oil spits. Patrick looks tired, she thinks. Perhaps she's laying too much on him. He's grieving, too.

'I'm sorry to land everything on you,' she says. 'Everything circles round and round in my mind. It's the not knowing that's so horrible.'

'It's fine,' he says. 'It's why I'm here. To be honest, it's probably helping me just as much as you. I've been feeling guilty about Tom.'

'Guilty? Why?'

'The depression,' Patrick says. 'I should have been there for him. I haven't been a very good friend. I should have done more for him, but I was finally starting to make something of my life. I was being selfish.'

Nicole stares. 'What depression?'

24

WEDNESDAY

Jen

Detective Jen Walsh watches Sasha closely. The evening has turned cloudy over the Manor, darkening Olly Palmer's study. Its windows, leaded and set deep in stone surrounds, don't let in much light.

She's just had a message from the Incident Room saying that there's no way to tell how or why the security cameras at the Barn weren't working on the morning of Tom's death. It's disappointing.

Sasha smiles serenely at Steen as he repeats questions that he already asked her the first time they met. She's a cool cat, Jen thinks. Most people are more perturbed by a death happening close to them, but Sasha appears poised and seemingly completely in control of how she presents. Her posture is impeccable, shoulders back, stomach in, legs carefully positioned so Jen and Steen can see the contours of her long thighs beneath the tight sheen of her yoga pants. Her trainers are shiny white, and Jen has never seen such perfectly groomed hair outside a salon.

This woman, Jen thinks, invests a lot of time in herself. She had the same impression of Olly, too. Even though he presented in a more disarming way, best described as shabby writer or academic, it felt studied, like a costume: Harry Potter glasses; a good shirt but with a delicately frayed collar; old, soft khaki trousers and desert boots that had seen better days.

They make an interesting couple. Different on the surface, but each of them displaying a certain command of themselves. It's not quite arrogance, but almost. They're like cats who've got the cream, Jen thinks.

But Sasha isn't completely in control. Watching her carefully, Jen decides that Steen is making her feel uncomfortable. Jen notes a subtle tightening in Sasha's posture and around her eyes. Discomfort is disrupting her poise. Interesting, Jen thinks, though it's not unusual for people to feel uneasy during police questioning.

'How long have you lived here?' Steen asks.

'Five years.'

He asks her the same question he asked Olly about whether they bought the Manor, and she provides almost identical responses, also naming the owner as Anna Creed.

'Where does Anna live now?' Steen asks.

Sasha blinks. 'She has a place in Portugal. A finca. She prefers to live there.'

'Does she come back here often?'

'No. She prefers Portugal.'

'Why doesn't she sell this place?'

Sasha shrugs. 'You'd have to ask her.'

'Do you and Olly act as house-sitters? Is that your role?'

She takes a moment before answering. 'Yes. I suppose you could say that. Actually I'd say we act more as managers than house-sitters.'

'It's an unusual arrangement.'

'We're very lucky.'

'I'd say so. Olly tells me you don't pay rent to Anna Creed.'

'That's correct. We maintain the property for her in exchange for living here.'

'And you run your yoga business from here?'

'It's the perfect location. My clients love it.'

'I expect they do. And just to confirm, on the morning when Tom Booth's body was found, how many people were here?'

'Me, Olly, Kitty and my yoga student, who was here between ten and eleven.'

'Kitty is your housekeeper?'

'Yes,' Sasha says. 'She lives in the old Coach House, on the estate, as she'll have told you.'

'Can you talk me through how you learned about Tom Booth's death?'

'I was outside, on the front yawn, practising yoga. Olly had just joined me when Nicole came running up the drive, screaming for help. Olly left me with her while he ran to their house. He wanted to see if there was something he could do. Nicole was practically catatonic; she was in shock. I asked Kitty to take care of her and I ran to join Olly. But obviously, we were too late. It's devastating. Tom was such a lovely man.'

Jen's work phone buzzes and she sneaks a look at it. The text is from a colleague.

We've had a message from Kitty, housekeeper at the Manor, saying to tell you she needs to speak to you while you're there.

Jen reads it twice and wonders why Kitty wouldn't say so directly. She texts back: When did this message come in? And gets an immediate answer: Ten minutes ago.

While we've been interviewing, she thinks.

Did she say anything else?

No.

The obvious conclusion is that Kitty has something to hide from her employers.

When Hal winds things up with Sasha, Jen says, 'We'd like to meet with your housekeeper, too. Could you call her for us?'

Intriguingly, Jen sees something in Sasha that makes her pulse quicken: it's a more significant fracture in Sasha's poise, a muscle twitching in her jaw, a lick of her lips. It only lasts a moment before Sasha's on her feet. 'I'll get her for you,' she says.

'One thing before you do,' Jen says. They've heard what Olly said about Kitty and now she wants to know what Sasha thinks. 'Is Kitty a good employee? Reliable?'

She keeps her eyes on Sasha, though she feels Hal glance at her, wondering why she's asking.

Sasha looks as if she's deciding how to answer. 'She's a good worker, mostly,' Sasha says. 'We wouldn't be without her. But she's not always truthful.'

'In what way?'

Sasha repeats what Olly told them about Kitty, almost word for word. Jen doesn't ask any questions, and Hal follows her cue, letting Sasha talk freely. Sasha seems to warm up as she does. They learn nothing new, but she uses the word 'delusional' just as Olly did and something about it seems rehearsed to Jen. She's got no proof, it's just what her gut is telling her. There's something off about Sasha.

'Thank you,' Jen says when Sasha finishes. 'That's very helpful. Could you get her for us?'

When Sasha's left the room, Hal says, 'They don't have rock-solid alibis, this couple, or the housekeeper. If this is murder, I don't think we can rule them out.'

She leans towards Hal and shows him the texts. He reads and looks at her, eyebrows raised. 'Interesting,' she mouths at him. Hal nods. He's about to reply when there's a knock on the door. He says, 'Come in!' and they exchange a glance as the door opens.

25

FIVE YEARS EARLIER

Anna's Journal

The noises that used to terrorise me at night have stopped. Sasha asked me about it the other day and I realised that I'd forgotten about them. I don't think I've heard anything since you moved in, I said. It was hard to remember. My days are no longer lonely. I'm busy, now.

She smiled. 'Well, it's good that we're staying a little longer, then.'

I persuaded them to stay on. I'm so happy. It took a bit of doing. They found a flat and were getting ready to move out, but then Sasha unexpectedly lost the use of her space at the yoga centre. She was very upset. The details of how it happened weren't clear – she muttered about politics and people's selfishness, and it was an extra blow because it meant the flat that they found might not be the right choice for them because they'd picked it for its proximity to her workplace. She didn't tell me about any of this for days. I noticed she was looking strained and worried it was something I'd done. I made an extra effort to behave how I thought she'd want me to, keeping out of their way but also making sure things were nice for them in the house. Eventually, I found her crying in the kitchen and she told me.

'You can stay here and teach in the Great Hall,' I told her. I'd been thinking a lot about what a good space the Hall would make for her, and how she would be able to host retreats here. I didn't want people staying in the house, but they could camp, or stay nearby. She could build her business. I hadn't dared mention it before for fear of seeming overbearing, but the words came tumbling out now.

'Do you know what?' she said. 'That's actually a brilliant idea.' I felt so happy, though she seemed to think twice. 'But I couldn't possibly be so reliant on your generosity.'

'Nonsense!' I said. 'What am I going to do on my own here? This is what the Manor needs. It's crying out for people to use it.'

'Can I pay you rent at least?'

'No! Absolutely not!'

'I'll talk to Olly,' she said. She took my hand and gave it a gentle squeeze. 'Thank you. You really are a wonderful person.' It was the loveliest moment.

Things have been busy since then! We worked very hard to get the Hall ready to host classes. We thought pupils could park around the back of the Manor and enter by a side door, but Olly requested that they not pass by his study when they arrive, so Sasha will let them in through the main door. I wasn't sure about it at first, all those strangers coming into my home, but

I've got used to the idea. They'll feel part of the Manor. As Olly said, it'll enhance their experience of coming to learn here. He also said that it takes someone with vision to bring an idea like this to fruition so beautifully and I felt very flattered.

The only downside is that Sasha doesn't want me to come to class any more, which, I admit, was a surprise. She said she'll give me some private lessons, which is nice, but I'll miss being in the group. When I asked her why, she said it might be a weird dynamic if I was there, especially for the ladies who know me already. She thought people might focus on me, the hostess, and it might be distracting. 'We don't have to tell them I own the Manor,' I said.

'It might slip out, though, mightn't it? If not in your words, then in your behaviour,' she said, and I supposed she was right.

I'm still losing things regularly, which is an inconvenience now that life has got so much busier. I try to cover it up, because the last thing I want is for Olly and Sasha to think I'm becoming a senile old woman.

Kitty has got a lot quieter, lately. I asked her if she was happy with the new arrangements.

'I am, but it's a lot more work.'

I felt very guilty because I should have thought of that. I didn't consult Kitty at all regarding these changes and she's been remarkably accommodating of Olly and Sasha moving in. I think she likes the Manor being livelier, too. For a moment I considered hiring more help, but I knew that would put a squeeze on my finances. The Manor is an expensive property to run, and Nick didn't leave me with a fortune in cash. I have enough to cover most things if I live frugally, but only just.

I said, 'I'll help you. Tell me what I can do.'

'Are you sure?' she said.

'Of course.' We worked out what she couldn't manage, and I've taken it on. Mostly, I make sure the Great Hall is kept ready for yoga lessons and tidied and cleaned afterwards. It really is a pleasure. The more I do, the happier I seem to feel. Sasha says she always thought part of my problem was that I didn't fill my time enough after Nick died, and if I did, it was with the wrong things and the wrong people.

Sasha said that one of my old acquaintances had joined her yoga class and was asking after me. 'Who?' I asked.

'Catherine,' she said. I remembered Catherine. She was one of the nicer women.

'I should say hello,' I said. 'Perhaps I should invite her to have a cup of tea after class next time.'

'Hmm,' Sasha said. 'Is that a good idea?'

'Isn't it?' I felt nervous.

'I don't love her energy,' Sasha said. 'She's very competitive.'

I remembered this about Catherine. Conversation with her could be tiring because she took everything you said as a provocation to prove that her life was better. But she was also quick to laugh and sometimes good fun.

'Perhaps she's changed,' I said. I was nervous about upsetting Sasha. She was so protective of me and, as she told me often, she was also fragile because she gave so much of herself to other people. But the pull of old friendships was still something I couldn't ignore.

'Maybe,' Sasha said.

'Could you mention it to her? Ask her if she'd like a cuppa?' I said, knowing Sasha wouldn't want me to lurk at the end of class to see Catherine.

'Sure,' she said. Her voice sounded strained.

I waited a week to ask her if she'd had a chance to pass on my invitation. I'd been looking out for Catherine arriving at class, thinking I might find an excuse to run into her, but hadn't seen her.

'Oh, Catherine?' she said. 'She didn't show up again.'

I kept my disappointment to myself. 'Do you have contact details for her?' I asked. A week ago, I lost all my contacts when I left my phone in my trouser pocket when I put them in the wash. It was another of those terrible moments when I thought I was losing my mind because I was sure I'd checked the pockets. But when I heard an awful noise coming from the machine and I went to check, there was my phone, spinning. I haven't got around to replacing it, yet.

'I might have her email address,' Sasha said. 'But not a phone number.'

'Could I have it?' I asked. It felt brave. I would also have to ask to borrow Sasha's laptop to send an email, but I was certain that would be okay.

'Sure,' she said. But she hasn't given it to me and, when I reminded her, she snapped at me, saying couldn't I see that she was a little busy trying to run a business. I'll ask again when she's less up against it.

Olly seems very content. He's really settled into the study and says he's never been so productive as he is now. Apparently, the words are flowing onto the page! I think a lot about Olly's novel, about how exciting it is to have something potentially special written here in the Manor. I can't help feeling that by supporting him I'm a contributor to the book (in the humblest way possible, of course).

Sometimes, I dream that Olly and Sasha might start a family here. We could raise the child between us. I wouldn't dream of saying it, though. I think I've found a balance of being there for them but also allowing them their privacy, and not interfering. Time will tell!

26

WEDNESDAY

Hal

Hal watches Kitty carefully as she enters Olly's study for her interview. Her smile is uncertain, and she sidles around the open door rather than striding through it. There's a slight stoop to her shoulders, her head held forward a little. Her body language reads as submission to Hal. She looks like someone who has been summoned to the headmaster's office. And yet, they know she wants to be here.

As soon as the door is shut behind her, her posture improves; she walks across the room with a straighter back and a more composed expression. She looks anything but 'simple', as Olly described her, though Hal wouldn't say she looks confident. It's more that she doesn't seem as cowed as she did around her employers. Hal's intrigued.

Kitty perches on the edge of the sofa cushion, as if she feels she doesn't belong there, or isn't going to be with them for long.

She slides a handwritten note across the table. Hal reads it and passes it to Jen. The note says: 'Every word we say in this room can be clearly overheard.'

Hal meets Kitty's eye and nods to let her know they understand. He's done a lot of interviews during his career and this one is already the strangest. When they spoke to Kitty briefly a few days ago, she presented as sensible and reliable, there were no nutty vibes, but this has taken a bit of a turn and he's mindful of how her employers described her.

He wonders if her note is implying that her employers will be listening from behind the door and glances at it, to confirm that it's a very substantial door, thick, fitting snugly into its frame. Hal doesn't believe it would be easy to hear what they're saying from outside this room. Olly's study is large and they're sitting at the far end of it from the door.

Kitty shakes her head, as if she can read his mind and is telling him that that's not what she means.

He clears his throat and makes the decision to choose his words carefully in case they are being overheard. Better to play along for now. 'Thank you for talking to us again. Shall we make a start?'

'Absolutely,' Kitty says. Her hands are folded neatly in her lap. Hal can see tension in her neck and shoulders.

'I'm keen to go over everybody's movements on the morning Tom Booth died and also the night before,' he says.

'Yes.' She answers quickly and her tone is bright and keen in a way that reminds him of a primary-school teacher; it wrong-foots him a little. When he and Jen interviewed Kitty on the day Tom Booth's body was found, they found her to be mousy and quiet, her voice almost a whisper. He supposes shock could have accounted for it, but it was notably different to how she's presenting now. She seems to slip between different versions of herself.

'Right,' he says. 'So perhaps you could start on the morning that Mr Booth's body was found and talk us through what happened from the time you woke up.'

'I got up at six-thirty when my alarm went off. I live in the Coach House, as you know. I did my yoga exercises early because it was a hot day, had some breakfast and came to the Manor at around seven-thirty to get breakfast ready for Sasha and Olly. That's my usual routine. Olly likes his porridge to be slow-cooked and Sasha has a fruit salad and a smoothie. She's into her superfoods. They're both very particular. They ate and I cleaned up before starting my tasks for the day. First, I tidied and dusted the Great Hall, where Sasha does her classes, in time for the private lesson she does on Saturdays. Then I did some weeding in the walled garden, but it gets a lot of sun, and I got too hot, so I went inside to start on the ironing. I saw Olly come in here on my way to the laundry room, but I'm not sure what time that was. He spends all hours working. I didn't see or hear either of them after that because I was tucked away in the laundry room, and I had the radio on. The next thing I knew Sasha came bursting in and said that Nicole Booth had run over here screaming that her husband had drowned in their pool. Sasha asked me to take care of Nicole while she went to the Barn with Olly, to see what had happened and to see if they could help him. But obviously, they were too late.'

'Did you know Nicole Booth?'

'No, not really. I was introduced to them once when they came here for a drink. I think they've been round here twice altogether. Sasha and Olly have been there a few times, but I wasn't invited. The first time they came here was for a meeting. It was after they'd just bought the land from us, and they wanted to show Olly and Sasha the architect's plans for converting the barns into their new home. Olly said it was because they were hoping that if they had a face-to-face meeting, he and Sasha wouldn't object to the plans formally. He said it was a smart move. He appreciated it.'

'Do you know what your employers made of the plans?'

She stares at him intently. There's an answer in her eyes, but she won't articulate it. She puts a finger first to her lips then moves it, pointing to the walls, as if to indicate that they have ears. She says, overly loudly, and obviously for the benefit of whoever she believes is listening: 'So far as I know, they were very happy.' But she's shaking her head.

Steen nods to indicate that he understands, but inside, he feels as if he's sagging. There are truth tellers, there are liars, and then there are fruitcakes. He's not one hundred percent sure which she is, but his suspicions are mounting, and he doesn't want her to waste any more of his time. He snaps his notebook shut. They need to continue the conversation, but not now, not here.

He's about to signal an end to the interview when Jen takes over and runs through the rest of the questions they planned to ask. He's disinclined to interrupt because he doesn't want to undermine her. Clearly, she thinks it's important to finish the interview and he respects that. Resigned to having to sit there, he watches Kitty closely. The questions are banal, and she seems to give a straight answer most of the time. Yes, she observed Tom and Nicole together once, walking down the lane. They looked happy together. No, she didn't speak to them and can't comment any further on their relationship. She never saw or heard them argue and never observed personal visitors at the Barn, just a lot of tradespeople. 'But I don't get out much,' she adds.

Jen keeps her tone light and steady and he admires her for it. He wonders if she has a boyfriend then chides himself for losing concentration.

'One final question, if you don't mind?' Jen says. 'Did your employers ever fall out with the neighbours? It could be over anything, large or small.'

'No, not to my knowledge,' Kitty says, but she nods her head vigorously, implying that the opposite is true.

Jen looks satisfied. Hal understands that she asked that question for their eavesdropper, if there is one, so that Kitty could deliver the response she wants or needs to. And he's glad she did. This is interesting. Especially since Olly and Sasha are relying on each other for an alibi and there are periods of time during Saturday morning when they were in separate spaces in the Manor.

'Thank you, I think that's everything,' Jen says.

He opens his notebook and scrawls a note, shows it to Kitty.

She mouths the words as she reads them. 'Can you come and talk to us at the station?'

She holds out her hand for his pen and his book and he gives both to her. She writes a reply and hands it to him: 'It's difficult but I'll try.'

'Thank you very much,' Jen says. 'For talking to us. I know you must be very busy.'

'I enjoy my work,' Kitty says.

'Tomorrow?' Hal writes.

Kitty reads the note and nods. He nods back.

'Well,' Jen says. 'Isn't that lovely? You're certainly in a gorgeous spot here.'

Kitty smiles, apparently without an edge. 'It really is a dream,' she says. He thinks he can see both pain and joy in her expression, which strikes him as weird, or complicated, or both.

Kitty shows them out. Olly and Sasha don't reappear.

As soon as the car doors are shut, he and Jen speak simultaneously.

'The housekeeper's a fruitcake,' he says, as Jen says, 'Something's very wrong in that home.'

27

WEDNESDAY

Nicole

Nicole tears through Tom's bathroom cupboards, looking for antidepressants.

Patrick told her that Tom called him just a month ago. That was a shock. Tom promised that they hadn't spoken, but apparently, they've had a few conversations since the fall-out over money and in this last one Tom admitted that he was struggling with his mental health.

She feels betrayed by Tom. He promised her that he wouldn't have contact with Patrick until they'd agreed together to resume communication. To hear this from Patrick and then to hear that Tom confided something in him that Nicole doesn't know is to have some of her worst fears come true.

She opens the only drawer she hasn't searched yet and rifles through it urgently. There's nothing there except for some nail clippers and bottles from the expensive skincare ranges Tom has been trying. She slams the drawer shut and catches sight of her reflection, flinching at how haggard she looks, the dark circles beneath her eyes, her puffy skin.

She knows this search is pointless because the police have already looked through every drawer and cupboard and trawled all his devices, so they've been everywhere before her. If they'd found evidence of an affair, or of mental health issues, then surely they'd have told her.

She lies down on their bed and tries to will her brain to think clearly enough to remember whether Tom had been showing signs of depression. Was it right under her nose? Did she not notice that he was struggling because their life was so crazy and busy?

She knows they were happy before they won the money, and she thinks back through all the stages of them getting here. The shock and thrill of the win, combined with Tom's pain at losing his granny; the planning for a new life and letting go of the old one; the practical demands of negotiating to purchase the land; the design of the house, the build, the decoration, the landscaping and planting. It's been a lot. Did she lose him somewhere along the way?

She thinks about it. He seemed okay. He tuned out of some of the practical arrangements, but he was super-engaged with lots of things like the tech elements of the design and build and he was so proud and happy when they moved in, wandering around with a big grin on his face, chatting with the removal guys. That's how she remembers it, anyway.

She wonders if she could have been projecting, attributing all sorts of wonderful feelings to him, when in fact it was her who was experiencing them? Or was he pretending? But could he really have faked his happiness when he opened the champagne on their first night here after all the men had left? Or when he tried to dance with her, or led her to their new bed, the mattress still wrapped, and they made love on the sticky plastic before falling asleep in each other's arms and were woken up early the next morning by the blinds rising in time to show them a beautiful dawn breaking over their beloved view on a crisp, clear winter morning.

To Nicole, it was bliss. Was Tom really hiding sadness? It wasn't in his nature to hide things. Except, perhaps, where Patrick was concerned. Which raises the uncomfortable question: if he was willing to lie about Patrick, were there other things?

She tries to focus on the matter in hand: the detail of what Patrick learned. According to Patrick, Tom told him that he was considering speaking to a therapist and a doctor. Nicole had pressed him on that. Did Tom say why he was unhappy?

'He said he was rich now, but he was still him. He thought things would be more different.'

She wonders what this could mean, whether it implies that Tom was already unhappy and the disappointment that their win hadn't changed things for the better was acute. She remembers moments from after their win when Tom seemed uncomfortable. There was the time that his burgeoning enthusiasm for starting a wine collection was tempered by paranoia that the wine merchant was looking down on him. But he wasn't alone. They'd both felt the same way. Setting up their new, larger life was overwhelming at times after the small existence they'd had. They had so much to learn.

'Fake it till you make it!' Nicole had told him. 'I do!' While Tom played with his new gadgets, she compulsively studied articles and photographs for ideas on how to dress and how to decorate in their new life. Almost everyone she follows on Instagram and TikTok is a fashion or interiors influencer. From the moment she called the National Lottery winners' line she's felt the pressure to live up to the win, to be good at being rich. Her perfectionism kicked in in spades and she's proud of what she's achieved.

But Tom has never been as nimble as her, or as practical. Nicole does what she has to do to achieve something. She's outcome focused. Have I been dragging him along unwillingly, unhappily? she asks herself. The thought is devastating, and she can't accept it. It doesn't feel right. She knows, *knew*, her man.

She hears a gentle knock on the door and considers ignoring it and pretending to be asleep, but she'd better not. It's not fair on Patrick. 'Hi,' she says.

'Are you okay?' Patrick calls.

'Yes.'

'Food's ready if you want some.'

'I'm coming.' She stands up and smooths down her clothing, takes a deep breath and opens the bedroom door. The corridor is empty. She walks down it, towards the kitchen. Her limbs feel weighted.

An idea occurs to her: perhaps Tom told Patrick that he was depressed to make his friend feel better about their good fortune. It would be typical of Tom to make a gesture like that. He was so protective of Patrick, always. The thought makes sense and she feels slightly better. She takes a seat at the kitchen island, alongside Patrick. I don't care what you think, she tells him silently. Tom was happy.

Patrick's phone starts to vibrate as he's serving up. It's on the island between them. 'Shall I get it?' she asks, reaching for it.

'No!' he snaps, and she snatches her hand back, shocked.

He grabs the phone and declines the call before slipping it into his pocket. 'Sorry. I just don't want to answer it right now. I'm not in the mood. Tom is on my mind too much.'

'Oh,' she says. 'I understand.' Though she's not sure that she does. It seems to her that he didn't want her to know who was calling.

Patrick puts a plate of tacos in front of her. The food smells fragrant and looks wonderful but she can only pick at it. They don't speak for a while.

'You don't like it?' he asks when his plate is clean but she's still pushing food around hers.

'It's lovely. I'm just, I've got no appetite.'

'I'm sorry I landed that on you earlier, about Tom's depression,' Patrick says. 'I didn't think it would be a shock.'

Feeling defensive, she watches him carefully for signs that he's relishing knowing something about Tom that she didn't know, the way he used to, but it's hard to read him. He seems so calm these days, so stable, and it's weird. She wonders if he's medicated and if that's what has evened his temperament out.

'Tom and I didn't have secrets from each other,' she says.

'If he kept this from you, I'm sure he didn't think of it as keeping a secret from you. He probably didn't want to upset you.'

'Was he unhappy here? Tell me again, what exactly did he say?'

'Just what I told you before. Nothing else. It's my bad. I should have questioned him more and tried to get to the bottom of it. I've been a terrible friend.'

Patrick's phone pings. He ignores it and it pings a few more times.

'Get that if you want,' she says.

'No, it's okay.' He takes the phone out of his pocket, mutes it and puts it face-down on the table without glancing at the screen to see who's calling.

'What shall we do tomorrow?' he asks.

The question takes her by surprise; it's as if they're on holiday.

'I'm exhausted. I don't think I can think about it until the morning. I might go to bed.' She wants some time alone. It's tiring talking to him, trying to read him, trying to figure out if the last year of her relationship has been a lie.

'No worries. You go ahead, I'll finish up here.'

'Thanks for dinner.'

He looks away from her briefly, as if bashful, and nods. Has he still not learned to take a compliment? It's a welcome glimpse of his childhood self and as usual this makes her feel a twinge of affection for him. There's the Patrick I know, she thinks. Tom's friend. Your friend. She values loyalty. And where are her so-called friends or Tom's other mates? When push has come to shove, Patrick has turned up to help her.

Still, it's a relief when she shuts her bedroom door behind her. The bedroom is gloomy, the cliffs outside invisible now. She can only see an oblique patch of lawn, off to the side where the light from the living area lands crisply on the grass.

The blinds won't descend when she asks them to so she doesn't bother to turn the bedroom lights on but undresses quickly in the bathroom, brushes her teeth and falls into bed where she sits, propped up against a bank of pillows, and stares out, clutching a handful of sheet to her chest.

Her thoughts are jumbled and distressing; scraps of grief, fragments of memory that she can't help scouring for signs that Tom was depressed but still finds none. Eventually, her eyelids become heavy, and she slips into sleep as if it were drug-induced.

Waking, she's disorientated. There is shouting. She is still propped up in the position she fell asleep in. Her mouth is dry. Her heart thumps. 'Hello?' she tries to call out, but her voice is barely more than a whisper. 'Patrick?' she says, but so quietly that he probably wouldn't hear her even if he was in the room.

It's a man's voice she can hear, and it sounds like Patrick. He's very angry, but his words are indistinct. She gets out of bed and stands, riddled with anxiety, in the middle of her bedroom, unsure what to do. Would it be better to hide? Has someone broken in? Is Patrick confronting them? Wouldn't the house security system have gone into action if someone was here who shouldn't be? Or would it? She looks for her phone, thinking to call 999, but she must have left it in the living area.

Her hands are shaking. The shouting stops and the quiet that follows is almost more frightening. She remains standing, as still as her body will let her, and counts slowly to one hundred. By the time she's finished the silence seems to have settled permanently like a blanket over a bird cage and it feels safe enough to move.

She's only taken one step towards the sanctuary of her bed when she hears the slightest of noises outside the bedroom door. Her head whips round in time to see the door handle turn and she screams.

28

FIVE YEARS EARLIER

Anna's Journal

A terrible thing happened and it's my fault. Sasha finished giving me a private yoga session and was dashing to teach a class and she gave me her necklace to look after. 'I forgot to take it off,' she said. She doesn't like to wear jewellery when she teaches the public; she prefers to look impersonal. 'Can you please put it somewhere super-safe?'

'Of course,' I said. I recognised the necklace. She'd inherited it from her mother and I knew it was precious to her, so I took it into the kitchen and put it inside a small bowl that lives on a high shelf on the dresser. Kitty was peeling potatoes at the sink. 'I've put Sasha's necklace in the Spode bowl,' I told her. 'Hmm,' she said. She barely seemed to pay attention.

After class, Sasha was tired. I made a pot of mint tea and put it on the kitchen table with some cups. I don't make a fuss of serving it to her these days; I just make sure it's there. She came in and sat down and I busied myself at the kitchen counter so she wouldn't think I was hovering. I love talking to her after class, hearing about how it went and who did what. 'Have some tea with me,' she said, and I felt pleased. We talked about the afternoon and about what was planned for tomorrow. 'Where did you put my necklace?' she asked, her hand on her chest. I went to retrieve it, but the bowl was empty.

'Have you seen the necklace?' I asked Kitty.

'No,' she said. 'What necklace?'

'Sasha's necklace. I told you I was putting it in here for safekeeping.'

'You didn't.'

'I did. You saw me put it in here.'

She shook her head. 'I'm sorry, Anna, but I didn't.' Sometime since Olly and Sasha moved in, she'd stopped calling me Mrs Creed and started calling me Anna. I wanted it that way because we felt more like a family.

'You did,' I insisted. 'You were right here.'

'Then where's the necklace?'

I couldn't answer that, and I felt so stupid.

Kitty looked sympathetic. 'You'll remember in a minute. Don't worry.'

'Yes,' Sasha said. 'Don't worry.' But I could see that she was concerned.

I went hunting for it, trying to remember where I might have put it. I checked all my other safe places but there was no sign of it. I was so ashamed of my memory lapse and the fact that I'd let

Sasha down that I began to feel shaky. The necklace was not easily replaceable; its value was emotional.

'Anna!' Sasha called.

I could hardly face her and lingered in the Yellow Room where I was checking if the necklace could have fallen out of my pocket. She came to me. The necklace was dangling from her hand. 'Oh, my goodness!' I felt almost tearful with relief. 'Where was it?'

'Kitty found it in the hall. You must have dropped it.'

'I'm so sorry,' I said. 'What must you think of me?'

'I think that you made a mistake, but I wish you'd admitted it instead of insisting the necklace was in the bowl.'

What could I say? I didn't want to say that I remembered putting it in the bowl, because, clearly, I hadn't. It would make me sound gaga.

'You're right,' I said. 'I'm so sorry. I don't know what I was thinking.'

'That's okay. But remember, trust is everything.' She slipped her arm through mine and walked me back to the kitchen. 'Shall we make a new pot of tea?'

It was just one of a few funny things that have happened lately. When I was trying to read in the drawing room last week, while Olly and Sasha were working, I heard a tapping sound, slow and insistent, coming from behind the fireplace. I called Kitty and asked her if she could hear it and she said no, and I said it had just stopped and she gave me a look so full of pity that I hardly knew what to do with myself. I definitely heard it. It was a rhythmic, deliberate sound. I checked the openings behind the panelling, thinking, as I had before, that

165

there might be an animal stuck back there, but there was nothing.

Another difficult thing happened last night. The three of us hadn't eaten together in a while since we'd decided that there should be no expectation that we should, because Olly and Sasha felt it put pressure on them. I didn't mind at all. It was tiring to be 'on' every night when I was with them, no matter how much I like their company. But last night they suggested we have supper together as it was Sunday. I cooked because it was Kitty's day off and we shared a bottle of wine. It was lovely. We talked about families. I explained a little more about Nick and my failed attempts at fertility treatment and they were very sympathetic. 'Maybe you were just meant to give in a different way,' Olly said.

'You're such a beautiful person,' Sasha said. 'Our life wouldn't be nearly as rich without you and everything you do for us.' Her necklace glinted in the candlelight, and I felt so grateful for their lovely words because I still felt afraid that my grip on things was loosening.

I went to bed feeling a bit tipsy after drinking wine and slept very deeply. In the morning, the mood at breakfast was different. Sasha and Olly's faces were grim.

'Do you remember anything from last night?' Sasha said.

'No! I slept so well.'

'You didn't get up in the night?'

'Not that I recall.' For once, my bladder hadn't woken me up, which was a small victory for me these days, but I wasn't going to share anything so personal. 'Why?'

'You came into our bedroom.'

'What?'

'We woke up at half past two and you were standing in the door of our bedroom, staring at us.'

'No!'

'I'm afraid so,' Olly said. 'It scared the life out of us. Your eyes were open and everything. We talked to you, but you didn't reply. After a few minutes you walked back to your room.'

'Do you have any history of sleepwalking?' Sasha asked.

'No, none. I'm so sorry.' I thought of how I must have looked, standing there in my nightgown, which I would never normally let them see me in. It appalled me to think that it might have revealed anything.

'I'm sure it won't happen again,' she said.

But I've been worried about it ever since, and I've decided to move to a bedroom in a different wing of the house. It's not as large, but I don't need anything fancy. I could ask Olly and Sasha to move, but it seems silly since there are two of them and only one of me. It's a relief to have made the decision.

Tonight, all feels well, though. It's been a good day and I've been able to forget some of this stuff and concentrate on working to make everything run smoothly. We have a group of guests here for a weekend retreat. They're camping at the end of the drive and Olly has lit a bonfire on the front lawn so we can gather around it. It's my favourite part of the retreats. Sasha is happy for me to join the guests and help serve food.

Kitty isn't with us. It's another day off for her, and although I could have used her help I don't like to ask. It's easier to do it myself.

When I'd finished helping, I sat on one of the logs around the bonfire. I kept myself to myself the way Sasha prefers me to, not pestering the guests with conversation, but I felt free and loose, able to forget the things that had been plaguing me and to enjoy the sight of everyone talking and meditating in little groups on the lawn.

Olly came to sit by me, which was a nice surprise. He told me he was on the verge of a breakthrough with his book. He was so excited about it; he almost seemed a little feverish, or drunk. 'Do you realise that without you, this couldn't have happened?' he said. 'Do we tell you enough how special you are to us?' He hugged me, which shocked me. It was the first time we'd touched, and it felt a little bit like electricity.

'It's my pleasure,' I told him. I hoped he wasn't drunk, that this was genuine.

'Anna,' he said, 'do you want to help me with something later?'

'With what?' I asked. From the look of him, it was something exciting.

He tapped the side of his nose. 'Don't move from here,' he said. 'All will be revealed in good time.'

'Okay,' I said. His excitement was infectious. No part of us was in contact now the hug was over, but I wanted to feel his touch again. It was confusing. And inappropriate. But someone else's passion for something is a powerful aphrodisiac.

'Can you tell me more?' I asked.

He leaned over towards me, until I could feel his breath on my neck. He whispered in my ear and my stomach flipped.

29

THURSDAY

Sasha

Sasha tests the water temperature in the bath. It's perfect. She pulls the window open wider. A honeysuckle-scented breeze cools the skin on her arms. Wispy clouds idle in the sky. It's not often she starts the day with a soak in the tub, but she woke with tight muscles, and she could do with some time for herself. The last few days have taken their toll. She feels as if she's spinning a lot of plates.

She turns off the taps and gets into the bath, submerging herself completely. She holds her breath and floats underwater for a few moments, enjoying the dense silence, but a vision of Tom appears, his face nose-to-nose with hers, as if he was floating above her, a waking nightmare. She sits up quickly, pulling in air, letting out a cry, rakes back the damp curtains of her hair and wipes water from her eyes and face. Her breathing is laboured. The breeze is still circulating, but now it feels too cool on her wet skin and the scent of her bath oil no longer seems pretty or invigorating. It's sickly, too strong.

She tries to calm herself down, to count her blessings. She wants to enjoy her bath.

Olly is her first blessing. It all starts with him, her complicated, beautiful man. If he hurts her emotionally sometimes, the little twists of pain he inflicts are quickly numbed by how much she loves him. It's been that way since she first met him.

When they met, it was a classic meet-cute and she loves to remember it. She was trying to complain about something at the reception desk of the university gym – what it was exactly has been lost in time and retelling – but she was inarticulate and flustered about it, faced with an unsympathetic receptionist, and struggling to find the right word to describe how she was feeling when, from over her shoulder, she heard it: the exact word she'd been searching for. She turned to see Olly. 'I'm so sorry,' he said. 'I couldn't help overhearing. It's really none of my business.'

It would be an exaggeration to say that she melted when their eyes met, but the instant attraction between her and Olly that day was undeniable. The receptionist she'd been arguing with stared and said, 'You two should get a room.'

They got a coffee and talked. She found Olly to be clever, sweet, and very attractive. She fell hard for his rumpled, academic look, and fell harder for his attentiveness and confidence, his thoughtful focus, and his certainty. He was clearly an achiever, too; he hadn't dated much during uni, he told her, because he was totally dedicated to his studies and was hoping to graduate with a first-class degree.

The physical attraction between them was strong – she could tell he felt it, too – but he behaved like a gentleman, giving her his number, asking her to message him if she wanted to meet up again. We could see a film, he said, or go for a walk. She'd been teaching yoga at the gym for six months and been hit on plenty of times by students, but this felt different. Olly seemed more mature and interesting than the other young men she'd met.

Only four hours passed before she cracked and messaged him to ask him out for a drink. She had to wait overnight, until she came out of class at eleven the next morning, before he replied. Her stomach lurched when she saw he'd said yes. She felt as if she was fifteen again.

The memory brings a smile to her face, as it always does, but it fades fast. It will be nice when the police leave them alone. Their presence isn't entirely unhelpful, because it seems to ramp up Nicole's vulnerability, but it's a lot to manage. Sasha shudders involuntarily and another image of Tom's body in the pool, this time with Olly sitting beside it, comes to her. She feels uneasy. In another effort to relax, she applies a thick face mask and tries not to think about anything apart from the sensation of it tightening her skin, but her mind keeps whirring.

She thinks, we've been so focused on the practicalities since Tom's body was found, and on supporting Nicole and trying to figure out what Patrick's presence means, that we haven't dealt with the trauma of the morning. Olly would never mention if he was feeling troubled by it because he pushes away anything difficult, but this was a truly horrible event. He can't be unaffected. Nicole's wails are still ringing in her ears. The shock on Kitty's face when Sasha told her what had happened is still fresh in her mind. Though come to think of it, was it shock?

Sasha replays that moment. She recalls running through the Manor, towards the laundry room. The sound of her own breathing comes back to her: sharp, panicky intakes and out-takes. She opened the door. The radio was on. Kitty always listens to Radio 4, nothing cheerful. She was standing at the ironing board, pressing one of Olly's shirts, or it could have been some bedlinen. Sasha recalls that it was a pale fabric. Steam was rising from the iron, and it hissed as she began to blurt out the story about Nicole. She tries to recall how Kitty looked. *Think.* Was there something off about it? Why does she suddenly feel so certain of it?

She remembers Kitty looking up and meeting her eye and replays that instant again, and again. Kitty's expression was as slack as usual, but in her eyes there was a hint of, what? Knowledge? Sasha tenses. Knowledge of what?

Her thoughts are interrupted by the door inching open. It startles her. She thought she'd locked it. Olly peers in. 'Hey,' he says. 'Mind if I join you?'

She's self-conscious about the face mask she's wearing. Sasha hates Olly to see her looking less than perfect. She often gets up before him to put on make-up and brush her hair. It's not that he's ever said anything, but he's such a perfectionist in every other way that she feels it's necessary.

'I look stupid,' she says.

'You want me to wipe that off for you?' he asks. 'Has it been on long enough?'

172

He likes to do small, intimate things for her. He likes to shave her, to brush her hair.

'Sure,' she says. This invasion of her privacy is both intensely wanted and also uncomfortable, sometimes. It's when she feels at her most vulnerable.

He takes a face cloth from the towel rail and comes to kneel beside the tub. He dunks the cloth in the water, and she inhales sharply as it brushes her side. Olly doesn't react, though he's watching her intently. He squeezes excess water out of the cloth. Sasha's mouth feels dry.

'Shut your eyes,' he says.

She balks, momentarily, at this command, a reflex when he wants to get intimately involved in her grooming, but instead of her usual worry that he's going to see her imperfections and be put off by them, she thinks, he's going to push me underwater and hold me there. I'm going to drown like Tom. Immediately, she talks herself back from this fantasy. How ridiculous! Olly would never do that to her. She doesn't know why she's even thinking it. Her brain must be overtired.

She shuts her eyes, partly because he's told her to, but mostly she doesn't want him to see that she was afraid, even for a moment. If he does, he'll make her tell him why, and he'll see it, quite rightly, as a betrayal of her trust in him. He wants her to trust him absolutely. He has one rule: don't lie to *me*. Trust is everything, he tells her. Without it, who are we?

He begins to wipe the mask from her face. He applies just the right amount of pressure and moves the cloth gently over her skin. She relaxes a little. He notices.

'You were tense before.' He touches her collar bone lightly, where it meets her neck, and she flinches, her eyes flickering open. 'Easy,' he says. 'Nearly finished.'

When he's done, she sits up and splashes her face. Beads of water hang on her lashes. She wipes them away. Olly comes into focus. His arm rests on the side of the bath; his fingers trail the water.

'Kitty's gone out,' he says.

'*Out* out? Where?'

'I've no idea. She didn't even ask if we needed the car, just took it.'

Sasha considers this. It's unusual behaviour. Kitty barely leaves the Manor and Sasha can't remember the last time she did. Most of what they need gets delivered, or Sasha and Olly pick things up in town or in the village. Kitty makes an occasional trip to the hairdresser, but that's about it, and she always tells them where she's going and when she'll be back.

'It could be nothing,' she says, although her gut's telling her otherwise. 'I'll speak to her when she gets home and ask her where she's been. She's terrible at lying, so I'll know if she does.'

'I don't like it.'

'I don't either,' she admits. 'But her interview was fine.'

She eavesdropped on Kitty's conversation with the detectives, slipping into the space in the wall between the Music Room and Olly's study. Kitty's interview was as bland as they could have hoped.

'It's paranoid to worry,' Sasha says. Saying it out loud helps her to believe it herself. 'Forget about it. I'll talk to her later. She's probably getting her hair cut or going to the dentist. I mean, everything's up in the air right now. These aren't normal times. She probably forgot to tell us.'

He scratches his cheek with the back of his nails. He doesn't look convinced.

She says, 'We have enough to worry about, don't you think? Let's not waste time dwelling on a problem before we're sure it exists.'

He looks uncertain. 'Preparation is everything.'

'I know that. But let's get the facts straight first.' It annoys her how he expects her to listen unquestioningly to him and take his word for things, but he won't reciprocate. She has an idea of how to distract him. 'Do you think it's time I messaged Nicole again?'

'Yes. We could invite her and Patrick over,' he suggests. Always, he wants to go too far, too fast.

'Maybe it's a little too soon for a full-on social invitation. I could ask her if she wants to meet up with me for a walk, or a coffee. Just us girls. She might spill about Patrick.'

Olly smiles. It transforms his face. 'Great idea,' he says. He looks boyish, raffish, again. There are so many sides to him, Sasha thinks, and this one is her favourite because it's the one she fell in love with.

At the time, she had no idea what he was hiding.

30

FIVE YEARS EARLIER

Anna's Journal

When Olly whispered in my ear he said, 'Kitty's in desperate need of our help. Have you ever staged an intervention?'

He was so close it made my stomach flip, even though I know that's not how a woman my age should feel around a man his age, but it did. I probably should have taken his words more seriously, or given them more thought before I followed him, but I was too busy enjoying the sense that he and I were embarking on something together. I wanted to bask in his attention.

When he pulled away his eyes gleamed, refracting the firelight. 'You in?' he asked. 'How do you think she's going to react?'

'Why does she need an intervention?' I wasn't exactly sure what it was but was too embarrassed to ask.

'You'll see,' he said.

I trusted him completely so of course I was 'in', and I had no idea how Kitty would react because I didn't really understand what was happening. I should have asked more questions. I was like a lamb to the slaughter.

Once the last few guests at the retreat had gone back to their tents, he stood up and walked towards the Coach House. I followed and Sasha joined us. One moment I was walking a few steps behind Olly and the next I felt eyes on the back of my neck, and I turned to find her close behind. She smiled and I smiled back. My sense of belonging and of anticipation grew.

Olly rapped on the door of the Coach House assertively. If I'd been inside, the sound would have startled me. He turned to smile at us as we waited for Kitty to answer. That strange energy of his was still coming off him.

At first there was just a glow from the back of the house, where the bedroom was, but Kitty must have flicked a switch inside, because we were suddenly harshly illuminated by the porch light. Shadows dragged Olly and Sasha's features down, ageing them.

Kitty opened the door. She wore a silky nightdress styled like an oversized man's shirt and held its neckline closed to disguise her cleavage. Her feet were bare. I felt embarrassed on her behalf. I'd never seen her like this, and I had an uncomfortable vision of myself standing, similarly undressed, in the doorway of Olly and Sasha's bedroom.

'What's wrong?' she asked. She sensed trouble before I did.

'Can we come in and have a quick word?' Olly said.

'Now?'

'I'm afraid so.' His tone suggested that she didn't have any choice. She looked at Sasha, who smiled, and then at me. I looked away, still embarrassed and increasingly aware that I didn't know what was going on. Kitty held the door open for us. 'Let me get covered up,' she said.

We sat in the small sitting area. Kitty returned wrapped up in a dressing gown, the belt tightly cinched. Olly and Sasha were side by side on the little sofa and I perched on the window seat. Kitty took the rocking chair.

'What are we doing?' Kitty asked, directing the question at Olly. 'Are we doing this now?'

I thought it was an odd thing to ask. 'Doing what?' I said but they ignored me.

'It can't wait,' Olly said, his words slow and deliberate. 'Anna's suffered enough.'

I frowned and Kitty did, too. It was confusing. Olly leaned forward and addressed her. 'Sasha and I want to put it to you that you've been tormenting Anna, purposely. You've been moving or hiding her things and lying about it; you put her phone in the washing machine and you've also been making noises at night to terrorise her.'

'What?' Kitty said. She looked astonished.

'Hold on a minute,' I said. I wanted to press pause and rewind, to try to understand what was happening, but nobody paid any attention to me.

Kitty's face was contorted as it cycled through a variety of expressions. She looked angry, and, to my horror, guilty. 'Kitty, is this true?' I asked.

She licked her lips. Her nerves were contagious. 'I think what Olly means to say is that *we* – me, Olly and Sasha – want to talk to you, Anna, about what's been happening. We all feel that you might need to seek some treatment because you've been letting so much slip and we're afraid that you might have been imagining things.'

'What?' My heart sank. I'd been afraid of this.

'Let me stop you there, Kitty,' Olly said. 'This is exactly what I thought might happen. Faced with an accusation about your behaviour, you're not honest enough to own up to what you've been doing and instead you're turning on poor Anna. Hasn't she been through enough?'

Kitty's eyes hardened as she looked at him.

Sasha spoke for the first time. 'We're very keen to move on in the best way possible for all of us. Clearly, given this behaviour, you can't stay on here. If you'll agree to go nicely, we'll provide you with a good reference. This doesn't need to hang over you.'

'Really? Are you joking?' Kitty said.

'Sasha's right,' Olly said. 'Are you willing to do the right thing and go quietly, or not?'

'You're having me on,' Kitty said. 'This isn't what we agreed.'

'We didn't "agree" anything,' Olly said. 'What are you talking about? Come on, Kitty. The game's up. Don't make it difficult for us all.'

'You worm.' Kitty looked as if she'd like to hit him. 'How do you sleep at night?'

'What's it to be? A graceful exit or are you going to fight me all the way to the door and lose your references on the way out?'

I felt like I had to interrupt him. Kitty was my employee after all. 'Can't we talk about this? I'm not sure I understand what's happening. Did you do this, Kitty?'

Sasha reached over and put her hand on my knee. 'Anna, it's okay. Olly and I want to do this for you. Kitty's been using you very badly.'

'Have you?' I asked her.

She met my eye but she looked shifty, as if she was trying to decide what to say. I knew then that she was guilty of deceiving me and the sense of betrayal was shocking and painful.

'They're taking you for a ride,' she said. 'Don't trust them.' But I didn't believe her.

'Hey!' Olly snapped. 'How dare you?'

'Don't!' she told him. To me, she said, 'They've got you wrapped around their little fingers and they're never going to let you go.' Her face was red with anger, and I felt frightened of her. I was seeing a side of her that I never imagined existed.

Sasha got up and came to stand by me, as if shielding me from Kitty. I stood, too, suddenly claustrophobic, not wanting to be part of this any longer. Sasha caught my arm. 'Look at me,' she said. 'I'm sorry you had to learn about it in this way, but we thought it was better to have it out with everybody in the room.'

I shook my head. I didn't feel so good. I thought I might throw up, or faint.

'Your mother would be disgusted with you,' Kitty told Olly.

'What the hell has she got to do with anything? You're the kind of person who's eaten up with jealousy of others because you never achieved anything yourself. You might think that if you hang around you can exert your toxic influence over Anna and persuade her to keep you on, and you might have been right if we hadn't been here. But it's time for you to go.'

The last thing I saw before I passed out was Kitty launching herself at Olly.

31

THURSDAY

Jen

Jen jogs downstairs, the soles of her shoes squeaking on the treads, the squeak echoing painfully in the stairwell at the station.

She opens the door into the reception area. The receptionist sees her and indicates a seat in the corner where Kitty, the house-keeper from the Manor, sits, looking neat, prim and fearful.

Jen offers her hand and Kitty shakes it limply. The skin on Kitty's palm is hard. Jen can feel callouses. Working hands. She asks Kitty to follow her and leads her through the station, glancing back now and then with a smile that Kitty returns cautiously. Jen holds the door to the interview room open for her.

'Sorry this room isn't the most comfortable,' Jen says. 'It's all we could get at short notice.' Hal is already there. He gets to his feet, shakes Kitty's hand. Kitty looks around, taking everything in.

'Can I get you a drink?' Jen asks. 'I'll be honest, the coffee here is terrible but it's hot and caffeinated.'

Kitty shakes her head. She sits where indicated, takes her time getting comfortable. She rests her handbag on her lap and places her hands on top of it as if it's a safety barrier, between her and them. Jen notes something that she hasn't before: Kitty's wearing a chunky engagement ring with a very large stone in it – a diamond? – and a wedding band.

'What a lovely ring,' Jen says.

Kitty glances at it. 'Yes,' she says. 'Isn't it?' She twists it around her finger.

Jen doesn't remember Kitty saying that she was married, and she has the impression Kitty lives alone. Perhaps she's bereaved. Probably the reason Jen hasn't noticed the rings before is that Kitty takes them off when she's working.

'What can we do for you?' Hal asks.

Kitty swallows. She twists the ring a little faster. Jen can feel her nerves.

'They don't know I'm here,' she says.

'Who doesn't?' Hal asks.

'Olly and Sasha.'

'Is that important?'

'I didn't feel safe talking to you in the Manor. The walls have ears.'

Hal nods, ostensibly to encourage her, but Jen can sense his irritation building. He believes that Kitty is a fantasist. Eyeing the rings again, Jen wonders if he's right. Is the engagement ring costume jewellery? It's certainly at odds with the rest of her appearance.

183

At best, Kitty's clothes and hairstyle can be described as practical, at worst as aggressively plain. There's hardly a scrap of make-up on her face, only the slightest dull gleam of lipstick and some dark eyeliner, applied with a wobble, as if she was out of practice. Her hair is long and straight, grown to below her shoulders, and brushed though not styled. It hangs loose, mostly, though she's used a couple of kirby grips to anchor it behind her ears. A few dark, chestnut-brown strands of hair are visible, letting Jen imagine how Kitty might have looked when she was younger, but they're few and far between amongst the frosty grey.

'You can speak freely here,' Jen says.

Kitty nods and Jen senses a change coming over her. She wonders if Kitty's a narcissist. Is she relishing the attention? There are witnesses who love an audience, and some criminals, too. Or maybe Kitty's simply lonely, working in that house all the hours and living in isolation. How much can she have in common with Olly and Sasha, really? Jen's a firm believer that it takes an exceptional employer not to breed some level of contempt in their employees. Olly would be hell to work for. He preens constantly. And there's a glassy quality to Sasha, an impenetrability.

Jen has only recently ceased to be surprised by how many lonely people she meets in her job and become resigned to it. She's come to think of loneliness as a virus itself, sparing no sector of the population. If we solved loneliness, Hal once said, we'd solve a lot of crime before it happened. She thinks he has a point.

'You're going to think I'm stupid,' Kitty says. 'I am stupid.'

'We're not here to judge you,' Hal says. 'You can tell us anything.'

'This is a safe space,' Jen adds, though she thinks about how sometimes it isn't safe at all. This is a room where countless boring interviews have taken place, but it's also a space where what you hear can make the hairs on the back of your neck stand up.

'I used to feel safe,' Kitty says. 'Olly and Sasha made me feel safe when I first met them.'

She avoids meeting Jen's eyes or Hal's, instead fixing her gaze on her ring, as if it's the ring she's telling this tale to. She twists it more roughly now, backwards and forwards. It's uncomfortable to watch. Jen imagines the skin beneath it chafing. She wishes Kitty would stop.

'And now?' Hal asks.

'I think they've used me.'

Jen glances at Hal. A muscle twitches in his jaw, a sure sign that he's running out of patience. If this isn't directly related to Tom Booth's death, he won't want to know. Jen's heart sinks. She hopes Kitty isn't using this audience as an excuse to air some grievances about her employers. What a waste of time.

'Can you tell us what you mean by that?' Jen asks gently, before Hal can speak. She wants to give Kitty a chance. They wait in silence, Kitty's lips moving soundlessly as if she's rehearsing what she wants to say, until Hal clears his throat. Kitty looks up. She stops twiddling the ring.

'I'm not Kitty Ellis,' she says.

'What?' Hal asks.

'My name isn't Kitty. I've been coerced by Olly and Sasha into pretending that I'm her.'

Jen is stunned; Hal, too, by the look of him.

'Who are you, then?' Hal asks.

'I need you to keep this between us.'

Hal nods but doesn't confirm verbally.

'I'm Anna Creed. The Manor House belongs to me.'

She roots around in her handbag and removes a passport, which she hands to Hal. He opens it, looks and passes it to Jen. Jen notes that it's been out of date for four years. The photograph clearly shows the woman in front of them, and her name is Anna Elizabeth Creed, date of birth 5 June 1966. Anna digs around in her handbag again and pulls out a slim exercise book, which she hands to Jen.

'My story,' she says. 'How it happened. It's all in here.'

'Anna' is printed neatly on the top right-hand corner of the book's front cover, and just below it: 'Journal'.

'Read it,' Anna insists. 'But promise me you won't tell them I've told you.'

32

THE DAY OF HIS DEATH: 03:13

Tom

Tom wakes in the dark. The night air feels soft and warm on his skin. Nicole is beside him, sleeping on her back, her mouth open, snoring. He's never told her that she snores; she would hate it.

He's woken up because he's hungry. Nicole has them both on a diet. She took all the ice cream out of the freezer last week and it melted in the sink. Tom thought it was a terrible shame, like watching pleasure itself ooze away. Last night they sat morosely over bowls of salad and chicken at supper, and now he's ravenous.

'Nicole,' he whispers and, when she doesn't react and he's satisfied she's out cold, he climbs carefully out of bed, taking care not to wake her. He picks his way across the floor and heads for the kitchen. Walking through the glass corridors at night is one of his favourite things to do. He looks up to see a bright scattering of stars and the moon, which is almost full and the colour of cream, casting a milky light over everything. He loves the moon; the sight of it makes him feel childlike, in a good way, the way you feel when you fall asleep at night knowing that your family loves you and there'll be pancakes in the morning.

Maybe I should get a telescope, he thinks. He remembers a television show he watched about astronomers. They had huge telescopes, very cool. His thoughts gather: we could build a special observatory in the garden for it and invite friends and neighbours to come round and look through it. Olly might even like it, which would be good. Tom has tried to make friends with Olly but finding something they have in common has proved impossible even after six months.

Tom misses his old friends, misses meeting in the pub, watching the rugby together, playing pool and darts, even misses the lads he worked with at the garage. After the win, he treated his colleagues and mates to a big night out in the West End, but some of the lads got snide about the money. Patrick was downright nasty and the two of them nearly came to blows.

'I thought you'd be happy for me,' he said in the aftermath, when Patrick had been pulled off him. He was shocked by the almost-violence. Even as the words came out of Tom's mouth, a little slurred, a little needy, he knew something had happened that would be hard to reverse. Positions had been staked. Tom no longer felt as if he was 'one of the lads'.

'Mate, we are happy,' one of them mumbled but his words died in the air as Tom turned away and headed for the tube, forgetting the limo he'd hired, forgetting that he was rich enough to take a taxi, thinking only about Patrick's betrayal. That was a bond he'd thought couldn't be broken. For the first time in his life, he felt lonely. It hurts to think back on it even though Patrick apologised within hours. Tom never told Nicole about it. She has a lower tolerance for Patrick than he does, and he feared she would want to cut Patrick out of their lives, when Tom didn't want to do that. He couldn't bring himself to sever their childhood bond completely. Ignorant, she went ahead and approved Tom's suggestion that they give Patrick a gift of a lump sum. Tom hoped it would appease Patrick, but he can't deny it left a nasty taste in his mouth that's lingering.

He opens the fridge. The shelves present a bleak sight because Nicole has emptied them of everything unhealthy. He's against the diet in general but Nicole won't be swayed. She's explained again and again how much it means to her that they slim down. All his arguments against it – that he adores her the way she is, that he's happy with how he looks, that who-the-fuck cares? – have fallen on deaf ears.

It's to do with their new neighbour, Sasha, Tom's sure of it. She spouts all sorts of boring self-care crap, and she's whippet-thin, not like Nicole whose shape he adores. She's the sort of woman who makes Nicole feel lousy about herself. They couldn't have had more unfortunate neighbours. All Nicole wants from a friend is to have a chat and a laugh and a glass or two of prosecco, and all Tom's after is someone to share a few beers with, invite over for a swim, maybe play a round of golf with. As soon as he's learned to play, that is. Instead, they got these two smug-as-hell characters out of a posh Sunday supplement.

We should buy another house in Swindon, he thinks, so we can see old friends and get our social life back. Maybe I could try again with the lads, treat them to an escape room or to Laser Quest. He decides he'll talk to Nicole about it.

He shuts the fridge and checks the freezer in case the ice cream has miraculously replenished but the shelves are almost empty there, too. He bangs the door shut, grumpy because he won't be able to get back to sleep unless he eats. It feels like enough of an emergency to raid his secret stash.

He makes his way through the Barn to the wing that contains his den and thinks, not for the first time, how amazing it is that Nicole knew exactly what she wanted to do with the money right after it landed. She told him she'd been visualising something like the Glass Barn her whole life. 'I knew something like this would happen to us,' she said. 'I felt it in my bones. I could see this house.'

'You have such an imagination,' he told her. Since they met in childhood, she's amazed him often. When he thinks about how he loves her, he comes up with two words that he'd never share with his male friends: sweetly and intensely.

'Stop it, Tom Booth,' she told him back, sternly, because she isn't good at taking a compliment, but she blushed with pleasure.

He couldn't bring himself to tell her that he would rather she'd dreamed of a grand town house, instead, where they'd have some life on the doorstep.

As Tom moves through the house, night lighting comes on; dim, floor-level lights that show him the way. He's pleased to see them working. The system has been playing up lately.

He pushes the door of his den open. The digital clock projected on his wall glows red, informing him that it's 03:29. He yawns and moves a wedding photograph of him and Nicole aside, revealing four chunky bars of chocolate hidden behind it. He opens one and swivels his easy chair so that it's facing the window. He sits and breaks the first row of chocolate off the bar. It melts on his tongue, and he relaxes instantly.

The blinds are open, and he can see out to the side of the Glass Barn where a wildflower meadow planted by the landscaper is bordered by tall grasses. Tonight, they're swaying gently, bleached by the moonlight, as if he's looking at a sepia photograph. The sight is almost otherworldly. He breaks off another line of chocolate, steps outside into a warm, gusty wind and breathes in the soft, loamy air. He considers waking Nicole to enjoy the moonlight with him. It's romantic.

Something catches his eye, a movement in the grasses. Curious, he steps off the deck into the meadow to see better. Fronds of dry grass tickle his ankles. There it is again: it looks like a person, walking through the long grass around the side of the Barn, coming from the swimming-pool area, heading towards the woods, just their head visible. But it's hard to see clearly. It's like trying to track a seal's head in a choppy ocean as the grass undulates in the chalky light.

The person stops, as if he or she can feel Tom's gaze, and turns towards him. He sucks in his breath sharply and stares back, but he can't identify whether it's a friend or a stranger.

33

THURSDAY

Anna

Anna walks slowly away from the police station. She feels as if all the strength it took her to get through that meeting is draining out of her and her legs might give way. She gave the detectives the journal and left right away, refusing to answer any more questions. She didn't want to say more because she's not sure she comes over as believable in person. She wants the journal to tell her story. She thinks it went about as well as she could have hoped and she's as confident as she can be that they'll keep this to themselves for now, because Sasha and Olly mustn't know she's done this. Not yet.

She crosses the road and walks towards the centre of town. It's so long since she's been here; in fact, she doesn't think it's more than a handful of times since Sasha and Olly moved in. Some of the shops have changed hands, but not everything is different. She walks past Dal Baffo's, the restaurant where she and Nick sometimes used to eat. It's empty now; a waitress is laying the tables for dinner service, the barman is polishing glasses. She wonders if he would even recognise her if she went in. There was a time when he greeted her and Nick by their first names.

She fantasises about looking through their reservations book – even though she supposes that these days it's probably electronic – to see how often their old friends – if you can even call them that – still dine here. She asks herself, as she has done so often over the years, whether it was something specific she did that made them drop her after Nick died, but she knows in her heart that socially she was always hard work for those women. She was too serious; she wasn't posh enough and therefore not fun or frivolous enough. Plus – the ultimate sin – she was childless. They only let her into their circle because she was married to Nick; that was the truth of it that she learned brutally quickly after he died.

She wonders if she could have tried harder after Nick died, to stay in touch with the women. If it was partly her fault. If she'd never met Sasha, would she have been able to make those friendships work? She doubts it. She was too broken. She was damaged goods, and those women didn't have the time or inclination to help fix her.

'Anna?' She swings around at the sound of her name to see Lucy Samson, and her heart sinks. Of all the people. Lucy's dressed as if she's just stepped out of a sleek Netflix drama. Beautifully cut trousers and jacket, a white silk shirt. Her pale blue handbag looks expensive. The clasps gleam.

Anna's painfully aware of how frumpy she must look by comparison. Since taking on Kitty's role she's found no need to buy good clothes. Her dress is old, aeons out of date. She has better clothes, but they've been stored for years because she's had no need for them since becoming the housekeeper at the Manor. She did consider trying to dress better to meet the police, thinking it would give her more credibility, but that would have attracted Olly and Sasha's attention if they'd seen her.

'How are you?' she says. She desperately wants to bluff this out, to convince Lucy that she's okay, to will Lucy not to judge her. But Lucy's already clocked that Anna's fortunes have taken a turn. Her eyes rake across Anna, assessing her outfit, her shoes, the extra weight she's carrying, her limp hair, understanding everything a woman like Lucy needs to.

'I'm fine, really well, actually,' Lucy says. She's holding her phone in one hand and Anna suspects that she's dying to message her posse of friends to tell them how low Anna has sunk. 'We're just back from the Seychelles. Amy's doing her marine biology placement there.'

Of course you are, Anna thinks, and, of course Amy's placement is in the Seychelles. She's starting to remember why it was so hard to fit in with these women. Amongst other reasons, she was never able to keep up with their naked competitiveness. Children and their achievements were weaponised to score socially. Gargantuan efforts were made to ensure the success of even the dullest and least promising offspring. It was one reason Anna liked Sasha and Olly so much when she met them: they hadn't been handed life on a silver platter.

'That sounds nice,' Anna says, trying to keep the flat note out of her voice.

'Are you still living at the Manor?' Lucy asks.

Anna nods but she's ready for this conversation to end.

'I'm sorry but I have to go,' she lies. 'I have an appointment.'

'Oh, sure,' Lucy says and, unexpectedly, she looks disappointed. 'I've missed you,' she adds. 'I felt bad for ages because you texted me about a coffee and I lost my phone and all my contacts before I texted you back. I felt terrible. You were always such a breath of fresh air. You used to make me laugh.'

Did I? Anna thinks as Lucy leans in to hug her. Anna stiffens, but confusingly Lucy's embrace is affectionate, and Anna has the same dawning sense that she had when she read Olly's novel that she's been blind, not just to Sasha and Olly, but to everyone. Lucy didn't snub her. She lost her phone. It's a crushing feeling; it almost knocks the wind out of her completely and it makes her wonder about Catherine trying to get in touch with her when she came to yoga at the Manor. If she'd not been so absorbed with Sasha and so quick to assume that others didn't like her, life could have been very different.

'Shall we get together sometime?' Lucy asks.

Anna nods. 'Can you write down your number? I forgot my phone today.' She doesn't mention that she hasn't had a mobile phone for years. After hers broke, Olly and Sasha persuaded her that she didn't need one, that she'd be happier and healthier without. How did I not object to that, she thinks, when they're glued to theirs all the time? How did I let any of this happen to me? But she knows why. It's because they made her feel worthless outside of their orbit.

She takes the note with Lucy's number on it. She won't message her any time soon because that would take more social courage than she has right now, but maybe she'll get in touch, one day, and that gives her some hope.

She dwells on this as she walks to the hair salon and while she's having her hair washed, recoiling a little at the feel of a stranger's fingers on her scalp, she thinks, who am I? No longer Kitty, that's for sure, and I never will be again. But who am I, now?

Emboldened by seeing Lucy, she can brush away the shame of what's happened to her more easily than usual. I will be Anna again, she tells herself. But not Anna who is awash with grief, driven crazy by it; not Anna who feels totally worthless. I'll be new Anna, whole Anna. I'll be worth something. She knows it'll be hard to make herself believe this every day, but she will.

When she sits in front of the mirror, the temptation to tell her stylist to make a radical change to her hair is strong, but she can't, not yet. She wants Olly and Sasha to pay for what they've done to her, and she's gambling that the best way to achieve that is to stick to her plan and do whatever she can to remain invisible for a little while longer.

34

THURSDAY

Nicole

Nicole wakes to find her bedlinen tangled around her and her mattress damp with sweat. She feels as if she barely slept.

Patrick frightened me, she thinks. The memory of last night is as vivid as if it happened just seconds ago: how she watched with horror as the handle of her bedroom door turned slowly, before the door inched open and she screamed, long and piercingly loud, and Patrick rushed to her saying shush and I'm sorry. He tried to pull her into his arms, but the feel of his hands on her through her skimpy nightie was too intimate. She pushed him away and got back into bed and pulled up the covers. He took a seat at the end of the bed. When he put a hand down on the duvet, she drew her feet up.

He explained that he'd had a horrible row, with a friend, on the phone. He was worried she'd overheard and was coming to check on her and he was terribly sorry that he'd frightened her.

'Which friend?' she asked. 'You sounded so angry.' His voice had been ugly with rage. Even in the aftermath, she felt as if she could hear an echo of it, as if it was a soundtrack playing, muted, beneath the calmer tone he was adopting with her. Light from the corridor was falling across Patrick, making the scene feel unreal, as if she was watching a film.

He hesitated. Why? 'A fling who thought she was my girl-friend,' he said. 'I broke up with her. She didn't want me to. She got a bit nasty.'

'Oh,' she said. The way he spoke about it makes this girl sound sordid. She wonders how he treated her. Didn't he tell her before that he hadn't had any significant relationships? Perhaps this ugly break-up is why he's been coy about that. 'Did she do something bad? Why were you so upset with her?'

'Did you hear what I was saying?'

She shakes her head, although she thought she'd heard him shout something troubling. He'd yelled, 'Try that and I'll hurt you.' Or that's what it sounded like. She can't be sure, and she's afraid to ask because she's heard it before, the night he attacked and hospitalised a man.

'I got more upset than I should have. I guess I'm not up to having a domestic right now. I told her it wasn't the time, but she can't cut me any slack even when I'm grieving.'

She heard weariness in his voice, then, which was just what she was feeling beneath her fear. At that point, she had no energy to ask for more details; she just wanted him to go.

'I'm sorry it happened,' she said. 'I'm fine. We should try to sleep.'

After he shut the door behind him she stayed awake for a long time, and now it feels as if she's only been asleep for a few minutes, and she's woken up feeling less rested than she did last night.

'Blinds up,' she says, but the blackout blinds remain stubbornly closed. Of course. A thin strip of light beneath the door tells her that it's after dawn. She prays that the police will come today and tell her that Tom's death was an accident, and she can be released from this nightmare of not knowing and of fear, and try to work out how to live without him.

Patrick calls her, his voice a stage whisper, and knocks softly on her bedroom door. It's so different from last night. 'Are you awake? Would you like a cup of tea?'

No, she thinks. I'm not ready to see you or talk to you, yet. Go away. She bites down on her lip before forcing herself to respond: 'Yes, please.'

She gets out of bed and finds a robe. 'Blinds up,' she repeats and this time her command works. She wraps the robe around her, gets back into bed and pulls up the covers, feeling slightly less vulnerable than she did last night.

Patrick delivers her tea a few minutes later, barely meeting her eye, carefully moving things on her bedside table so he can put the mug down within her reach, and as he does, he fumbles, dropping a book and then kneeling to retrieve it from beneath the bed. He seems nervous and embarrassed, too. She doesn't know what to say, apart from, 'Thank you.'

'You're welcome,' he says. She wants him to go but he lingers.

'Can I ask you a favour?' he says.

She nods.

'My car's playing up. I had a warning light on when I drove to the supermarket yesterday. I could wait until I go home to have it looked at, but I'd rather not especially because I'm not sure how long I'll be staying. I called the garage in Chepstow, and they can look at it today, but I would need to borrow a car from you while it's with them. Would that be okay?'

She's relieved it's such a banal request, that they don't have to talk about what happened last night. 'Oh, of course,' she says. 'You can borrow the Maserati.'

'Are you sure?'

'Absolutely. Do you want me to drive you to the garage?' It might be nice to get out of the house for a while.

'No, you don't need to trouble yourself. I'll drive the Jag there and get a cab back. I'll probably take it over there now if you don't need me.'

'I don't.'

'I'll see you later,' he says. 'Is there anything you need?'

'No,' she says. He stocked the fridge yesterday.

She feels strange after he's gone. Lonely and relieved. Still troubled by what she heard last night. Did his shouting have echoes of that night when she saw him lose control? It did. She can't deny it.

Get up, she tells herself. Stop thinking about it. When she gets out of bed, her foot lands on something and she slips and almost falls, just catching herself. The culprit is Patrick's phone. It must have dropped out of his pocket.

She picks it up and hurries towards the kitchen in case he hasn't left yet. As she goes downstairs, the phone starts to vibrate in her hand.

'Patrick!' she calls. 'Your phone's ringing! I've got your phone.'

He's nowhere to be seen. As she opens the front door, she sees his car disappear down the drive. She waves to attract his attention, but it's too late.

The phone stops vibrating but starts again almost immediately. The name on the screen is 'Peter F'. That can't be his ex-girlfriend so there's no harm in answering it. She can explain that Patrick's gone out and left his phone.

She takes the call. 'Hello, Patrick's phone.'

'Who the fuck is this?'

Nicole flinches. She dislikes bad language. 'This is Nicole Booth. Patrick's staying with me.'

'Nicole,' the voice says, flatly.

'Yes,' she confirms. 'Who is this?'

'Is Patrick there?'

This man is rude, she thinks, wishing she hadn't picked up. 'He's taking his car to be mended. I expect he'll be back in an hour or two, latest. Can I give him a message?'

'He's taking his car to be mended? Is that what he told you?'

'What do you mean?'

'What I mean is that if he doesn't call me back and tell me that he's going to pay me the money he owes me in full I'm going to hunt him down and break his fucking legs and his fucking arms and his fucking life. And if he ever threatens me again, I won't just break his life, I'll take it. So, where is he exactly, darling, because he's not at home? I'm sitting outside his gaff now.'

Nicole pulls the phone away from her ear and her hands shake as she ends the call. It buzzes again and she throws it onto the sofa.

Patrick has been lying. About everything. He's in debt, and a lot of it, by the sounds of things. He hasn't changed at all. These are the sort of people she and Tom warned him against.

She remembers the anger in his voice last night. The threat he made: *Try that and I'll hurt you.* She'll have to confront him and ask him to leave, but she's frightened by the prospect. Her mind searches for a solution. Perhaps she could lock him out. Tell the system not to accept his pin.

The security hub recognises her face and presents her with the same menu she saw when she and Patrick enabled his pin, but her mind's a blank. She can't remember what they did, and her brain is too jittery and fried to work it out. She'll have to go back to the Manor House and ask for help.

Questions pile up as she laces up her trainers. To have lied to her this completely, Patrick must be desperate. For what? For her money? She can't come up with anything else. It sickens her to think that his compassion for her has been fake. If Tom knew, he'd be devastated. She pulls her laces tight. She'll go to the Manor and ask Olly and Sasha for help, and she won't come back until Patrick has moved out of the Barn. She never wants to see him again.

She stands up, momentarily dizzy. At first, she thinks what she hears is the roar of her own blood in her ears, but a moment later she realises she's wrong. Patrick must have clocked that he left his phone behind. What she can hear is the throaty sound of his Jaguar coming back up the drive.

35

THURSDAY

Olly

Olly stands in the Coach House. He sneaks into Kitty's home periodically. It's easy to do. A spare key to the Coach House lives in a drawer in the Manor House's kitchen. Not that she locks it often.

When Kitty got back from town, she seemed quite normal, and when Sasha asked she said that she'd had her hair cut and done some shopping.

Olly couldn't see any difference in her hair, but Sasha said the split ends had been cut off and it looked better. Sasha asked what shopping she'd done, phrasing it beautifully as if she was truly interested, the way Sasha can, and Kitty said she'd seen a pop-up houseplant sale and gone in. 'I bought a lovely succulent for the Coach House, and I treated myself to a cup of tea and a slice of cake,' she said.

It sounded plausible, but neither he nor Sasha could get past the feeling that Kitty wasn't behaving quite as normal. And if there's one thing that they're expert at, it's observing her, and intervening if she seems to be thinking for herself too much. This behaviour is a small red flag, but it's a red flag, nonetheless.

He's here in the Coach House to check on her. If he can't see a new houseplant, he's going to know she was lying.

Olly looks around the living area. Kitty lives in three rooms: an open-plan sitting room and kitchen/diner, a bedroom and bathroom. They're compact spaces but reasonably pleasant and airy, in Olly's view. The word 'cosy' makes him shudder, but he supposes you could apply it here. The spaces are sparsely furnished because Kitty said that she didn't need much when she moved in. In fact, she insisted on it, blathering on about how it would be a relief not to be surrounded by all her old stuff from the Manor, that it would help her declutter her mind and allow her to focus on the new her. It was laughable. The only things of value she took were two oil paintings which Olly discovered were worth something when he googled the artist, though they're extremely dull and not nearly as valuable as the carriage clock that she displays on the mantel shelf. He has his eye on that. It would look much better in his study.

He inspects her bookshelves and isn't surprised to see that her paperbacks are still mostly romance or crime. Nothing of merit has been added since the last time he was here in spite of the recommendations he's given her.

Kitty's life is so depressing, it makes him shudder. The dreadful mundanity she embraces is exactly what Olly has

204

spent his whole life trying to escape. It would be so nice if Kitty wasn't in their lives at all. Sasha reminds him that they should consider themselves lucky that this is how Kitty wants to live; otherwise, they wouldn't have the Manor to themselves and wouldn't get the housekeeping support, and she's right, but, still, Olly does find Kitty very annoying. Her whole way of living feels like an insult to him; that chronic subservience, the ease with which she shed her identity. He's read Dostoyevsky and he can relate to the contempt Raskolnikov felt for his victim. Sometimes, it's hard not to wonder whether Kitty should meet the same fate.

He considers the ease with which they got Anna to move out of the Manor House and into the Coach House after Kitty was gone. All they had to do was tell Anna that she was sleepwalking regularly and behave as if it was troubling them. It freaked them out, they told her, and invaded their privacy, but Anna might also like to know that she wasn't always covered up when she appeared. They were even considering moving out. Anna was mortified and offered to take herself to the vacant Coach House. It was that easy. It will suit me more, she said.

The day Anna moved they helped her carry her stuff from the Manor to the Coach House. Sasha had spent a week helping her to paint the place and sew new curtains. When her few belongings were in place the two of them sat down for a little lunch with her and toasted her new home with prosecco. It was pitiable.

But in the afternoon, he and Sasha moved into the master suite at the Manor. He bought champagne. They shared the bottle, and it was so good to be able to make love, to talk, or even shout, without worrying that Anna might overhear them. It felt like a triumph and it's nice to remember it now because he thinks he's probably taken it for granted for a while, which is a shame, because it was some victory.

He thinks of what they've done to Anna over the years as an experiment, of sorts, an interesting study in psychology. He started to consider how far he could push it sometime after she had moved into the Coach House. He asked Sasha: 'Do you think we can persuade her to be called Kitty? Because to all intents and purposes she's become Kitty now.' It was true. She had slipped into Kitty's role wholly by then. 'Her jobs keep me busy,' she protested if they told her she was doing too much for them. 'I love supporting you both.'

'That's sick,' Sasha told him, and he took it as a challenge.

He decided on a soft start. He suggested laughingly that Anna should change her name to Kitty 2.0 because she was a better version of the original, and watched her reaction. She seemed confused, but not appalled. He called her Kitty once or twice, pretending it was a slip of the tongue, and she didn't protest. On one occasion she looked uncomfortable, and he said, 'Forgive me, dear lady. I'm such a twit.' She laughed and blushed. He tried again a few weeks later. 'I'm sorry, Anna, but when I see you these days, I keep thinking that Kitty Cat is actually a sweet nickname. I think it suits you.'

'She's desperate for attention,' he told Sasha when she told him to stop, told him he always went too far. 'She loves it. Watch and learn.' He kept it up, over months, until he called her Kitty more often than he called her Anna, always with a smile on his face. He wondered if she would ever work up the courage to ask him not to one day, but she never did. He found it extraordinary. Surely, she would prefer to be called by her real name.

Curious, he asked Sasha to check on Anna's feelings about it. 'I've never had a nickname before,' Anna told her. 'I quite like it. It feels like a fresh start.'

'I can have a word with Olly if you like,' Sasha told her, on his instructions. 'Tell him to stop.'

'No. Don't do that. I'm happy. I don't want him to think he's done anything wrong.'

There it was. Her greatest fear was that she would upset them. She was willing to trade her name, her very identity, for a sense of belonging. It was extraordinary. Shortly afterwards, they stopped calling her Anna altogether and it's been that way ever since.

Afraid of them and afraid of being without them, she was happy to agree to anything.

Anna's been living here in the Coach House for so long now that for a while he's thought of the Manor as truly belonging to him and Sasha. It was annoying to have to tell the police that they aren't its real owners. He believes they would have some claim to it by now, as long-term residents, if Anna were to try to kick them out, and he wonders if she's aware of that. But they've got no money to fight a legal battle, not until he's sold his book. Sasha doesn't earn enough.

He knows Anna doesn't have much cash either. When they met her, they assumed she would. Mrs Anna Creed of Lancaut Manor surely had money! It was a mistake. She had very few assets other than the house. Hence, they made the decision together to sell the land with the barns on it. It brought in some money, most of which got ploughed into much-needed maintenance at the Manor. Sasha's right, he supposes; they've done very well out of Anna. Perhaps he shouldn't be thinking of her as expendable just yet.

There's no houseplant in the living and dining area. He wonders what he'll do if Anna's lying about this. Wait and watch? Follow her if she goes out again? Confront her?

He pushes open the bedroom door. Her bed is neatly made, as he expected. She has a hideous, old-fashioned doll with a heavy ceramic head and eyes as hard as shiny wet pebbles, and as usual it's on the bed, leaning askew against her pillows, limbs splayed unnaturally, lips slightly parted. It's monstrous. Who would keep that where they sleep? And there on the windowsill is a succulent, its price tag still on. Of course, Anna's bought an ugly, meanly proportioned plant, but the sight of it relaxes him. She didn't lie, she's probably not capable of lying effectively.

Beside the plant, a notebook catches his eye. 'Journal' is written on the cover. Oh! he thinks. He picks it up and his heart rate quickens. 'Anna' is printed carefully on the top right-hand corner of the front cover in her small, pedantic handwriting, which he recognises from all the shopping and to-do lists she composes. Is this it? he thinks. Could this be the journal that he spent so long looking for after they dealt with the original Kitty? Sasha and he knew this journal existed because Anna told Sasha it did. When they asked about it after Kitty had gone, Anna was vague. 'I think I wrote a few entries in it,' she said, 'but I got bored and threw it out.'

'Are you *sure*?' they'd asked her. They were afraid of what Anna might have written. They wanted to be sure that the journal would never be discovered.

'I'm sure,' she'd insisted, and Olly and Sasha had to believe her in the end.

He checks his watch. Lots of time. Sasha promised to keep Kitty busy cleaning the glass in the Orangery.

He sits on the bed with the journal and starts to read. After a couple of pages, he shuts it. He needs to show this to Sasha. Now.

36

THE DAY OF HIS DEATH: 03:36

Tom

'Hey!' Tom calls. 'Hello!'

The person disappears into the moonlit grasses. Tom has the impression of them being swallowed up. The breeze picks up, pressing his T-shirt flat against his torso.

He feels unafraid. Mostly curious.

Should he follow them? Tour the property perimeter? No. He can't be bothered. It's probably one of the people who camp illegally on Lancaut occasionally, pitching tents on the riverbank or in woodland clearings. It doesn't bother Tom so long as they leave no trace behind. Live and let live, he thinks. Why shouldn't they enjoy this place, too, if that's what floats their boat? You shouldn't have to be a millionaire to have access to nature this beautiful. Sometimes, he enjoys chatting with them.

He eats the rest of the chocolate quickly, standing in the breeze, watching clouds scud across the moon. Nicole really would love this, he thinks, but she also loves her sleep. After a while, he goes back inside and eats more chocolate because he's still hungry.

On his way back to bed he wonders if he should check the security cameras to see if he can get a better look at the man he saw outside. He could do it on his laptop, but he'd need to go back to his den. He can look on the security hub instead. He taps the screen and peers into it, and it grants him access. The menus are complicated. He feels good when he navigates them successfully to find the cameras and tries to replay the footage, but he hits the wrong button. 'Whoops,' he says. The footage seems to disappear. He tries something else to get it back. 'Footage deleted,' the hub tells him. 'Shit,' Tom says. He makes a last attempt to salvage things. 'System disabled,' the hub tells him. 'Oh, bloody hell,' he says. 'I give up.' He decides he'll sort it out tomorrow. He can't be bothered now. He yawns. Time to go back to bed.

He smiles when he thinks of re-joining Nicole there. He knew she was the one the first day he saw her, and he feels the same, still.

Walking past the kitchen he sees a phone screen light up on the island. It's his phone, which he left here to charge. Who's sending messages at this time of night? He picks it up and his heart sinks when he sees a message from Patrick, but he reads it, because it's Patrick, and even though things are rocky between them, Patrick gets all the bad luck in life and always has done, and this is what his friends do for him. He makes Tom feel guilty. Even before the lottery win that was their dynamic, because even when Tom had very little, Patrick had less.

I'm not sure why this is so difficult for you. The shit has hit the fan for me, and you and Nicole are sitting like pigs on a pile of cash and you won't even give me a scrap more. This is too embarrassing to ask someone who isn't like family to me, but I guess I'm not like family to you? You're no better than me so why should you get to decide to ruin my life? What do I need to do? Beg? Would that make you feel like a big man?

Look, we go way too far back to fall out over money, and I know you'll do the right thing. When you do, these are my credit card details – the best way.

Tom shakes his head and puts the phone down. Patrick has crossed a line. He snatches his phone up again and types a devastating reply, unleashing feelings that have been building up for months, telling Patrick where he can go and what he can do with himself, advising him that they will never speak to or see each other again, but by the time he's finished typing his heart isn't in it because this is what always happens. The story of their friendship is that ultimately Tom forgives Patrick because he feels sorry for him, and because if you lose the mates who knew you when you were a kid, you can't replace them.

He takes a deep breath, deletes his reply and Patrick's message, puts the phone down and rubs his face hard with both hands. There. That'll do. He feels exhausted now. Why does Patrick always have to do this? But it'll blow over. It always does. I'll call him in the morning, Tom thinks. He won't tell Nicole this, hasn't told her about any of his difficulties with Patrick. If she knew what a menace Patrick has become, she would never forgive him.

The bedroom is pitch-dark. No lights come on when he enters. The system knows that Nicole is asleep. He gets into bed and relaxes instantly when he lies beside her. She's like a drug to him, a happy drug. He falls asleep within moments.

37

THURSDAY

Sasha

Sasha tries another take. She wants her content to be perfect. She's been getting good engagement across her social media platforms lately, but it's hard work.

She's filming in the Manor's entrance hall, where the Tudor staircase is the backdrop. Sasha has placed tea lights on each step and woven some foliage from the garden around the banister. It looks magical, a set fit for a costume drama, and it makes her posts stand out from the usual wellness and yoga content.

The dream is that if she increases her social media following, she can put her prices up and teach less. Or she can start to do some sponsored posts and get paid for them. She's the only person living at the Manor who earns money, and she feels the pressure. Olly likes a good lifestyle. He's drunk Nick Creed's wine cellar dry and he has a taste for expensive food. So, her efforts are important. And even if her and Olly's plan comes off, they will still be important to her because Sasha's dream is to become an influencer in the yoga and wellness world. She doesn't just want money. Why should he be the only one with career ambitions?

She walks down the stairs slowly, talking to camera. The take is going well until Olly bursts in. He shoves a book at her.

'Anna's journal,' he says. 'I found it.' He's amped up, shaking the book in her face. It's been forever since he referred to Kitty as Anna and it sounds jarring. 'And don't worry, I left everything as I found it. She won't know I was there. And there was a plant, by the way. She wasn't lying about that.'

She stares at the journal. 'Is this the one she said she'd thrown out?' They tried so hard to get Anna to hand it over after Kitty's last night. They were terrified it might incriminate them somehow. Wow. This is a much bigger lie than Sasha thought Anna was capable of. 'You shouldn't have taken it! What if she notices it's gone? Why didn't you just photograph the pages?'

'You said you'd keep her busy in the Orangery.'

'Just long enough for you to check for the plant,' she hisses. 'What if she decides to pop home for something and notices this is missing?'

'She won't,' he hisses back. 'Stop focusing on that and look at this.' He flicks through the book, and she sees pages and pages of handwriting. 'I've only read the beginning,' he says. 'You're going to want to, too.'

She takes it from him and opens it. Anna has written in ballpoint pen. Sasha runs her fingertips over the indentations it's made on the paper. I can feel her concentration, Sasha thinks.

'Where was it?' she asks.

'In her bedroom, in plain sight.'

Even more reason not to take it, Sasha thinks, but there's no point in saying it. He'll get tetchy. When she feels frustrated with him, she reminds herself that they're playing a long game, and she has to hand it to Olly: he gets things wrong, he can be overconfident, and dare she think it, just plain stupid sometimes, but if it wasn't for him, they wouldn't be living in the Manor at all. He saw how good Sasha was with people and encouraged her to be choosy about who she befriended, to spot opportunities. We're never going to get given anything on a plate, he insisted. We need to hustle for it. It made perfect sense to Sasha. She's a hard worker, a grafter, but she realised she'd been waiting for life to happen to her, rather than making it happen herself. Olly opened her eyes to another way. He told her about Libby Franklin.

She reads the first few lines of the journal: *'It's time you moved on,' Kitty said. I was reading my book in Nick's study, minding my own business, when she just walked in and blurted it out as if she'd been thinking about it for ages.*

This must be right before I met her, Sasha thinks. It takes her back to Anna turning up at her first yoga lesson, and how much of a deer in headlamps she was. The first time she came, Sasha was looking out for her, but she would have noticed her anyway. Unlike the other, chatty women, Anna's body language was depressed. She crept into the class, shoulders bowed, head down, and hovered anxiously before taking a place at the back. She repeatedly and awkwardly tugged down the hem of her T-shirt. It confirmed everything that Sasha had been told. Anna Creed was not in a good place.

Sasha didn't approach her right away, intuiting that if she was overbearing, Anna might scuttle off and never come back. Instead, she gave her a warm, welcoming smile, made just one or two encouraging interventions and kept the pace gentle with a focus on restorative poses. She knew it might annoy some of her regulars who were there for something more challenging, but they could put up with it. Sasha's goal was befriending Anna, and this was the first time she had her in her sights.

She flicks through more pages of the diary, skim-reading sentences here and there. Reliving their past from Anna's point of view is both familiar and strange.

There are things that Sasha had forgotten. It fascinates her to read Anna's account of how her actions unfolded. She takes pleasure from the sense of a job well executed and successfully completed, but there's something about seeing inside Anna's mind that's also disconcerting. She's never thought of how Anna experienced this period because she was too focused on her goal at the time: to convince Anna that everything they were doing was in Anna's best interests, while getting her to do what they wanted.

'Is that her?' Olly says. They listen.

Kitty's coming.

Sasha snaps the journal shut and hands it to Olly. 'Take it upstairs, photograph every page and then put it back exactly where you found it. I'll keep her busy.'

As he runs upstairs, she takes a deep breath. Thank goodness they found this. The thought of it getting into the hands of anyone else, and especially those detectives, makes her nervous.

Hal Steen and Jen, the female detective, are not the types to have the wool pulled over their eyes easily. She needs them to stay focused on Tom Booth and not on what's happening here at the Manor.

For a moment she's tempted to run up after Olly because she should have flicked to the end of the journal. It's the end that matters the most.

38

THURSDAY

Nicole

At the sound of Patrick's car, his phone falls from Nicole's trembling hand onto the stone floor. The corner dents and a spiderweb of cracks appears across the screen. When she picks it up, pieces of glass flake off. The phone is dead. Her hand shakes.

Outside, the car engine dies. A bass still thumps. She can feel it in her chest. Then the music goes off, too.

Move, she thinks. Flee. Patrick has been telling her lies. She can't forget the threatening words of the man on the phone this morning or the anger and intensity in Patrick's voice last night. It brings to mind the time years ago when Tom had to intervene as Patrick horribly assaulted that man, and she dreads to think what would have happened if he hadn't. Patrick's clearly desperate, and associating with ugly, violent people. She's afraid of what might happen if he discovers she knows he's been lying.

It's impossible to stop him from getting in. His pin gives him access to the house. She can only hide. She hurries through the open-plan space and into the corridor leading to their gym. His phone feels as if it's burning her hand. She wants to get rid of it, somewhere Patrick will never find it, will never know that she looked at it.

She hears Patrick call out, 'I forgot my phone!' Her heart thumps. She jogs down the corridor and slips into the Barn's fitness suite.

Patrick calls again. Frustration has crept into his voice. 'Nicole! Have you seen my phone?'

She runs through the gym and bolts herself into the shower room at the back, puts the lid down on the toilet and sits on it. I'm being stupid, she thinks. Hiding will make it worse if he finds me. Her brain is still fighting over the contradiction between the caring Patrick who has been looking after her and the man she's glimpsed over the last twelve hours.

She flinches at the sound of the door to the gym opening. He must have worked out this morning while she slept in. She should have thought of that. So, he's come to check for his phone here. Surely it's only moments before he discovers her.

She considers using her own phone to call the police, but he might hear. She wonders if it's possible to use it to set off an alarm in the house, but she'd still be stuck here, with him.

She stands up. It's impossible to access the cistern because it's built into the wall, so instead, she lifts the toilet seat carefully and drops the phone into it. It's all she can think to do. She flushes. The phone won't go anywhere, she knows, but she needs Patrick to believe she was using the loo. She washes her hands, dries them on one of her monogrammed hand towels – her and Tom's initials intertwined – opens the door and pretends to be startled.

'Patrick! You gave me a shock!' She puts her hand on her chest and doesn't have to fake its exaggerated rise and fall.

'Didn't you hear me? I'm looking for my phone.' He takes in her dressing gown, nightie and slippers. 'You working out in that?' he asks.

'No. Just using the bathroom. It's my favourite one on this floor of the house.' She shrugs. 'You know,' she adds. 'Comfort.'

Her heart is thumping so hard she's amazed he can't hear it. 'Where did you last have your phone?' she asks.

'I'm sure it was in the kitchen. You haven't seen it?'

She shakes her head. 'Sorry. How annoying.'

She swallows and it feels as if she's trying to choke down a tennis ball, but he seems oblivious. He's sighing and already on his way out of the room, the missing phone preoccupying him. It's only Patrick being himself, half her brain tells her, but the other half of her brain screams, *get away.*

'Do you think you might have dropped it in the car somewhere?' she asks, following him down the corridor.

'I'll check again.'

As soon as he's left the house, Nicole hurries to her craft room, at the back of the Barn, and lets herself out into the garden. She steps off the deck and slips between the tall grasses, taking the path that leads towards the woodland, from where she can make her way to the Manor without being seen. As she moves, she glances over her shoulder, imagining Patrick following her and grabbing her – and doing what? She's not sure, but she doesn't want to find out. If his temper is on a hair-trigger, so is her anxiety.

She pushes herself to keep running between the trees. She can feel her phone in her pocket. She should call the detective, Hal, and tell him what's happened, but she doesn't want to stop now. She'll do it when she reaches the Manor. Nettles whip at her ankles and the sound of the gate clanging shut behind her sends a shudder through her. She follows a path that's barely there, and keeps going, hoping she's heading towards the Manor House, towards safety, gasping with relief when she bursts out onto the lane. She crosses it and finds herself within sight of the Coach House.

39

THE DAY OF HIS DEATH: 09:09

Tom

When Tom wakes again sunlight is pushing through the narrow gaps between the bedroom blinds and the window frames. He sits up.

Nicole isn't in bed. He listens but can't hear her in the bathroom. 'Nic?' he calls but she doesn't answer. She's probably making coffee. He hopes she is. He feels disoriented, dry-mouthed and still tired. The memory of getting up last night is dreamlike. If it wasn't for the chocolate stain on his T-shirt, he might believe he dreamed it. He wants to tell Nicole about how surreal and beautiful it was out there, in the moonlight.

'Blinds up,' he says, but the blinds don't move. He tries saying it again, sitting up a little, as if that would help, but it doesn't. Tom's embarrassed that he can't get the house's systems to function the way they should. He's had the company who installed them back here a few times since moving in and tried to pay attention as the guy tweaked a few settings and explained exactly how everything worked, but Tom has always had a short attention span and became distracted as he felt increasingly paranoid that the man thought he was stupid. He was sure he detected some scorn in the man's eyes and he heard in his voice echoes of a teacher at school who told Tom that he would never amount to anything because he was by far the bluntest tool in the box and always would be.

It wasn't just that man, either. Tom was excited when they decided to build the house, but he felt inferior around their architect, then the wine merchant who stocked his wine wall and their garden designer. He thought winning the money would help him rise above feelings like these, but it turns out that it makes them worse, because the money has catapulted him and Nicole into an unfamiliar world, where there are new rules and where people know things that they don't, and whenever they spend time with these people he finds himself lurking at the periphery of meetings, the fear of saying something dumb gluing his mouth shut when they asked if he had any thoughts, even though he did.

It's been a shock, and humbling. He expected to enjoy the money, to revel in every aspect of being stinking rich, but apparently ten million quid doesn't buy you a pass to escape your insecurities, though thankfully it hasn't been the same for Nicole. She seems to have grown in confidence through the process and he's happy for her, but he wishes it could have been the same for him.

He gets up, presses the switch to override the blinds and curses when it doesn't work. Nicole has never said, 'I told you so,' about the cranky systems, but every failure makes him feel ashamed that he insisted on them. He jabs at the switch again and this time the blinds rise. 'Finally,' he mutters, letting himself out onto the terrace.

He cheers up immediately as he looks out over the pool, which appears perfect in the early light, as does the prairie planting around it, rustling and golden, and beyond, the cliffs, still partially in shade. The birds who nest there are swooping and vocal already, animating the sky. Tom shuts his eyes and angles his face to the sun. It's going to be another scorcher. The funny thing about living somewhere like this is that he permanently feels as if he's on holiday, though whenever he thinks that he remembers that even holidays can get dull after a while, and he tries not to take that thought further, to the truth that sometimes feels as if it's screaming in his face: he's bored here, and lonely. He misses their old life. He doesn't know what to do with himself at Lancaut.

He's been wanting to talk to Nicole about it, to try to articulate the sense of uselessness and dislocation that's bubbled up inside of him since they moved in, but every time he thinks he might have found the right moment he clams up, afraid to spoil things for her. She loves it here so much and envisages a long and happy future for them in this place. How can he put a dent in that? He can't. Instead, he's been trying to keep his feelings at bay with endless new toys – car, motorbike, golf clubs, and more.

As he stares at the view he remembers where Nicole is. She said she was going to the County Show, an agricultural fair. Perhaps he should have gone with her this morning, but if he's honest, farm animals aren't his bag. Nicole will love it, though. He hopes she's having a nice time.

He has a shower and heads to the kitchen. His phone catches his eye. He checks it with a knot in his stomach and feels relief that Patrick hasn't sent any more messages. He tips cereal into a bowl, splashes milk over it and sits at the island, spooning it into his mouth, chewing with his mouth open because Nicole isn't here to tell him not to. He reads the sports news and considers making a bet on the racing, but it's not as fun as it used to be because there's no thrill in winning money he doesn't need.

He hears the buzzer and is halfway to answering it when he remembers he should have tried doing it via his phone, because it's all set up to let people in remotely. He doubles back to get his phone but can't make the app work. Nothing works. He remembers that he disabled the security cameras by mistake last night and reminds himself to sort that out today. He's beginning to think the systems have it in for him, that they want to mess with his head. He should have listened to the architect's advice about not installing too many things.

The bell rings again and whoever's outside raps on the door. He puts his phone down and hurries to answer it, tripping over Nicole's nest of 'ghost' coffee tables on the way and giving his leg a scrape. He curses them. Why she had to buy see-through furniture, he does not know.

When he gets to the door, he finds a large cardboard box, almost waist height, outside and an unfamiliar car is on the drive, but Tom doesn't see anyone.

'Hello!' he calls and, as he does, he thinks he can hear someone calling back. He follows the path around the side of the Barn, towards the pool, to see a squat man in a baseball cap standing beside it. The man has thick legs, a beer belly and wears dark glasses which make it hard to age him.

'Hi,' Tom says.

The man turns. He's about forty, Tom thinks. He has a logo on his cap, a farmland motif, which seems familiar to Tom, but he can't place it. 'Can I help you?' he asks.

'Sorry, when you didn't answer the door, I came round to see if you were outside,' the man says. He gestures to the pool. 'This is something.'

'Thanks,' Tom says. 'Yeah. We like it.'

The man walks back towards him and Tom follows him round to the front of the house. Tom has no idea what's in the box – presumably something Nicole ordered. They've had so many deliveries. 'Do you want me to put the box somewhere?' the man says. 'I'm supposed to ask customers.'

'Is it heavy?'

'Not too bad. They make them out of fibreglass,' the man says.

Tom connects the logo on the man's cap and the comment about fibreglass.

'Is it the sheep?' he asks.

'It's the sheep.'

Tom pulls the box open a little to see a full-size sheep replica standing inside. It has kind eyes. 'Amazing. It's a surprise for my wife,' he says. 'She loves sheep. She collects models of sheep, but she's never had one that's life-size. She's going to be chuffed.'

'Lovely,' the man says.

'I didn't know it was coming today.'

'Boss didn't tell you?'

Tom shakes his head. He feels a bit annoyed because if Nicole had taken receipt of it, the surprise would have been ruined.

The man shrugs. 'Sorry, mate. I hope she likes it.'

'Thank ewe,' Tom says. He waits for the man to get his joke. 'Thank. Ewe,' he repeats.

'Haha!' the man says. 'Very good. Never heard that before. Have a good day then.'

Tom pulls the box indoors and wonders how to hide the sheep, because he wants to give it to Nicole on her birthday in September. She's going to love it. He can imagine getting a whole flock of them. Maybe they can stand around the pool. Or on the front drive. He looks at the row of small ceramic sheep she's arranged on a shelf. 'Ladies, meet your big sister,' he says, and adds, for good measure, a 'Baaa' sound.

He sets his mind to the problem of where to hide the sheep and realises he probably should have given it some thought before now, but it's nice to have a little problem to solve. It'll stave off the boredom.

He kneels to eyeball the sheep. 'Right, darling,' he says. 'Where shall we put ewe?'

40

THURSDAY

Hal

In his office at the station, Hal reads an email from his press officer:

> A local journalist, Dave Gittins, is getting persistent seeking info about the investigation. I know Jen spoke to him already, and I've asked him again to hold off. Not sure how long he'll be willing to, but he owes me a favour, so fingers crossed.

He replies:

> Thanks. Let's buy as much time as we can.

On the other side of his desk, Jen is sitting and reading Anna Creed's journal. He's read it already. Her eyebrows are raised, and he's not surprised. It's a hell of a story.

'Did you get to the end yet?' he asks.

She doesn't look up. 'Almost.'

'What do you—'

She shushes him. 'I'm nearly there.'

When Anna Creed handed over her journal, Hal felt irritated. Why couldn't she tell them what it contained, instead of making them read it? How much time did she think he had? But she left immediately after handing it over, saying she had to get back to the Manor and looking as anxious and browbeaten as when she'd arrived, so he had no choice but to dip in if he wanted to know what was in it.

'Done,' Jen says, closing the journal. She hands it back to him.

'The ending,' she says.

'I know. But let's start at the beginning. What do you think?'

'It's shocking in a few ways. And there's a lot to corroborate.'

She's not wrong. 'That's an understatement,' he says. 'Is it the work of a fantasist?'

Jen shakes her head. 'I don't know, but I'm leaning towards believing her. We've seen this kind of coercive control in so many domestic abuse cases. Olly and Sasha put in just as much time and dedication to controlling Anna as an abusive partner would. The journal lays out in black and white how they became intimately involved in her life and created an emotional dependency on them in order to use her.'

Hal nods. 'But isn't it a bit of a stretch to believe they persuaded her to change her name?'

'People do. Maybe not in domestic cases but there are cults that use similar methods of control, where an integral part of belonging is shedding your original identity and taking on a new one. It can be the culmination of a process of cutting people off from friends and family, from the entire outside world. I see that happening in the journal. When Anna writes about how "supportive"' – Jen mimes the inverted commas to Hal with her fingers – 'they are, she's really describing how they exploited her vulnerability, isolated her and never gave her a chance to get perspective on what was happening to her. Once she'd invited them to move in with her, they notched the manipulation up.'

'So that she works for them now. Under another name. The name of the former housekeeper.'

'Exactly.'

'I'm worried she's unreliable,' he says. 'When she writes, it seems intelligent, but in person, I'm not so sure.'

'Believing her is high stakes,' Jen says. 'If she's right—'

He cuts in. 'Then we're going to be running two murder investigations.'

She nods. 'If it's true, those people are monsters.'

I'm a little bit in love with her, Hal thinks. No, not a little, a lot. But she's a colleague and she's too good-looking for me. It's not worth trying.

'As I said, I'm leaning towards believing her at this point,' Jen says.

He reopens Anna's journal and finds the final paragraph. It's only about a third of the way through the little notebook. There are plenty of blank pages after it. He rereads Anna's last entry:

I haven't seen our housekeeper Kitty since the night we confronted her. When I woke late the next morning, nobody was in the Manor. The yoga guests had left. I found a note on the kitchen table from Sasha. 'At the Coach House,' it said. I walked down there, nervous. The night had been so ugly. I felt as if I had a hangover, even though I hadn't drunk any alcohol at all.

A lot of the furniture had been pulled out onto the gravel at the front of the Coach House. The curtains had been washed and were drying on the line. I went inside. Sasha was on her hands and knees scrubbing the bathroom floor. The place stank of bleach. The washing machine was turning with Kitty's bedlinen inside. Cupboard doors were open, the interiors spotless. The other floors were clean and striped with damp.

'I want every trace of her removed,' Sasha said, when she saw me.

'Where is she?' I asked. This was all shockingly quick. I'd thought discussions would continue today, once everyone had calmed down, that we might come to some sort of agreement with Kitty, obtain some answers from her.

'Olly's driving her to the station.'

'Where will she go?'

Sasha looked up at me. There was a sheen of sweat on her forehead. I noticed she wasn't wearing make-up, which was unusual.

'Anna,' she said. 'You must learn not to be such a pushover. Kitty terrorised you. She's toxic. Do you really care where she goes?'

I blinked at her. I did care, a bit, even after Kitty's betrayal. But I was afraid to say so.

'Or do you want her here, to do it all over again?'

Sasha's expression was harder than I'd ever seen before. She got to her feet and stood close. I felt intimidated. 'Answer me! Are you really so submissive that you want her to stay here and continue to make your life hell? Have you learned nothing from me? Have I wasted my time trying to help you?'

Her hands were shaking. I was shocked by her vehemence and struggled to find the words to reply. The energy in the room had changed from bad to something worse. It felt as if violence was hovering there. I took a step back.

'No,' I said. 'I'm so sorry. Of course, Kitty must go. Thank you for all of this.' I gestured to the room. 'Can I help?' I felt obliged to offer though I didn't want to. What I wanted was to get out of there. Kitty's downfall was hard to bear even in theory, let alone to observe the aftermath. Until last night I'd felt attached to her, I realised, because she'd been a thread connecting me to my old life with Nick.

Sasha's expression melted into something kinder and more familiar. 'No, I'm sorry,' she said. It was like she was a different person. 'I'm just so angry that Kitty was working against you. I can't believe I didn't figure it out and do something about it sooner.' She took my hands in hers. She'd stopped shaking, her grip was gentle and firm. Of course, she was right, and I was silly to cling onto old ideas.

'You didn't know,' I said. 'I'm glad we found out when we did. Before she did anything more, or worse.'

'You were brave last night,' Sasha said. 'I was proud of you.'

Those words warmed me. I decided I would help her. To run away would be unsupportive and she deserved better. I made a start on the kitchen, pulling pots, pans, crockery and cutlery out of the cupboards, and scrubbed everything. The meagre contents of the fridge went into a black sack, and I threw it all out. It felt like a waste but realistically which of us was going to want to eat Kitty's food? We'd have had to choke it down. I was almost finished when I saw the bread bin. It was one of those on-the-counter ones, made from wood, its door hinged. I opened it. Inside, was a small red bag, with a shoulder strap. I recognised it immediately. It was Kitty's bag, the one she carried with her always, because it contained the insulin, pens and needles that she needed to control her diabetes.

I opened it. It was stuffed full, with more vials of insulin than she normally carried – it could be a week's worth, at least a couple of days' – and two of the pens she used to inject herself with, one for the day and one for night. The bag contained at least twenty needles, too. They spilled out all over the countertop in their little containers.

I knew what everything was because she'd explained it to me once. I'd been fascinated by how she managed the condition when I first met her but hadn't thought about it for years. She seemed to manage it effortlessly, so long as she had that bag by her side. If she didn't have it, she told me, it wouldn't take long for her to become very sick indeed.

I stared at it. Why didn't she have it now, if she was on her way to the station? There was so much insulin in it, I could only think that this was all she had.

I heard Sasha calling me. Something, a sort of creeping panic, made me stuff everything back into the bag and replace it in the bread bin, and I didn't tell Sasha about it. Together, we pulled the furniture back into the house. I looked more carefully at the floor this time and at the bathroom. I wondered why Sasha had felt she *had to scrub everything so hard but couldn't bring myself to take that thought to any conclusion. It was too outlandish, too horrific.*

Olly joined us soon afterwards but didn't help for long. He said he was tired, and he went back to the Manor. Sasha didn't stop him. I was virtually mute, as if my voice had deserted me. I felt as if asking questions might open a can of worms because I kept wondering: did they do something to Kitty? But that was surely my silly brain running riot.

I hung up the bedsheets and we closed the place up. It was spick and span. Later, after a strange, queasy sort of afternoon where Sasha and I avoided each other and everyone was uncharacteristically silent, I walked back over to the Coach House and took the dried bedlinen off the line. I wanted to take it back to the Manor and iron it. It was the last job we had to do, the final purge of Kitty. Everything had changed in a heartbeat, it felt.

I couldn't resist going back into the Coach House while I was there. It wasn't locked.

Kitty's bag was gone, and the bread bin scrubbed clean like everything else.

The diary ends there. Hal shuts it. 'Why's she telling us this now? Is it something to do with Tom Booth's death?'

'Maybe she's been waiting to tell someone all these years. She's probably been scared to death, isolated in the Manor, and now we're here, on her doorstep, and she sees an opportunity.'

'Maybe,' Hal says. He knuckles his eyes.

'Let's find Kitty, then,' he says. 'The first Kitty. Then we'll know whether this is a load of hokum or not. But let's not forget, our priority is to find Tom Booth's murderer.'

41

THURSDAY

Olly

Olly photographs every page of Anna's journal, which doesn't take him long, because there aren't many. She's only filled about a third of the slim notebook; the rest is blank. He knows he should return it as soon as possible, but he can't resist looking at the last entry. He needs to know if she described the events around Kitty's disappearance, because he and Sasha could be in danger, if the police get their hands on this.

He turns to the final entry. So, her writing ends here, he thinks, the day she promised that she would destroy the journal. Except that she didn't. It's the first time he or Sasha have ever caught her in a lie. It makes him nervous.

He reads the entry carefully.

I've just got back to bed. It's still dark outside and I can barely see because I don't dare turn a light on so I'm working at the

236

window, using the dawn light, but I need to write this down before I forget any of it.

I woke up earlier when it was still pitch-dark. I'd come back here after fainting in the Coach House, and left Olly and Sasha with Kitty. I'd fallen asleep and had terrible dreams about the confrontation, and I knew I couldn't get back to sleep. I wondered what had happened after I left.

I started to worry about the bonfire because I wasn't sure if anyone had put it out at the end of the night, so I tiptoed downstairs and wasn't surprised to find the door unlocked after everything that had happened. I went outside. Clouds raced across a bright half-moon. The front lawn was empty of people. They'd all gone back to the field at the end of the drive where they were camping.

I checked the bonfire. The embers were glowing. If someone had tried to put the fire out, they hadn't done a good job. Before I dealt with it, I knelt beside it for a moment. It was chilly and I wanted to absorb some warmth.

I could see the Coach House from where I sat. Moonlight paled the slate tiles on its roof and cast shadows over the whole scene. For a few moments, I let myself imagine that what happened last night with Kitty had been a dream. I fervently wished it was so. I sat there, sleepy, woozy from hunger because I realised that I hadn't eaten the night before. I was rubbing my tired, itchy eyes when two figures emerged from the Coach House, and at first I thought I was seeing things. I made to stand up and was about to call out to them, but something – some feeling of dread – made me think better of it. I watched, instead. I couldn't see well, but I thought they were dragging something heavy. It made a similar sound to the one I hear behind the panelling in my room: a scraping noise.

They didn't speak at all.

'Olly? Sasha?' I asked under my breath. Was it them? It could be.

After a few seconds I couldn't see them any longer. They'd disappeared into shadow, where the woods meet the Coach House garden and where there's access to a footpath that leads down to the site of the ruined chapel and its graveyard, by the riverbank.

The night was ghostly quiet. I heard an owl; leaves rustled in a gust of wind. A few seconds later it was as if it had never happened, as if they were never there. Did I see something? I wondered. Or had I imagined it? I stood up, my bones creaking, and carefully kicked earth onto the fire until all the embers were covered. I stood still for a long time, half listening, half afraid to move, until I began to feel as if I was no more substantial than a shadow itself. I considered going to the Coach House, to check on Kitty, but I wasn't brave enough. Eventually, I worked up the courage to go back to the Manor.

I took my shoes off, turned out the light downstairs, and debated over whether to lock the door. I checked to see if Olly and Sasha's bedroom door was shut, and it was. I wondered if they were in there but didn't dare look. I left the front door unlocked because, if it was them that I'd seen outside, I didn't want them to know I'd been there.

And now I'm writing this because I don't know what I saw but I want to record it. I'm not sure I saw anything. It can't be what it looked like – that's surely my brain playing games with me

– because it looked like two people carrying a body. If I believe what Olly said, Kitty has been responsible for me thinking I'm losing my mind. But perhaps I am losing it. Perhaps it's not Kitty's doing.

I can only tell myself that everything will be fine in the morning. I'll go to the Coach House to check on Kitty first thing, to speak to her alone, because although this has been ugly, she and I go back years so I owe her that, at least.

I'll be kind and as understanding as possible, and steel myself to ask her to move out quickly. It'll be fine. Everything will be fine.

Olly rereads the passage, shuts the journal and drops it onto his desk, as if it has burned him.

He opens his study door and listens. Sasha and Kitty – or should he say Anna now? Has her mask slipped for good? – are talking as they walk down the hallway. The dull timbre of Anna's voice infuriates him. The fact that such an insignificant human being can put him in so much danger is enraging. He wants to wring her neck.

He sits heavily on his sofa and puts his head in his hands until he's managed to contain his anger and channel it into a coherent plan. His fists clench as he thinks, and his fingertips dig into his skull, but after a few minutes he has an idea of what he should do next.

First, he'll put the journal back, so Anna's none the wiser.

Tonight, he'll talk to Sasha about what he's thinking but he can't wait to warn her about this.

He texts Sasha: She knows.

42

THE DAY OF HIS DEATH: 09:31

Tom

Tom considers putting the model sheep in the garage but Nicole's likely to find it. She regularly inspects anything he leaves down there and insists he unpacks boxes and recycles the cardboard because she doesn't like clutter. Another option might be their unrestored outbuilding because Nicole's afraid of it so she never visits it. It's a tiny structure and was probably used for grain storage. They considered making something of it but when they toured with the architect, he pointed out witch's marks on the old beams and that was enough for Nicole to decide that they'd leave it well alone. It's partly ruined, but it has a roof. Tom decides to take a look at it. 'I'll be back,' he tells the sheep.

He walks around the side of the house, past the pool. The sound of crickets is becoming louder and sharper as the day warms. He takes the serpentine decked path that cuts through the prairie planting. Within moments banks of grasses close in around him. They're taller than him, they block the breeze, and he feels hotter and hotter as he walks. The path narrows until it's just wide enough for one person, and feathery fronds touch his shoulders and upper arms, spooking him. He tries to brush them away but it's a losing battle. He's relieved when the path ends.

He pushes open the door of the outbuilding and peers inside. It's stuffy. A shaft of sunlight penetrates a small, cobwebbed window and illuminates the poky space. A little creature scrabbles for cover, startling Tom. It must have been a mouse because there are droppings everywhere. His nose wrinkles. This won't do as a place to hide Nicole's sheep. It's filthy. He's about to close the door when he notices a canvas bag, shoved into a corner. He picks it up and opens it. It contains some books – fiction and what look like academic texts – and a set of juggling balls.

He studies it for a moment and concludes that somebody must have left it here on purpose, maybe for safekeeping. It could be one of the people who camp here sometimes. He wonders whether to leave it or remove it. Perhaps he could go looking for the person and hand it over, let them know that they can't store stuff here. He doesn't have a problem with people camping on his land occasionally, but if they're going to, they need to keep themselves to themselves. It occurs to him that whoever left this here could be the person he saw last night. If they're settled semi-permanently in the area, he's not happy with that and Nicole will be totally freaked out, especially if he tells her that he saw someone after dark.

Back on the path, the grasses irritate him even more and his claustrophobia intensifies. This path should have been built much wider. Why did he keep his mouth shut when the landscaper said he wanted this area of planting to feel like a maze? At the time, all Tom could think about was how that idea reminded him of *The Shining*, but he signed off on it because he felt too intimidated to disagree. It was another of those moments where he kept his real thoughts to himself and marvelled at how Nicole seemed to embrace the suggestions that were being made. One of his greatest fears is that she'll grow tired of him, because she'll transition smoothly into this new life and he'll be left behind, inadequate, a fish out of water.

He rounds the final bend in the path and glimpses the Barn but stops short when someone steps in front of him suddenly, blocking the way out. It startles him and for a moment he can't tell who it is – those damn swaying grasses – but then he recognises them.

'Oh, hi,' he says.

43

THURSDAY

Anna

Anna watches as Sasha climbs the ladder to demonstrate precisely how she wants the Orangery windows cleaned, even though Anna's already done a few of them and they're gleaming.

Confidence in yourself is a strange thing, Anna thinks. What makes Sasha believe that she's the expert here when she's hardly lifted a finger to do housework over the past five years?

Anna has a feeling that Sasha asked her to work in here because they want to check on whether she did what she said while she was out. She would bet that Olly has gone to the Coach House to see if she really did buy a houseplant. It wasn't difficult to lay a breadcrumb trail that they could follow and hopefully Olly has found the journal. She's realised that they think she's very stupid, and, honestly, she's not sure she can blame them. I would think the same thing, she tells herself, if I'd manipulated me that successfully for all those years, but she can use it to her advantage.

She's extremely angry with herself for letting them use her. She doesn't know which one of them she resents most: Sasha, for reeling her in, or Olly because once she developed a crush on him, he made her even more of a pushover. Probably she resents her own weakness and susceptibility to them the most.

It was a gamble, creating two journals. She can hardly believe she dared to. She kept the original journal all these years, even though she told Olly and Sasha that she threw it out. It has been very well hidden. She didn't think too much about why she was keeping it at the time. She even felt bad about deceiving them, but she couldn't bear to give it up. Maybe I did have some protective instincts, she thinks. It's nice to give herself a little credit for something.

The journal had functioned as it was supposed to, giving her somewhere to work out her thoughts. It had been a comfort in the aftermath of Nick's death. She'd enjoyed writing in it so much that she'd bought a second, identical journal, but never used it. Recording her thoughts felt too dangerous after Kitty was gone. But it's come in handy now. She's made a copy of her original journal in it. The only change she made in the copy was to write a different ending; otherwise, they're identical. After that, it was simple. Put one in the hands of the police and make sure Olly and Sasha 'discovered' the other.

Her plan isn't perfect. It's flawed and it could fail, it might put her in some legal jeopardy, or even in danger, but she doesn't care. She has two goals: to throw a bomb into Olly and Sasha's lives to reveal what they're truly capable of and get them out of the Manor forever. She could tell them what she knows and insist they leave, but why should they get the chance of an easy exit when they've made a fool of her? It wouldn't be fair. And besides, she's afraid that if she confronts them, they'll outmanoeuvre her and the police somehow. That option seems more dangerous than the one she's chosen.

The sun doesn't penetrate the Orangery directly, but the space is heating up. Anna used to love this room. She grew citrus trees, tended a bougainvillea that splashed pink blooms across the back wall and had a productive vine trained partially over the ceiling. She and Nick picked out pale blue wicker furniture and they used to have morning coffee and evening drinks in here. I wasn't simply dependent on him, she thinks. We were the best of friends. I gave myself to him because I loved him, and he loved me back.

Her eyes drift to the cabinet where her gardening tools have lain, wrapped up and mostly gathering dust since Nick's death. The snips and secateurs, the Hori Hori knife. She used to keep them sharp, clean and oiled, but hasn't used them regularly for years. Soon, hopefully, she can start to tend this place again, the way she wants to. She feels somehow confident that she'll be alright on her own if she can get rid of Olly and Sasha, but it feels like a big and terrifying 'if'.

'Anna?' Sasha says and Anna's attention snaps back.

'Sorry,' she says. It's not easy to keep her expression placid.

'Did you hear me say about rubbing each pane with newspaper after washing it, so we get a really good shine?'

I taught you that trick, Anna wants to tell her, because I learned it from watching Kitty clean, but she says, 'Absolutely.'

Sasha looks dubious. 'I'll show you again.'

Anna makes a show of watching and listening, but her head aches from looking up. While Sasha lectures her, she lets her

245

eyes drift down. Sasha's phone is on the table beside them and the screen lights up with a message. It's from Olly.

She knows, it says. That's all. It must be about the journal. Olly's read it. She wasn't expecting things to go this smoothly; nor was she expecting to feel so electrified when they did.

'Do you see?' Sasha calls.

Anna's pretty sure the phone is out of Sasha's sight. The screen will go black again before Sasha climbs down. She won't know Anna read the message. 'Amazing!' she calls to Sasha as if she's been rapt all this time. 'How clever. I'll do exactly that!'

She looks up the ladder. It's close to midday and the Orangery's glass roof is bright with reflected glare.

I'm like Icarus, she thinks. Flying close to the sun. But unlike Icarus, she thinks, I will not fly *too* close.

Sasha and Olly know one thing and the police know something else.

Her future depends on what they do next.

44

THURSDAY

Olly

Olly bounds across the front lawn and jogs the rest of the way to the Coach House. He lets himself back inside and replaces the journal in Anna's bedroom, exactly as he found it.

He's angry with her because she said she'd got rid of the journal. She's a liar. An urge to trash the Coach House wells up in him. He wants to take the cosy little domestic picture she's painted here and destroy it, because disloyalty gets under his skin. But it would be a stupid thing to do, an unforgivable loss of control and counterproductive. Better to get out of here and work out what to do. If she's going to pose a threat to him and Sasha she will have to be dealt with.

He hears someone knock urgently on the front door. He considers ducking behind the sofa until they go away, but before he can, the door opens. It's Nicole Booth.

'Olly!' she says. 'Thank God.' She doesn't seem surprised to find him here.

He takes in the state of her. She's dishevelled and sweaty, her face is tear-stained and she's wearing a nightie, a thin dressing gown and slippers. 'What happened?'

'Is Kitty here?'

'No. She's at the Manor.'

'Patrick lied to me.'

'What? Why?' he asks. 'Has he scared you?'

She nods and he moves towards her, hoping to herd her out. He's mindful that they need to leave the Coach House because he doesn't want Anna to know that he's been here. 'Shall I take you to the Manor?' he asks.

She's trying to catch her breath and looks as if she might faint.

After a moment of hesitation Olly helps her to sit on the sofa.

'What happened?' he asks.

She tells him about the phone call she took, and the lies Patrick has been telling. She's talking fast; she's almost hysterical. She says she's worried Patrick killed Tom, because if he's been lying about everything else, why not that? Perhaps he tried to get more money out of Tom and Tom refused. He's got angry when they didn't give him money before, and he's been violent before.

Olly pays close attention to everything she's saying. This feels too good to be true. 'Have you told the police?'

'I haven't had time. I wanted to get away. I can call now.' She pulls her phone out. Her hands are shaking.

'You've done the right thing.' Olly's mind is racing with possibilities, but he needs to get her out of the Coach House.

248

He's going to have to gamble that Nicole won't mention that she found him there because she'll be so preoccupied with what's just happened to her. 'Before you call, let's get you to the Manor,' he says.

'He hurt that person very badly.' Her voice cracks. 'Do you think he could have hurt Tom?'

'Let's get you to the Manor. Don't be afraid. I'm with you.'

He opens the door just a crack and looks carefully before they exit. Patrick is twice Olly's size, and Olly doesn't relish the idea of dealing with him, but there's no sign of anyone.

'Let's go,' he tells Nicole. Her breathing becomes even more laboured as they hurry towards the Manor. They find Sasha and Anna in the Orangery. Anna is up a ladder. She looks hot and sweaty. Sasha is on her phone. When she first meets his eye he can tell that she got his message.

Nicole bursts into tears when she sees them. Sasha hugs her and looks over Nicole's shoulder at Olly, a question in her eyes. He nods. Yes, I did put the journal back, it says.

'What's happened?' she asks.

'I found Nicole by the Coach House,' Olly says. He wants to get that in there, so they imagine him meeting her outside the Coach House, not inside.

Nicole is still breathing so hard she can scarcely be taking in what he's saying. 'Tell them what happened, Nicole. And I think we should call the police now.'

45

THURSDAY

Hal

Hal's mobile rings as he's waiting in line to buy a coffee.

'Steen,' he says.

'I've heard from forensics,' Jen says. 'They found a small amount of blood and human tissue on the edge of a table in the Booth home.'

'Whose?'

'They're testing and we won't know for a few days, but my money is on it belonging to Tom Booth. The height of the table matches the scrape on his leg.'

'Which table?'

'In the living room. It's a low table.'

Hal reaches the head of the queue. 'Americano,' he tells the barista.

Jen's talking in his ear. 'I mean, it could be an accident,' she says. 'But the scrape is very fresh, it fits with the timeline of his murder.'

'One shot or two?' the barista says. Hal holds up two fingers.

'If we rule out an accident for now, are we saying that the scrape could have been sustained in the course of a struggle in the home?' he asks, thinking of the pair of coffee cups they found.

'It's a possibility.'

'But there were no signs of disturbance in the house.'

'No,' she concurs.

'Any results back on the coffee-cup smear?' he asks.

'What's your name?' the barista asks as Jen tells him no, not yet, she'll chase it.

He gives his name. The space where people are waiting to pick up their drinks is cramped. A woman scowls at him as he inserts himself into the pack.

'Hal?' Jen says.

'I'm still here. I'm getting coffee. I didn't catch the last thing you said.'

'I tasked Dan with looking into Kitty, the original Kitty, Anna Creed's housekeeper.'

'Okay,' he says. The woman who scowled elbows him as she reaches for her drinks. He silently vows that he will never come to this coffee shop again while knowing that of course he will, because it's the closest one to the office.

'She grew up in Lydney, a village about a twenty-minute drive from Lancaut. She never married. In 2007 she moved out of the council home her parents brought her up in, after they both died, and she presumably started working at the Manor at some point after that and got that grace and favour cottage. The last official trace of her is a speeding ticket she got, but that was while she still worked at the Manor.'

'Does she have family?'

'Two sisters. One deceased. The good news is that Dan has tracked down the living one even though her surname is Jones. I'm going to visit her today.'

Hal's name is called. He grabs his coffee. His phone beeps as he steps outside.

'I've got another call,' he says. 'I'll see you in the office later.'

He cuts her off and says, 'Steen.' The street is busy. Traffic thunders past and people weave around him. 'Hello?' he says. He stops, to try to hear better.

'Detective Steen?'

'Yes.'

'This is Olly Palmer, from the Manor House at Lancaut. Nicole Booth has just arrived here again. She's terrified. Her friend, Patrick, who came to stay with her, has been behaving very erratically. It's a long story, but the short version is that she's in a bit of a state, and she needs you to come.'

Even though he can't hear him perfectly, Hal detects an irritating note of self-importance in Olly Palmer's voice.

'I'm on my way,' he says.

He starts to jog to the office. Coffee spills over his hand, scalding him. He stops beside a homeless guy lying in a doorway. Steen meets the guy's bloodshot eyes and hands him the coffee. 'It's hot,' he says.

He calls Jen back, lets her know what he's doing.

'Do you want me to come with you?' she asks.

'No. I'll check it out. You go and see the housekeeper's sister.'

When he tells his body to pick up the pace, it does. Hal runs 10K three times a week. He can move swiftly when he needs to, and often, nobody sees it coming.

46

THE DAY OF HIS DEATH: 10:03

Tom

'What are you doing here?' Tom asks.

Patrick squints at him. 'I wanted to talk to you.'

Tom feels caught off guard. 'I don't want to argue with you. If you keep this up, I'm going to have to tell Nicole we're talking and you're misbehaving again. I don't like keeping secrets from her. You're putting me in a crappy position. What the hell was that message last night?'

Patrick puts his hands up. 'I know, I know, mate. I'm sorry. I come in peace.'

'Let's go in.'

'Is Nicole here? I rang the bell, but no one answered.'

'She's out, lucky for you.'

'Thought so. I didn't see her car. Though I don't know what she drives these days. What is it? Something sporty? An SUV?'

Tom doesn't answer. Patrick follows him towards the house. Tom stops suddenly by the pool. 'How did you know I was on the path?' he asks. Last night comes back to him. The figure in the grass. Might it have been Patrick and not a stranger? Has he been lurking around the property, watching and waiting for Nicole to go out because he knows she's not a pushover like himself? He curses himself again for trashing the camera footage.

'I didn't. I was looking around for you.'

'I didn't hear you calling for me.'

Patrick shrugs. 'How about a cold drink? It's been a long drive.'

Tom feels himself giving in, going for the easy option when he should probably send Patrick on his way. It might put a stop to his begging. But when has he ever laid down the law with his friend?

Patrick looks at the pool longingly. 'Beautiful,' he says. 'I mean, really. Amazing to see it on such a sunny day. You've done an incredible job.' He grins. 'Didn't think you had it in you.'

'Nicole had most of the ideas.'

'She always did love luxury.'

'Did she?' Tom says. He's not sure that's entirely true.

'Oh, yes. She used to save up her pennies to get the best products, don't you remember?'

Tom does, but he's not sure it speaks to a longing for luxury. He feels defensive. 'She likes nice things, what's wrong with that? Loads of people do.'

He beckons to Patrick to follow and walks brusquely towards the front door. He'll make Patrick a drink, keep the conversation away from money then tell him that he's busy. It's true. He has to hide the sheep before Nicole gets back.

Patrick notes the package when they go in. 'That's a big box.' He reaches out to pull the flaps open.

'Leave it,' Tom says. He doesn't want Patrick to mock Nicole's present, or him for buying it.

'Fine.' Patrick holds up his hands as if surrendering.

'Coffee?' Tom asks.

'Just water please, mate.'

Tom drops the bag he found on the floor, makes himself a coffee and fetches iced water for Patrick. As he does, he watches Patrick rubbernecking and his unease increases. Patrick takes his time checking everything out. Tom tenses when he picks up Nicole's various sheep ornaments in case he drops one. Patrick gets his nose right up to the artworks that the art consultant chose for them, the wine wall, the glass sculpture on the dining table, the designer furniture, and Tom can almost see the numbers clocking up in his head. Tom sighs to himself. This can't lead to anything good – being here is only going to stoke up Patrick's resentment about money.

Patrick drinks the water and puts the glass in the sink. 'More?' Tom asks.

'No, I'm good.'

Tom puts the glass in the dishwasher.

'Let's go to the den, shall we?' he suggests. It'll be better there; they'll be surrounded by souvenirs from their shared past. There will be less to wind Patrick up.

'Sure,' Patrick says.

Tom puts his coffee cup down on the table in his den and signals to Patrick that he should sit opposite.

'What brings you here?' Tom asks. 'Your message last night was horrible.'

'I know, I'm sorry. I was a dick. I've been stressed. I'm here because I want to show you something in person. It's a business opportunity that I'm not going to get again. I want to look at the numbers with you. When you see the numbers, you'll know it's gold.'

Tom sighs. This wouldn't be the first time he's lost patience with Patrick – it's happened once or twice over the years – but it's the first time Tom feels that he might be at the absolute end of his tether.

'Couldn't you have emailed?'

Patrick looks hurt. 'Look, I'm sorry about last night, if that's why you're upset.'

'I am upset. That was a shitty message.'

'Forget about it. I wasn't myself last night. Things have been stressful, but this can't wait. It's time-sensitive. If I don't invest next week, I won't get the chance again.'

'This "opportunity" is why you want money?' Tom's confused. Every time Patrick asks for money, he seems to have a different reason for it. 'You didn't mention it last night.'

'Forget last night!' Patrick's voice rises. 'Sorry.' He moderates his tone. 'Please, forget last night. Delete the message. I shouldn't have sent it, but this is real, it's a good business opportunity. Look at the numbers. I'm not asking for something for nothing. If you invest, you can make something back and so can I.'

He digs into his backpack and pulls out a sheaf of papers in a plastic folder and a laptop.

I wonder if I paid for that, Tom thinks. He's not interested in seeing whatever it is that Patrick wants to show him.

'Since when did I get good at numbers?' he asks, trying to lighten the tone. He was renowned for being terrible at maths at school. 'That's Nicole's department.'

'Then I'll show Nicole.'

That can't happen. 'I think we'll keep this between us, mate.'

Tom reaches for his coffee and drinks, but it's cold. He realises it's the one he made earlier.

Patrick puts the folder on the table and pushes it towards Tom. Tom ignores it.

'You're not going to look at it?'

'We're not handing out more money.' He feels bad saying 'we'. He should be strong enough to say 'I', but this is easier, somehow, if he invokes Nicole.

'It's not a handout, it's an investment.'

'We're not investing money.'

'I'm not asking for much.'

Tom shakes his head, though he feels a touch of uncertainty. The soft part of him wonders if giving Patrick some of what he's asking for would get rid of him, let him have a punt at whatever this venture is.

'Honestly,' Patrick says. 'I wouldn't be asking if I didn't believe in this one hundred percent. It's such a small investment you won't even notice the money's gone until it comes back with interest.'

Tom knows what Nicole would say. She'd say that they've heard this all before, on numerous occasions, that giving Patrick money is enabling him to continue to avoid properly supporting himself, that he's taking advantage of Tom and always has done.

'I know you understand that I just need this chance, mate,' Patrick says. 'Nicole, she's always been harder on me.'

'What's stopping you getting a proper job?' Tom asks. 'Why does it always have to be a scheme? We gave you a deposit for a flat. Have you still got the flat?'

'Yes, I've got the flat,' Patrick answers after a beat. It's hard to know if he's telling the truth.

Tom musters up his courage. He needs to get Patrick out of here before Nicole comes home. 'I'm not giving you money for a scheme. It's not the right thing to do.'

Patrick's eyes harden. 'Not the right thing to do? What the fuck do you mean? Do you know what your problem is, mate? You're whipped by Nicole, and you always have been. You're her bitch.'

'What did you say?'

'She's controlling. It's worse since you won the money. Too good for me now, is she? Is that what this is about?'

'Take that back.'

'I'm not taking back what's true.'

Tom stands up and Patrick stands too. They face off across the table. 'Don't you ever speak badly of Nicole,' Tom says. 'Never.' He jabs his finger at Patrick on every word for emphasis. 'Apologise.'

'You should wake up,' Patrick says. 'You might be rich but you're pathetic.'

'Get out. Now.'

'If I go now, you'll never see me again.'

Even in the heat of the moment Tom feels that as a hard pinch to his heart, but he stands his ground. 'If that's what you want.'

Patrick stares him down and Tom can feel his courage contracting, but he holds Patrick's gaze and tries not to let his doubt show. Both are breathing heavily. Tom feels his resolve cracking, but before it does Patrick turns and walks away. Tom steps into the hallway behind him and follows until Patrick has left the house. Patrick kicks the package on the way out and tries to slam the door, but its mechanism won't allow it. It closes softly behind him.

Tom returns to the den and slumps on the sofa. He sips his coffee but it's lukewarm and his enjoyment of it has been spoiled by the conversation. He pushes it away in disgust. I'll make another one, he thinks. It's been the strangest day, so far. Not at all what he was expecting. It's not even eleven in the morning and he's already starting to wish it was over.

47

THURSDAY

Hal

Hal listens as Nicole Booth tells him why she's fled her home. She's highly agitated, he notes. She tells him she was so scared of Patrick that she fled the Barn in her nightclothes and has had to borrow a hoodie and some trousers from Sasha. She picks at the tight waistband. Her slippers are dirty. He writes down everything she says about Patrick: his serious history of violence, the aggressive petitioning for money after their lottery win, the angry phone call she overheard last night, the threat she thought she heard Patrick make, and the man she spoke to on the phone today, who demanded money and made threats of his own.

'Do you believe Patrick is a danger to you, personally?' he asks.

'I don't know.'

'Do you think he had any reason to harm Tom?'

Her eyes widen. 'I don't want to say.'

'Because you think he did harm Tom?'

'Because I don't know. But maybe. He has been lying to me. He's been pretending to be rich.'

'Do you know why?'

'I told Tom we shouldn't have contact with Patrick after he pestered us for money. I wanted Patrick to back off and to learn a lesson. Tom was his friend, not his bank. So maybe Patrick thought if he turned up here looking successful, I wouldn't judge him. Maybe he wants money from me.' She looks desperately anxious.

Hal knows what he suspects: that Patrick is certainly still after money, and he thought the best way to get it was to turn up looking like he didn't need it. The question is, did he kill for it?

'I'll speak to him now,' he says. 'My officers are with him at the Barn. Are you happy for me to talk to him there? I can ask him to leave and have a chat with him elsewhere.'

'I don't know.' She looks shattered. Adrenalin crash, he thinks. He has a sense of what she's going to say next. He's seen it happen in cases of domestic violence when the fight goes out of the victims. Once the initial rush of fear has ebbed, there's a stubbornness about believing that someone truly wants to do you harm. Sometimes it's easier to pass people's behaviour off as a misunderstanding, or an isolated incident, than to accept that you're the victim of targeted, malicious intent from someone close to you.

'What if I've got all this wrong? I'd feel so bad.'

'I'll talk to him,' Hal says. 'You sit tight here.'

'It's fine to talk to him at the Barn,' she says.

He nods, leaves her. He wants to get the measure of Patrick and then he'll advise her if she'll listen. He drives to the Barn. The rear-view mirror reflects nothing but dust and blue sky.

A squad car is parked in the drive. The front door is ajar, and inside Hal finds two officers sitting with Patrick, who stands when Hal enters. His body language looks tense, as if he's coiled and ready to spring. One of the officers stands, too.

'What the fuck is going on?' Patrick says.

'Hello, Mr Young,' Hal says. He introduces himself, nods at the officers, and keeps his tone level. He doesn't want to escalate this when Patrick's temper is already flaring. 'Shall we have a chat and see if we can sort this out?'

Patrick sits, but he's agitated. Hal says, 'Have the officers explained what the problem is?'

'They've explained that Nicole felt threatened, but I've got no idea why. I'm here to help her. I've been doing everything right. I mean, she heard me have a row on the phone last night, and I might have shouted a bit, but I apologised for that. She wasn't even in the room. I don't know what else to tell you. These two are treating me like a criminal.' He gestures dismissively at the uniformed officers. His leg jigs up and down.

'As I understand it, this morning you left your phone here when you went out and Nicole answered it because she wanted to be helpful. She got an earful of abuse and some horrible physical threats from someone who said you owe them money. It terrified her.'

He watches this sink in and notes Patrick's expensive-looking watch and clothes. He's certainly making the effort to present as someone well off.

'I do owe money. I owe a lot of money.'

Hal nods. 'So, you haven't represented yourself accurately to Nicole?'

Patrick shakes his head. 'Where is she?'

Hal doesn't answer. 'Is this person you owe money to a threat to you?'

'Maybe.'

'Is he a threat to Nicole?'

'Where is she?' Patrick asks again. 'She's with those neighbours, is she? Because she didn't take her car.'

'Let's talk about why you came here.'

'To help her. Tom was my best friend. And I know, she's probably told you I badgered them for money, but it was a stupid mistake. I wish I'd never done it. I apologised for it.'

'Did you want to borrow money from Nicole?'

'No. Fuck you. I came to help.' He tears up. He looks as spent as Nicole did.

Hal decides to take a different tack. 'What was Tom and Nicole's relationship like?' he asks.

'Amazing. It's like they were born for each other. I can't imagine many other couples meeting as young as they did and still being together.'

'Was there ever any conflict between them?'

'They argued less than any other couple I know.'

'Sounds pretty perfect.'

'They weren't perfect. He didn't tell her everything.'

'Such as?'

Patrick pauses, thinking. 'Stuff that might wind her up.'

'Anything in particular?' Hal is intrigued.

Patrick shrugs. 'She kept him on a pretty tight leash sometimes.'

'Do you want to be more specific?'

'He was depressed, and he didn't tell her.'

'He told you this himself?'

'He wasn't supposed to be talking to me, but he did and that's what he told me. He wouldn't have wanted her to know. He was protective of Nicole.'

'Do you think he was suicidal?'

Patrick shakes his head. 'No.'

'When did you last speak to him?'

There's another hesitation before Patrick says, 'About a month ago.'

'Was that when he told you how he was feeling?'

'Yes, and I know, I should have followed up. I feel bad about it. I called him because I wanted to make amends after rowing about the money. It didn't work. Tom said that it would take a bit of time for Nicole to forgive me so I should keep laying low for a while.'

'Did he tell you if he was seeking help for his depression?'

'No. I told him he should, though.'

'How did you find out he had passed away?'

'She posted on Facebook.'

'When did you last see him in person?'

'I came here to visit the site, while this place was still being built. It was last autumn.'

'And where were you on the morning Tom died?' Hal says.

'I was at home in Birmingham.'

'Were you with anyone?'

'I was at my gym.'

Hal notes the details. They need checking asap.

'You gave Nicole quite a scare,' he says. 'She's very shaken up.'

'Look, I'm a lowlife. I'm a lying scum sometimes. But I'm a lowlife with a big heart. I loved Tom and I love Nicole. End of story. Can I please apologise to her? I shouldn't have put her through this. Let me explain everything. I owe it to her.'

'We'll have to ask her if she's happy with that.'

Patrick nods. 'This is all she needs, isn't it?'

'I'll talk to her shortly. I'll let you know how she feels.'

Hal asks a few more questions and Patrick answers them in a monotone. He paints a pretty depressing picture of his life.

'Tom died in an accident,' Patrick calls after Hal as he leaves. 'It was an accident!'

Hal steps out and stands in the deep shade of the porch for a few moments, thinking. Heat comes off the driveway. Solar panels on an outbuilding glint.

He needs to know more about Patrick Young. The man seems to have an identity crisis, lurching from saviour to victim, from aggressive to self-abasing. He has a history of violence – Hal wants to see the details of that – and he needs money. Hal will feel a lot happier if Nicole tells Patrick to leave.

A notification on his phone tells him he has a message from a colleague.

We have a good lead on the card found in Tom Booth's pocket. 'Sadie' works at a massage parlour in Bristol.

He tries to phone his colleague but can't get through. Jen needs to know about this, too. And about Patrick. Things are moving fast, and he doesn't want anything to slip through their fingers. He tries phoning Jen, but she doesn't pick up.

He texts her: CALL ME!

48

THURSDAY

Jen

Jen turns the car into a small village and drives past a row of quaint cottages with thatched roofs and blooming gardens. She passes a village green, neatly mown so the grass is almost glossy, a cricket clubhouse sitting smartly on the edge of it, strung with bunting that's reflected in the glassy surface of a duck pond. Weeping willow fronds trail the surface of the water. Beyond the pretty centre of the village, the picture-postcard houses dwindle until there are no more thatched cottages in sight.

The outskirts are first dominated by bungalows, clustered in neat cul-de-sacs, but these quickly give way to barely maintained social housing, where some of the front yards have become junk yards. Jen grew up in a place like this. She knows how claustrophobic it can be when your family can't afford to run a car and the bus only comes twice a day.

She crawls down a street and pulls up outside a small house. Its meanly proportioned door and windows depress her. She gets out of the car and walks to the front door on a drive made from badly poured tarmac, its edges crumbling into tarry rubble. A pocket-sized lawn has become a bed of daisies and dandelions, straining towards the sun.

The doorbell chimes elaborately when she presses it, and a shadow grows behind the reeded glass panel in the door.

'Hello?' A female voice. Jen announces herself, holds her badge up to the glass, though who knows whether it can be seen. 'I'm here to see Melanie Jones,' she says.

The door opens. 'I'm Melanie.' She's dressed in slippers, polka dot leggings and a loose striped sweater which bags over a protruding stomach, though the rest of her frame is skinny. Most of her hair is dyed raven-black but an inch of roots is the colour of slate.

'Are you the sister of Kitty Ellis?'

She looks surprised. 'I am.'

'Could I ask you a few questions?'

Jen follows her down a short hallway that's practically impassable because there's so much clutter, mostly stuffed supermarket plastic bags, heaps of magazines. The compact sitting room is no better. There are two small spaces to sit on sofas set at right angles to one another, though they're barely recognisable as sofas beneath the junk. A cat sleeps on top of a stacked pile of cardboard boxes, curled tight into a lick of sunshine. The room stinks of dust and there's a sour undernote that Jen doesn't want to think too much about, but she suspects it might be something to do with the cat.

'Anyone else home?' Jen asks.

'Just me. My husband died a year ago. Drink?' Melanie offers and in a fleeting moment of eye contact Jen can see that she doesn't want to talk about her loss and that she's embarrassed by the state of her home.

'No, thanks, I've just had a coffee.' It's a lie, but she won't eat or drink anything here, it's too dirty, and Melanie nods as if she expected that's what the answer would be, and it suits her.

'So, Kitty Ellis is your sister?'

Melanie's eyebrows raise. She glances at Jen. 'She is. Christened Karen but we all called her Kitty. She married Jack Ellis right out of school. It only lasted a year, but she kept his surname.'

'We're trying to establish contact with her so we can ask her a few questions related to an enquiry that we're pursuing.'

'What's she done?' The words are barked out roughly. Melanie starts to wheeze and Jen wonders if she has a respiratory condition before realising that she's laughing.

'Kitty's not in any trouble but we believe she might be able to help us with an enquiry. Do you have contact details for her, by any chance?'

Melanie's mouth sets into a tense line and her expression clouds.

'A phone number?' Jen offers. 'Address?'

The other woman shakes her head. 'I haven't had sight or sound of her for the best part of twenty years. She disappeared from here first chance she got. Kitty thought she was better than the rest of us.'

Jen swallows. It sounds like her own story, but she's not going to share that. She also feels the bite of disappointment.

Melanie's the only living family member of Kitty Ellis that they've been able to locate.

'Was she working at Lancaut Manor, then?'

'Where? No, she had a job at the Co-op. Hated it. She thought she was too good for that, too.'

'Are there any other family members who might be in touch with her?'

'None that I'm in contact with.'

'Anyone whose name you can give me?'

Melanie licks her lips. It's clear her sister isn't a comfortable subject for her. Her nerves and hostility are visibly building and Jen senses that her time in this house is running out. Flattery might be needed.

'It's so kind of you to help us,' she adds. 'Really.'

Melanie looks as if she's uncomfortable acknowledging the compliment. Jen has a sinking feeling that she's not going to get anything else out of her.

'So, just to confirm. You haven't heard from Kitty at any point in the last two decades?'

'I just said that, didn't I?'

Jen snaps her notebook shut. 'You did. You said you hadn't seen her for twenty years, but I wanted to check whether you'd spoken or been in touch any other way. Thank you. I should get going. You've been more than helpful,' she lies.

Melanie visibly relaxes, almost attempting a smile, and begins the painful-looking process of raising herself up out of her seat. She needs help, Jen thinks, and makes a note to check if she's on social services' radar.

Jen waits until her hand is on the front-door handle to lob a final question at Melanie now that her guard is down somewhat. Sometimes, people only open up when they know you're on your way out.

'Are you sure there are no other family members we can contact?'

Melanie's lips twist, deciding whether to help or not. 'Our other sister died but you could try our nephew, her son. He was close to Kitty after he lost his mum. If any family are still in touch with her, he'll be. He had the same sense of entitlement as her.'

'What's his name?' Jen asks.

Melanie makes a face, as if even saying the name disgusts her. 'Oliver,' she says. 'She called him Olly, but he was always Oliver to me. Nasty little prick.'

'What's his surname?' Jen asks. She feels her excitement building. Could it be the same Olly who lives at the Manor House? Or is that a stretch? It would mean he might have done something unthinkable to his own aunt, with the emphasis on *might*. But still, the back of her neck crawls.

'Palmer,' Melanie says. 'Oliver Palmer.'

It is the same man. Jen can't get out of the house quickly enough.

She pulls her phone from her pocket to call Hal and sees she has a message from him: CALL ME. She remembers Hal went to the emergency at the Manor. She dials his number. She has the sense that things are about to get exciting.

49

THURSDAY

Anna

Anna watches Nicole closely. She has so much sympathy for her. Widowhood makes you vulnerable. She should know. Nicole is looking out of the Yellow Room window, down the drive. She's waiting for the detective to come back and tell her what happened with Patrick. He's bad news, Anna can feel it in her bones. He arrived at the Barn too quickly, and it hasn't taken long for Nicole to feel terrified of him. He can't be a true friend. Not the kind of friend you'd want by your side at a time like this. It sounds as if he's a man on the edge. But, as she knows, a misplaced sense of loyalty can bind you to the worst of people.

Anna watches Olly and Sasha, too, but more subtly. Now that they've read the journal, it's a waiting game to see if they'll make the move she expects. She didn't just buy a potted plant when she went to town; she also collected a motion-triggered

272

wildlife camera she'd ordered. It wasn't easy to buy. With no phone and no laptop, she purchased it via her TV. But installing it was easier than she thought, and she made sure it was well hidden.

Her only worry is that Olly and Sasha might turn on her before she can entrap them. She's seen what they can do. Hopefully, the police presence offers her some protection. She can't believe they'd hurt her right under the noses of the detectives.

'He's here,' Nicole says.

Anna moves to stand by her, and they watch Steen get out of the car. Nicole puts her hand on her chest, as if trying to stop her heart from thumping. She's very pale. 'Kitty, get the door, please,' Sasha calls from the hallway.

She lets the detective in and directs him to the Yellow Room. Neither of them mentions Anna's visit to the station. A uniformed officer trails behind them. Olly and Sasha have slipped into the Yellow Room in the meantime. Nicole is sitting down, Sasha beside her. Olly hovers behind them, tall and stooped, his hands on the back of the sofa. Sasha reaches out to hold Nicole's hand. Nicole tolerates it for a moment then pulls her hand away. Anna doesn't think she's ever hated him or Sasha more. They're going to move in on Nicole, she thinks. They want the Barn, just like they wanted the Manor. I'm right to be doing what I'm doing. I just hope it works. She silently prays that reading her journal will prompt them to try to move Kitty's body and that she'll be able to catch it on camera.

'Could we have the room, please?' the detective asks.

Anna steps into the hall. Olly and Sasha stand up. 'Are you sure you don't want one of us to stay with you?' Olly asks.

Nicole looks at him and at Sasha, then looks past them towards Anna. 'Kitty,' she says. 'Will you?'

Anna hesitates. 'Me? Are you sure?'

Nicole nods. 'Please. Do you mind?'

'Of course not.' She doesn't meet Olly and Sasha's eyes as she takes her seat beside Nicole. The uniformed officer indicates that they should leave and shuts the door behind them.

Steen clears his throat. 'Patrick is still at the Barn. I've spoken to him at length, and he told me that he lied to you about having money and his current situation and that he's sorry. The truth, according to him, is that he owes money, and he's being pursued for it. He would like an opportunity to explain this to you himself and to apologise. I'm not sure that's a good idea, but it's up to you. He's happy to leave before you get back if that's what you prefer.'

'I don't know. Was he angry?'

'No. He's very remorseful about the anger he displayed, what you overheard and the conversation you had on his phone. The man you spoke to is someone he owes money to.'

'But he seemed like he has money.'

Steen shakes his head.

'What about his car?'

'It's not his. He rented it for a couple of days to give the impression that he's doing well for himself. He was going to return it today. The story about it needing to have work done was a cover for that.'

'He told you this?'

'He did.'

'So, he's in trouble?'

'He's in debt, yes.'

'He made out that he's Mr Big now.'

Steen nods. Anna bows her head. It's not just Olly and Sasha that are circling around Nicole, but Patrick, too. Anna admires the way that Steen is handling Nicole. He seems truthful but also compassionate. It's so tempting to tell him everything she knows about Olly and Sasha, to hand the whole problem over to him, but she can't. Not yet.

It would be her word against theirs, and they are so clever, they'd wriggle out of it somehow and she dreads to think what would happen then. She needs to force Olly and Sasha to show their hand if she's going to be safe from them. This is a long game, she reminds herself. Be patient.

'Tell Patrick to leave the Barn, please,' Nicole says. Her voice wobbles. 'Can you do that? I don't want to see him again.'

She's brave, Anna thinks. It's inspiring.

'Of course,' Steen says. 'Can you tell me more about the row that you and Tom had with Patrick over money?'

'It was after we won. We gave him a good chunk of cash as a goodwill gift but it wasn't enough for him. He hounded us for more, absolutely hounded us. We didn't give in. I told Tom we had to break off contact with him for a while.'

'And did you?'

Nicole nods.

'Did Tom?' Steen asks.

She doesn't answer immediately. Anna looks at her and sees the muscles in her cheeks twitching. 'No. He kept in touch behind my back,' she says. 'I only just learned this from Patrick.'

'We're going to make some enquiries into Patrick,' Steen says.

'Do you think . . .?' Her voice tails off. Anna's tempted to finish the sentence for her: Do you think Patrick harmed Tom? But it's not her place to.

Steen understands what she's asking. 'We're looking into all possibilities.'

Nicole reaches out a hand towards Anna and Anna looks at it for a moment, before realising that Nicole wants her to hold it. She reciprocates and Nicole grips her fingers tightly. Anna hasn't touched another person for years. It feels intense, and powerful. Steen looks at their hands, and then at Anna. She sees questions in his eyes. He's an intelligent man. Just the person she needs to deliver Olly and Sasha to.

Be patient, she tells him silently. Look after this woman. And please, follow up what's in the journal I gave you. She wants him to search for Kitty and discover that she's disappeared. It will help when she reveals her video evidence. *If* she can get it.

'Is there anyone else who can come and stay with you?' he asks Nicole. 'Unless you're happy to be at the Barn alone. We could help you book a hotel if that's what you'd prefer.'

Nicole's grip on Anna's hand tightens, briefly. This question upsets her, Anna thinks. She feels a rush of empathy. Nicole shakes her head. 'No, there's nobody.'

'I could stay,' Anna says. The words leave her mouth before she's thought them through. 'If Olly and Sasha don't mind,' she adds, glancing at Steen.

'Would you?' Nicole says. 'I would love that.'

'I'll ask,' Anna says. 'I'm sure they can spare me.'

She avoids meeting Steen's eyes and the questions in them. He'll surely want to know why she needs to have permission from them and why she's still calling herself Kitty. She hopes he understands that it's because she's afraid.

'Okay,' he says. 'If that works for you?'

Nicole nods. 'It would make me feel a lot better.'

Steen looks at Anna. There's some scepticism in his eyes. He's not sure about me, she thinks, but I need him to be. She wills him to believe in her.

'Please, call me or Jen if you need anything,' he tells Nicole.

His officer follows him out of the room. Anna can see Olly and Sasha waiting in the hallway. Nicole says goodbye to him at the door and shuts it, leaving Olly and Sasha outside.

'Are you sure you don't mind asking if you can stay?' she says. 'I'd be so grateful.'

'I don't mind at all,' Anna says.

Nicole's phone buzzes. She pulls it from her bag. 'Oh,' she says. She's already pale but Anna watches her turn an even more bloodless shade. She angles her phone so that Anna can read the message. Anna fishes her reading glasses out of her apron pocket and takes the phone from her. She has a Facebook message from Patrick.

I'm so sorry. I'm ashamed of myself. Tom would kill me if he knew I'd upset you when I'm here to help you. Please forgive me. You deserve better. When the police have gone, I can explain, if you'll let me. But if not, I totally understand. I want you to know something, though. I won't ever desert you.

50

THE DAY OF HIS DEATH: 10:47

Tom

Tom grabs a fresh cup and as he makes a new coffee he wonders if this really is the end of his friendship with Patrick. It feels like it might be and that hollows him out a little inside.

His mouth and lips still feel as dry as they did earlier. It's unpleasant. He drinks a glass of water and searches the vanity cupboard in the downstairs bathroom for a chapstick. Nicole usually keeps one in there. He finds one and applies it. Too late, he realises it's tinted pink. He goes to wipe it off but it feels good on his lips, so he purses them instead and blows himself a kiss in the mirror.

He sips his coffee while it's hot and feels it restoring his equilibrium a little, but Patrick keeps creeping back into his thoughts. He wonders if Patrick left anything in his den, any paperwork. He doesn't want Nicole to find it and ask questions, so he hurries to check, but it's okay. There's no trace of Patrick.

He sinks down onto the sofa and finishes his coffee. It tastes good. When he puts the cup down beside the one he rejected earlier, he notices that his lips, pink from Nicole's chapstick, have left an imprint on the side of it and he smiles.

He remembers the sheep, suddenly. How could he forget it? He needs to hide it before Nicole gets home. He hurries back to the atrium. The box has a dent in the side of it where Patrick kicked it. He opens it and peers inside. The sheep doesn't seem to be damaged. An idea occurs to him and he drags the box into the living area. It's unwieldy and he wonders if it would be best to take out the sheep. He wraps his arms around its belly and lifts it from the box and carries it up the stairs that way.

The guest bedrooms are up here, and a room that he and Nicole have chosen for a nursery. He'd love to be a dad; he can't wait.

In the corner of one of the bedrooms he places the sheep beneath an almost invisible panel cut into the ceiling, which gives entry to the attic. Their roof space is a little mean, but useful for some storage. The sheep should fit up there. He decides he wants to protect it while it's being stored because it'll get dusty otherwise, so he fetches the box.

He pushes a button on the wall that controls the ceiling ladder. The hatch is supposed to open smoothly, and the ladder extend down. It doesn't work. Tom punches at the buttons and curses. He's had enough of things not functioning in this house. He needs this to work, now.

He hits the buttons, knowing how stupid that is, hearing Nicole's voice in his ear telling him not to get worked up, but he's rewarded by the sight of the hatch opening smoothly. He can see the ladder, folded up in the space. It's supposed to come down automatically. Or is it? Does he have to do something else? He presses the buttons again, not sure which one controls what. The hatch closes then opens again but the ladder doesn't budge.

Tom looks at the sheep. 'Shit,' he says. The sheep's poker-face is pleasing to him. Nicole is going to love it so much.

He jumps up to see if he can grab the end of the ladder and give it a tug to get it down but can't reach. He jumps again and this time he gets hold of it. He manages to pull it, but the ladder doesn't budge. Tom sighs. He punches at the buttons again and hears the mechanism start. Hallelujah, he says. He goes closer to see if it's working and looks up expectantly. For a few inches, the ladder moves slowly out of the hatch, then all at once, it drops quickly and one of its feet hits Tom's forehead.

He staggers and holds his hand to his head. That hurt. He looks at his fingers to check for blood but there is none. He blinks, waiting to feel pain, but it's no worse than a small ache. It's nothing.

He looks at the sheep again. 'Are you going to climb up there first, or am I?'

51

THURSDAY

Jen

Jen and Hal sit in the Incident Room, catching up. Jen feels pumped from her discovery about Olly Palmer. Hal, just back from the Glass Barn where he told Patrick to leave and not to return, is giving off the same energy. 'He wasn't happy at all,' Hal says.

'It's for the best,' Jen says. 'Horrible to think of her alone there with him.'

Hal shifts his attention to Jen's news. 'So, Olly Palmer is related to Kitty Ellis, the original housekeeper at the Manor House.' He knows this already, but repeating information to make it sink into his head is a tic he has.

'Olly Palmer is Kitty's nephew,' Jen confirms.

'Remind me how Anna Creed met Sasha and Olly.'

'According to her journal, Anna first went to Sasha's yoga class because Auntie Kitty, who was obviously Anna's housekeeper at the time, encouraged her to; she told Anna it would help her get over her bereavement.'

'She set up the meeting between Anna and Sasha, then,' Hal says.

'She did.'

'Thinking out loud, here. This is how it could have gone: once Nick Creed dies, Kitty identifies Anna Creed as a mark. She knows she's a soft touch anyway and now Anna's grief-stricken, lonely, and the owner of a large Manor House and presumably some money, too. She doesn't have a support network. She's isolated. Kitty says to Sasha, I'll persuade this woman I work for to come to your class. You should make friends with her. And she does that with a view to, what? Getting Sasha to become close to Anna so she can get some money out of her? Was that a plan they had right from the start?'

'They could have,' Jen says. 'And then it goes better than expected. The relationship develops, Sasha introduces Olly into the equation, and they discover it's easy to persuade poor, lonely Anna to like them both. She's such a patsy that she even invites them to move in. They're very happy about that. They've probably got more than they dreamed of. Then, over a number of years, they push things farther and farther and eventually complete the coup by turning on Kitty and getting her to leave, then coercing Anna into taking on her role and moving out of her own home and into the Coach House, which Kitty has vacated.'

'It's extraordinary if it's true. But I want to think about that first step for a moment, the first move they made. Why wouldn't Kitty develop a friendship with Anna herself, if it's money they want? Why involve Sasha when Kitty's already much better positioned to do it? She's living in the Coach House, has been working for Anna for a while and presumably knows her well.'

'Maybe she didn't have the skills. Perhaps Anna and she didn't get on very well. From what Anna writes in the journal, the relationship doesn't sound warm.'

'How did Kitty have the confidence that Sasha could do it?' Hal asks.

Jen thinks about this. It would have been a very long shot for Kitty. Though she wouldn't have had anything to lose by trying. Perhaps they're missing something. Or— 'What if Sasha had done it before?' she says. 'What if there was a successful track record and Kitty knew about it?'

'A previous con?'

'Yes.'

'That's good thinking,' he says, and Jen feels a glow of pleasure. It's not normal for her. She takes praise the way she takes criticism, usually, with pragmatism. But it's different, coming from Hal.

'I'll get someone to dig deeper into Sasha,' she says. 'What do we need? Prior living arrangements? Relationships?'

'All of the above. And not just her. Olly, too. He's in as deep as she is. If it's not her that did this before, it might have been him.'

'Anna won't want us to turn up and ask,' Jen says. They've talked about whether to bring Anna in again, or to visit her for an interview, but decided against it, for now. She hasn't expressed unhappiness with her circumstances, so there's no action they can take without her cooperation. Hal's decided it's a watch and wait situation.

'It might be easier to speak to her now she's moving into the Barn,' Hal says. 'Though presumably she doesn't want Nicole Booth to know about her past. Unless she's confided in her.' He remembers the two women holding hands during his last interview. They're either close already or moving that way.

Jen considers this. 'Do you think Olly and Sasha are planning to make the same move on Nicole Booth that they made on Anna?'

'They could be.'

'And if you follow that logic, we need to continue to consider whether they murdered Tom. Their only alibis for that morning are the ones they've given each other.'

'And they've got holes in them. How you keep track of someone else if you're in the Manor House, I don't know. One or other of them could easily have slipped out undetected for a short time.' He sighs. 'I don't think I've ever worked a case where we have so many potential suspects, and I think it's the money that has them circling. Patrick Young being a case in point. He's a piece of work. Which reminds me. His alibi.'

'I can make some calls to check on it.'

'I'll get someone else to. We've got enough on today.'

She waits while he messages a colleague. When he puts his phone down, she says, 'What do you make of Patrick?'

'He strikes me as a coward behind all that bluff. And cowards often flee with their tails between their legs. Except when they're cornered. It depends how desperate he is. To be honest, I'd be happier if Nicole was in a hotel. Even if Anna Creed moves in with her, that doesn't exactly fill me with confidence from a security point of view. I wonder if we should send some officers to the Barn overnight.' He winces at this. It'll be expensive. 'If Patrick didn't have this history of assault, I wouldn't be so worried, but he does. Actually, I want to see exactly what happened with that.'

He opens his laptop and logs in. Jen shifts her chair so she can see the screen. Hal accesses the PNC database. There are a few Patrick Youngs to sift through, but they find him.

Hal reads from the screen: 'Section 18 Offences Against the Person Act 1861. GBH with intent. Twelve years ago.'

'That's not pretty,' Jen says.

'He could have got a substantial sentence if they'd convicted him, but it says the charge was dropped.'

'I'd like to know why.'

'We'll find out,' Hal says. He stands, looks out of the window. 'Patrick's clearly capable of beating someone to a pulp and our Olly and Sasha are capable of coercing someone into becoming a maid in her own home and changing her name. What a lovely bunch of people.'

'We also still have the possibility of it being a stranger,' Jen says. 'Robbery gone wrong, maybe. Don't forget the camper or vagrant guy. We've had three reports of someone on the peninsula, two from the last week, one from the last month. These properties aren't as insulated from the outside world as they feel.' If this is what happened, they both know it'll be almost impossible to find the perpetrator.

'And then there's Nicole, our widow,' Hal says. 'Did she do it? So many persons of interest.'

285

'We can do this, boss.'

'Yes. We'll get there.' He sighs. 'Any other leads on finding the original Kitty?'

'Nothing so far. The team is turning over as many stones as they can. If there's something to find, they'll find it.'

Jen checks her watch. 'We should go.' They have a lead on the business card found in Tom's pocket and they need to drive to Bristol to check it out. The trip will make it a very long day but neither of them mentions it. Both have empty homes waiting for them and both understand that an investigation like this requires dedication.

Sat nav guides them into the heart of the city, to Stokes Croft, where signs of gentrification contrast with the street life. They park on a side street near a small triangle of wasteland where men and women are gathered, drinking, perched on a filthy mattress. A dog sleeps on a bed of cardboard. Jen spots an original Banksy amongst the graffiti smothering the buildings. Rubbish has collected in the gutters. The energy couldn't be more different from Lancaut Peninsula. From what she knows of Tom Booth, she can't imagine him here. But people surprise you. If you don't learn that as a detective, you're never going to learn anything.

The place they're looking for is across the street; access is via a metal door. 'Are you sure this is right?' Jen asks. Sadie's business card suggested somewhere classier.

'I hope so,' Hal says. He presses the buzzer.

A woman lets them in after a delay. Jen steels herself. The last thing a place like this wants is a pair of detectives walking in. The door opens to a short, dark hallway and a staircase, leading up. They climb, Hal first. The stair carpet is crimson, and filthy. A woman opens a door at the top.

She's young, maybe mid-twenties, possibly younger, and tall, dressed in a short skirt and barely there top. Hal shakes her hand. He's good with people, Jen thinks. There are detectives she's worked with who would talk down to a woman like this, but Hal will treat her as a person, as she deserves.

'Thank you for speaking with us,' he says. He introduces Jen.

'You were lucky it was me that picked up the phone when your officer called,' she says. 'No one else knows me as Sadie here. I go by Poppy. Follow me.'

Poppy takes them up another flight of stairs to a small attic room, built into the eaves. Unlike the rest of the establishment, it's brightly lit with natural light falling from two skylights. 'Staff room,' she says and laughs. 'I know this place doesn't look nice from the outside but it's alright.'

A futon sofa is crammed in beside a tiny kitchenette with a kettle. Jen and Hal fit onto the futon together.

Hal shows her the card in the evidence bag. She looks at it closely and hands it back. 'Yeah, that's mine,' she says. 'I made that.'

'Is Sadie your real name?'

'No! Come on. I have work names. Poppy, Sadie, whatever I fancy. So long as it's not the same as the name that's going to be on my degree certificate.'

'You're a student?'

She nods. 'At the uni.'

'What are you studying?'

'Physics.'

'Impressive.'

She smiles. 'Yeah, I'm a clever girl. I just don't have any money. Uni's expensive if your parents don't pay for everything, and mine can't.'

'What's your real name?'

She hesitates. 'Martha Hayward. I know, don't you just dream of having a massage from her?' She laughs at herself. Jen warms to her.

Hal shows her a photograph of Tom Booth on his iPad, a picture that Nicole provided. It shows Tom's head and shoulders. He's outdoors, facing the camera and smiling. Jen's impression of him from the photograph is that he's one of those men who isn't going to win any prizes for most handsome but is attractive because he has a lovely smile. He looks just the way Nicole describes him.

Martha studies the photograph and shakes her head.

'I've never had him as a client,' she says.

'Are you sure?'

'I'd remember him. He's got a nice smile.'

'How long have you been doing this?' Jen asks.

'Two months. Very part time. I can make more on a couple of shifts here than I could working minimum wage for a month.'

'Are you sure you'd remember if you met him?'

'I don't see that many guys.'

'Where do you think he got your card?'

'That's the puzzling thing. I've never distributed them, so I've got no idea. I had a few made but then I didn't need them because business has been good. The rest are in my dorm room.'

'You didn't bring any here?'

288

'No. I have to be Poppy here, because the owner's wife's called Sadie, would you believe it, so they're no good to me.'

'Right,' Hal says. 'Who are your room-mates?'

'I share a flat with three girls.'

'Does anyone else have access to your room? Do you have a boyfriend?'

She shakes her head. 'No. Too complicated.' She shrugs. 'But I did have a stalker for a while. That was strange. I thought someone broke into my room once while it was happening.'

'Did they take anything?'

'Not that I noticed and I wouldn't have if one of these was all that had gone. I had a stack of them.'

'Who was your stalker?'

'I never knew. They left me little love letters. It was sweet at first, and then it got creepy.'

'What happened?'

'Nothing. They just stopped one day.'

'Did you ever take any calls on the phone number listed on the card?'

'No. Like I said, I never gave out the cards. It was a crappy phone. Cheap. I chucked it when I got my first money from here, bought myself a smartphone and got a new number.'

'Can you show me the letters the stalker sent you?'

'I chucked them, too. Sorry.'

'Did you have any idea who sent them?'

'I thought it was a guy in the flat next door. He was a bit weird. He dropped out and left Bristol around the time the letters stopped coming.'

'Can you remember what the letters said?'

'At first it was "I love you" with a bit of "You're so pretty" thrown in. Schoolboy stuff. The last two mentioned what I'd been wearing which was well creepy.'

'Any abuse?'

'"You think you're too good for me." That sort of thing. Incel stuff. But mild and, again, it was only in the last two notes that his tone started to change.'

'Do you know what triggered the notes? Did you have contact with the man in the flat next door? Was there an incident that made you think it might be him?'

'The first note mentioned that he'd seen me at a festival on the Downs, and I looked like I was having fun. I could only think he'd seen me doing a job for a car dealership. I'm with a modelling agency and they got it for me. A few students I know do events for them. It was one of those promotions where they hire girls to stand around a car and hand out merch. I was working for Maserati.'

'Maserati?' Hal says.

'Yes.'

'When was this?'

'It was last spring. I remember because we had to wear almost nothing, and I was freezing. We all were.'

Jen and Hal exchange a glance. She can tell Hal is thinking what she's thinking: that Tom Booth drove a Maserati.

52

THURSDAY

Sasha

Sasha pours hot water over her camomile tea bag and sets the timer on her phone for three minutes, so it infuses the perfect amount.

'Sasha?' She turns to see Anna in the doorway.

'What's wrong?' Sasha asks. Anna is usually back at the Coach House by now. The Manor belongs to Olly and Sasha at night.

She looked at Anna with new eyes this afternoon, appraising her. Olly's discovery of the journal is a game changer. He texted her photos of the last pages, and she read them with a building sense of horror that past events were finally catching up with them and that Anna has become a liability. Or is she overreacting? Can they relax because Anna has kept this quiet for so long that she's hardly going to blab now?

'Nothing's wrong,' Anna says. 'I just wanted to ask you something. I was going to earlier, but there never seemed to be a good time.'

'Go ahead.'

'I was wondering if I should offer, well, what I mean is that I sort of already offered to stay with Nicole for a few days now that Patrick has been sent away. Because I don't think she should be on her own. But, of course, I won't if that's not okay with you and Olly.'

Sasha stirs her tea bag around her cup to give her a moment or two to think. The advantages of this are that Anna could help them get close to Nicole. It would look like a big favour they were extending Nicole, which it is because if Anna moves next door, Sasha will have to take on a lot of work around the Manor. Which is a disadvantage. Another is that they won't be able to keep such a close eye on Anna. And that feels important just now. But if she's only at the Barn during the evenings, that shouldn't make too much difference.

'How lovely of you,' she says. 'I'm all for it. I think poor Nicole needs all the help she can get. Of course you can go. Will you be helping her with the house, or just staying the night?'

'Just staying the nights. I don't want to let you down.'

Then why are you even asking? Sasha wonders, once again marvelling at the extent to which this woman behaves as if she has no agency. She says, 'Well, that would be wonderful, but don't desert Nicole if she needs you. We'll be fine here.'

'Thank you,' Anna says. 'Goodnight.'

'Goodnight.'

After Anna's gone, Sasha stays in the kitchen, thinking, until she's finished her tea. Sometimes, she likes to get her own thoughts in order before she shares them with Olly.

Olly is in bed already when she gets upstairs, apparently asleep. She climbs in beside him and turns out the light. All the sounds of Lancaut are audible through the open window. She listens to an owl hooting, and another replying.

'Are you awake?' she whispers to Olly. He reaches for her, running his hand down her neck to her chest, touching her carefully. Her body responds and their lovemaking is quick. She's desperate for the release and he gives it to her efficiently, as if he needed the same.

When they're finished, he moves to the other side of the bed, where he lies, hands behind his head, staring at the ceiling. She's grateful he doesn't want more intimacy. The night is too hot. Too much is happening, too fast. Her nerves are shot.

'Anna is going to spend the nights staying at the Barn with Nicole,' she says. 'She asked me if it was okay.'

'What for?'

'To protect Nicole now that Patrick has gone.'

Olly snorts. 'What did you say?'

'I said yes. What else could I say?'

Olly is silent for a little while. She listens to his breathing. He says, 'She knows.'

They've only managed to exchange a few words about this today.

'Yes,' she says. 'But what does she know exactly?' Although she's panicking inside, she wants this conversation to be clear-headed.

'She saw us move Kitty's body,' he says.

'The journal says she isn't sure what she saw.'

'I think it's crystal clear.'

'Surely, she'd have run a mile if she suspected us of something like this, if she thought we were capable of murder,' Sasha says. 'I'm betting she's not certain what she saw, or she might be exaggerating. She'd have gone to the police before now if she was.'

Olly shifts a little. Sasha can feel his eyes on her. 'Unless she's frightened of us,' he says.

Sasha thinks of the way Anna asked her if she could stay with Nicole earlier. She didn't need to do that. She could go to the Barn every night and they'd never know. They hold a lot of power over her and based on the journal Olly's point is fair, but Sasha isn't convinced it's the whole story.

'I don't think she's scared,' Sasha says. 'I think that whatever she saw, or thought she saw, she still wants us and needs us just like she did when we first met her. She has no life beyond these walls. She doesn't know who she is without us.'

'Maybe she knows what she saw, but she's loyal to us,' he says. Sasha thinks about this but considers it delusional. Olly craves grandeur. Submission in others is an attractive concept to him. He conflates it with loyalty. 'She wouldn't have sold the land to the Booths if she didn't want to keep supporting us. She had an opportunity right there to say no. She could have sold the Manor, moved on, be done with it all. She's loyal.'

'Jesus. This isn't *Game of Thrones*,' Sasha says. 'She hasn't sworn an oath of fealty to us. If anything, it's just not in her DNA to say no. She's a pleaser.'

'She's weak.'

'Exactly,' Sasha says and repeats the mantra that they've used all along to justify their actions. 'She needs us.'

They fall quiet, listening to the night sounds. Everything inside the Manor feels heavy and still. Sometimes, Sasha thinks the place feels a bit rotten, with all those soft stone windowsills that are crumbling and worn, the beams, panels and doors honeycombed with woodworm. It's why she loves the Glass Barn so much, why she keeps imagining herself living there and teaching there. It would be sensational to wake up to that view every day.

Olly yawns. He'll be asleep soon. He never has trouble sleeping except when there's a problem with his book. She looks over at him and sees his profile in shadow: his long nose, the contours of his lips, full eyelashes and his closed eyelids, two small, pale moons. It startles her when he opens his eyes suddenly and turns to look right at her, as if he could feel her gaze on him.

He says, 'But we need to move the body.'

53

FRIDAY

Anna

Anna wakes up early and checks the time. It's 04:36. Almost dawn. She's in the guest suite at the Barn. It's luxurious. The bathroom alone is almost as big as her entire living space in the Coach House.

She left the blinds open last night and on the bedside table she can dimly see the pin that Nicole gave her. She must remember to wear it. Nicole spent a long time on the hub screen last night, trying to work out how to enable Anna's pin, and treated it like a small triumph when she succeeded. Anna couldn't help but smile.

'Do you wear a pin?' she asked.

'No. The system knows me by facial recognition,' Nicole said.

'Amazing,' Anna murmured.

'It's complicated,' Nicole said. 'And I need to learn how to use it properly myself because Tom did it all.' Anna sat with her while

Nicole went online and researched how to master the systems. She downloaded an app. 'Oh! It knows my phone,' she said. 'Tom must have linked them. I have no idea if this'll make me better or worse at controlling everything, mind you, but it's worth a try.'

Anna admired Nicole's independence, and her bravery.

She wonders if Sasha and Olly made their move during the night. If she was them, she would have. She wouldn't want to waste any time. She gets up and pulls on sweatpants and a top over her nightie and slips on her trainers. She attaches the pin to her top and makes her way downstairs and out of the front door.

Outside, the birds are beginning to sing and the sky is a deep velvet navy, turning pale blue at the edges. The shadows between the trees are as black as tar.

She hurries towards the Coach House, just able to pick out her way in the lightening sky. She feels nervous. She's not sure she's right, but she has a good idea of where they hid Kitty's body because she believes she found Kitty's grave a few days after she went missing.

It's not all she has to go on. Olly was fond of posing questions to her; often they related to his novel in some way. Usually, she learned, he didn't want to listen to her answer, but wanted to tell her what he thought. It flattered her that he would use her as a sounding board.

One night, after a few glasses of wine, before Kitty disappeared, he asked where she would bury a body. It was for a plot point in his book, he said. Anna can't remember her reply, but she hasn't forgotten what Olly said. He told her that if he was going to bury a body, he'd do it where there were already bones. It made sense, he said. If the body was dug up years later, it wouldn't be nearly so likely to raise alarm bells. She thought it was clever and the old graveyard beside the ruined chapel came to mind.

She picks her way down the path behind the Coach House. It's steep and uneven. She knows the lie of the land well, but she walks with intense concentration because she doesn't want to slip or turn her ankle, and emerges with relief into a parched meadow where the ruined chapel stands on steep ground just above the riverbank, a small wall around it almost completely tumbled down and in places invisible amongst the long grass. It's nearly light now. Anna walks alongside the wall, through the scratchy foliage, until she finds the opening where a gate once hung. She enters the old graveyard and navigates past fallen and tilted gravestones.

The chapel roof is long fallen in. Ferns grow between the chunks of stone on the inside and outside of the building. Anna stoops to enter. It's tiny inside. When it was in use, it can't have held more than twenty people; maybe thirty, if it was crammed full.

Parts of the stone traceries in the window in the west wall remain. She finds her footing on a stone ledge built into the wall below the window and heaves herself up, so she can better see out. Behind the chapel is a shady, scrubby area where the boughs of an oak hang so low they almost touch the grass.

This spot is where she stood three days after Kitty disappeared. They were long, lonely days when she missed Kitty keenly, and was disturbed by Olly and Sasha's indifference to her absence. They didn't want to discuss Kitty at all, and Anna wondered how they could so easily let go of someone who had been closely involved in their lives. If Anna mentioned her, she was met with silence, or with a swift change of subject.

The truth is that she didn't actually see Olly and Sasha drag a body from the Coach House, but after she came here, and based on what Olly said, she's certain they must have. She wrote a fictional description of them removing Kitty's body from the Coach House in the version of the journal she gave to Sasha and Olly to try to smoke them out. The journal she gave the police is the original one. She did find Kitty's insulin, and she did find Sasha cleaning out the Coach House, and that, along with her discovery of the grave site, convinced her that they had killed Kitty, but she never saw them.

It was a coincidence that she found this grave site. She was simply walking to one of her favourite places, trying to make sense of what she was thinking and feeling, and of Olly and Sasha's behaviour since that night. When she got here, she thought of Olly's comment about where he would bury a body and, as if living a nightmare, she began to notice unusual signs around her: the imprint of a foot, some flattened nettles and a long, narrow area of earth that looked disturbed. A torn branch had fallen over it, the leaves only slightly drooping but soon to crisp and fall. This looked like a fresh grave to her. She didn't think she was imagining it.

She pressed her hands over her lips, trying to seal in her fears, before dropping into a crouch, her back against the chapel wall, the stone blocks, the ledge digging into the middle of her spine. Since then she's asked herself many times why she didn't go to the police immediately, why she ran away and hasn't returned. Why she continued to live and work alongside them without doing anything. The answer is never easy. But she knows she thought then that she could never beat them, that they would control her, always. She was so divorced from her former life at the time that there was even a sort of twisted comfort in believing it.

But the idea that they killed Kitty and buried her here has been a dark suspicion that she's held inside since that night. It's been burning a hole in her for far too long.

She finds the camera where she left it, tucked into the stone tracery overlooking the burial site, and removes the card before replacing it with a fresh one. She can't tell if the ground has been disturbed. There's a branch lying over the area, just like there was yesterday, but she thinks it might have been moved. She pockets the card. She'll take it to the Coach House and have a look at it before she returns to the Barn. She can tell Nicole that she just popped home to collect some more of her stuff.

A breeze picks up and the branches shudder, leaves rustling. As Anna turns away from the chapel a chill crawls across the back of her neck and she thinks of Kitty, lying here amongst the other dead.

Just as she steps back onto the path, branches crack in the undergrowth and she freezes. She stands still for a few minutes, her heart beating too fast, too hard. When she starts to move again, she walks as quietly as possible, and it occurs to her to wonder why, although Sasha and Olly show so much concern about Nicole staying in the Barn alone, they've never once asked Anna if she's alright in the Coach House alone. Not. Once. Nor did Sasha ask her if she would be alright walking to the Barn in the dark last night. Is it because they don't care, because she's nothing to them? Or could it be because they know she's fine, because they know who killed Tom Booth? And the only way they would know that is if it was one of them.

54

THE DAY OF HIS DEATH: 11:12

Tom

Tom picks the sheep up under one arm and climbs the ladder. The sheep's size and shape make it awkward to get it through the hatch and he grapples with it until he works up a sweat but gets it through eventually. He climbs back down to retrieve the box it came in and takes the box up, too. The attic space is tidy. Nicole has strict rules about what they can store up here; she doesn't want it full of junk. In the middle of the space, where the headroom is greatest, he hefts the sheep back into its box. It's not easy because the box is tall, and Tom can't quite stand upright. He looks in at the sheep and says, 'Sleep tight for a while.'

He closes the box flaps and feels very satisfied. Nicole told him she didn't want an expensive birthday present, but something thoughtful instead, and he hopes this will work. At the least, he knows it will make her laugh.

The attic is stuffy, and the temperature is rising. He climbs back down and presses the button on the wall, making sure he's well out of the way as the ladder ascends and disappears into the hatch, which closes as it should.

'Fine,' he says. 'Good.'

He returns downstairs and wonders what to do. A walk would be sensible, he supposes. He's found it hard to motivate himself lately, though he hasn't told Nicole. He wouldn't do that to her. She always dreamed of having a different, more special life when they were younger, and now she has it, he can't burst her balloon. His insecurities and his bouts of lethargy will remain hidden. He'll figure out how to get through it himself.

He feels weary. Dealing with Patrick was exhausting, and sad. Tom struggles to come to terms with what just happened; he wants to find some hope in it, but part of him also knows this is the culmination of months of Patrick's behaviour degenerating. It hurts that Patrick is the only person he admitted his true feelings to, telling him in one of their better conversations about his struggles with their new life, and Patrick has responded with total selfishness, fixating on the money. Tom sighs. It annoys him, too, that Patrick has put a blight on this morning.

Perhaps some music would help. He's been trying to educate himself in opera. Nicole wants to go and see one at Covent Garden. She wants a box and a fancy dinner and a lovely new outfit. He's totally up for it, but he also wants to understand opera a little before he goes because he's tired of feeling ignorant, so he bought an album by the Three Tenors.

He tells the house to play it, now, and to play it loudly, and the sound swells from the speakers, pleasing him until a little headache starts to press behind his eyes, but he ignores it and concentrates on listening. When 'Nessun Dorma' comes on, he conducts, humming along, and chipping in with the one or two words he's picked up. It's his favourite. His mood lifts and he sets it to play on a loop.

He sees the bag that he dropped on the floor, the one he found in the outbuilding. It would be good if he can track down whoever stashed it there and ask them to leave before Nicole finds out they were ever on their property.

He steps outside, carrying the bag. The music in the house is supposed to stop playing and transfer to the outdoor speakers, but it doesn't. He mutters his disapproval, but who cares, really? Let it play in the house. There's no one out here to be disturbed by it. He enjoys hearing it as he walks down the meadow.

He reckons that if there's someone camping near enough to want to use the outbuilding for storage, they're probably in the treeline close to the river. He can still hear the Three Tenors faintly. When he reaches the trees, it's a relief to get out of the sun. In the shade of an oak tree, he wipes a sheen of sweat from his forehead and presses on through the woodland until he reaches the boundary of his property.

He follows the fence line. When they bought the land they replaced the old barbed wire with new wooden fencing. It looks more beautiful and is less likely to harm wildlife, but it occurs to him that it also makes it a lot easier for people to sneak over it.

The ground crunches underfoot as he walks, twigs and leaves bone-dry after the weeks of heat. His nostrils curl as a distinctive odour reaches them. It smells like fire and there shouldn't be any fire here. He finds the smoking embers soon after, in a clearing beside the fence. The fire is part of a wild campsite: a one-man tent and a small cooking stove, a pile of rubbish. There's no sign of the camper and Tom's furious. This is the height of stupid behaviour. What if the fire spread? He can imagine it ripping up the dry meadow towards the Barn, catching the tall grasses, creating a wall of flame.

'Hello?' he calls. He hates confrontation normally, preferring to see the best in others and considers himself a benevolent landowner, but this is one of those moments when his outrage exceeds his better intentions. 'Hello?'

He sees a man approaching, coming up the riverbank. He's carrying a jerry can, water spilling messily from the top of it. The man is about Tom's age but dishevelled, wearing a T-shirt and knee-length cargo shorts, well-worn trainers. His hair is messy and quite long. He has a few days' growth of patchy beard, and bloodshot eyes.

'Is this your fire?' Tom asks.

'Just got some water to put it out, mate.' The man lifts the jerry can. He says it as casually as if this were his property, his land, as if Tom is being a jerk.

'You shouldn't have lit it. It's dangerous.'

The man pushes the jerry can beneath the fence and leaps it effortlessly. He takes his time dousing the fire with water. It's like a performance, as if he's trying to make the point that Tom is being unreasonable.

Tom's temper rises. It doesn't happen often, but he's annoyed that the man is assuming him to be hostile, when he came here with the intention of giving him his bag and asking him nicely to move on.

When the can is empty and the fire's a sodden pile of ashes, the man looks Tom up and down and Tom feels judged for his nice clothes and his relative cleanliness. He tries to stand taller, straighter. 'Is this yours?' he asks, holding out the bag.

'Yes,' the man says. He takes it.

'You can't store stuff on my property. How long have you been here?'

'Not long. I only left the bag in your hut because I don't want to carry everything with me every day. I'm moving on today so I would have got it. It's not like it's doing you any harm.'

Tom isn't satisfied. He wants more contrition. 'And you shouldn't have a fire. Can't you see? It's a tinderbox here.'

The man clutches the bag to his chest. 'I was careful with the fire.'

'Lighting it wasn't careful, mate.'

Tom doesn't want to escalate things, but he does want the man to acknowledge that he's in the wrong and the little headache he felt earlier is intensifying. It's not helping his temper. The man turns his back on Tom and begins to gather his stuff up, slowly, as if he's in no rush. He mutters something. To Tom it sounds like 'fuck you'.

'What did you say?' he asks.

'Nothing, mate. Think you're imagining things.'

'You've got a nerve,' Tom says. 'I could call the police, have you arrested.'

'Go on, then,' the man says but he doesn't look bothered and he doesn't move. Tom's fists clench with frustration. All he wants is for his authority as landowner to be recognised, and it would be nice if the guy could also acknowledge that Tom is being reasonable *and* trying to be nice.

He briefly wonders if he could physically intimidate the man, if necessary, and force him to leave. Tom is bigger, but the man has a wiry sort of fitness that worries him. He fears that if the man struck him, it would be with accuracy. And Tom hasn't had a physical altercation for decades. He might go down quickly.

'Well, if you go now, I won't,' Tom says. 'If you hurry up.'

He's relieved when the man starts to pack up, but he does it with frustratingly slow movements as if to provoke Tom. Occasionally, he makes eye contact with Tom, but it's more disconcerting than reassuring. He has a dead look in his eyes. Tom doesn't want him anywhere near Nicole, ever.

'Hurry up.' He tries to sound authoritative, but he finds himself swallowing nervously. To speed things along, he begins to pick up the trash himself, gathering it in a plastic bag. As he does, the ground briefly lurches towards him, but he finds his balance and picks up the rest of the rubbish, hoping the guy didn't notice. He can't lose face. By the time he's done, the man is finishing stuffing everything into his pack and looks like he's ready to leave.

Tom holds out the bag of rubbish. The man ignores it.

'Here,' Tom says. 'This is yours. Take it away and dispose of it properly.'

'You take it.'

Tom's temper snaps and he tosses the bag at the man, not hard, but the man makes no attempt to catch it. It hits his arm and falls to the ground and some of the rubbish spills out. Tom picks it up, and the bag, as the man turns and walks away. Tom runs to get in front of him and shoves the bag into the man's chest. 'Take it,' he says. 'Take. It.'

There must be something in his face, finally, that convinces the man he's serious. He accepts the bag from Tom. 'Alright,' he says. 'Keep your hair on, cunt.'

The word shocks Tom. 'Fuck off,' he says as the man walks away, but his heart skips a beat as the man stops in his tracks and turns to stare hard at Tom.

'Feels good, does it, to step all over the little people?' he asks. 'Does it make you feel like a big man? Because here's the thing: I've been here for weeks. I've been all over your property. I've looked in your windows at night and seen you and your fat wife living your smug life. And I'll be back. You won't know when. But I'll remember how you spoke to me today.'

'And I'll remember you!' Tom shouts.

'You won't see me, mate. Not until it's too late.' The man climbs the fence, his pack lurching on his back. Tom feels tempted to shove him so he falls – he wants to see this man humiliate himself the way Tom feels humiliated – but the man drops easily onto the other side of the fence. He laughs at Tom. 'See ya,' he says. He points two fingers at his own eyes then one at Tom before melting away into the woods.

Tom stares at the spot in the woodland where the man disappeared until his adrenalin ebbs. He feels completely drained. He walks back to the fire and checks it again. It's fine. Completely waterlogged and dead. There's one stray piece of litter left on the ground, a card with a name and number on it. He stoops to pick it up and shoves it into his pocket then kicks some leaves and sticks over the area where the tent was pitched. He wants to erase all trace of the man.

The walk home is uphill, and he suffers in the heat. His mind churns with all the things he wishes he'd said to the man. Should he have been more of an asshole? Is that what you have to do when you're rich? He doesn't want to be like that.

As he approaches the Barn, he can hear the Three Tenors again. Beside the pool, he pulls one of the sunbeds into the shade and lies down on it, shutting his eyes for a moment. This morning sucks. But he's managed to get rid of Patrick and this other guy and now he can't wait for Nicole to come home so they can hang out and not be bothered by any of that. He smiles as he remembers that he also managed to hide the sheep. At least one good thing has happened.

55

FRIDAY

Olly

Olly scrubs his hands. His skin is sore, the soap stinging around his fingernails and over his knuckles which are rubbed red and raw.

The dawn chorus has begun, and light is creeping across the peninsula from the east.

'Stop,' Sasha says. 'They were clean when you went to bed. They're clean now.' In the mirror, he sees her standing behind him. She puts her arms around him, gently takes his hands in hers. Their eyes meet. Water drips from his fingers, through hers, and hits the bathroom floor with a soft spatter.

'It didn't bother me when she died,' he says. 'I've never given it much thought since then because it was the right thing to do. Kitty was so *useless*. An *idiot* could do what she did. There was no art to her, no beauty; she injected ugliness into our lives. She held us back. It felt so right when it happened, and it was so clean.'

'This will pass,' she says. 'You did a good job last night. You're having a reaction, that's all. A reaction to last night and a delayed reaction to when she died. I mean, it's understandable. She was family.'

It's true that he didn't cope well with moving the body, though Olly hates to admit it. He was prepared for bones, even for hair, but the body was partly mummified. Olly likes to consider himself a detached observer of life, a *flâneur*, but the body got to him. The stretched skin and open mouth. Her teeth. It was a horrible shock. He didn't love Sasha seeing him double over and retch, but she said nothing, just got on with the job until he was over it.

He looks into her eyes. They're so still. He can never see past the surface of them. Sasha is unreadable. Sphinx-like. It draws people to her. It drew him. 'Why aren't you feeling it?' he asks. She was right beside him last night, digging, filling IKEA bags with remains.

'I don't know,' she says. She puts her hands on his shoulders and digs in deep. It's painful, but he leans into it.

'You're tight,' she says. Olly's body aches everywhere. It's been a while since he did manual labour and he's seizing up. The digging put blisters on his hands, as well as dirt. He looks at them, sees sore patches but clean, wet palms and fingers. The backs of his hands are the same. At least the basin is clean. Sasha must have done it. When he walked away from it last night, rivulets of filthy water stained the sides of the basin and bits of earth and grit and God knows what else collected in the plughole. An involuntary sob escapes him. Even if they look it, his hands still don't feel clean.

Sasha stops kneading his shoulders. She moves to stand between him and the basin and cups his cheek with her palm. 'Shhh,' she says. 'You're okay. Why don't you go out this morning? Get away. I'll handle everything here.'

'This is Anna's fault,' he says.

'I know.'

'After everything we've done for her.'

'I know,' she repeats.

He follows her downstairs, watches as she makes breakfast for them both. He's glad Anna isn't here this morning. It would be hard to stop his anger with her from showing.

'How can you be so calm?' he asks.

'We have no choice,' Sasha says. 'We have to be strong.' She hands him a bowl of porridge.

'Are you teaching this morning?'

She nods.

'I'll eat in my study,' he says. 'I don't want to see Anna.'

'That's probably for the best. Stay out of her way until you've calmed down. Don't let this spiral. Remember the endgame.'

He settles into his study. Sasha is a better partner than he could ever have dreamed of. She knows how to keep him steady. He takes a seat on the sofa facing the orchard. The porridge makes him feel a bit more human. The coffee, too. He consumes both greedily. Last night was horrific, he tells himself, but death is a part of life, and as a novelist, he should treat it with curiosity and not let it overwhelm him. If Sasha can keep her cool, he can, too.

Once he's finished his food and drink, he sits for a while, looking out. The orchard is densely planted and, if you ignore the fallen and rotten fruit, it's beautiful. Moving Kitty's body was essential to protect their lives at the Manor and their plans for the future, he thinks. If you're not willing to take extreme action when it's needed, you will always be a slave to other people. He believes deeply in this.

He thinks how a life of crime is not so different from the creative life. You take risks in both, you gamble. You're not subject to the normal rules. Sasha was right to warn him to keep his head. Just like his novel, this game has been carefully planned and, so far, almost perfectly executed. It's nearly over and they should be prepared to do whatever it takes to reach the end.

At first, he thinks what he sees is just a shadow at the edge of the woodland. But it's not. He watches as a man emerges from the treeline and stands facing Olly directly. He can't see me, Olly thinks, not from there. The windows are old, and leaded. But he feels uncomfortable in the man's gaze.

He stands, thinking to open the window and call out, to let this person know that they are trespassing. It occurs to him that this could be the person Nicole Booth saw wandering around, the one she told the police about. If he's not a camper perhaps he's a vagrant. They discover them in the woodland here occasionally. He's certainly got a nerve, approaching the Manor like this.

Olly stands and opens the window. He leans out. 'Hey! You! You're on private property! You shouldn't be here!'

The man sees him. He glances left and right and walks towards Olly, weaving between the trees, sometimes in view, sometimes disappearing momentarily.

'Hey!' Olly shouts again. 'Did you hear me? Get lost!'

The man emerges and Olly is shocked to find that he recognises him.

'Patrick?' he says.

It looks like Nicole's friend, so far as he can remember his face.

'I need to talk to you,' Patrick says.

'Why are you sneaking up on the house?'

'Come outside.'

Olly balks. He knows that Patrick is capable of violence. But he's also curious.

'Why?'

'I want to talk to you.'

'What about?'

Patrick shakes his head; he doesn't want to say unless Olly comes out. Olly feels his curiosity get the better of him. Perhaps Patrick will tell him something that will be useful in terms of Nicole. He slips out of his study and hurries down the corridor to a door that leads directly into the orchard. It's low and set into the deep stone walls and opens into a small porch. Patrick joins him there. They sit on either side of the porch on narrow stone benches, facing one another.

Patrick looks dishevelled, his nice shirt crumpled, and his chinos dirt-stained. 'Are you sleeping rough?' Olly asks. Patrick ignores the question.

'I saw you last night,' he says. 'In the woods. You buried something.'

Olly feels his blood run cold. 'You saw no such thing,' he says.

'It looked like a body,' Patrick says. 'Was it? No. Don't deny it. I know what it was, and I know where it is. I could tell the police.'

Blackmail, Olly thinks. Of course, Patrick would be this crude. He's a chancer.

'What do you want?' he asks.

'Ten thousand quid.'

'That's a lot of money.' Olly doesn't have access to anything like that amount and, even if he did, he wouldn't give it to Patrick. Stalling Patrick is his only option. Then he and Sasha can work out what to do, because this is a problem.

'You need to come back,' he says. 'I can't lay my hands on that kind of money quickly.'

'I need it soon,' Patrick says. 'Or I'll tell the police.'

'I understand. But I need time.'

'How much?'

'Two days,' Olly says. 'At least.'

'You have until tonight.'

56

FRIDAY

Anna

Anna puts the memory card into her TV in the Coach House and looks at the footage from the camera. She needs to get back to the Barn so Nicole doesn't miss her, but she must do this first. She can't go a whole day without knowing. She feels a small, hopeful thrill that she's been able to manage this, at all.

On the footage, the area at the back of the chapel shows up as a patchwork of grainy greys and blacks. A hare bounds across the screen, quick as a flash. The next clip shows a badger, ambling, taking its time to explore nooks and crannies for something to eat. She's startled by the size of it and its muscularity. She tries to remember if the positioning of the fallen branches at the start of the tape looks the same as when she collected the memory card.

It's not clear what triggered the next clip, because the scene looks still. Perhaps a branch moved in the breeze. Anna stares deep into the shadows. Her excitement quickens. If she sees either Olly or Sasha – and it could well be both – she'll be elated. It's the best revenge. She'll walk out of here, get into the car and drive so fast to the police station that she'll have handed this over before Sasha and Olly have even noticed that they must fix their own breakfast.

But after that little clip, there's nothing more on the card. Anna rewinds the footage and rewatches it. If Olly and Sasha visited the grave site, they haven't been recorded. Nothing happened there last night. Her stomach sinks. But surely, they moved the body. *Surely*. If she was them, she would have done it right away. And that's what they're like: brutally efficient.

Disappointment bites hard and is followed by a wave of uncertainty. Clearly, she's either wrong or she's been stupid and isn't capable of outwitting them. After all, they've been leading her up the garden path for years. Maybe they're still one step ahead.

She works hard to calm herself down and to retain the crispness of her thinking. Perhaps, she forces herself to consider, I'm not wrong. Perhaps I just need to be patient and they'll do it tonight, or tomorrow. Because they must do it if they think I know, mustn't they? It's too much of a risk otherwise.

Maybe they need some equipment, or they're waiting for some other reason, though she can't imagine what that might be. There will be a reason, though. They must both be determined to hold onto what they've got at all costs. If they need to move that body, they'll do it soon.

Unless they didn't kill Kitty, and she's got it wrong. But she *knows* they did. She knows what she saw in the Coach House when she found Sasha cleaning there and she discovered Kitty's insulin. And she's certain she saw a grave beside the chapel.

She fingers the security pin that Nicole gave her. Staying at the Barn will give her some protection, as will the police presence, but she doesn't underestimate what Olly and Sasha are capable of. She needs proof of what they did, and she needs it fast, before they move against her.

57

FRIDAY

Hal

Hal pulls the car into the Maserati dealership and parks.

'Wait,' Jen says as he's about to open the car door. 'I've been sent some CCTV footage from the location where Patrick Young claimed to be on the morning Tom died.'

It takes a frustrating amount of time to download, but once it has, Jen hits play. The venue is a gym called Snap Fitness. 'Apparently this is the only way in and out,' she says. They watch as a few people enter, mostly women, clearly none of them Patrick. Jen hits pause when a man comes in who might be him. His hood is pulled up and his stature is similar to Patrick's. She looks closely. 'It's not him,' she says. Hal looks, too. She's right. They play through the remaining footage, pausing again a few times, until it ends.

'He didn't go to the gym that morning,' she says. 'He's lying.'

'It's a shame we didn't get this earlier,' Hal says. 'Tell Finn Macdonald to track him down. I want to bring him in.' If they'd got the footage yesterday, they could have questioned Patrick last night, instead of sending him packing. Now, who knows where he's gone? Hal feels his stress levels rise.

He gets out of the car while she makes the call. The dealership is as swanky as he expected. He feels out of place. When Jen is ready, he pushes open the door, and she follows. The air inside is cold and thickly laden with scents of leather, polish and whatever else they're pumping around to persuade people to part with their cash. Hal hates car salesmen, hates the way they try to obfuscate and tie you in knots when all you want is a fair price on a driveable motor.

The young man at reception plasters on a smile for them. Hal pulls out his badge before there's any foolishness. He doesn't want this young man to have to pretend he believes Hal can afford one of these cars.

'I'm interested in an event your dealership held up on the Downs,' he says. 'We'd like to know if someone attended it. Do you keep records?'

Hal watches as the chain of command is invoked. The receptionist knocks on a glass office door and has a word with the man inside. He, in turn, leaves his space with a smile at Hal and speaks to another man, working in a corner office.

The salesroom manager, Mick, is a big man, in chinos and a branded polo shirt. He towers over Hal and presents as affable, a man's man, a slew of pleasantries and mild jokes on the tip of his tongue, but Hal senses a cut-throat edge to him, too. He's met enough senior officers in the police force to recognise his type in an instant. Mick shakes both their hands but addresses himself exclusively to Hal, which embarrasses Hal.

'We have a database of clients: some have purchased from us; some are interested parties. I'm happy to search it for you if you give me the name you're looking for.'

'His name is Tom Booth. He's already bought a car from you. What we'd like to know is whether he attended an event you held on the Downs as part of a local business festival.'

'We were sponsors,' Mick says.

'Indeed.'

'Let me see. We try to take names at these things, but we don't always get to everyone.'

His computer screen is angled out of Hal's view. He spends a few moments staring at it, scrolling and clicking. 'Tom Booth bought a lovely Quattroporte from us in the spring. Canary yellow. All the trimmings. Lovely guy.'

He looks up, as if just realising that talking to the police about Tom might not be what Tom wants.

'I'm sorry to say that Tom died,' Jen says.

'What? No! That's terrible. He was young. What happened?'

'We're currently investigating,' Hal says.

'Oh, I see,' Mick says. 'Tragic. Say no more.' He mimes zipping his mouth shut and Hal finds it distasteful.

'Anything?' Hal says, nodding at the computer.

Mick has another look. 'Spouse is Nicole. No kids. We collect a bit of information about clients, and oh, yes, here it is – we had first contact with Tom at the event. There's a note here.'

He swivels the screen and Hal reads the note: 'Lottery winner!!!! Chatted to Darryl. Priority follow-up!'

Bingo, Hal thinks. That means Tom could have met Martha. But it would be nice to have confirmation.

'Do you know if he spoke to anyone else at the event?'

'I don't know myself. I can ask Darryl.'

'Is he here today?'

They find Darryl at his desk, drinking coffee from a branded mug. 'Tom Booth was a legend. A pleasure to do business with.'

'Do you remember him at the event?' Hal asks.

'Yeah. Lovely guy. He said he used to work as a mechanic but him and his wife won the lottery. I didn't believe him at first. He was almost embarrassed. But he called me for a test drive a few days later and I sold him a Quattroporte.'

'Did he speak to anyone other than you?'

Darryl smiles. 'He spoke to the girls. I mean, that was their job, to hand out merch and pull in the guys, make them feel comfortable.'

'Did he speak to any one of them in particular?'

'Not that I remember. I mean, I didn't know their names. We only hire them in for the day. Eye candy.' He winks at Hal who tenses just as Jen does beside him.

'Thank you,' he says.

'Please give our regards to the widow,' Mick says.

'Sure,' he says, but he has no intention of doing so. He suspects they only want to buy the Maserati back off her.

In the car park, he looks at Jen over the roof of their car.

She says, 'I'm used to it. Every woman is.'

He nods. 'I'm wondering if it was Tom Booth who stalked Martha. Why else would he have her business card? She said she didn't give any out, so he has to have got it from the break-in to her university room. I think we need to know if Martha Hayward has an alibi and whether anyone else might have taken offence at someone stalking her.'

'*If* he did,' Jen says. 'Meeting her doesn't mean he stalked her. It doesn't sound like him. We only have her word for it.'

'True,' he says. They both thought well of Martha Hayward, but that doesn't mean she's reliable.

'Why do I feel as if stalking isn't something our Tom would do?' Jen asks.

'Perhaps because everyone talks about him as a stellar guy? The guy who wouldn't hurt a fly.'

Sometimes, it's Hal's greatest wish to meet murder victims. He gets to know them so intimately in death that he can find himself mourning their loss, even if they're far from perfect. People talk about detective work as the process of solving crime, but it can also be the process of making a victim rise from the dead, bringing them alive through all the traces they left, on paper, online, through the words and memories of others, to try to find out what happened to them. It's a part of his job that fascinates him: the slow unboxing of someone's psyche.

But the jury's out on Tom for him, still. Jen has good instincts, but he's not sure she's right in this instance. Hal has met plenty of men and women who present as mild or inoffensive, as the boy or girl next door, but who are capable of terrible things.

'You think he could have done this? It seems so out of left field,' Jen says.

'I want someone to take another look at his devices to see if we can find any trace that he stalked Martha Hayward.'

'Surely, we'd have found something already. Stalking is a behaviour pattern,' Jen says. 'If he did it to her, he might have done it to others. Do we ask Nicole Booth about it?'

He winces. 'Not yet. Let's dig around first. If you were stinking rich, how would you go about stalking someone?'

Jen has a think. 'Send very expensive unwanted gifts instead of crap ones.'

'She didn't mention gifts.'

'I'm not sure money makes a difference.' She thinks through the classic stalker traits. 'I suppose he could pay someone to damage her property, if that was his game, but there'd be no point in getting another person to follow her because the point is that she sees him.'

'We should check the sat nav on his car for previous destinations.'

'That could be useful. But I don't buy it, Hal.'

He feels a little irritated. 'We don't have to buy it. We have to investigate it.'

She doesn't reply and he regrets sounding snappish, but this investigation gets more tangled by the day. When they should be homing in on leads, more possibilities seem to be presenting themselves. It's threatening to become overwhelming.

He releases the brake and they make their way out of the dealership and into traffic, and the silence is excruciating until Jen's phone rings.

'Finn?' he says. She nods and puts the phone on speaker. 'Have you got any word on Patrick Young?' Hal asks.

'Not yet, boss. We've sent someone to his home address to see if he's there.'

Hal feels cold. He's got a bad feeling about Patrick Young. 'Finn, organise a car to sit outside the Barn tonight and for the next few nights. I want to make sure Nicole Booth is safe until we find this guy. She's got Anna Creed there with her but that's hardly going to protect her if Patrick comes back.'

'Will do. I've got something else. Have you heard anyone mention Libby Franklin?'

58

THE DAY OF HIS DEATH: 12:10

Tom

On the sunbed by the pool, Tom feels himself falling asleep and forces himself to open his eyes. He doesn't want Nicole to find him napping. His headache hasn't gone away. Perhaps he needs to drink some water. It occurs to him that he might have a concussion. He had plenty during his rugby years and he knows the signs, but the hit to his head earlier was barely anything.

Distraction is what he needs, something to keep him awake. He reads some sports news on his phone, but his eyelids still feel weighted.

He checks the time. Should he call Nicole? There might be no point. She said she'd be home by lunchtime. She's probably in the car by now. Perhaps he'll get some lunch, but it's a bit early for that. He wonders if she'll bring him anything from the County Show.

The urge to see her is overwhelming, so strong that it takes him by surprise. A tear slips down his cheek and he's not sure why, but he feels a huge sense of loss, suddenly, as if he is about to be robbed of something, of her, of all this. It must be the accumulation of all the unpleasant things that have happened to him this morning, little mishaps, threats. He experiences them sometimes, these small disintegrations of his self-worth.

He tries to sit up and his head swims. Could it be concussion? Perhaps he should go to A&E if it doesn't settle soon. He'll ask Nicole when she gets home.

The Three Tenors are still playing from the house on a loop. He's had enough now but can't be bothered to go in and try to turn the music off. He scrolls through emails, all boring until one that offers him a link to a luxury-watch website. He browses for a while then googles local golf clubs but gets bored trying to navigate the membership requirements.

He yawns and thinks about googling some porn to pass the time. It's not something he does often. He switches his internet browser to private mode and watches couples banging each other but he's not feeling it. The sunlight is so bright that it's hard to see the screen properly and there's no question of masturbating in case he's disturbed, not that the signals are getting through his aching head to his groin, anyway. He's totally limp down there.

He hears a shout in the distance, and it shocks him so much that he fumbles his phone in his haste to close the browser window and click out of private mode. It falls and when he bends down to pick it up his brain feels as if it's sloshing inside his skull like a yolk in an egg. Cracks have spider-webbed across the phone's screen. He sighs, slips the phone into his pocket and wonders if he imagined what he heard. Or perhaps Nicole's home. Thank God.

He gets up gingerly and walks around the side of the Barn towards the front door. He feels dizzy and trails a hand along the walls to steady himself as he walks. With every step, he feels as if the ground is shifting beneath him. Thank goodness Nicole's home. He is starting to feel quite unwell.

There are no cars in the drive. Disappointment that it's not Nicole hits him hard. 'Hello?' he calls. Is it a neighbour? The neighbours' housekeeper? He doesn't recall Nicole saying anyone else was coming over so maybe they've called in on spec. 'Hello?' he says again.

He leans against the porch to quell the bout of dizziness. The heat's getting to him; he should go indoors. Whoever dropped round, he's got no idea where they went. He tries the front door, but it's locked. The thought of walking all the way back around the building is daunting. What he'd really love to do is take a swim. The water would be so soothing and cool. But he knows that's not a good idea because he's feeling too woozy.

Wobbly and slow, he makes his way back the way he came. At the edge of the pool, he lowers himself down carefully, takes off his shoes and puts his bare feet in the water. He kicks gently and watches ripples expand until they lap the sides. A bright red dragonfly hovers and the sun beats down on his head and shoulders, but the water cools his feet, and he feels confident that it'll keep him alert for a while. He wants Nicole.

His mind is sending out mixed signals. He feels sleepy but also strangely hyperalert, as if all his senses are receiving signals that are too unwieldy for him to process. He turns around suddenly, looking over his shoulder. Was someone there? He catches sight of something in the corner of his eye. A figure, moving towards the house. Two figures? He blinks, trying not to see double. The figure has gone. He stands up. The decking is hot beneath his bare feet. He struggles to put his flip-flops on.

'Hey,' he calls once, but his voice is drowned out by the opera. His head pounds.

He walks towards the Barn following the figure, who went in the direction of the gym suite.

Tom rounds the corner and sees him, standing by the door into Tom's den.

'What are you doing?' he says.

59

FRIDAY

Sasha

In the Great Hall, Sasha places her yoga mat in the middle of the room and sits in Padmasana. She needs to keep herself calm and this is the best way she knows how.

Olly told her what happened with Patrick this morning, the blackmail attempt. Olly was fuming. Spitting, almost. She told him to go out for a while, to get some air, and to think. She didn't want Anna to come back and find him so overwrought. Everything needs to seem calm, and as normal as possible. It's essential. Not that Anna has turned up, yet.

She tries to put the drama out of her mind. If she relaxes, then a solution might come to her, something she can present to Olly, but her brain has other ideas. She sifts through images of last night. The state of the remains wasn't pleasant but nor was it unexpected. Olly's reaction was disappointing. He retched and coughed so much that she did most of the dirty work herself.

She kept control of herself around the body. They had a job to do, and she wanted to do it well. If anything spooked her, it was the site. They buried Kitty deep in the woods, at the site of a medieval plague pit. They chose that location because Olly had a theory that if bones were discovered on such an old burial site, they'd be less likely to attract attention if found. It was nonsense, Sasha thought at the time and still thinks, because any human remains found would be tested and proved to be modern, but Olly loves to tell himself little fictions, and who is she to contradict him when those fictions often suit her.

She tries to focus, reminding herself that however traumatic it was, she's pleased with the outcome. They moved Kitty's remains to the Manor's septic tank. It was only installed last year, a replacement for the old one, after they got the money for selling the barns and land to the Booths. Nobody would think to look there for a body that disappeared five years ago. Her idea, naturally. Olly was all for throwing Kitty's remains in the river, but water has a habit of washing things up and Sasha doesn't want to live in fear of that.

She inhales and exhales deeply, but her mind still won't rest. It's destabilising, thinking of Olly as fallible. She knows he's not perfect, and there have been times when she's been grateful for that because the weight of his confidence, his ego, would be too much for her otherwise. But she's never thought of him with contempt before last night. It happened as she worked while he was doubled over, vomiting. It makes her feel as if a fissure has snaked through their relationship and she wants to close it because she wants to be with Olly; she wants this life. She tries to tell herself that what she felt wasn't a true reflection of their relationship, but simply her reaction to what was happening in the moment. The body was horrible. Even she can't be unscathed by what they did, no matter how calmly she behaved at the time.

The grandfather clock in the hall strikes the hour. She listens to the chimes, counts them. Olly has popped out to the local village and will be back in about half an hour, probably. An idea creeps up on her, something forbidden, but it would remind her what she admires about him and why they're doing this. She wants to look at his book. She knows he won't let her if she asks, because she's asked before and been refused, and if she so much as walks past when he's writing, he pulls the lid of his laptop down in case she should read something over his shoulder. He doesn't want her to see it until it's finished, he insists.

But if she were to take a little peek at it now, she thinks, it might reassure her. She's never once harboured any doubt that he's writing something brilliant, so might this be the time to have a little taste of what's wonderful about Olly? It could help to seal that fissure; it could give her some strength.

She goes into Olly's study and shuts the door behind her. She opens his laptop. It's password protected, but she doesn't hesitate before typing in a word: Hemingway. His hero. Many of Olly's abilities leave her in awe, but he's hopeless and transparent on others. He uses the same password for everything.

She inhales sharply when the novel comes up on-screen. The moment feels huge, partly because she shouldn't be looking and partly because she's anticipated it for so long. She notes what page the document has been left on so she can return there and scrolls to the first page. The beginning. And reads.

It's brilliant for a few pages. It sweeps her up and carries her along. But on page 4, it suddenly doesn't make sense. She wonders if Olly has been clever, if this is one of those original novel structures that he likes to talk about, and if she just doesn't get it. She rereads it, flicks through the novel. It gets more and more jumbled. She tries to detect a pattern to it, or any meaning or point to it at all, but it reads like nonsense and the more she tries to detect brilliance, the less it makes sense and the lower her heart sinks, because Sasha's no connoisseur of literature but she can tell that this book is really, truly terrible. Nobody is going to publish this.

She scrolls hurriedly to return the document to the page she found it on and closes the laptop. Is this what she's given up years for? She has tiptoed around this man, worked like a beast to earn their spending money, protected him from the day-to-day crap of life. And all for this mess of a novel?

She walks from the room slowly, closing the door behind her so he won't know she was in there. She feels as if she's in shock.

The sound of a car engine dying comes to her faintly. Olly is back already. She stands in the hallway, beneath the ranks of oil paintings, uncertain what to do. He's a fraud, she thinks. But is he conning himself? Or me? Am I as much of a mark as Libby Franklin and Anna Creed and anyone else he's suckered onto and bled dry over the years? What's worse? A man who lies to others or to himself?

She opens the heavy front door as he's walking towards it. He lifts a hand to acknowledge her. He looks calmer than he did earlier. She opens her mouth to say something to him but finds she doesn't know where to start. Wait, she tells herself. Before you challenge him: wait and think.

60

FRIDAY

Jen

A young DC called Finn is talking. Jen and Hal are in the car outside the Maserati dealership, listening to him on speakerphone. 'First things first, we can't find anything to raise suspicion on Sasha Dempsey. We've done a deep dive on her background but it's unremarkable. She's worked as a yoga instructor for years and was never in trouble before meeting Olly Palmer.'

'Tell us about Libby Franklin,' Hal says.

'Libby Franklin was a student at Bristol University when Olly Palmer was there. They met at a party in the English department when they were both second-year undergraduates and hit it off. Libby ran a group for wannabe writers. They would meet in cafés and various other venues across the city, including Libby's nice one-bed flat in Clifton, purchased for her by her parents, and share their work. At first Olly impressed everyone in the group. He had talent and they could see it. Libby told me that soon people became obviously jealous of him. The group would be generous with their praise towards everyone except Olly. They'd savage whatever it was he'd written. Libby thought it was unfair and she told him so in private.

'Here's where it gets interesting. A friendship developed. He told her that she was the only person ever to understand him. They got closer and became lovers. He involved her in his work, asking her advice, seeking her reassurance, appointing her to be the only other reader of what he'd written. She told me she felt privileged, so much so that she stopped working on her own writing and became obsessed with helping him improve his. She handed over the writing group to someone else to run and she and Olly got very tight, barely seeing anyone else.

'What happens next starts to sound familiar in the context of Anna Creed's journal. Olly tells Libby that he has a housing crisis. Apparently, he'd been renting a studio flat – she'd never been there for various reasons that she accepted at the time: it was a bit out of town, it had damp, her flat was much more convenient – and he was going to get kicked out of it at short notice. The landlord wasn't playing nice, and Olly was about to be homeless. He tells Libby he's very afraid, that this is his worst fear because stress stops him from writing, from doing anything. He confesses he's got so obsessed with his novel that he's stopped going to class, too.'

Hal sighs. 'It sounds very familiar. And she buys this?'

'She buys it hook, line and sinker. She's very much in love with this man who she believes will be the next big thing in

334

literature. She's still diligently going to her lectures and seminars so she can get her degree, because that's a condition of Daddy buying her the flat, but every spare minute of her time is spent with Olly. She's started to do things for him so he can write.'

'Let me guess, she tells him he can move in with her,' Jen says.

'Yes. And he does. He brings one small suitcase containing books and clothing and a laptop. She sets him up a desk in her sitting room and they share a bed. The flat is converted from an old chapel. It's beautiful. His desk has a view, the kitchen is well stocked with a weekly Waitrose delivery, and she even has a takeout allowance.'

'She told you this?'

'She wanted to spill. She's had ten years to get some distance. She said herself that she was incredibly naïve at the time. She still lives in the same place, she works at the university and is raising a baby with her new partner. But she hasn't forgiven Olly.'

'What burst the bubble for her and Olly?' Hal says. 'I presume it did burst?'

'It did. Spectacularly. He tried to steal money from her, and she caught him. She said it was an extraordinary moment. She realised that he'd been taking her for a ride. Her whole perception of her life changed in that instant. Up until then, she'd felt privileged to be doing what she did for him. Her exact words were, "He made a slave out of me, and I let him. I even *liked* it." She's mortified. She said she never thought of herself as the type to be so convinced by someone and she struck me as an intelligent woman. Her parents were incredibly relieved. They'd sensed something was wrong and tried to get her to talk to them about it, but Olly had persuaded her that he and she only needed one another.'

'Coercive control,' Hal says. He glances at Jen. 'How did she get rid of him?'

'She told him her father was coming over with some of his friends and wanted a word. Apparently, Olly's a coward. He packed up and was out of there within the hour. Before he left, he told her she was a talentless nobody who wouldn't amount to anything.'

'That's nice,' Jen says.

'She said she's struggled to trust anyone since.'

'How did you find her?' Jen asks.

'A deep dive on Facebook. She re-joined her writing group and made some disparaging comments about him there. We contacted her and got more than we bargained for.'

'Olly has form being coercive, then,' Jen says. 'This backs up Anna Creed's story. I wonder about Sasha. Is she his victim too?'

Hal says, 'If she is, it's in a Stockholm Syndrome sort of way. If we believe what we read in Anna Creed's journal, Sasha's as guilty as he is of coercing Anna Creed. Finn, do we have any update on the whereabouts of Olly's Aunt Kitty?'

'Nothing. No official record of her existing since she left her position at the Manor. She seems to have disappeared off the face of the earth at that point.'

'Can you find out if there's any update on the visit to Patrick Young's home yet?' Hal asks.

'Hold on.' They wait while Finn checks. He's back on the line quickly: 'They've been there but there was no sign of him.'

'ANPR on the Jaguar?'

'No trace so far.'

Hal grimaces. 'We should never have let him go.'

'I agree, boss,' Jen says, 'but we couldn't arrest him, and I think Olly Palmer is possibly a bigger threat.'

'Patrick has form being violent,' Hal says. 'And he might still be in the area. He must be a priority.'

'Olly and Sasha are playing a long game,' she says, 'but that doesn't mean they're not just as dangerous. I'd feel happier about them if we'd found Aunt Kitty, but we haven't.'

'You think they're a direct risk to Nicole?'

'I think they're potentially very dangerous.'

He believes she might be right, but in this case, he sees danger in many other places, too, and he can't focus on all of them. The decisions he makes at this stage of the investigation could have very serious consequences.

'Get that car organised, Finn,' he says. 'I don't want Nicole Booth unprotected.'

61

FRIDAY

Nicole

Nicole wakes up late, at nearly half past ten, and comes downstairs to find Kitty in the kitchen, cutting fruit. It's a relief not to see Patrick and not to be alone.

'Morning,' Kitty says. 'How did you sleep?'

'I can't believe I slept that long,' Nicole says. She's been in bed for almost twelve hours. Her sleep was deep and dreamless, and this is the first time since Tom died that she feels a bit more like herself. It makes her feel guilty.

'How about you?' she asks. Kitty looks a little tired.

'The bed was very comfortable. I woke up early and popped home to get a few things. I hope I didn't disturb you.'

'You didn't at all. Did your security pin work okay?'

'Like a charm. Can I just say, this place is sensational,' Kitty says. 'Absolutely gorgeous. The house and the view. There's so much light. Did you tell the architect what you wanted?'

'We said we wanted to make the most of the view and we let them have free rein on the first design, but we got more involved in the process after that. We wanted to make sure it included all the things that were personal to us.'

'You two put your heart and soul into this place, didn't you?'

'It was our baby. *Is* our baby.'

'It's very special.'

Nicole looks around. There are traces of Patrick still here: cushions that haven't been plumped and arranged how she likes them, a dirty coffee cup on a side table. She picks it up. 'Thank you. I wish it wasn't in such a state. I haven't been keeping it as clean and tidy as I'd like.'

'Do you do all the work yourself?'

Nicole nods.

'It's a lot.'

'I know. I've been thinking I might get some help, but I didn't want to hire anyone at first. I didn't want us to get above ourselves, you know? I mean, I know you work for Olly and Sasha, but no one in my family has ever had a cleaning lady, let alone a housekeeper.'

'If you need help, you should get it. You must be kind to yourself. Especially now. You're going through something terrible. After my husband died, I felt totally at sea for a very long time. I still feel that way, sometimes, and he died of cancer. So, we knew what was coming. We understood that he'd been let down by his body. Tom's sudden death is so much worse.'

Nicole feels her eyes brimming with tears. 'There's all this noise about how Tom died and why he died, which are things I want to know, *need* to know, but in the middle of all of that, the worst thing is that I miss him terribly.'

'I know that feeling well,' Kitty says.

'I'm sorry your husband died, too,' Nicole says.

'Permission to hug?' Kitty asks, and Nicole nods. Kitty hugs her briefly, gently. She smells clean and fresh, of laundry detergent and soap; her blouse is soft on Nicole's cheek. When she lets go of Nicole, she says, 'While I'm here, I would love to help.'

'Thank you, but you're my guest. It's very good of you to be here at all.'

'Can I give you some unsolicited advice?' Nicole nods. 'While you're in such a vulnerable place emotionally, you must be careful that nobody takes advantage of you. Being a widow isn't easy. Be on your guard, especially with everything you have.'

'They warned us about that when we won the money,' Nicole says. 'We've been very careful.'

'Be even more careful, now. Don't let anyone else tell you what's best for you.'

'I will.' Nicole thinks about this for a moment. 'Can I ask you something? Do you think I should be leaning harder on the police? I'm afraid it's going to get in the press and turn into something sensational if they don't figure out what happened soon. Tom's death, this place, it's a story. Especially if people think he was murdered.'

Kitty looks thoughtful. 'There is another way of thinking about this. If you consider that outside attention is inevitable.'

'What's that?'

'Let's say, just for the sake of argument, that Tom's death wasn't an accident. Don't you want the police to leave no stone unturned?'

'Do *you* think it wasn't an accident?'

'I don't know what happened to Tom. But *if* it wasn't an accident, I'd want whoever did this to pay for it.'

'What are you saying?'

'Maybe you shouldn't be afraid of the press but use them to ask for information and to put pressure on the police. Maybe someone else has seen this vagrant man who has been lurking around.'

'I could offer a reward.'

'You could.'

'I should ask, though.'

She messages Jen: Should I offer a reward for information?

Jen replies. We would advise you against that. It can lead to an excessive amount of public interest and bring out the crazies. This investigation is already complex.

Nicole considers this. 'They don't want me to,' she says.

'They can't stop you. But it's up to you to decide if you think it will help, or not. Sometimes, it's nice not to feel helpless.'

She thinks about it. She doesn't want to annoy the police but she's ready for something to happen, so she's not stuck in this limbo of not knowing. Surely, money can help. She opens Facebook and begins to type. She makes an appeal for information, offers £50K for any that leads to a resolution of the case, and hits 'Post'.

62

FRIDAY

Jen

Jen sits at her desk, feeling fretful. Earlier this morning she had a worrying message from Nicole Booth, asking if she should offer a reward for information. She told her not to do it but didn't mention it to Hal, and now she wonders if she should have. She's been preoccupied with trying to dig up some background on Anna Creed. Now she wonders if she should go to see Nicole just to make sure she's not going to go ahead with it.

The research on Anna hasn't turned up much. Jen wants to know more about why Anna allowed herself to be suckered in by Olly and Sasha but hasn't found out a lot apart from some sparse details that piece together a picture of a quiet life. Anna's husband Nick Creed started a company that made them some money. They used it to buy the Manor House and settle down there, so far as Jen can tell. And that's it. But what she has learned about the couple reminds her of Nicole and Tom Booth's situation. They came into money and moved here, too, and Jen gets the impression that integrating hasn't been easy for them either. Anna and Nicole might have more in common than they know. Jen wonders if that makes Nicole a possible target for Olly and Sasha and if that means they could have had something to do with Tom's death.

Finn appears by her desk, and she switches screens. Hal's told her not to spend too much time on Anna Creed while the focus is on finding Patrick Young.

'Hal wants to see you,' Finn says. Jen glances at his office. He's putting the blinds down. That's a bad sign. Hal only shuts himself away when he wants to give someone a dressing-down. She crosses the room with trepidation, knocks softly. In the Incident Room the phones are ringing as if something has happened.

'In,' he says and gestures to her to take a seat.

'Boss.' Her heart is thumping. She was hoping to find someone else in here, but it's her he wants to talk to. He looks pained, as if he doesn't want to do this, and hands her a piece of paper, a printout of an email sent to him by Nicole Booth. Jen reads it:

I've decided to offer a reward for information about Tom's death. £50K. I'm not unhappy with what you've done, and I want to work with you, but he was the love of my life and if this can help us discover who murdered him, I don't see why we wouldn't do it. There are tips coming in already. I've attached a link to the post on my Facebook page. It's spreading fast.

Jen groans softly and swears. She looks at Hal. 'She called me earlier to ask about offering a reward and I advised against it, but clearly, she didn't listen. I thought she had. I thought I'd put it to bed. I'm sorry.'

'Why didn't you tell me?'

She stares at him, her face reddening. 'I should have. I got distracted. I made a mistake.'

'The point of your role is to support Nicole Booth, to watch her closely and also to make sure she's working with us.'

Humiliation creeps through her veins. She's mortified that she's let him down. It's obvious that he's feeling the pressure. 'I thought I was doing my job,' she says. 'There's been so much going on. I let this slip.'

He looks as if he's deciding what to say next and she barely breathes while she waits. Is he the type to defend her or throw her under a bus for this? She knows what she hopes.

'Alright, I know you were doing your best,' he says. She nods tightly, and exhales with relief. 'The boss is furious,' he says. 'There are already so many calls and emails coming in that they think we're going to have to take manpower from elsewhere to handle it.'

'And most of the calls are the crazies, I bet,' she says. 'I told her they would be.'

He nods.

'I'm so sorry, Hal. I didn't have her pegged as being so headstrong. I should have.'

He doesn't reply to that, and she appreciates him not making her squirm any more than she is already.

'The £50K is going to bring every single worm out of its hole,' Hal says. 'And the story is already on the online news sites so it's only going to get worse. Anything on Patrick Young?'

She swallows uncomfortably and decides to come clean about what she was doing. 'Finn is on it, and I know I should have been concentrating on Nicole, but I was looking into Anna Creed and—'

'I told you we don't have time to look into Anna Creed now.'

'I think what happened to her might be connected to Tom Booth's death.'

He shakes his head. 'Don't let Anna Creed distract you, Jen. She's not credible.'

'I think she is.'

He lets his hand fall, and his palm slaps the top of his desk. Jen jumps. 'Sorry,' he says. 'But this is how it is now. When we've found Tom Booth's murderer, or if we find evidence that something bad happened to Olly's Aunt Kitty, we'll take a closer look at what Anna Creed is saying. Okay? Let's not get distracted. Not now.'

She looks at him, every cell in her body wanting to fight this, to try to persuade him that he might be wrong. 'Jen,' he says. 'This is coming from above me. But I agree.'

'Okay,' she says. 'But I think you're wrong.'

'You're entitled to think what you like, but please do your job.'

That stings. She stands. His phone pings with another message. 'Wait,' he says. 'Another email from Nicole. Patrick Young is still in possession of the pin that allows him access to the Barn. She thinks she's disabled it but she's not sure.' He swears. 'That's not good. I'll reply and tell her that we have a car on the way for protection. I'll copy you in.'

She tries to maintain a composed expression as she leaves his office. The phones in the Incident Room are still ringing and now she understands that it's because of Nicole Booth's Facebook post, that she could have helped avoid this and that everything just took a turn for the worse.

She pauses. 'Hal,' she says. 'Has anyone gone to talk to the car rental people about Patrick Young in person?' He shakes his head.

'I'd like to, and I'll make enquiries at local taxi firms and the train station while I'm out. You're right. We need to find him.'

63

FRIDAY

Anna

Anna makes her way to the Manor in time to prepare lunch for Olly and Sasha. It's hard to tear herself away from the Barn. She feels so much safer there.

She has some doubts about whether she should have persuaded Nicole to post a reward for information, but the way she saw it was that the more attention focused on what's happening here at Lancaut, the safer she is personally. And the safer Nicole is, too. Olly and Sasha would be very foolhardy to make a move against either of them if the world is watching. She's convinced that they killed Tom but doesn't have a scrap of proof.

She lets herself into the main hall. 'Hello!' she calls. Olly's study door is shut. She finds Sasha in the kitchen.

'Oh, hi!' Sasha says. 'How was your night? How's Nicole?'

Anna works hard to appear her normal self. 'It was fine,' she says. It's probably not a good idea to say much more, and it's definitely not a good idea to let Sasha know how much better it was at the Barn than being here, or in the Coach House. 'I mean, it's not my home, but it's nice to be of help.'

'Are you working for her now?' Sasha asks.

'No, I'm just sleeping the night. She hasn't asked me to do anything.'

'It sounded like you were going to work for her.'

'Sorry,' Anna says. 'That's not what I meant. Would you like some soup for lunch?'

'That would be lovely,' Sasha says. 'Gazpacho?'

'Of course.'

Anna goes out to the kitchen garden to pick some tomatoes. Sasha seems more tense than usual. Perhaps that's a good sign. Maybe she's trying to work out how to move the body. Perhaps Anna will capture them on video tonight.

Her tomato plants are tall and strong, bearing lots of ripe fruit. She's been watering and feeding them assiduously and she waters them again now, before selecting the best fruits for her soup.

Olly comes into the kitchen while she's preparing it. Like Sasha, he seems distracted and tense. Anna tries to sound like her usual self. 'Morning,' she says, and smiles.

'How was your night at the Barn?' Olly asks. 'Was it better than here?'

'No,' Anna says. 'Of course not. This is home.'

He has a bad energy about him. She keeps her head down and focuses on making the soup. He doesn't leave the room.

'Kitty,' he says.

'Yes,' she replies. The tomatoes are in a bowl. She slits their skins, pours boiling water over them, and keeps her back to him.

'Do you remember the diary you used to write?'

It takes every ounce of her self-control not to tense up physically. She can feel his eyes on her back.

'Yes,' she says. 'I enjoyed it at first, but it got boring very quickly.'

'Do you ever look over it? I was thinking that must be a nice thing to do. Nostalgic.'

She turns to face him and keeps her expression slack and innocent. 'No. I think I threw it away. There wasn't a word in it worth rereading. I'm no writer. Not like you.'

'Right,' he says, after a beat. She turns back to the countertop and reaches for an onion to slice. Her heart is thumping. She's got no choice but to stick to her original story but it feels danger-ous. After a moment or two he leaves the room. When she hears the door to his study slam, she flinches. For a moment the world seems to tilt and she fears she might lose her nerve but forces herself to carry on preparing the soup. As soon as it's done, she'll leave. She wants to get back to the Barn as soon as she can. She no longer feels safe here.

She has a strong urge to confide in Nicole. I want to be her friend, she realises, but I can't be if I'm lying to her. How would she drop her bombshell on a total stranger? She'd have to just come out and say it: *I'm not Kitty. I'm Anna Creed. I'm the true lady of the Manor.* But she doesn't know if she dares.

As she works, she begins to feel calmer. She puts the radio on, quietly, as she normally would. It's important that she doesn't

349

seem different to Olly and Sasha. She sees Sasha walk past the kitchen door and a few seconds later hears a faint knock and then the sound of Olly's study door opening and shutting.

I could eavesdrop on them, she thinks. The idea of it is terrifying, but compelling. It might tell her what they're thinking and planning. She leaves the vegetables on the side, walks softly down the corridor and slips into the room next door to Olly's study without making a sound. It's called the Map Room because of a large and very old map of the peninsula hanging on one wall, but it isn't much used. There are many rooms in the Manor like this. They keep them largely shut, and the furniture is draped with dust sheets.

She easily moves a section of wall panel to give her access to the space between the Map Room and Olly's study. Olly and Sasha's voices are instantly audible, but she can't hear what they're saying. She'll need to be inside the space and put her ear to the back of the study panelling for that. She clambers into it, as slowly and carefully as she can, to avoid them hearing her.

'It's Anna!' Olly says. His voice is raised. 'She started all this. It's her bloody fault.'

Anna feels her chest tighten.

Sasha shushes him and says something back to him in a low voice that Anna can't hear. It doesn't reassure him.

'I swear to God, I'll kill—' Olly says. Anna doesn't wait to hear the rest. She pulls herself out of the alcove, puts the panel back in place, then moves to the door, hoping to get out, but she hears Olly's study door open and a set of footsteps coming down the hall. What if they're looking for her?

She stands behind the door, her back to the wall. Opposite her, on the wall, is a very old map of Lancaut. Nick loved it. When they bought the Manor, he made it a condition of sale that the previous owner left it here. She stares at it, trying to moderate her breathing, trying not to make a sound, wishing with all her heart that Nick had never died, that none of this had happened.

She takes in every detail of the map, to try to distract her from what might be happening outside the room. If they find her in here, she has nowhere to run. The map shows the Manor, when only the oldest parts of it were complete. The chapel is there, too, and the medieval village. The mapmaker has drawn in the woodland, and it covers the whole peninsula. There are no fields, no sign of the barns that Nicole and Tom Booth converted. This map is too old. She sees it, then, a detail that makes her catch her breath: the plague pit.

Of course, she thinks. That's it. How could she have forgotten about it? Olly didn't bury Kitty in the graveyard, he buried her in the plague pit. She had the right idea about him using a place where bodies were already buried, but the wrong location. She needs to move the camera. But just as this gives her a little bit of hope, she realises that she might be too late and have missed her chance to catch them moving the body.

She'll have to go to the plague pit and see for herself.

64

THE DAY OF HIS DEATH: 12:27

Tom

It's the man from the wood, the camper.

'I told you to go,' Tom says. He can't believe the audacity of the guy.

'Nice place,' the man says. 'What did you do? Win the lottery?' The look on his face is contemptuous. You feel morally superior, Tom thinks, because I'm rich and you're not. You think you can come here and steal from me and not feel guilty about it. He fingers the phone in his pocket, thinking of ringing emergency services, before remembering that his phone is dead.

'There are cameras filming you right now,' he says, even though he recalls that he disabled them.

'Give me what I want, erase the footage and I won't hurt you. I'll go.'

'I'm just like you,' Tom says. He feels desperate to make this point, because perhaps if the man gets it they can come to an understanding and avoid this ugliness, but he laughs.

'No, mate, you're not. You're a privileged little shit.'

Tom sees it, then, in the man's hand, a sharp blade, a camping knife, the edge serrated and vicious. 'Take whatever you want,' he says. 'I don't care. Please, don't hurt me.'

He badly needs to sit down. The dizziness has returned. It's impossible to stay upright any longer. He doesn't care what this guy does so long as he leaves Tom intact. All he wants is his life with Nicole. He turns to walk back to the sunlounger, each step harder than the last. His body feels as if it's as broken as the house system, no signals getting through, stubbornly malfunctioning. He staggers, half falls, and rights himself.

He hears the man's footsteps approach but can't bring himself to look behind him. It doesn't feel possible, physically. He stares at the ground to keep himself upright, watches his feet land flat-footed on the decking. Raising his head is out of the question.

The man's feet appear in front of him. 'Please,' Tom says. 'I'm not feeling so good.' He steps to the side, but the man mirrors his movement, blocking his way. Tom sees the knife dangling from his hand and knows he should feel fear, or terror, or something in that realm of emotion, but all he feels is terribly vulnerable and extremely sad.

'What's wrong with you?' the man asks.

Tom forces himself to look up, to meet those bloodshot eyes. He touches his hairline. 'I hit my fucking head,' he says. He makes a gesture of frustration. 'I was hiding a sheep.'

'What?'

'Help me,' Tom says. 'Take what you want but help me sit down.'

He feels as if the scaffolding of his body is collapsing. He's going to fall, hard.

'I'm a nice guy,' he says. 'Don't hurt me. My wife.'

He can't get another word out. He collapses towards the man, falling forward, seeing the knife rise in the other's hand, and shuts his eyes. Whatever's coming next, he doesn't want to see it.

When he next opens his eyes, he's lying on the sunbed in full sun. He groans. It's very bright. He shuts his eyes, and for a few moments they flicker open and shut until he can stand the light and the blueness of the sky, the chalky whiteness at its edges.

Swivelling his head is painful. His brain is soup. The Three Tenors are still singing. A dark shadow blocks the light to his left. Someone. Sitting on the sunbed. The man? Tom feels an urge to talk, to explain. He has something he wants to get off his chest.

'You see, we did win the lottery,' Tom says. 'Recently. And it changed everything, but I also realised it changed nothing because we already had that thing, that thing where you can be happy anywhere if it's just the two of you. Nicole doesn't see it like I do. She's looking for other ways to be happy, she wants to be thinner, she wants to have a house that other people admire, she's not ready to listen to me when I tell her none of it matters.'

He squints at the silhouette. Is it the man? A dragonfly hovers above his face and Tom tries to bat it away. It hurts to stare into the brightness, so he shuts his eyes again.

He wants to talk more, to share the things he's been thinking about. 'The thing is,' he says, 'I love her. She's all I want. They can take the pool and the Maserati, the smart house, the golf clubs, the cinema room, they can take it all. You can take it all. All I want is Nicole.'

Why isn't the man replying? Is he even there?

'I think I need to go to A&E,' he says. 'Now.'

He touches his face. It's wet with tears.

65

FRIDAY

Jen

Jen sits in the car rental office with a young man. The place is on an industrial estate on the outside of Chepstow.

'I was here when he brought the car back yesterday,' he says.

'Do you remember what time that was?'

He checks the computer. 'He brought it back at six, just before closing.'

A few hours after we told him to leave the Barn, Jen thinks. She wonders what Patrick did in the meantime.

'Did you speak to him?'

'No, but I saw him.'

'Did any of your colleagues speak to him?'

'I was the only one here. He parked and left the keys in the ignition without coming in. I saw him walk away. I couldn't go after him because I'm not allowed to leave the site unattended.

He owes us money. He left us a cash deposit, but his card payment was declined.'

'In which direction did he walk?'

'Towards the bus stop.'

'Where's that?'

He points down the road. 'It's about a quarter of a mile that way. You can get the bus into Chepstow or Swansea.'

'Did he have anything with him?'

'Two bags, a duffel and a backpack.'

'Do you have any CCTV?'

He accesses the footage for her. Filmed from the roof of the building, Patrick does exactly as the man described.

'Is there a building near the bus stop that might have CCTV?'

'I doubt it.'

'Please call me immediately if Patrick Young contacts you.'

'What's he done?'

'We'd like him to help us with some enquiries.'

She finds the bus stop. It's on a country lane, no CCTV near it. She sighs. They're going to have to check cameras on the buses travelling in both directions, but that shouldn't be too hard. They know what time Patrick left here.

She has a thought as she arrives back at the rental place to pick up her own car.

'Is it possible to look at the sat nav in the Jag to see where Mr Young might have been?' she asks.

'We can try.'

She sits in the passenger seat as he looks at the previous destinations. There are four postcodes of interest. She looks them up. The first is the Glass Barn and the second is the supermarket in

Chepstow. The fourth is the car rental place. It's the third location that's a mystery to her. She finds the street on Google Maps and uses Street View to look at it.

It's a long residential street and she feels frustrated. They'll have to do house-to-house enquiries if they want to find out what he was doing there. But then she sees it: a hostel. She looks it up and gets on the phone to them.

'Could you please put me through to one of your guests, Patrick Young.'

'We don't have phones in our rooms, but I can take a message. Hold on.' Bingo! Jen hears muffled talking in the background before the receptionist comes back on the line.

'Sorry, I'm afraid I've just been told that Mr Young was here for a night, but he cleared out of his room and didn't settle his bill. He's done a runner. If you get hold of him, will you let us know?'

'Sure,' Jen says. She hangs up. She'd be willing to bet quite a lot of money that Patrick's still in the area and not intending to leave any time soon.

66

FRIDAY

Hal

Hal watches his team file out of the Incident Room after their afternoon meeting. Jen didn't attend. She's still out trying to track down Patrick Young's movements.

The strain is showing on his team, in their faces and postures. Nicole Booth's Facebook post has gone viral and they can't get to all the calls and messages that are coming in. Leads are piling up and they're obliged to investigate them all, but finding one that's helpful will be like locating a needle in a haystack. And that's on top of the work they were already planning.

Hal wants nothing more than to lean back in his chair and take a nap. He's been running on just a few hours of sleep every night since taking on the case and it's starting to catch up with him. He can sense his decision-making slowing, uncertainty creeping in.

To be fair to Jen, it surprised him, too, that Nicole would do this. She didn't present as someone difficult. She seemed placid and happy to let the police lead. He wonders if she was numbed by shock at first, and now that it's wearing off, she's coming to life. Whatever the reason, it's a problem.

The phone on his desk lights up and he answers.

'There's an Anna Creed on the line. She wants to talk to you or Jen.'

He groans. 'Can you take a message?' In the corner of his eye, he sees a small disturbance. No, he thinks. Not now. When he's under pressure, he's susceptible to migraines. Visual disturbances are a precursor.

'She's very insistent and she sounds distressed.'

He weighs up whether ignoring the call will make things worse with Anna Creed and decides it might. 'Put her through.'

Anna doesn't introduce herself. She sounds breathless. 'I know where they buried Kitty Ellis. It's in the plague pit. You need to come.'

He sighs. 'Who buried her and where?' He feels his forehead wrinkle into a frown and smooths it out with his fingers. The corner of his vision distorts again and his heart sinks.

'Five years ago, Olly and Sasha killed Kitty, our house-keeper, and buried her body in the plague pit at Lancaut. It's within the Manor House grounds. It's hard to find but I went there, and the ground was disturbed. They've dug her up and moved her remains, but I don't know where to. You need to come.'

Hal swivels his chair to look out of the window. A seagull stalks the roof of a nearby building. The sun is falling, casting long shadows. Golden light rims the rooftops. His vision warps. Plague pit, he thinks. Really? It sounds fantastical to him, much like the rest of what Anna Creed says, or writes. But then, Kitty has been untraceable so far.

'Are you there?' she asks. He doesn't like her bossy tone. He wants her off the phone so he can concentrate on the job in hand. This is a distraction.

'I'll send an officer around to take a look,' he says.

'Today?'

'Probably not. I have limited resources and Tom Booth's death to investigate.'

'What if their deaths are linked?'

He can't get past the idea that she's a delusional pest as he scrabbles through his desk drawer, looking for his migraine meds. He finds aspirin, drops three into a glass of water, waits for them to dissolve.

'Olly and Sasha have an alibi for the period of Tom Booth's death,' he says.

'But they've given each other an alibi. They could be covering up for each other.'

'We're aware of that, Mrs Creed. You need to let us do our job.' He drinks down the aspirin. He's starting to feel nauseous.

'I'll send an officer,' he says. 'We'll be in touch.'

'I don't have a phone.'

'Where are you calling from?'

'The Barn.'

'Landline?' he asks.

'No,' she says. 'I'm borrowing Nicole's mobile. But she doesn't know.'

'Can we reach you on that number?' His vision is getting worse. He looks at a piece of paper on his desk and finds it almost unreadable.

'Yes,' she says. 'But don't tell her that I called. I'm going to delete this from the call log.'

He realises she sounds breathless because she's whispering. 'Come today,' she says. 'I'm afraid of them.'

Hal's patience snaps. 'Mrs Creed, I'll send men when I think it's fit to. I'm in charge of this investigation. Not you. Not any of my junior officers. Thank you for the tip, it's noted, but unless you have anything further to add, you are denting your own credibility and wasting my time and I don't like time wasters.'

He hangs up. It was wrong to speak to her like that, he knows, and he's been in trouble for this sort of thing before, but everybody's patience has a limit. He has a thousand different demands on his time, a killer on the loose and the neighbours have an alibi, even if it's not the most solid. Without evidence that they hurt Tom Booth or had intention to, he's not inclined to prioritise her ramblings. If Kitty Ellis is found alive and well and playing bingo in Droitwich in the next few days, he'll have egg all over his face and all over his career.

His phone rings once more. The receptionist says, 'It's Anna Creed again.'

He swears then apologises. 'Take a message, please,' he instructs and hangs up. He manages to focus on his phone just long enough to call an Uber to take him home because he can't drive himself like this, but he needs to sleep off this migraine. There's no other way through it. As he waits for the car he

362

squints, attempting to minimise his warped vision. His head aches and he knows that the pain will morph into something much more severe very soon.

He tries calling Jen, to run this by her, but she doesn't answer. He gets a notification telling him his car is here and makes his way to reception. He signals to the driver to wait. He can just make out enough of his phone screen to message Jen:

Anna Creed is claiming that Olly and Sasha buried Kitty Ellis on the site of an old plague pit. Could you go over there and talk to her and eyeball the site for me before you go home? Might be an opportunity to drop in on Nicole too and make sure she's not going to do anything else we don't want her to do.

He hesitates, then adds:

I may have been a bit short with Anna on the phone.

He thinks and edits the message to read: I was too short with Anna on the phone. I was getting a migraine.

Oversharing? No. He wants to be honest with her. If he's feeling overwhelmed that's not Jen's problem, nor is it Nicole Booth's. They deserve that every lead gets followed. He sends the message to Jen.

His headache notches up another level. Even as he leaves the office, in the distance he can still hear the phones ringing. And tomorrow morning he'll have to give a press conference, because of Nicole Booth's offer of a reward.

When he's in the car he manages to compose a few more words for Jen and sends them:

Thanks, Jen. I know you'll handle this beautifully. I'll be at home for a few hours while I sleep this off.

67

FRIDAY

Nicole

Nicole carries a tray with mugs of tea on it out to the officers parked in her driveway.

The one on the passenger side rolls down the window. 'Thank you.'

She hears a shout from the end of the drive. A man is getting out of his car. He holds a long-lens camera up to his face and starts taking photos.

'Oh, God,' Nicole says.

'Go inside. I'll talk to him,' the officer says. She hurries in. She needs to warn Kitty.

'Kitty!' she calls. She doesn't hear an answer and goes to look for her.

She opens the door to her den and finds Kitty sitting there, with a phone. But Kitty doesn't have a phone of her own and she looks guilty.

'Is that my phone?' Nicole says. 'I mean, it's fine, you can use it, but please ask.' Kitty looks distraught. 'What's wrong? Are Olly and Sasha making it difficult for you to come here?'

She's wondered if they might. Having witnessed first-hand what Kitty does for them and how they barely acknowledge her, she's not sure how much they value her as a person. She's toying with trying to poach Kitty. She hasn't been able to imagine having help before, but now that she's met Kitty, she can see that it could work. It's too soon to make her an offer yet, but perhaps, if things continue to work well for a few weeks, she will.

'No,' Kitty says. 'That's not it. Did you know there are journalists in the lane? I saw them on my way back from the Manor.'

'I was coming to tell you that. Are you okay? Did something happen?'

'I'm sorry I used your phone without asking,' Kitty says. She hands it back. Nicole feels worried about her. She looks desperate.

'You can talk to me,' Nicole says. 'Really. Whatever it is.'

Kitty breathes out, as if mustering up courage. 'Alright,' she says. 'It's Olly and Sasha. But it's not what you think. My name isn't Kitty.'

Nicole sits, rapt, listening to the story of how Anna became Kitty, of how she was courted by Olly and Sasha up until the point where her mind was being controlled by them, and was then manipulated so constantly by them that she had no space left in her head to consider what was really happening to her. 'That's the only way I can explain it,' she says. 'I don't know why

365

I let them refer to me as Kitty. It makes me sick to even think of it now. I'm Anna.'

Nicole finds it hard to watch the other woman's pain as she talks, and she feels appalled and angry on her behalf. It's an extraordinary story and she can hardly believe it, but she knows this sort of thing happens. She's read articles and seen it on TV.

'This is unbelievable,' Nicole says, when Anna finishes. 'They're like parasites. You have to get them out of your house.'

'There's more,' Anna says. 'I wasn't going to tell you this, any of it, because I've reported it all to the police, but they aren't interested, they don't see the urgency. The detective spoke to me as if he thinks I'm a fantasist.' She takes a deep breath. 'I'm afraid of them. I think Olly and Sasha killed Kitty and buried her in the plague pit here, on Lancaut. And I think they may have had something to do with Tom's death, too.'

'What?' Nicole says. 'What did you say?'

While Anna repeats her words, slowly, carefully, and answers Nicole's questions, Nicole feels as if she can hardly take it all in. This is a lot. It's crazy. But Tom really is dead. Possibly murdered. She must face up to that now, and in a world where you allow for the possibility that the unlikely, the truly terrible, can happen, this version of events that Anna is outlining actually *makes sense*.

Her mind races as she considers how to respond. Before she can begin to sort any of it out, they're disturbed by a whining sound. Outside the bedroom they see a drone, hovering. It looks menacing.

'Oh no!' Nicole says. She backs away from the window.

'It's the journalists,' Anna says. 'They're trying to photograph you.'

'Blinds down!' Nicole shouts.

They do nothing.

'BLINDS. DOWN,' she screams. They descend in synchrony, blocking the drone out, and Anna and Nicole wait in silence until they can't hear it any longer.

Their eyes meet. 'Don't go back to the Manor again,' Nicole says. 'Not until you've worked out what to do. You're safe here with me.'

68

THE DAY OF HIS DEATH: 12:32

Tom

Tom tries to focus on the silhouette sitting on the sunbed beside him. It stands, casting shadow over him, which would be welcome if Tom didn't feel so powerless. Instead, it feels sinister.

'I'm sorry,' he says. 'I'm sorry I told you not to camp here. You can. It's fine. But no fire, okay? Don't light a fire.'

He sees the silhouette shake their head. It's not the man, he thinks. He was wearing shorts. But it's hard to make out more of this person. They're standing in front of a hedge and the sun is shining behind them.

'Patrick?' he says. 'Is that you? Was I asleep?' He puts out his arm, trying to make contact. 'Thank God it's you. Can you help me? I think I need to go to A&E.'

The silhouette speaks. 'It's not Patrick.'

'Olly?' Tom says. He peers up. Yes, it's Olly from next door. Tom feels a surge of relief. 'Where's the man?' he asks.

'What man?'

'He was here. He wanted to steal from us.'

'Really? I didn't see anyone.'

'Where did he go?'

'I've no idea.'

'Perhaps you scared him off when you came. He wanted to steal from me. I told him he was being filmed but I broke the security cameras and I need to mend them in case he comes back,' Tom says.

'You broke them? They're not working?' Olly asks.

Tom feels very confused. What was he just talking about? He says, 'I've hurt my head. I think I'm concussed.'

'How did you do that?'

He's not going to mention the sheep because he strongly suspects that behind their backs, Olly and Sasha judge him and Nicole, and judge them harshly, and he doesn't want any shade cast on the sheep, or Nicole, so he says, 'It was an accident.'

His longing for Nicole has become a physical pain, emanating from his chest, from the exact place where his heart is, and radiating out. It's worse than his head pain, worse than anything else he's ever experienced.

'Can you take me to A&E?' he asks. 'Can you get Nicole? Please?'

'Sorry,' Olly says. 'But I don't drive.'

Frowning hurts, but Tom can't help it because he thinks that's a lie. He's seen Olly driving, hasn't he? 'Can you get Sasha or try to call Nicole?' he asks. 'My phone's dead.'

'I don't have my phone with me. Where did the man go?'

'I don't know,' Tom says. 'I told him the security cameras were filming him. Maybe he ran off because of that. Or because he saw you. But you know, it was a lie. The cameras are broken. I broke the system. Do you hear that? The opera? I can't turn it off. But I was talking to him then I fell over and I think I blacked out and next thing I know I'm lying here with you. I need Nicole.' He tries to stand.

'Whoah,' Olly says. 'Careful. We should get you inside. Here. Let me help.'

Tom feels his hands on him, bony and insistent. What a terrible day this has been. Perhaps it's to counter all the good fortune he's had. 'I'm a lucky man,' he tells Olly.

'Yes, you are.'

He feels Olly steering him towards the house. He's so unsteady on his feet that he wants to give the pool a wide berth.

'What time is Nicole getting back?' Olly asks.

'I don't know. I've been waiting for her. Maybe a quarter of an hour.' He's slurring his words again. He has to say the sentence twice for it to be comprehensible. Olly puts a hand in the small of Tom's back to guide him and pushes Tom a little hard, towards the pool. Tom stumbles. 'Hey,' he says. 'Careful. I said careful.'

They walk a few more steps. Tom's vision fills with the beautiful pool water, all the gorgeous shades of turquoise and aquamarine, the foliage around it dancing with wildlife, those psychedelic red dragonflies, and the play of the sunshine on its surface.

They stand beside the pool together, Tom supported by Olly. His symptoms steady and he finds a moment of clarity. 'What are you doing here?' he asks.

69

FRIDAY

Olly

Olly sits in his study. Anna lied to him outright about her journal earlier and it's difficult to suppress his anger at her, but he must focus.

He's rehearsing what he and Sasha have agreed that he'll say to Patrick. They're going to try to do a deal with him, tell him that they can't possibly get him £10K now, but if he can be patient, the rewards will be much greater in a few months' time. He might even be able to get the Maserati if he's willing to be very patient.

It's a risky strategy. They decided not to tell him that they have Nicole's wealth in their sights because that would complicate things. It relies on Patrick not questioning how they will deliver but believing they're capable of it. If he agrees, it buys them time to decide exactly what they're going to do about him. Time is what they need. They need the press and police to leave and attention to be diverted somewhere else, away from the peninsula. Then, they can make a move on Patrick. And Anna.

Patrick raps sharply on Olly's study window as it's getting dark. Olly indicates that Patrick should meet him by the small porch where they spoke this morning. He unlocks the door and lets Patrick in.

'How are you?' he says.

'Have you got my money?'

'Why don't you come in? We can have a chat.'

'No chat. I want my money.'

Olly peers outside. 'There's been a drone buzzing around this evening because, as I'm sure you're aware, the press are gathering, desperate for a story. Do you want to be seen?' He holds the door open a little wider. 'Come in. You won't regret it. I have a proposition for you and it's a good one.'

Patrick enters cautiously, clearly suspicious. He ducks to pass through the low doorway. Olly shows him into his study. 'Do you mind if Sasha, my partner, joins us?' he asks. Patrick shrugs and Olly beckons to Sasha who's watching from the shadows at the end of the hall. The soles of her shoes squeak on the flagstones as she enters the room.

They sit, Olly and Sasha opposite Patrick. Patrick looks dishevelled. He has a backpack with him and a duffel bag. Olly suspects he slept rough last night.

'I just want my money,' Patrick says.

Olly smiles. 'Here's the thing. Have you heard of the Stanford marshmallow experiment?'

'What?' Patrick says. He looks at Sasha.

'Humour him,' she says.

She's wearing make-up and dressed in skinny jeans and a loose white shirt that's showing off beautifully tanned skin and cleavage. Olly notes that Patrick can't help checking her out. She's always an asset.

'So, in the Stanford experiment, researchers gave a group of children a choice: have one small treat – a marshmallow – immediately or wait fifteen minutes and get two small marshmallows. They left the children alone in a room with the one marshmallow to see how many of them would be able to resist that instant gratification—'

'For fuck's sake,' Patrick interrupts. 'What are you talking about?'

Olly feels irritated. He hates to be interrupted and he's tempted to snap at Patrick, but Sasha lays a hand on his thigh and leans forward, towards Patrick. 'You're right,' she says. 'Let's not waste time. We have a proposition for you. Take ten K now or wait for six months and we'll give you more than that. Much more.'

'How?' he says. 'And how much?'

'You'll have to trust us.'

'That's ridiculous. I don't know you.'

'You know what we did. You could go to the police at any time. It's not in our interests to lie to you.'

'And what if I can't afford to wait?' Patrick's tone is aggressive; he sounds as if he's running out of patience and Olly suddenly has a very bad feeling about this.

Sasha doesn't seem to pick up on it. She persists in talking to him in a reasonable tone, reassuring him that if he can wait, it would be a very smart investment, that it makes sense for him, that she and Olly are clearly successful people, but Olly has the sense that this isn't going to work. Patrick's too desperate and too emotional.

Olly interrupts her. 'Listen, as a gesture of how much we'd like you to trust us, we'd like to offer you a bed here in the Manor tonight, while you think about this. You can't stay in the house because our housekeeper will be here in the morning, but we can put you up in the old stables. There's a small apartment there, with a shower room. If the police come, we'll deny that we've seen you because I don't think they'll be happy to hear that you haven't left Lancaut. Would that work for you? I get the feeling you don't have anywhere else to go tonight, am I right?' He doesn't wait for an answer. 'In return for our hospitality over-night all we ask is that you think about this offer, and we can talk again in the morning. Whatever you decide then, we'll accept it and we'll help you get off the peninsula without being seen.'

He can sense Sasha's frustration that they haven't discussed this. He avoids looking at her and focuses on Patrick. 'You need a place to stay tonight, don't you?'

'But what's going to be different in six months? How will you get me more money then?' Patrick asks.

Sasha draws breath to answer but Olly cuts in again. 'That's for us to worry about, not you. We're just asking you for time. You can go to the police whenever you want so it's not a bluff. It can't be. You hold the power here. So, what do you say? Do you need a place for the night?'

Patrick looks from one to the other of them. He's tempted, Olly can tell. 'Yes. And food.'

'We can get you food. Sasha, why don't you rustle something up and I'll show Patrick where he's staying.'

She glares at him, and he knows she's trying to tell him that she had this, and that he shouldn't have gone off piste, but he ignores her. Olly can tell that Patrick isn't going to go for their offer. He has an air of desperation hanging about him like a bad stink.

Olly leads him out of the study. In the hall he pauses to tell Patrick a little about the house, as if he was a regular guest. Patrick seems to relax.

'Do you ever get used to those old dudes staring at you?' he asks, gesturing to the portraits.

Olly forces a laugh. 'Would you like to see the Great Hall?' he asks.

Patrick shrugs. 'Sure.'

'It's the finest and oldest room in the house. I'm sure you'll appreciate it.'

He opens the door to the Hall. Patrick enters and Olly steps in behind him. 'Wow,' Patrick says, taking in the huge stone fireplace with its heraldic carvings, the thickly beamed roof, the ancient staircase leading up to a balcony on the wall opposite the fireplace. 'It's old,' he says.

'Very,' Olly agrees. 'Isn't it spectacular? Sasha uses it to teach yoga now.'

Patrick is drawn to a large tapestry, hanging on one wall. He stands in front of it, his back to Olly. Olly picks up one of the yoga belts that Sasha keeps neatly rolled on a shelf.

'This is incredible,' Patrick says.

375

'It's a rare depiction of a hunting scene,' Olly says. He unrolls the yoga belt and wraps the ends around his wrists. 'Though obviously it's just a fragment. If it was complete, it would probably be best kept in a museum. You see the hunting dogs? I guess the missing fragment shows a dead stag. You can imagine it, can't you? Collapsed and bleeding.'

He steps behind Patrick, so he's within touching distance. 'It's probably a blessing that that bit is missing,' he says. 'I doubt Sasha's yoga students would want to look at such a gory scene.'

In one swift movement he loops the yoga belt over Patrick's head and tightens it around his neck. He pulls as hard as he can. Patrick is a big guy but he's not taller than Olly. All Olly must do is hang on. It's not easy. Patrick thrashes around, grabbing at the belt, trying to pull it away from his neck, throwing himself from side to side, but Olly doesn't give up; he keeps up the pressure until, finally, Patrick collapses onto the floor. Olly, panting, kneels to check his pulse.

Sasha walks in, carrying a tray. 'Here you are,' she says. 'I went to the stables. Oh my God.'

Olly can't feel any sign of life. 'He's gone,' he says. He notices a pin on Patrick's lapel and recognises it as one of the guest pins from the Barn. He removes it and slips it into his pocket. It could come in useful.

He looks up at Sasha. She's frozen in place, staring at Patrick. He glances at the tray she's carrying. It's sweet that she brought Patrick a sandwich, some fruit and one of Kitty's brownies.

'You bothered to bring him supper,' he says. 'You didn't need to.'

'What have you done? You—'

His temper rises swiftly, and he cuts her off. 'I did what needed to be done.'

'We're right under the noses of the police! Or haven't you noticed?'

'He was a loose cannon! Didn't *you* notice? We can put him in the septic tank with Kitty. It's not a problem. Give me some credit.'

She throws the tray at him, hard, and he ducks, but the food splatters him and the tray clatters across the medieval tiles.

She storms out. 'Clean up your fucking mess!' she shouts and the door slams behind her.

He stands, staring at the back of the door, feeling a twitch in his eye and a queasy and unwelcome mixture of anger and doubt.

70

FRIDAY

Jen

As Jen drives up the lane leading towards the Manor House and Barn, she sees the reporters gathered at the end of the Barn's drive, one of them operating a drone. She curses. How horrible for Nicole.

She tries to call Hal to ask what she should do about it, but he doesn't pick up. He must still be sleeping off his migraine.

The squad car has moved from its position in front of the Barn to block the entrance to the drive. Jen pulls in and gives the instruction to the officers in the car to move the press right back to the main road. 'Keep them away, but drive by the Barn now and then,' she says. 'I'll call for more help.'

'Get that drone down,' she tells one man. 'Or I'll nick you for trespass.'

She drives on past the Barn and the Manor and parks at the very end of the lane, where a wooden gate blocks vehicles from going any further. She and Finn let themselves through it. Finn found an old map of Lancaut online, which suggests a location for the plague pit, and he has a screenshot of it on his phone. Jen can't read maps to save her life but he's promising he can take her there.

Beneath the trees, it feels like night already. Finn switches on a powerful flashlight and leads the way down a steep path.

'Wait here a moment,' he says when they're part of the way down. He studies the map and directs them to step off the path and immediately the going gets tougher as they wade through dense undergrowth. Finn walks ahead and tries to hold back branches for Jen but some whip into her anyway. They arrive in a dense thicket of saplings, difficult to push through. 'Are you sure this is the right way?' Jen calls.

'Yep,' Finn calls back. He's getting a bit ahead of her, and she scrambles to catch up. He leads the way across a flatter patch of ground, where mature trees soar above them. The undergrowth is less dense here, and the light between the trees ahead is paler than that behind them and to the sides, suggesting a clearing. Jen's senses prickle.

On the map, Finn showed her that the plague pit was some distance from the abandoned village. They wouldn't have wanted the diseased to be buried too close, he said. It makes sense. He stops at the edge of the clearing, a small terrace of land. It's covered in thick, tufty turf and there's a deep quietness about it that gives her the chills, even though she doesn't believe in the supernatural.

'I think this is it,' Finn says.

He rakes the torchlight across the turf. 'There,' he says. 'It looks different.'

Jen doesn't see it at first, but then she does, a patch of ground where the turf is a little wilted, splaying in the wrong directions. The patch is about the size and shape of a burial site.

'Holy shit,' she says. They approach the area and Jen gets on her hands and knees. Chunks of turf come up easily. Their regular edges could have been cut by a spade. Beneath, the dirt is loose and uncompacted. 'It looks as if it's been dug up very recently,' she says. 'I'll call this in.'

She reaches for her phone, but she has no reception. 'Use your radio,' she tells him, but it's out of range. He moves a short distance away and tries again. Jen stands close to him, hands on her hips, surveying the site, thinking about what this means. The radio is crackling as he tries to use it, but she thinks she hears something in the woods behind her. A rustle, something cracking underfoot. She sees a dark shadow move between the trees and disappear. 'Hey!' she shouts and starts to make her way into the woodland, running and stumbling. 'Police! Stop!' Finn swings the torch towards the sound and follows, catching up with Jen when she finally stops running and stands, out of breath, realising she has to give up because if it was a person, she can't hear them any longer and she has no idea what direction they went in.

'Let's get back to the road,' she says. 'We need to get forensics in to see if there are signs that there was a body buried here.'

Jen remembers that there are probably plenty of bodies in the ground and she hopes that won't complicate things. Finn is looking around as if he's not sure which way to go. She's lost all sense of direction. 'Do you know where we are?' she asks.

'It's this way,' he says. 'I think.'

'Are you sure?'

'No,' he admits. 'We ran quite far. But I think we need to go uphill.'

'Let's go.' She walks behind him, and she can't shake the feeling that they're being watched. She compulsively checks over her shoulder, seeing nothing apart from a patchwork of shifting shadows, and she hopes they're not hosting some kind of horror.

71

FRIDAY

Sasha

Sasha walks carefully through the woods, as silently as possible, forcing herself not to cry out when she almost trips, or is whipped by a branch or a bramble. Her left arm feels ablaze after it was raked by nettles. Her breathing is heavy. She had to run hard from the plague pit. What were the police doing there? They've already searched the peninsula thoroughly.

She shouldn't have gone back, but she had to get out of the Manor, away from Olly, because what he did to Patrick horrified her. It was reckless and stupid. He didn't give her a chance to get Patrick onside and she's certain she could have. Olly's arrogance has gone too far. He's so sure of his own brilliance that he's put them in jeopardy, even more than they were already in. It's hard to know if she can keep getting up every day and putting on a 'normal' face while everything is in tatters around them.

She didn't know where to go once she'd left the Manor. She was afraid of being seen by the police or the press, so she avoided the lanes and headed straight into the woodland, thinking she might walk down to the river and try to get some peace by sitting on its banks, watching the water, feeling its flow, enjoying the anonymity of the darkness.

On her way, she felt drawn to revisit the plague pit because of a sudden paranoia that they'd left something there when they moved the body. When she's anxious, her perfectionism ramps up. She feels a pressing urge to check and double-check things. Even as she was walking to the pit, she thought, this is dumb, I should turn back and return to the Manor, I should trouble-shoot there, make sure that Olly has cleaned up properly and there's no trace of Patrick anywhere. But she couldn't face Olly yet, so she kept going.

What Sasha was not expecting to see at the plague pit was torchlight. She was walking by the light of her phone's torch and extinguished it before she was noticed, but when she hastily turned to leave, she gave her presence away by stepping carelessly and snapping a twig. She was very close to being discovered by the police.

Tonight isn't just unnerving her; it's threatening to unravel them completely.

She skirts around the edge of the orchard and slips into the Manor House by a back entrance. A strip of light shows beneath Olly's study door. She opens it. He's at his desk but his laptop is closed. He looks as pale and shattered as she feels.

'Where have you been?' he asks.

'The police are at the plague pit.'

'What?' His eyes look a little wild. 'Is that where you went? Why?'

'Did you clean up?' she asks.

He nods. 'He's in the septic tank. I'm sorry,' he says. 'I don't know if I did the right thing.'

Well, it's too late now, she wants to spit at him, but she's not one hundred percent sure he's being honest, or whether he's trying to suck up to her by hinting that she might have been right. Olly doesn't suffer from doubt or regret much. Not the way she does. She says, 'What's done is done. What did you do with his bags?'

'In the tank, with him. I cleared up properly.'

She knows she'll check anyway. 'I'm going to get changed.'

'Your arm's scratched and stung.'

'I know,' she says.

'We don't want anyone to see that.'

'I know!' Her voice is raised. She has a feeling that they're going to get a visit from the police tonight.

Upstairs, she pulls off the leggings, T-shirt and socks she was wearing and replaces them with a shift dress. She uses a flannel to wipe under her armpits and her breasts, washes her face and the cuts on her arms, dries everything, then pulls her hair out of its ponytail and brushes it in front of the mirror until it shines. A small twig falls from her hair onto her lap. She throws it out of the window. Finally, she shrugs on a light cardigan that covers her arms and checks herself in the mirror. She no longer looks like someone who's been chased through the woods.

She hears a car parking on the drive as she walks downstairs. She stands in the hall and takes a few deep breaths. A silver lining occurs to her: she's thankful that Kitty isn't here tonight. Though perhaps, if she was, Patrick would still be alive.

The doorbell clangs. To maintain her composure, she counts slowly to fifteen before opening it. The porch light is on, casting an unflattering glow over the pair at the door. It's the detective, Jen, who she presumably just heard in the woods, and another, younger man, who she doesn't know. He was probably there too.

'Hello,' Sasha says. Her mouth becomes instantly dry. 'You're here late,' she says, and hopes they can't hear her nerves.

Jen smiles. 'Hi. I'm sorry to call on you at this hour. This is Detective Constable Finn Macdonald. Would it be possible to borrow a minute or two of your time?' Sasha sees that Jen has a small twig in her hair, like the one she just removed from her own head. Finn Macdonald looks dishevelled and sweaty, too. It was definitely them she just ran from.

'Has something happened?'

'It might be easier to have this chat inside. Is Olly here?'

Sasha considers saying no, but that could have consequences. 'He is.'

'If we could talk to you both that would be great.'

'Let's go into the kitchen.' She leads the way and puts the kettle on.

'Is your housekeeper here?' Jen asks.

'She's staying at the Barn at nights. To help Nicole,' she says, though she suspects that Jen must know this already. 'I'll fetch Olly.'

She goes to his study and knocks softly at the door.

'Come in,' he calls. He stands in front of the window, his back to her. His shoulders are raised and tense. She can see his reflection in the windowpane. His expression is dark, and she wonders if they're going to be able to get through this without giving anything away.

'It's the police,' she says. 'They want a word with us.'

'Can't they make an appointment?'

It's not what she was expecting him to say, and it aggravates her to the point of wanting to scream. Why does he have to be so arrogant when everything he's doing, his occupation of this room, the years he's spent in here, the time everyone else has donated to support him and his work, is predicated on the lie that he's talented when in fact, based on what she's read, he hasn't got a gift at all? And why does he have to be so arrogant when he's just murdered a man?

'Let's just do this,' she says.

He doesn't move. She forces herself to go to him and wrap her arms around his chest. She leans her head against his shoulder. 'Please,' she says. 'I don't want them thinking we have something to hide. I want them to go away. They'll only be back tomorrow if we refuse.'

He sighs, a cross little exhalation that she hears and feels beneath her hands.

'Alright,' he says. 'Let's go and find out which tree they're barking up now.'

She marvels at his confidence that he can stay a step ahead of the detectives. She's not so sure that she can; she feels dangerously unmoored, though she's going to give it her best shot to stay ahead of everyone.

72

FRIDAY

Nicole

Nicole lies, exhausted, on the chaise longue in her living area. The drone has been gone for a while and she put the blinds back up and turned off all but the dimmest of lights, so she didn't feel on display. Having the police outside makes her feel safer, though they're not there now because they've had to move to the end of the lane to keep the press away. They told her they're going to check on her every half-hour.

The sun has gone down and the cliffs glow pale in the watery light of the moon. She's missing Tom terribly. I must keep his memory alive, she thinks. His face, his words, the looks they shared, the moments of quiet magic. Even after they won the money, those were the most important things in her life. Her hand moves to her belly. If only, she thinks. They'd just begun trying for a baby. If only they'd had a chance to try for longer.

On a whim, or maybe because grief is making her masochistic, she checks the fertility app on her phone. It tells her that her period was due yesterday. She blinks and double-checks. She's usually incredibly regular. Most likely her period is late because of the trauma of Tom's death, but she can't help feeling a spark of hope. She'll get a pregnancy test if her period still hasn't come in a few days, she decides, but not yet, and in the meantime, she mustn't let that hope grow into anything bigger, because it could be nothing. It's most likely to be nothing.

The idea makes her restless, though. What if she is pregnant? That would be incredible. Feeling energised, she gets up. She feels drawn to the pool. Maybe if she goes out there, she'll feel close to Tom again. It's so much nicer to think about this than all the negative things. Those horrible clues that might add up to him being murdered or having an affair. She doesn't care if she's in denial; this is what she wants to think about: her and Tom and the possibility of their baby.

She's glad Anna's gone to bed, or she might be tempted to share the news, and she shouldn't. Not until she knows it's true. She's only one day late, for goodness' sake.

Nicole steps out of the house and onto the decking around the pool. The lights come on automatically as they should do, a mellow configuration that Tom programmed just for her. She slips off her sandals and sits on the side with her feet in the shallow end. The water is cool enough to be a small shock at first, but she soon gets used to it. Stars fill the sky in the breathtaking way they do here, where there's so little light pollution. Many nights this summer she and Tom have lain on the sunbeds out here at night, gazing up, guessing at the constellations, making up names for them, because neither of them can recognise anything apart from Orion's Belt.

She looks across to the sunbeds, and screams. A man is standing between them. He's a dark silhouette against one of the lights.

'No,' he says. 'It's okay. Please don't be afraid.'

She scrambles to her feet, almost slipping, feeling as if this is it, she's going to die, the same way Tom did. She's stepped out of the house into the arms of Tom's murderer and, sickeningly, she thinks she knows who it is.

'Patrick?' she says.

'No. I'm not going to hurt you; I just want to talk to you. Are you Nicole?'

It's not Patrick. She considers whether to scream for Anna, but he's moved close enough to grab her. 'Yes,' she says. 'Keep back.'

'I'll sit here.' He lowers himself onto one of the sunbeds. 'Please don't run away. I saw your appeal online and I have something to tell you. It's about your husband.'

'What is it?'

He tells her a story about camping on their land the night before Tom was murdered. As he talks her eyes acclimatise and she's able to see more of him and to make out his scruffy clothes and his unshaven face, the battered trainers. His small backpack lies in a limp heap beside the chair. He tells her that he met Tom in the woods, and Tom was angry with him because he'd lit a fire. 'I was an asshole,' the man says. 'I behaved badly because I knew he was right, and I felt like a twat. He was being nice to me, I mean, totally reasonable.' She remains standing, feeling the evening breeze move around her, catching the smell of some sweet fragrance in the air, and listens to his words as if they're a fairy tale, as if she's being given something precious back, some minutes of Tom's life that she thought were lost.

The man keeps talking. 'When I don't take my meds, I can be like that. I didn't think much of it afterwards, but when I saw the news, I realised that it was him I saw. Because the thing is, I didn't leave when he told me to. I came up to the house. I was angry at him. I thought *he* was being the asshole, a rich fucker, you know. So, I acted like I was leaving but I followed him up here to give him another piece of my mind, and I saw him on the sunbed, on this sunbed here. I was watching from over there.' He points, indicating the long grasses abutting the edge of the decking. 'And I saw that he looked unwell. He seemed alright down by the river but when I saw him up here, I felt guilty because he wasn't quite right.'

Nicole can hardly bear to hear this; it's hurting her, but she doesn't want him to stop because she's desperate to know. The man keeps talking, his voice low and confessional. 'I was going to ask him if I could help him, like get him some water or something, but someone came around the house and your husband said "Hi" and so I shrank back into the shadows.'

She can imagine it. This man has barely emerged from the shadows to talk to her. He's like an apparition.

'Why are you here now?' Her voice is a whisper. 'Why didn't you call the tip line?'

'Because they'll think I did it. I'm homeless. I live out here in the woods, not just here but in the area. I walk every day and I try to move on every few days. I was a student at Bristol Uni but I lost my way a bit. I made a girl feel uncomfortable. It was bad behaviour and it's over. I got help and got diagnosed with something – it doesn't matter what, but that's why I live like this, so nothing like that happens again. I'm not a bad person. I wanted to tell you what I saw, but I can't talk to the police. You understand?'

She feels as if someone has picked her up and shaken her so that all her joints, all the parts of her body, are a little loose and can't be easily put back together. She feels that if the breeze gets any stronger bits of herself might blow away. Understanding other people isn't easy just now.

There are lots of things she wants to ask, like how did Tom seem unwell? But one question is the most pressing.

'Who did you see?'

73

FRIDAY

Olly

Olly strides into the kitchen. The detectives are sitting at the table. He recognises the female, Jen.

'Evening,' he says. 'You're working late.'

Jen smiles. 'Sometimes that's unavoidable. I'm sorry to disturb you.'

He takes a seat. 'What can we do for you?' Olly asks. He drums his fingers on the tabletop. Sasha serves a pot of tea and some milk. He notices her hand has a little shake.

'Is your housekeeper here?' Jen asks him.

'She's at the Barn, being a Good Samaritan.'

Jen nods. 'And can you remind me of her name?'

He looks at her in disbelief. 'Kitty,' he says. 'Don't you keep a note of this stuff?'

'Are you sure that's her name?' Jen asks.

He feels the smallest stab of danger and glances at Sasha. She's looking at Jen attentively. 'I'm sure,' he says.

'Has that name changed since you've known her?'

Sasha remains silent, leaving him to answer.

'Her name hasn't changed, per se. But it's a new name in the sense that it's her nickname. A sort of in-joke.' He laughs and means it to sound light, but the sound seems to coalesce into something clumsy and forced. This isn't how he wants things to go. He glances at Sasha again and notes how studiously she seems to be keeping her profile turned to him. Perhaps she's frozen up and needs him to lead this.

'What did you call Kitty before she acquired her nickname?' Jen asks.

'How is this relevant to anything?' Olly says. He hates the way she's looking at him, like a cat who has a mouse cornered. How dare she? 'Aren't you supposed to be investigating Tom Booth's death, or am I missing something?'

'I'd appreciate it if you could answer the question, please,' Jen says. She smiles at him. Something feels off about this. He feels that little twitch in the corner of his eye again, and forces his expression into a smile for Jen, because women like smiles, but feels it's unconvincing. He glances back at Sasha. She looks like a Pre-Raphaelite beauty, sitting there in that dress and pretty cardigan, her hair down. His instinct to protect her kicks in. Come on, he tells himself. Pull yourself together. This is nothing more than a dance and I must lead it.

'Her name was Anna,' he says.

'Why did you start to call her Kitty?'

'Well, we had a previous housekeeper called Kitty, and when Anna took over her duties, we joked that the transition was so seamless that we might as well call her Kitty, too. I'm the first to admit that working around me isn't easy when I'm writing and I had concerns over whether somebody new could fill Kitty's shoes, yet Anna did it perfectly. We're very fond of her, in spite of her flaws.'

'Whose idea was it to call her Kitty?' Jen asks.

'I don't remember who said it first, do you, Sash?' Sasha doesn't respond and Olly carries on, 'Like I said, it started as a joke, and it stuck. Though I think, to be more serious for a moment, to delve into personality or character, if you'll permit me to, that Anna was ready for a change. She'd had an unhappy life until then. As Kitty, she thrives.'

He beams around the table, feeling as if he's pulled that off perfectly. Like the best lies, it's almost all the truth. He's only omitted who Anna was before she became Kitty. And what became of Kitty.

Jen nods and in the silence that follows, Olly's confidence grows a little. He stifles a yawn and hopes they'll take it as a cue to go. Sasha meets his eye and her expression is very flat. Hang in there, he thinks, I've got this. She must be rattled by Patrick's death. She was strong for me when we moved Kitty's remains, so it's my turn to be strong for her now.

He watches as Jen flicks back through her notebook. She stops after a few pages and reads, then looks up at him and says, 'I thought the name "Anna" rang a bell. Didn't you tell us that the owner of this property is called Anna?'

Olly swallows and shrugs, as if to say, So what?

'And can I ask,' Jen continues, 'what became of the original Kitty? The one who worked here first?'

He struggles to maintain his composure. 'She upped and left one night. No explanation. Honestly, we felt betrayed, but we realised that the way we were taking things business-wise at the Manor was probably too much for her. The yoga classes and the like. She was rather possessive of the place, and she'd worked here when it was just a private house for so long that I think she felt a bit violated – is that too strong a word? – no, I think it's right. She felt violated by the commerce. But this house does not pay for itself.'

'No,' Jen says. 'I don't suppose it does. And have you had any contact with the original Kitty since she left?'

He shakes his head. 'None whatsoever. Sad, really.'

'You don't miss your Auntie Kitty?'

Olly's heart skips a beat. He takes a moment to process the fact that they know Kitty was his aunt before answering as lightly as he can. 'Life is full of loves and losses, don't you think, detective?'

'You're not wrong,' Jen says. 'Thank you for your time. I might have a few more questions for you over the coming days.'

He can hardly believe it's over so suddenly. 'Of course. We're delighted to help, aren't we, Sasha?'

'Yes,' she says. She turns to Jen. 'Detective, I remembered there's something that I didn't tell you.'

'I'm all ears.'

'On the morning Tom Booth was murdered, Olly went out for a while in the morning. For about an hour. Didn't you, Olly?'

74

THE DAY OF HIS DEATH: 12:35

Tom

'I came to ask you and Nicole over for a drink tonight,' Olly says.

'That's nice,' Tom says. 'We'd love to.' He knows Nicole will want him to say yes to this, because she still seeks friendship with Sasha. He would rather decline, give up on the relationship, and accept that Sasha and Olly aren't worth bothering with.

'But now that I'm here,' Olly says, 'I'm thinking I might have changed my mind. Sasha, what do you think?'

'Sasha's here?' Tom asks. He can't see her. Is that her standing in front of the Barn? Now, he sees two of her. He looks up at Olly and sees two of him, too.

'Do it,' Sasha says. It is her.

Tom starts to say, 'Hi, Sasha,' but doesn't get the words out. Olly shoves him hard, in the back, and he falls forward, into the pool. His mouth fills with water.

He flails underwater, his arms thrashing until he feels a hand on his head, and he reaches upwards to cling onto the arm it belongs to, but instead of helping him up, to where he can breathe, to where he can live, he feels only downward pressure.

Looking up, he sees Olly's face through the water, distorted and determined.

The last breath to leave his lips carries a word, 'Nicole', but it never reaches anyone's ears. It becomes a cascade of bubbles that drift upwards until they burst at the surface, watched impassively by Olly and Sasha.

75

FRIDAY

Sasha

'What?' Olly says.

Sasha turns to him and smiles. 'When we were interviewed previously, we forgot to tell the detectives that you went around to see Tom on the morning he was murdered. Didn't you?'

He stares at her, and his expression says it all, speaking to his shock and to his anger with her which is nascent, but will grow fast and furiously until it consumes him. Sasha is taking a risk, she knows, but she's willing to.

She almost wants to laugh as the cogs turn behind his eyes and outrage and betrayal play out across his expression first, soon to be replaced by a tense calm that she knows is costing him every effort to maintain. He's making calculations. Olly hates to be wrongfooted so much that, in spite of the danger she's put herself in, the fact that he might say that she was at the Barn that morning, too, she also feels glee. And some curiosity. What's he going to say? How's he going to play this?

She's amazed to find that she feels no regret at throwing him under the bus. Instead, she feels liberated.

All eyes are on him. She sees he's come to a decision. It'd better be a good one, boyo, she thinks. She tries to keep a smirk off her face.

'I don't recollect that at all,' he says.

'What time was that?' Jen asks.

'I think it was about an hour before Nicole Booth appeared in our drive here,' Sasha says.

Olly coughs. He stands up. 'Sorry. I need a glass of water.' He stands at the sink and fills a large glass. He drinks with his back to them. To Sasha, it feels as if it's happening in slow motion.

'Do you recall this, Mr Palmer?' Jen asks him.

He pivots slowly to face them. Sasha watches him closely. He'll try to talk himself out of this. She expects him to turn the tables on her.

'No, I don't recall it. I think Sasha must have made a mistake. I was here all morning.'

'I didn't make a mistake,' she says. 'I'm absolutely certain of it.'

His eyes narrow. She sees hatred in them and stares back, letting him know that she's not afraid, that this is it.

He starts to walk back to the table, but just as she expects him to sit, he ducks out of the room. They hear his footsteps quickening as he goes down the hall.

Jen's chair scrapes on the floor as she stands. 'Mr Palmer? I have a few more questions.'

He doesn't answer. Sasha jumps up and runs after him. The detectives follow. There's no sign of him. They look outside, though none of them heard the front door.

'Did he go upstairs?' Jen asks.

Sasha pictures all the hidden places in the Manor. 'I think he's hiding inside the walls,' she says.

76

FRIDAY

Nicole

Nicole watches the man sitting on the sunbed opposite hers. His face is lit blue by the pool lights. She sees something in him that makes her feel sad. She no longer feels afraid of him.

He says, 'It was a man I saw. He was tall and thin, with round glasses.'

'Olly,' she says. 'Oh my God. Did you talk to him?'

'I didn't want him to see me. Your husband was the first person to give me the benefit of the doubt in a long time. I know what most people think of me when they meet me. And I thought your husband was safe because he was on the sunbed, and he clearly knew the visitor. I promise I thought it was okay to leave. I haven't been able to sleep thinking that perhaps I left him with the person who killed him.'

'What's your name?' Nicole asks.

'I'd rather not say.'

'I need to tell the police what you've said, but how will I make them believe me if I don't know your name?'

He looks agitated. 'Just say that I came to see you.'

'I have no proof you exist. They could accuse me of making it up.'

'You're the widow. They'll believe you.'

'Being the widow makes me a suspect, too, doesn't it?'

He stands. He's going to leave. 'I can't. I'm sorry.'

'Is this true? Or are you making it up to get the money? How long have you been at Lancaut, watching us?'

'I'm not making it up. You recognised him from my description. I haven't been watching you and I haven't asked you for any money.'

'You might have seen him here before.'

'I'm not making it up, I promise you. I could have stayed away. I don't have to be here.'

'But ten grand makes it very tempting to be here, I imagine.'

He looks at his feet. 'Obviously, I need money, but I swear I'm telling you the truth. The money isn't why I came.'

'But you won't give me your name or speak to the police yourself?'

'I can't. I'm sorry. I really am, but I can't have contact with the police.'

She sees how nervous he is, eyes darting, hands that are never still. This is more than being afraid that he'll be falsely accused of Tom's murder, she thinks.

'What do the police want you for?' she asks.

'I don't know if they do. But I stalked someone at university. Another student. I didn't do anything bad to her, I just wrote to her, and once I took some stuff from her room, but nothing valuable. I don't want to get into trouble. I'm not well when I'm in the world. But I'm mostly okay out here. I keep away from people. It's why I feel so bad about getting in a row with your husband. I wasn't myself that day. But I can't give you my name. I can't get messed up with the authorities.'

'What about your family? Do they know you're living rough? How old are you?' He looks young, she thinks, beneath the stubble and the dirt. He's just a kid.

'Look, I'm sorry he died, your husband. He was trying to be nice to me that day. I could tell he was a good man. I wish I hadn't made his day worse.' He steps back into the shadows.

'He was a good man,' she says. I believe this person, she thinks. I do. The pool water glimmers darkly in front of her. 'How did he seem unwell?' she asks.

'He said he banged his head. He seemed a bit disoriented.'

Tom, she thinks. I should have been there for you. 'How did he hurt his head? Did he say anything about that?'

'I don't know. He didn't say.' He backs away again, but she wants more from him. She wants to know anything and everything about Tom that morning.

'And he was kind to you?'

'He tried to be. I'm sorry I didn't let him. I hadn't taken my meds. I keep thinking about him.'

'Tell this to the police, and I'll give you the money. I'll give you more.'

'I can't.'

'Please.'

He shakes his head.

'What if I call them now? They're here, around the front, or they will be in a few minutes.'

'I know they are. I'll be long gone before they find me. I know every inch of this place. But now you know what I saw, I can feel better about it in here and here.' He covers his heart with his palm and points to his head.

'Tell me your first name, at least, so I can thank you properly.'

'Ben,' he says after a moment.

'Thank you, Ben,' she says and, before she can say another word, he's gone.

77

FRIDAY

Olly

Olly slips behind the panelling in the Map Room and moves as quickly as he can through the space between the walls, feeling his way until he reaches a brick wall with a vertical beam set within it. Carefully, he reaches upward and pushes on the top of the beam, and it moves like a see-saw, the bottom coming away from the wall.

Olly crawls behind it. The space he enters is small and pitch-dark. Forced to his hands and knees by the low ceiling, he inches forward until he feels a void in front of him in the floor, and he manoeuvres himself into it, finding crude wooden footholds on the side of the tunnel beneath. He climbs down as fast as he dares, praying the footholds won't crumble. The air smells damp and rotten. Summer's heat hasn't penetrated here.

He makes a hard landing at the bottom and for a moment he fears that he's hurt his ankle, but he's okay. He's at basement level, deep below the Manor, in a stone chamber. There's no light here whatsoever, but he knows that he has three options. The first is to take refuge here in the priest hole, but Sasha knows about it, so it doesn't feel safe to stay. The other options will get him out of the Manor and into its grounds. One tunnel leads to the front of the house and emerges near the Coach House; the other will take him out the back where he'll emerge near the stable block. He hesitates. Sasha will think he'll go to the back. She'll assume he'll cut down to the nature reserve and follow the path along the river there. It's the quickest way to get off the peninsula. The path emerges far from the lane where the police and the journalists are gathered.

He takes the tunnel that leads out to the front. It's claustrophobic. He's afraid it will fall in on him. It's so dark he feels the wall as he moves along, to help him keep his balance. The walls are crumbly. He hears debris fall from them as he passes. He begins to cough and can't stop. When he finally reaches the steps, he's gasping with relief. He climbs and pushes on the underside of the wooden trap door that leads out. It's a struggle. When he makes it out, he falls onto the grass, lying on his back for a few moments, sucking in the sweet night air. His heart pounds.

He thinks of Sasha. That bitch. They got too greedy. The plan to move in on Tom and Nicole has stretched them too far. Would he have embarked on it if Sasha hadn't encouraged him? Never. He already knows that he will never work with someone again, the way he has with her. He let her get too close. She seduced him into making decisions that he wouldn't have made on his own. Men are fallible creatures around women, he knows that, and he has proved himself a part of that club.

Olly will disappear. He's done it before. He will also make sure that Sasha is destroyed.

He considers his options. He knows that a police car is in the area, and they will undoubtedly be looking out for him already. He must leave Lancaut quickly, before they call for enough back-up to watch all the ways he could get off the peninsula.

When he reaches the lane, he doesn't walk along it, but behind the hedges bordering it, out of sight. Soon, he sees the Glass Barn, dimly lit tonight.

He pushes on a few more yards before a pair of headlights crawl up the lane. He ducks down and waits for them to pass. A squad car swings into the Barn's driveway and idles there for a few minutes, before leaving. It must be patrolling and if it's just been here, it probably won't come right back.

A thought occurs to him. If he could sneak into the Barn, he could hide for the night and creep away at first light. Nobody will think of looking for him there. He would be hiding in plain sight, which is just what he suggested Patrick do. It was a good idea and it's very tempting. By morning, the police will assume he's long gone. The Barn is plenty big enough for him to remain hidden.

He approaches it carefully. He spent enough time being shown the place by Tom to be very familiar with its layout. There are plenty of areas that Nicole is unlikely to use at night. Something else occurs to him, something brilliant. He puts his hand in his pocket and pulls out Patrick's pin. He forgot he had it. But now it might come in very useful.

He hesitates when he remembers the security cameras. Tom told him that he disabled them. He's going to gamble that they're still out of action. By the time anyone checks them he hopes to be gone, anyway. Keeping under cover as much as he can, he creeps slowly around the edge of the property, scoping out which rooms are lit and where he might be able to sneak in, until he gets a bit of luck.

The doors by the pool are wide open.

78

FRIDAY

Nicole

Nicole tries calling Jen, to tell her what she's just heard about Olly and Sasha, but she doesn't pick up. She tries Detective Steen instead. He takes a while to answer, so long that she's considering calling 999, but he does eventually, and she breathes a sigh of relief and gives Anna a thumbs-up. Since she woke Anna with the news, Anna hasn't left her side.

Steen sounds groggy, as if he was asleep, and the dissonance of that, when every nerve in Nicole's body is humming, feels startling. She blurts out the story about the camper. 'It's Olly Palmer,' she says. 'He was here the morning Tom died.'

For a moment she wonders if he's still on the line, but then he says, 'I'm on my way. I'll see you in about forty minutes.'

She hangs up. 'He's coming,' she tells Anna.

'Good,' Anna says. She looks tense, and Nicole knows she's worried about Steen, afraid that he's not going to listen to them, convinced that the police won't take them seriously.

'So, we wait,' Nicole says. She shudders.

She feels a breeze on her arms and remembers that she left the doors open when she stepped out to the pool earlier. She should shut them. It was stupid of her not to have done it before. She hurries through, closes them and locks up, feeling relief that she remembered. She peers out to the front and sees headlamps coming down the drive. The squad car does a slow turn then creeps away. It's reassuring, though she's glad it wasn't here when Ben, the camper, came by. What if he'd been frightened off before he told her what he saw?

'Do you want something to eat?' Anna asks when she returns to the living area.

'I couldn't eat.'

'Me neither.'

They sit together. 'I suspected it,' Anna says. 'I suspected that Olly and Sasha could do a thing like this, but I didn't think anyone would believe me.'

Nicole doesn't ask her why she didn't say anything. She understands how broken Anna must have been.

She thinks about Olly and Sasha, how they present as so charming when one or both might be cold-blooded killers. They're certainly liars, telling the police they were at the Manor House all morning last Saturday.

Though none of us are what we seem, she thinks. Kitty was Anna. And I, she thinks, have killed, too. Though it was different. Granny was old, and sick. It was almost a mercy.

She used to go to see Tom's granny every week, even when she was dog-tired, even when Tom made an excuse not to. She brought Granny her shopping and her weekly Lucky Dip lottery ticket, helped Granny out with jobs, listened to her complain about everything Nicole did. She did it out of a sense of duty and for Tom, because he loved his granny, but Granny made her life a misery. Never grateful, increasingly demanding and unpleasant. She only wanted Tom. Nicole felt like a servant. No, a slave.

Tom never saw it. He loved Granny too much. Nicole was careful not to complain about her because she wanted to protect him from the hurt of them not getting on. But it got to her. Things might have carried on like that if she hadn't overheard Tom talking to Granny on speakerphone. He tried to turn it off, dropped his phone in his eagerness to, so they ended up both listening, the phone spinning on the floor at Nicole's feet as Granny explained how much she disliked Nicole. Tom snatched it up and ended the call but it was too late.

'She loves you, really,' Tom said, some difficult hours later. He was pleading with Nicole not to give Granny a piece of her mind. 'Honestly, she does.'

'Why didn't you defend me?' Nicole asked.

He winced. 'It's easier to let her vent. I don't agree with her, but she's my only family apart from you. It's just what she's like. She's not going to change now.'

It's just what she's like. She's not going to change now. Granny's words haunted Nicole. They eroded the good and wonderful thing she and Tom had together, they were contemptuous of the hours and hours of effort Nicole had made with Granny, and

411

she didn't see how age was any excuse for being horrible, but she loved Tom and wasn't prepared to give him a 'me or her' ultimatum, so she tried to carry on as normal.

The next time she visited Granny, though, she couldn't help remembering what she said, and thinking of how many years Granny might live. She was sick, but not at death's door. As she emptied Granny's sharps bin and restocked her medical supplies under Granny's beady eye, as she plumped her cushions, made her dinner and cups of tea just how she liked them and poured the perfect amount of sherry in Granny's favourite glass and handed her the TV remote control so they could watch the lottery results, because Granny didn't like Nicole to change the channel, Nicole felt less able to tolerate these behaviours as eccentricities and saw malice in them, as she was sure Granny intended her to.

She decided to give it one more week. If nothing improved, she would tell Granny that if she couldn't be more pleasant, Nicole would not come again. She would tell Tom that he would have to do it all on his own.

It was a rainy Saturday night. Tom was playing darts with his mates. Nicole forgot her umbrella, had trouble with the buses. She arrived wet and late as a result and found Granny snappish and horrible, picking fault with everything. By the time they settled down to watch the lottery results, Nicole was burning with resentment but tongue-tied and afraid to confront Granny. She knew Granny would bite back.

Tucked like a bitter old crow in her armchair, Granny fixed her beady eyes on the television. Nicole felt a profound contempt for her. I hate you, she thought. I always have. It was as if something had snapped inside her.

'Have you got the ticket?' Granny asked.

Nicole held it up. This was her job. To hold the lottery ticket and check off the numbers. Granny's eyesight was too bad. Though Nicole suspected she could see more than she claimed to.

She barely listened as they reeled off the numbers.

'Well?' Granny said. 'Wake up! What have we got?'

Nicole cleared her throat. She looked at the ticket, and then at the TV. A shower of glittering silver confetti was released onto the set. The numbers were displayed on the screen. She looked back at the ticket. 'Well?' Granny said. She poked Nicole's arm. Nicole looked at the TV and at the ticket once more. They had all the numbers, every single one.

Granny poked her again.

'Sorry,' Nicole said. 'It's another week of food stamps.' This was the joke Granny was expecting her to make. Nicole made it every week. She sat very still, the ticket in her hand. Usually, she would put it on the arm of the chair and throw it away later, but that day she slipped it into her pocket, out of sight of Granny.

She felt as if she was moving, hearing, speaking underwater as she went through the motions of helping Granny get to bed. Everything was the same, but different. When she finally got Granny settled, the old woman looked up at her from her lovely, plumped-up pillow and said, 'My neck hurts. Why don't you put the pillow at the angle I like it?'

Nicole stared at her. 'Let's get you more comfortable, then.' She eased the pillow out from underneath Granny's head.

'But I don't want—' Granny started to protest, and Nicole said, 'Shhh,' and she pressed the pillow over Granny's mouth and held it there until the old woman stopped moving. Then she put the pillow back and made sure it was nicely plumped and Granny looked comfortable before leaving Granny in bed and going home. The ticket felt as if it was burning a hole in her pocket. The next day she suggested to Tom that they make a surprise visit to see Granny.

'She hates surprises,' he said.

'She won't if you're there. She seemed lonely yesterday.'

Tom found Granny's lifeless body moments after arriving. 'She looks so peaceful,' he said, choked up. 'She does,' Nicole murmured. 'She had a good life,' he said to the GP who came to certify the death. 'She raised me,' he told the undertakers who collected her body. When everyone had left, he said to Nicole, 'At least she didn't suffer.'

Nicole pretended to find the ticket on Granny's kitchen table when they started to clear out the flat. A few days later she said to Tom, 'Shall we check the numbers? We might as well.'

Bless him, when he realised Granny's ticket was a winner, the first thing he said was, 'It's like she's trying to look after me, from beyond the grave.'

'Definitely,' Nicole agreed. 'Isn't that lovely?'

She shakes herself a little, to rid herself of the memory. She wishes Hal Steen would arrive and considers going out and telling the officers in the squad car to expect him, but there's no sign of them through the window. He told her to sit tight and she will.

79

FRIDAY

Hal

Hal parks at the Manor House. The front door is open, and lights are blazing from it and from the windows. He's spoken to Jen on his way here. He knows what Sasha Dempsey told them and he knows that Olly Palmer is missing as a result.

Jen's there to meet him. 'What's happening?' he asks as soon as he gets out.

'We've searched the Manor House comprehensively, but I think he's melted into the woods.'

'So, we search the woods.'

'Shouldn't we wait for back-up?'

More officers are on their way, but there won't be many of them. Not at this time of night. They'll have to wait until morning for a full response. 'How long has he been gone?'

'About forty minutes.'

'Add another half an hour to that by the time anyone else

gets here and he's already got too much of a chance of getting away from us completely. But Olly Palmer's no athlete. I'll bet he hasn't got very far yet. I'm going to have a word with Nicole Booth, and I'll join you.'

'We've searched the house and the immediate area outside,' Jen says, 'but the house and grounds are a rabbit warren. He could be anywhere. We'll go wider if you want.'

'Good,' he says, though he has the feeling they've already lost Olly and Jen knows it too. He makes the short drive to the Barn.

Nicole opens the door. She stands, arms hugging her chest, Anna Creed beside her. He updates them. 'Keep all doors and windows shut and locked. Don't let anyone in except us, okay?'

'Okay,' Nicole says. His heart goes out to her. The pair of them look vulnerable; he'd like to have someone here, but he needs his officers to cover the main road, where Olly could escape the peninsula.

'Alright,' he says. 'If you see Olly Palmer, call us immediately. Don't approach him under any circumstances. We'll check in on you regularly.'

He re-joins Jen and Finn at the Manor. Everything is still tonight. The trees, lit from beneath by the torchlight, tower over them. The three of them are never going to find Olly, he thinks, but they must try. He curses himself for not paying closer attention to Sasha and Olly during the investigation, for not listening better to Jen and Anna. There were so many other leads and distractions. He's made mistakes and he's going to have to live with them.

Jen talks quietly, almost in a whisper. 'We've done the area around the stables. I thought we should fan out, take an area each. Hal, you take the orchard.'

416

He makes his way around the side of the Manor. You could hide anywhere here, he thinks. Almost every tree trunk in the woods could conceal a man behind it, and in the moonlight the gnarled fruit trees in the orchard create pools of deep shadow where a man could easily crouch, unseen.

Hal walks quietly, torchlight swinging. His migraine has gone, but in the aftermath everything feels heightened to him. He's hyperaware. His breathing seems too loud. All his senses are on overdrive. A feeling of failure is creeping up on him and he tries to shake it off, but his brain nags at him. You're the guy who colleagues don't always back, but who prides himself on being ahead of an investigation, of approaching things in smart ways, of coming through when he needs to and having the energy and the mental and physical agility to give it everything, but you're failing. This investigation is too much. Another suspect has got away.

He listens hard for the sound of someone else nearby. Where the hell are you, Olly Palmer? Olly is a man who Hal had a lot of contempt for before he considered him a suspect. He didn't think he had this in him, not even after Anna Creed's accusations. He should have believed her. If Olly gets away, or hurts someone else, he won't forgive himself for that. He has no doubt that Olly's guilty. Nobody runs unless they have something to hide.

He stops at the far end of the orchard, trying to orient himself. He imagines what he would do if he was Olly. He would try to get off the peninsula. Perhaps before the search teams arrive, their time is better spent trying to help his officers cover the places where Olly might emerge onto the road. He is doubting himself and struggling to make a decision when he hears a scream.

80

FRIDAY

Nicole

When she shuts the door behind Hal, Nicole wants to double-check that every door and window is locked as he told her to. She thinks they are, but she was dumb enough to leave the pool doors open earlier. She's spooked, too scared to walk around the whole building in the dark, even with Anna beside her. She wonders if she can use the app on her phone to do it.

She pulls up the app and taps the menu labelled 'Security'. She taps on 'Outside Doors'. It offers her a variety of options, not all of which she understands, but she selects 'Lock All' and taps that. She does the same for the windows. Both show on-screen as 'Locked'.

'There,' she says to Anna. 'We're secure.' Anna is very pale. 'Thank goodness you're here,' Nicole says.

'Can I see?' Anna asks, pointing to the phone. Nicole shows her. 'What's that?' she asks. 'Does it show you a plan of the whole house?'

Nicole taps the button named 'Plan' and then selects 'Downstairs'.

A plan of the ground floor of the Barn appears on-screen, and within it she sees two flashing dots. 'I think that's us,' she says. 'Look. We're in the living area. It knows I'm here because of facial recognition and it can trace you because of your pin.'

Anna uses two fingers to move the plan across the screen so that they can see more of the rooms. 'That's very cool,' she says. 'How clever.' Nicole hands her the phone. 'Play with it,' she says. 'But don't unlock the doors.' It's a grim joke. Neither of them laughs.

Anna looks at the plan closely. 'It's so detailed,' she says. She frowns. 'But if we're in here, then who's that?'

She shows Nicole another flashing dot on the screen, in the fitness suite.

'Oh my God,' Nicole says. 'I forgot to ask the detectives to get Patrick's pin off him when he left. I didn't even think of it. I could have tried to disable it if I'd remembered after he'd gone but I didn't think of that either. Not even when we were doing your pin. How could I have been so dumb?' She feels cold at the thought of it. The sheer stupidity. The danger she might have put them in.

'Could he have dropped it here before he left?'

'I don't know,' Nicole whispers. She glances towards the glass corridor that leads to the fitness suite.

'What do we do?' Anna asks.

Nicole tries to think. Maybe Patrick did leave the pin here. According to her phone, it's in the changing area by the gym and it's not moving. If he has snuck back into the house, is he a threat? Instinctually she thinks he is, based on what happened last week, but there's new information to process. If it's Olly who harmed Tom, then Patrick isn't an immediate danger even if he has crept into the Barn. If he's skint, perhaps he had nowhere else to stay. She wonders if he really did buy a flat, like he told her, or if he squandered the money and carried on sofa surfing the way he used to.

'I'm going to go and see,' she says. 'You stay. If you hear trouble, call the detective.'

'Are you sure?'

'He didn't hurt Tom,' Nicole says. 'Olly did.' Patrick needs to know this, and she realises that this could be a good thing. Having him here is safer for her and Anna.

She doesn't want to alarm him by calling out to him. He might run. He doesn't know what's happening. With her phone in her hand, she walks towards the dot that indicates where Patrick is.

As she steps into the glass corridor, she sees in its walls a reflection of movement at the other end of it, somebody passing swiftly from one side of the fitness suite to the other, the dim, floor-level lights briefly flashing on and following him as he moves. He's trying to stay concealed, but he must have forgotten that there are default lighting settings for guests.

She covers her mouth. It's not Patrick. This man has a completely different shape. The lights are only on for a second and, right before they go out, she sees who it is.

As silently as she can, her heart thudding, she moves back to the living area and whispers in Anna's ear: 'It's not Patrick. It's Olly.'

She shows Anna her phone. The dot has moved. Olly has shut himself in the sauna.

81

FRIDAY

Sasha

Sasha's scream pierces the night. She was outside when she ran into the detective. Jen didn't scream but Sasha gave her a scare.

'What are you doing here?' Jen snaps. 'We told you to stay inside.'

'I can't stay in the house on my own. He might still be in there, or he might creep back in. I'm afraid he'll hurt me.' She doesn't need to try to sound convincing because it's not a lie. If Olly finds her, she's pretty sure he'll hurt her. She's got to hand it to him, she never expected him to flee. She thought he would stand his ground, try to talk himself out of trouble. She feels as if he's outwitted her. Her betrayal of him hasn't quite worked out as expected. She hoped he would be in handcuffs by now, or at least being questioned, giving her a chance to plan her next move.

Hal arrives, out of breath, and Finn is there a few seconds behind him. 'Is everyone okay?' Hal asks.

'It's nothing. I ran into Sasha out here,' Jen says. 'After I asked her to stay inside.'

'Please,' Sasha says. 'I don't feel safe on my own. Can I stay with you?'

'Jen,' Hal says. 'Could you drive her to the Barn? She can sit tight with Nicole and Anna.'

Sasha would rather be here, where she can steer the police away from the septic tank if necessary. She also doesn't want to be on her own, and she very much doesn't want to be at the Barn. She needs to get her head and her story straight before she sees Anna or Nicole again.

'Don't you need me here?' she asks. 'I know this place way better than any of you.'

82

FRIDAY

Nicole

Nicole and Anna look at one another. The dot on Nicole's phone remains in the sauna.

'Can you lock him in there with the app?' Anna whispers.

'I don't know,' Nicole says. 'I don't think the sauna door has a lock. It's a safety measure.'

'Can you lock him in that area of the house?'

'I can try.'

She brings up the menu and they look at the options. The house is divided into zones. Nicole taps on 'Fitness Suite' and gets menus relating to lighting and climate control. There are also specific controls for the steam room and sauna so you can turn them on and off.

'Go back to "Security",' Anna suggests.

They look at the security options. It's hard to see one that will lock internal doors.

She checks the plan. The dot remains in the sauna. But for how long? Hopefully the lights coming on spooked him and he reckons his best bet is to stay there if he wants to remain undetected. Nicole doesn't think he knows she saw him. She feels sick at the thought of him hiding in her home.

'Should we call the police?' Anna asks.

'Just a minute,' Nicole says.

She returns to the main menu. *Think,* she tells herself. Tom was proud of their systems; he over-specced every one of them. There must be something she can do to confine Olly to the fitness suite. *Come on, Tom,* she implores him, in her head. *Tell me what to do.*

Her eyes run down the options once more. What she needs must be in the 'Security' menu. She taps on it again and focuses.

Anna points. 'What about this?' she asks.

Nicole taps on an option titled 'Emergency' and it offers her two choices: 'Lockdown' and 'Alert emergency services'.

'Shall I?' she asks, her finger hovering over the 'Lockdown' button. Anna nods.

She taps it and a small menu appears, offering a total home lockdown or separate zones.

'Bloody menus!' she says. Her hands are shaking.

'Fitness suite,' Anna points.

Nicole taps on it and is offered 'Fitness suite lockdown internal' and 'Fitness suite lockdown external'.

'Internal,' Anna says. 'That's the one.'

Nicole taps it. Their heads turn to look down the glass corridor towards the fitness suite. The glass door at the end of the corridor swings shut, as does a door behind it that leads to the gym. They hear multiple locking mechanisms engaging.

Nicole exhales. Her breath sounds shuddery. 'Did we do it?' she asks.

Anna nods. 'I think so.'

Cautiously, they walk down the corridor and peer through the glass door. Every door they can see from there is shut, including the sauna. Nicole checks her phone. The dot is still glowing inside it.

'Even if the sauna door hasn't locked, he won't be able to get far,' she says.

'We've got him,' Anna says. She looks as if she can hardly believe it. 'If not in the sauna, then in here. Shall we call the police?'

Nicole looks at her phone, but hesitates. Instead of calling, she returns to the menus, searching for something she saw earlier, an option titled 'Sauna'. She taps on it and is offered a range of temperature settings. Anna is watching. Nicole hears her swallow, but Anna says nothing. Nicole turns the sauna temperature up to the highest level possible. 'Before we do, let's just see how trapped he is.'

They wait. After a while, they hear a very faint, rhythmic sound, as if someone is banging on the back of a door.

'It locked him in,' Nicole says. 'It must have a hidden security lock. Because normally you can't lock it.' For the first time, she congratulates Tom for his insistence on having the best of every system.

Her eyes meet Anna's. 'Can he turn down the temperature from inside the sauna?' Anna asks.

'The manual controls are just outside the door. I don't think there's anything inside because, normally, there's no option to lock it, it's not an issue.'

'There's no emergency cord?'

'I don't think so. There was no need for one. There was no possibility of being shut in there.'

'Unless this situation arises.'

'Yes,' Nicole says.

Olly is shut in her sauna, trapped in there. He could be in handcuffs within a few minutes. But what evidence is there that he killed Tom, apart from the word of a homeless guy? Nicole believes him, but will the police? Nicole is an avid watcher of police drama on TV. She knows you need evidence to convict someone. She's certain of his guilt, but would a jury be?

She feels strangely, preternaturally calm, just the way she did when she pushed that pillow over Granny's face. 'What if we don't tell the police that he's here? How many years of your life has Olly stolen?'

Anna holds up one hand, all fingers extended.

'How much has he robbed you of?' Nicole asks. She sees something in Anna crumble. 'He hollowed you out, didn't he?'

A tear slips down Anna's cheek and she wipes it away roughly. Another falls and Nicole reaches out this time, using a fingertip to wipe it gently herself.

'What would you say if I suggest we don't call the police?' she asks.

Anna is looking at her intently, making calculations of her own. 'They could be back here any minute.'

426

'But they won't be wanting to search the Barn. Why would they?' She walks away from the fitness suite, back into the main living area, and Anna follows. 'Can you hear anything from here?' she asks.

They listen and can't hear Olly banging on the sauna door any longer.

She thinks they can do this and do it right under the noses of the police. She remembers the famous Roald Dahl story about the leg of lamb. If that housewife got away with it, why can't she? She just needs Anna on board.

'I can't hear a thing,' Anna says, and Nicole sees that she understands exactly what Nicole is proposing and that she hates Olly as much as Nicole does.

'So, we wait,' Nicole says.

'There will be a body,' Anna says softly.

'I know.' Nicole hasn't worked out what to do about that, but they're resourceful women, they'll think of something.

'I have an idea what to do about that,' Anna says and Nicole smiles.

'How long do you think it will take?' Anna asks.

'I don't know. A few hours?'

Nicole picks up her phone. She feels pleased with the house and with Tom. They protected her today. It is some sort of justice. She returns to the menu on the systems app, feeling emboldened now, and after a few minutes finds the correct way to disable Patrick's guest pin. She wonders how Olly got hold of it. To check she's disabled the pin correctly, she looks at the plan of the house. There are red lines around the perimeter of every room in the fitness suite, indicating that it's locked down, but the light has disappeared from the sauna. Now, not even the house knows that Olly is in there.

She works through a few more menus, connecting her phone to the house's speaker system. Why didn't she do this before? It's so much easier than she thought it would be. She looks up at Anna.

'Do you like opera?' she asks.

83

FRIDAY

Anna

Anna lies in bed in Nicole's guest suite at the Barn. She can't sleep. Her window is open, and she listens to all the familiar sounds of Lancaut at night yet knows that everything is different.

She thinks about Olly, downstairs. Is he dead yet?

She thinks about Nicole, presumably in bed in her room down the hall and presumably awake, too, because who could sleep tonight?

The police came back briefly, at around eleven, to say that they were ceasing their search for the time being and that the squad car would remain in Nicole's drive for the rest of the night, for protection. They told Nicole that Sasha had given a statement suggesting that Olly left the Manor House on the morning of Tom's death.

She and Nicole chewed that over. Why did Sasha say it now? Did she know all along that Olly killed Tom and was covering for him? Or did she just find out? It's hard to know. They agreed it's probably nothing to do with Sasha having a conscience and more to do with her saving her own skin. Anna wonders if Sasha is staying in the Manor tonight. If I'd thrown Olly under the bus, I wouldn't stay there on my own, she thinks. Perhaps Sasha has police protection, too.

She yawns. Her body and mind feel shattered, but both are humming. I want to have my home back, she thinks. I want myself back. She will deal with Sasha, somehow, and reclaim the Manor. She has no doubt that Nicole will help her.

Anna lies awake for a long time, but eventually she starts to feel drowsy.

When I wake up in the morning, she thinks, it'll be done, and she feels incredibly peaceful. Sleep comes easily then.

84

SATURDAY

Nicole

Nicole wakes early, just before it's light. She knocks softly on Anna's door and slips in.

'Help me?' she asks.

Anna gets up quickly. They move downstairs silently. In the glass corridor they can see stars in the dark navy sky but also the suggestion of a rim of light on the horizon. They must hurry. Nicole turns off the sauna, reverses the emergency lockdown and the door at the end of the glass corridor swings open.

Outside the sauna the heat can be felt in the corridor. Through the strip of glass in the door, Nicole can see Olly lying limply across the bench. He's dead. It's not a pretty sight. In his efforts to get out, he's skinned his knuckles and done some damage to the room, but not much.

They wrap him in a sheet and pull him along the glass corridor as swiftly as possible. Nicole can't stop the floor lights coming on as they move through. If the police were to look in at this moment, they'd see them. But they have no sightline to here from where they're parked at the front, and she's got to hope they're not patrolling at this hour. But still, it feels like the riskiest part of the operation and she's relieved to have him in the living area. From there, they drag him down the stairs to the basement garage. His body is very hot and heavy. Nicole opens the boot of her Mini and can see that they won't be able to fit him in.

'We'll have to use the Maserati,' she says. 'But I don't know how to drive it.'

'We'll work it out,' Anna says. She wipes her forehead. 'Come on.'

Nicole finds the keys and they get Olly's body into the car.

A few hours later, when she's showered and dressed, when dawn has broken and Anna has taken tea and toast out to the officers in the squad car, when the freshly arrived police search teams have begun to gather in the lane, she gives Jen a formal statement about the camper and what he said about seeing Olly. Then she asks if they can go out.

'We can't stand to be here all day just waiting.'

'Understandable,' Jen says. 'I'm sure that's fine. Where will you go?'

'For a walk, and then maybe to town. Call us when you've finished. I hope you find him.'

'We'll do our best. I'll be in touch with any news.'

'Thank you,' Nicole says.

In the garage, Nicole settles into the driving seat, Anna beside her. The Maserati dash is intimidating. She gets the car started and tries the accelerator. It has bite.

432

'Ready?' she asks. Anna nods. Nicole opens the garage doors and the police in the drive move aside. Nicole leans out to have a final word with Jen. 'Do you want a set of house keys? So you can use the loo?'

She says it sincerely. Her gamble is that the more open and helpful she is, the less likely they are to suspect her and Anna of anything. It was natural that they suspected her when Tom died, but this is different. Now, she's very much the victim.

'No, thanks. We'll be alright. See you shortly.' Jen waves her on and she eases her foot down onto the accelerator, hoping the car will move smoothly, worried that if it doesn't, they'll realise it's the first time she's driven it and wonder why. But it behaves.

They don't drive a long way once they've left Lancaut. When they get Olly out of the boot, his body feels warm, still, but it's cooling rapidly. Getting him out of the car is easier than getting him in. They're on a small pebbly beach beside the river. It's not overlooked. They pack Olly's pockets with stones.

'It suddenly gets very deep here,' Anna says. 'If we get this right he'll be down there for a long time. I'll take him in.'

If the body is ever discovered, they hope that the water will complicate a post-mortem. They hope the stones in his pocket will suggest suicide.

Anna takes her clothes off and drags Olly into the river. As soon as she's out of her depth, Nicole can see the struggle she has to stay afloat and worries for her, but Anna lets go of him suddenly and he's gone, completely taken, invisible in the murky water. Nicole piles stones onto the sheet they wrapped him in and ties it around them. She tosses it far out into the water and watches it sink.

Anna climbs out, dripping, shivering. 'We forgot to bring anything to dry you,' Nicole says.

'I didn't.' Anna pulls a small towel from the shopping bag she brought and dries herself then packs the towel neatly away. She dresses and they get back into the car.

As they pull out, she says, 'Nick and I used to swim here,' and Nicole says, 'That's a lovely memory.'

EPILOGUE

85

TWO WEEKS LATER

Nicole

The house feels quiet when Nicole wakes. It's the first time she's woken up to an empty home in weeks. Anna moved back to the Manor yesterday, and Nicole helped her.

Sasha has cleared out all of her stuff and Olly's. Anna's letting her stay in the Coach House for now though Sasha says she doesn't feel safe anywhere, that she's afraid Olly is out there somewhere, just waiting to take revenge on her.

Anna made Sasha an offer: move out of the Manor and disappear or stay in the Coach House and continue to run your yoga classes in the Manor. They hoped it was a tempting enough offer for Sasha, and it turned out that it was. She accepted.

Revenge on Sasha is going to be a long game, but it's started.

Nicole likes the thought of Anna and her as close neighbours. She feels connected to her for life after what happened, and she's looking forward to spending more time with Anna. They get on beautifully.

Anna has offered to help with Tom's funeral and plans are underway. It's going to be the perfect tribute to her perfect man and the father of her child. Nicole has done a pregnancy test and she's expecting. It's the most glorious and scary thing that could have happened to her since Tom died.

She makes herself a green tea and a light breakfast and returns to her bedroom. She finds it hard seeing Tom's clothes hanging in their dressing room but can't bear to get rid of them for good, yet. She decides to box them up and move them out of the room as a sort of first stage. It takes her a while to fold everything carefully and pack it away. She can still smell him on the clothes in a way she no longer can on their bedsheets, or around the house.

Tom's clothes fill six boxes. She tapes them up so moths can't get at them and carries them to the guest bedroom where she has access to the attic. Standing well back, she holds her breath and hits the wall button that controls the attic ladder. It doesn't work. She tries again and this time the ladder shoots down very quickly and she's glad she wasn't in its way. That could do someone some damage, she thinks.

She climbs up cautiously, hefting the first box into the attic space then retrieving the others and shoving them in too. She considers leaving them like that, but her perfectionism kicks in and she climbs up into the attic with the intention of stacking them tidily.

The big box in the middle of the attic gives her pause.

She's never seen it before. Surely, Tom would have told her if he was putting anything up here. He knows she's particular about how they store things.

She examines the box. It's unmarked. She pulls back the lid flaps and at first isn't at all sure what she's seeing, but she quickly realises and tears at the box until it's in shreds, and standing proud in the middle of the attic is the replica sheep she longed to have. It's beautiful. Tom must have bought it for her as a surprise. She throws her arms around its thick neck and sheds a few tears, but mostly, she thinks about how lovely Tom was, and how their child will love this as much as she does.

Getting the sheep down from the attic isn't easy. She manages it after some cursing and grunting and feels satisfied when it's safely on the landing. 'There,' she tells it. 'You don't have to live in the attic any longer. We can find you a proper home now.'

She looks up. It must have been even more of a pain to get it up there, she thinks as she presses the button that will draw up the ladder and watches it judder slowly back into place. And as she does, her eyes light on the ladder's metal feet, and she wonders, just for a moment, if one of them could have caused Tom's head injury. Perhaps he didn't stand well enough out of the way when the ladder came down.

But she shakes her head. No. It can't be that doing such a wonderful thing could have caused him an injury. That wouldn't be right. Life isn't that unfair.

86

ONE MONTH LATER

Jen

Hal mutters as he steps out of the coffee shop.

'What is it?' Jen asks.

'They never get my name right. It's the simplest name in the world, but everybody loves to overcomplicate.'

He shows her his cup. 'HAIL' is written on the side of it.

'All hail Hal,' she says.

'If only,' he says. She hears a bitter edge in his voice. They've drawn a blank on the Tom Booth case. They never found Olly Palmer, and nor did they find any evidence that he murdered Tom Booth, but he's still wanted as a person of interest. Jen's hopeful he might turn up somewhere. They also haven't been able to make any progress with regard to Kitty Ellis. And they didn't find Patrick Young, either. She wonders where he went. They won't follow up because he ceased to be a person of interest, but Hal warned Nicole to remain wary of his intentions.

Anna Creed called Hal and apologised for harassing him about the grave site at the plague pit at Lancaut. She said she was spooked, that she didn't know what had got into her. It was just a fantasy. Jen knew what she and Finn saw there, and she told Hal. He wanted to examine the site forensically to see if a body had been buried there, but without anyone looking for Kitty Ellis, and the fact that there were human remains there already, he was leaned on by his superiors to drop it. The press tired of the story after reporting that Olly Palmer had vanished. It disappeared into the news cycle like everything else.

A few small loose ends got tied up. They learned the name of the man suspected of stalking Martha Hayward and stealing her 'Sadie' business cards. He was a Bristol University student called Ben Padden, but there was no need to track him down. There was still a lack of clarity over how Tom got her card, as she insisted that she didn't give any out at the Maserati event, but, again, it wasn't something they would be pursuing. Jen understands that there are some things you never get to know.

She has marvelled at the fact that Sasha is still living with Anna Creed at the Manor, even if Sasha is in the Coach House now and Anna back in the Manor. Sasha really is a friend, Anna told her. Olly coerced us both. Jen can't understand it. That's not the story the journal told. She puts it down to Stockholm Syndrome, to the general craziness of human beings. She warned Anna to look after herself but could do nothing more.

Hal and Jen have ended up feeling that something great was almost within their grasp with this case, that it could have been a career-defining moment for them both, Hal especially, but it slipped through their fingers.

She feels they did good work, that you can't win them all, but it got under Hal's skin. He can't stand the thought of Olly Palmer out there somewhere, having got away with this. What he needs, she thinks, is another case to get his teeth into. He's despondent about his chances of working on something meaty after this failure, but she's sure he will. Talent will out.

They walk back to the car. He's frowning. He seems to live in a permanent state of discontent at present. She wants him to relax, to recognise what he has achieved, to look forward to what he will achieve. One failure shouldn't bring anyone down.

'It just feels odd to me, all those women living together at Lancaut,' he says.

She thinks about this. 'Lancaut's a strange place, that's for sure. But trauma can bond people. And they're in separate houses.'

He stares through the windscreen. 'I know,' he says. 'I think about it too much. I can't let it go. It makes me uneasy, for some reason.'

He reaches to start the ignition and, before she can stop herself, a question pops out.

'Would you like to go on a date with me?'

His hand drops back onto his lap, and she waits for his rebuff.

'I know it's not strictly allowed,' she says. 'I'm sorry. I shouldn't have said it. Forget it.'

He turns to look at her and he's smiling for the first time in ages, and it's such a wide smile it's almost splitting his face in two and she doesn't think she could feel happier.

He says, 'It's definitely not encouraged, and it could cause us all sorts of problems, but it would make me very happy, and I think we can work it out so, yes, Jen, I would like to go on a date with you.'

'So long as we don't talk about work. You have to promise.'

'That might be a deal breaker.' He smiles.

'Half work talk, half nice talk?' she offers.

'I think I can agree to that.'

87

TEN MONTHS LATER

Sasha

Sasha looks out of the aeroplane window as they descend. London sprawls below, looking grey and rainy, but she doesn't care. She feels refreshed after an overnight flight. Business class is a revelation. She had a glass of champagne and ate in the lounge before boarding then slept through her journey back from the Caribbean. Now she feels amazing.

On landing, she texts Nicole and Anna: Just down.

Nicole replies: Super!

Anna, who took immediately to the new smartphone she got at Nicole's insistence, replies too: See you soon x

It's been a strange ten months. Immediately after Olly left, Sasha thought she'd have no choice but to move on from the Manor and set up her business elsewhere, somewhere Olly couldn't find her if he came looking. It wasn't going to be easy because leaving meant losing her home and her business venue and she had no savings. She would have to start from scratch. But Anna made her a surprising and generous offer and Sasha stayed on.

She struggled to make it work, though. Living in the Coach House was lonely; she felt vulnerable there, always looking over her shoulder for Olly. She lost her enthusiasm for yoga and clients noticed and stopped coming. It was impossible to save a meaningful amount of money, even without rent. After a couple of months, she gave up trying, cut her classes down to just two a week and diagnosed herself with depression.

Anna noticed. 'You can't carry on like this. I'll pay you to help me around the house.' She was insistent and Sasha agreed because nothing better felt achievable. The cleaning was horrible at first and the irony of the situation wasn't lost on her as she swabbed floors while Anna spent time in the study, which she'd converted to a craft room.

Nicole called around a lot. She and Anna sat in the kitchen, chatting and laughing, sharing memories of their husbands. Sasha thought of them as the Widows. They invited her to join them, one day, and they asked her about Olly. They said they understood that whatever he'd done she must miss him, because clearly, she hadn't known what he was capable of. Nicole said Sasha had been brave to tell the police about Olly leaving the Manor on the morning of Tom's murder. Sasha said she wished she'd said something sooner but she was afraid of him.

She watched Nicole's belly grow with interest. By Christmas, Nicole was showing. She spent Christmas Day at the Manor, eating lunch with Anna. They invited Sasha to eat with them. After lunch they played card games together. Sasha felt sleepy and full. She even felt a small sense of belonging for which she was grateful. She didn't want the day to end.

Nicole brought her a gift, which embarrassed Sasha. 'I didn't get you anything,' she said.

'It doesn't matter. Open it.'

The package was so beautifully wrapped it almost brought a tear to Sasha's eye. She tore off the paper and found a credit card inside it, with her name on it.

'What's this?' she asked.

'It's for the new outfits you're going to need,' Nicole said. 'For your new job.'

'What do you mean?' Sasha asked.

'This baby's due in a few months,' Nicole said, patting her belly. 'And I'm going to need help. I don't want you to do childcare, that's my job, but I could use an assistant. And if you're going to represent me you need to wear something other than tatty yoga clothes. So go shopping, kit yourself out with whatever you need and treat yourself, too.'

'Is this real?' Sasha asked.

'Absolutely, it's real. Do you want the job? Or shall I cancel the card?'

Sasha accepted the offer and loved her new role. Nicole was an amazing boss. The work was easy, mostly paperwork, running errands and the house, helping to get ready for the baby. After a successful trial period, Nicole encouraged her to get her hair and nails done as a reward. She continued to be generous with bonuses whenever Sasha did well, treating her to something, or telling her to take cash out on the card. After baby Tom was born, she declared Sasha to be indispensable.

Sasha began to go the extra mile for both women, working longer hours, showing them how helpful she could be. In return she got jewellery, and more clothes. She began to feel as if she herself was rich. And then, the crème de la crème, as a reward for doing so well at her job, Nicole gave her a holiday.

It's been a lovely fortnight away in the luxurious resort Nicole suggested. Sasha's enjoyed more than a few cocktails and spent a few satisfying nights with a hot waiter, exorcising the memory of Olly completely. She's been allowed to pay for everything on the card.

As she disembarks from the plane she realises she's looking forward to getting home and that it's the first time she's thought of Lancaut as home since Olly disappeared.

On arrival, she says goodbye to her driver and lets herself into the Glass Barn, dragging her new luggage with her. 'Hello,' she calls, brightly.

'Through here!' Nicole replies.

Sasha walks into the living area. Nicole sits on the sofa with baby Tom in her arms and Anna beside her. Opposite them, also seated, are two uniformed police officers.

'What's happening?' Sasha asks.

One of the officers stands up. 'Sasha Dempsey?' he says.

'Yes. What's wrong?' Has Olly resurfaced? Have they found Kitty's remains? Her heart skips a beat.

'I'm Detective Constable Phil O'Leary and this is Detective Constable Audrey Pope. We're arresting you on a charge of Fraud by Abuse of Position.'

'What is this?' she says.

'You're accused of misusing your employer's credit card to buy goods and services for personal use.'

'What? I'm authorised to use that card. I've been encouraged to use it.'

'You were not authorised,' Nicole says. 'You abused your position. You've been stealing from me.' Her voice breaks a little. 'Not just little treats, though there were plenty of those. You've been on a Caribbean holiday on my money. How did you think I wouldn't notice? Did you think I was too distracted by the baby to check what you're spending? Is that it? Shame on you!'

Her expression is a picture of betrayal, though Sasha wonders if it isn't a flash of satisfaction that she can see deep in Nicole's eyes. The baby starts to cry. Nicole holds him close and shushes him gently.

'I'll read you your rights, and we'll explain more at the station,' the officer says.

Sasha looks at Anna, who shakes her head to signal that she's appalled by Sasha, too, and when the police walk her out of the building and guide her into their car, Sasha laughs, because what else is she going to do?

She's been played.

ACKNOWLEDGEMENTS

Thanks as ever to my agent, Helen Heller, for steering the ship and providing so much support.

To my editors, Emily Krump in New York and Emily Griffin in London, thank you very much for your patience, enthusiasm and sharp editorial notes. This book is immeasurably better after your input, and you're a delight to work with.

Huge thanks, too, to the wider publishing teams who work so hard and so brilliantly on bringing my books to the market. In New York, Camille Collins, DJ De Smyter, Carla Parker, Elsie Lyons and Tessa James. In London, Isabelle Ralphs, Lydia Weigel, Helen Wynn-Smith, Joanna Taylor, Mathew Watterson, Ceara Elliott and Jess Muscio. In Canada, Cory Beatty, Rebecca Silver and Shamin Ali. I'm very grateful to every one of you.

I'm also very thankful for the support of Liate Stehlik and Jennifer Hart at William Morrow, Leo MacDonald at Harper-Collins Canada, and Selina Walker at Century.

Jemma McDonagh, Camilla Ferrier and everyone at the Marsh Agency, thank you for being such a joy to work with. Thanks, too, to all the editors and publishers of my books in translation. I'm so grateful to you for bringing them to a wider audience.

Readers, booksellers, bloggers and reviewers enrich my writing life and career immeasurably. I'm very grateful to know many of you, and for your support.

To my fellow authors in the thriller writing community, thank you for being amazing, inspiring and supportive. Special thanks to Shari Lapena, Claire Douglas and Tim Weaver for the chat and the encouragement.

To my family, thank you as ever. Jules, the aubergine parmigiana was fantastic this year. Rose, Max and Louis, love you.